Praise for
You Will Know Me by My Deeds

"A bracing historical thriller that further enriches this top-notch series."

Kirkus Reviews

"Mike Cobb's *You Will Know Me by My Deeds* is a taut, propulsive tale set against the harrowing backdrop of the 1980's Atlanta Child Murders. Entertainingly addictive and menacing."

Robert Gwaltney,
award-winning author of *The Cicada Tree*
and Georgia Author of the Year

"Mike Cobb's Atlanta-based historical fiction easily holds its place on the bookshelf next to Caleb Carr's *Alienist* novels."

Joey Madia,
author of *Sherlock Holmes and the Mystery of M*
and the *Stanton Chronicles* historical fiction series

"Mike Cobb is a master at weaving together a fictional story with real historical events, in particular ones in Atlanta and its surroundings."

Bill Stueck,
Professor Emeritus, Department of History
University of Georgia

YOU WILL KNOW ME BY MY DEEDS

MIKE COBB

Waterside Productions

First Printing, 2025

ISBN-13: 978-1-962984-72-0 print edition
ISBN-13: 978-1-962984-73-7 e-book edition

Waterside Productions
2055 Oxford Ave
Cardiff, CA 92007
www.waterside.com

A Word of Caution

IN A WORK OF PERIOD FICTION, THERE IS OFTEN TENSION between fidelity to the time period and the risk of offending the reader. Certain offensive words and cultural norms, which are unacceptable today, are used in this work. While the decision to use them was not taken lightly, their presence is important to the accuracy and integrity of the period. It is hoped that their incorporation will, at the very least, shed light on a time in our history when attitudes and mores that are taboo today were commonplace. Their use is not intended in any way to disrespect the reader or any group of people.

For Stella, Poppy, Emma, and Ruby

Prelude

This is a work of fiction. While elements are true, including details regarding the Atlanta Child Murders, Wayne Williams' trial and conviction for killing two adults, and suspicion of Klan involvement in the murder of at least one of the children, significant liberties have been taken throughout this book.

Billy and Cynthia Tarwater thought they had left the troubled past behind, until a series of ominous incidents threaten to destroy everything they hold dear.

Someone is out to get them, and Billy is determined to uncover the truth before it's too late. But as he delves deeper into the mystery, he realizes that the dark forces at play may be connected to the events of seventeen years ago. Or they may be connected to the Atlanta Child Murders. Or both.

Over a two-year period beginning in July 1979, at least twenty-nine black children, adolescents, and adults—mostly male—were kidnapped and murdered in Atlanta. At first, the incidents were believed to be isolated. But as more victims turned up dead, and given the similarities in the specific style and manner of the killings, law enforcement authorities began to suspect they were the work of a serial killer.

On June 21, 1981, police arrested Wayne Williams, an Atlanta native who was twenty-three at the time of the last murder. A grand jury indicted him for first-degree murder in the deaths of two adults. The trial date was set for early 1982. He was never charged with the killings of any of the children or adolescents, although law enforcement and the media suspected him of being guilty of those murders as well.

Williams was convicted in the court of public opinion for all the murders, and the saga of a horrific crime spree, one of the worst in the annals of Atlanta history, was laid to rest.

However, there were other forces at play in the city that may have played a role in the murders of the children. According to various sources, including WXIA TV and *Spin* Magazine, for over a year, the Georgia Bureau of Investigation had been working on a parallel inquest and allegedly had evidence tying members of the Ku Klux Klan to the murder of one small boy, and further evidence linking them to at least fourteen of the other killings, but suppressed it, fearing a race war. When Williams, conveniently black, was caught, the GBI allegedly "quietly, gratefully closed the book on their case, and, in the immortal words of Mark Twain, suddenly remembered another appointment."

LATE '81

CHAPTER ONE

Cynthia Tarwater

Monday, December 14ᵗʰ, 1981

TWO BLURRED HEADLIGHTS, RAGGED HALOS IN THE REARVIEW, broke the Stygian pitch.

Cynthia gripped the steering wheel so hard her knuckles blanched.

The rain cascaded down the windshield in gelid sheets. The wiper blades thwacked the edge of the Suburban's cowl like a metronome.

For the past twenty-four hours, Atlanta had been beset by a heavy downfall and scant visibility.

She struggled to make out the road ahead.

For the first five minutes of the drive, Billy Jr. and Addie had jabbered away in the back seat like sugar-high Energizer Bunnies. Then they sank into oblivion. *Just like that,* she thought. *Nothing like a weekend sleepover at Grandma Alice's to wear the kids out.*

She stopped at the intersection of Flat Shoals and Glenwood. The barbershop to her left was long gone, a victim of white flight, its plate glass windows boarded up with fly-posted plywood. She could almost hear the snip snip of Mr. Batson's clippers beckoning from yore. The snap of Sam Jepperson's shoeshine cloth beseeching a generous tip. The redolence of Bay Rum and Kiwi polish. Not that she ever got *her* hair cut—or her shoes shined—there. But her father Cecil dragged her along on more than one occasion with the promise that they'd go next door for a vanilla shake if only she'd sit like a "good girl" and watch him get trimmed. She had often wondered whether he did things like that just to piss her off. His way of controlling. Or did he really want her company?

The car that had been following her since she pulled out of Billy's mother's driveway lingered half a block behind. When the light changed, she turned left onto Glenwood. She looked in the mirror. The car turned left and kept its distance. *Probably nothing.*

At the Gresham Avenue intersection, she glanced over at what had been Harry's Army Surplus. Now, like the barbershop, just another padlocked casualty.

A long-suppressed memory welled up. Saturday, September 28th, 1963. She was thirteen. So capricious and carefree, like most girls her age. She left the East Atlanta Pharmacy by the front door and headed west toward Moreland Avenue. Just past Harry's, she looked back and saw a car following her. When she stopped, it stopped. When she went, it went.

That had been her last recollection from before *the erasure*—what she later came to know by its medical name. Localized psychogenic amnesia. For seventeen years, the next thing she had remembered was waking up at Grady Hospital with an officer standing guard outside her door. The nurse had said *You're not*

Cynthia now. You're Patti. With an i. Or something to that effect. She would later learn that the police had contrived the alias to protect her from her abductor.

It wasn't until October a year ago that everything began coming back to Cynthia in a torrent. What had been an eradication of five weeks of her past, leaving in its wake a deep, dark abyss, had begun to come back in a matter of days. This wouldn't have happened without Billy's help. And his dogged determination.

Did she welcome the recovered memory? There were times when she wondered whether knowing was better than incognizance. *Closure would feel right. But knowledge alone doesn't bring closure.*

And could closure ever come for the families of the girls who *didn't* survive? Why had she made it out alive, and the others hadn't?

She inched her way down Glenwood past Moreland Avenue. At the Boulevard intersection, she glanced across the street at Fire Station No. 10. A half dozen firemen were huddled under the overhang in front of the station. For a moment, she thought she saw Billy's brother Chester standing there smoking a cigarette and chatting up the others. But Chester hadn't lasted a year as a fireman before bugging out for the merchant marines, thinking he could avoid the draft. He ended up on the SS Mayaguez ferrying supplies through combat zones in Vietnam. Came home intact but with a chip on his shoulder.

She turned right.

She drove up Boulevard past Memorial Drive, hugging the eastern edge of Oakland Cemetery before assuming a northwesterly course past the shuttered Fulton Cotton Mill and through the railroad underpass.

She looked back. The car continued to follow her. That's when she realized that it wasn't *nothing*.

Perhaps she should have taken the expressway. But she had chosen not to. Visibility was bad enough on the surface roads.

As she neared the intersection with Ponce de Leon, the light turned yellow. She accelerated and took a hard left, hoping the car would stop on red. It didn't. When she turned right on Peachtree, then left on Fifth, the driver continued to dog her.

Cynthia eased into The Belmont courtyard. The other car stopped briefly at the turn-in then crept down Fifth. She craned her neck, trying to get a good look at it. At the driver. But she could see little through the relentless downpour and the fogged windshield.

She parked the Suburban at The Belmont entrance. She waited for the rain to abate enough for her to get the kids inside without a drenching. Then she hurried them into the lobby under her flimsy throwaway umbrella made for one.

She closed the umbrella and hooked it on her wrist. She held Billy Jr. and Addie's hands tight, lest they slip on the marble floor.

They crossed the threshold into the elevator cab, leaving a trail of dripping water behind. She punched 4.

When the doors opened, Billy was standing in the fourth-floor vestibule. He was in his light beige mackintosh and floppy yellow rain hat.

"Clairvoyant, are we?" Cynthia said.

"I saw you out the window and was on my way down to help. But you beat me to it." He placed his hand on her upper arm. "Cynthia, you're trembling."

"It's just the biting cold. I'm fine. I need to get these rug rats out of their wet clothes and into their PJs. And then sit for a while. You can park the car if you don't mind."

"Of course I don't mind. That's the least I can do."

She held out the umbrella. "Want this?"

"No thanks." He knelt in front of Billy Jr. and Addie. "How's Grandma?"

"Feisty as ever," Cynthia answered. "She sure knows how to cut a look. But the kids adore her, and that's what matters most. And compared to *my* mother…let's just say you're the lucky one and leave it at that."

When Billy returned, Cynthia was already curled up in her favorite overstuffed chair with a glass of Merlot. Her socks and Clarks slip-ons lay pell-mell on the floor about her. The open umbrella stood atilt in the corner of the room.

"That was quick," he said.

She took a sip. Notes of black cherry, of vanilla and sandalwood, teased her throat. "I'm sure the kids are deep into sugar-plum dreams by now. Grab a pour and join me. There's something you need to know."

Billy, glass in hand, plopped into the chair beside her. "What is it?"

"I need to tell you about a flashback I had. And about a car."

He listened as Cynthia told him about the car that had followed her from his mother's house. "Could you tell what kind it was?" he asked.

"I couldn't tell a thing, Billy." She ran her finger along the chair's piping, tracing in her mind the path she had taken. "All I know is it looked big. Maybe a sedan."

"I don't think you should be out late at night by yourself, Cynthia. It seems like every day more shit happens. Carjackings. Murders."

"At least Wayne Williams is locked up." She searched her thoughts. "Those poor children. And their grieving families."

Billy's hesitation baffled her. He just sat there for a minute without saying a word. He finally spoke. "Tell me about the flashback."

"The whole thing with the kidnapping came rushing back tonight. It hit me hard, just as I passed the old army surplus. I guess it was my being right there where my thirteen-year-old self had been lured away." She held her glass in the air. "More, please."

He refilled it and topped his off. He set the bottle on the side table, leaned over, and took her hand. "I'm so sorry, Cynthia."

"It wasn't what I expected. I thought I had finally put it all behind me, with Kilgallon…excuse me, the *Reverend* Kilgallon… dead and Sam Jepperson exonerated and freed. But now I'm not so certain. Maybe it'll haunt me forever."

"I hope not. I just wish there was something I could do to make things better."

"I'll be okay."

"Are you sure?"

"I'm sure. Life goes on, doesn't it? And I don't believe I have a choice in the matter."

CHAPTER TWO

Billy Tarwater

Monday, December 14ᵗʰ, 1981

BILLY PONDERED THE PINCH OF CYNTHIA'S EYES. THE downturned corners of her mouth.

"How about this," he said. "With Christmas less than two weeks away, and the Wayne Williams jury selection three days after that and then the trial, I'll be knee-deep at the courthouse. But as soon as it's over, maybe we can get away with the kids for a few days. Someplace where it's warmer. Maybe Florida."

Billy thought back to his Binky days. Every summer, his mom and dad would load up the Brookwood Wagon in the wee hours. They would practically carry him and Chester, half-asleep and still in their pajamas, from the house to the back seat. They would pull out of the driveway and head south to Ormond Beach. Somewhere along US 23—Billy seemed to recall it was this side of Hazelhurst— his dad would ease the car off the road. They would all pile out.

Dad would set up the folding chairs and the camp stove. Mom would throw a generous ration of bacon into the cast-iron skillet, cook it 'til it was crisp, crack some eggs in the bacon grease, and they'd have breakfast right there along the side of the road, as the sun came up and the cars and eighteen-wheelers and Greyhounds went whizzing by. When the meal was done, they would pack up everything and pile back into the car. But only after Chester and Billy had relieved themselves at the base of the same loblolly pine each year—the one just across the embankment from the road. And only after Chester had marveled at how much the tree had grown since the prior year, surely because he and Billy had nourished it.

For years, Billy thought the family ate along the side of the road for the adventure of it all. He and Chester always got a kick out of it. It wasn't until he grew older, and the trips became a bit tedious and less enjoyable, that he realized it had more to do with the old man's insufferable thrift.

"That'd be nice," Cynthia said. "But not before Spring break. I have two classes to teach between now and then. One's new, and I haven't even begun to pull together the course material for it."

"They're giving the Williams trial two months at the outside, so it should be well over by then."

"Okay. Let's plan on it."

"Can we go back to what we were talking about earlier?"

She raised her empty glass as before. "About another refill?"

"Again? Don't you think you should maybe slow down a little?"

"It's been a hard day, Billy. Indulge me."

He complied. "How about let's agree this is your last for the evening?"

She stared daggers. "Now, you were saying?"

"I was saying you don't need to be out late at night by yourself."

"I *wasn't* by myself. Billy Jr. and Addie were with me."

"You know what I mean, Cynthia. *I* should have picked them up from my mom's. Not you."

"Your mother likes my company." She smirked. "And anyway, you were busy. I'm off for winter break with little to do except take care of the kids and build a lesson plan."

"I know, but it's not worth putting you in harm's way. I could have left work early. And I should have."

"Billy, I hate the long hours you're logging."

That night, Billy couldn't sleep. He looked over at Cynthia. She was out like a light and hugging the pillow in deep embrace.

After two hours of his tossing and turning, of fits and starts and frustrated attempts to drift off, he got up and plodded to the kitchen.

The clock over the sink said 1:47. But he knew it was six minutes slow. For weeks, Cynthia had been imploring him to get the stepstool from the closet and adjust it. *Later today*, he thought.

He brewed a half-pot of Maxwell House Master Blend. The rich aroma of roasted nuts filled the kitchen. He realized as soon as the thick, dark liquid hit the cup that drinking coffee in the middle of the night wasn't the best decision. But what the hell. He couldn't sleep anyway. May as well make the best of wide awake.

Billy recalled his first coffee encounter. *What was I, three?*

Granny Tarwater would fill the blue-and-white porcelain saucer—the one with the cow and the milkmaid—with just enough to wet a little boy's whistle. *Blow on it, Binky*, she would say. *You don't want to burn your tongue.* His mother was livid when she learned of his toddler coffee encounters. But it was too late. He was hooked for life.

He sat at the table, savored a generous quaff, and endeavored to take account of things.

Maybe she wasn't followed. Maybe it was just a coincidence. But six miles? From Mom's? To here?

Maybe it was random. Somebody with too much time on his hands and less than honorable intentions driving by on a rainy night. He happens to see a young woman in the car all alone—as far as he can tell—and something clicks. He decides to follow her.

Maybe it has to do with the kidnapping eighteen years ago. Kilgallon had to have had an accomplice. And Cynthia was the only one to survive. Could it be that somebody is out to finish the job?

I'll call Gary later this morning and see if he can meet me at Marnie's after work.

By the inexact clock it was 2:23. He would stumble back to bed. Give it another try.

He knew morning would come too soon.

But the caffeine had kicked in.

He crawled into bed. Cynthia didn't budge.

He lay there, breathing in and out in concert with the gentle rise and fall of her chest. She had captivated him in '63. Breezy and flirtatious. Prancing down the street in her Daisy Dukes. Paying eleven-year-old Binky *no nevermind*, as her mother surely would have said. And here she was now, melancholic and dreamy, like a Vermeer painting in fawns and ambers and ultramarine blues. If only she could shake off the past once and for all and just be herself.

CHAPTER THREE

Cynthia Tarwater

Tuesday, December 15ᵗʰ, 1981

THE FIRST THING CYNTHIA SAW WHEN SHE WOKE WAS THE note on the nightstand. Scrawled in blue on a Chinet napkin.

CAN'T SLEEP. GOING IN EARLY. MAY BE HOME LATE. LOVE YOU. BILLY

She rubbed her eyes. It was 6:15.

She stumbled into the bathroom, quickly disrobed, and hopped into the shower. The surging water, cold at first but hot to the touch within seconds, pummeled her face and splashed off her shoulders. The stall filled with hot steam. She breathed deep and took it in. Her body absorbed the heat like a sponge. She cherished these brief times of solitude. Freed from the imperatives of the outside world. Before the kids roused and took command of her attention. Before the preoccupations of the day. Before anything, really, except her private shower thoughts.

Most mornings, those thoughts ran from the capricious to the sublime, gently nudging her passions and inspiring her to seize the moment. But this morning, her ponderings quickly ran to a darker, a more somber place.

Gibran wrote that the strongest souls emerge out of suffering. *The most massive characters are seared with scars.*

She instinctively ran her hand down the back of her thigh and across the snag of scarred flesh. A forever vestige left from an adolescent girl's plight for survival. From the twisted, "redemptive" soul of a sick man.

Some scars are visible to the world. But the ones you can't see—those are the deepest.

Cynthia had learned to overcome the unsettling feeling that Billy sometimes stared at it when they were intimate. He never spoke a word of it.

She toweled off and dressed.

The most massive characters are seared with scars.

* * *

Cynthia pulled out onto Fifth Street from the courtyard on her way to the Montessori preschool. She glanced over at the car parked in the lot across the street. Its motor was running. She thought little of it until she headed north on Peachtree and looked in the mirror. She saw the car turn onto Peachtree from Fifth, following a block or so behind her. Was it the same car that had followed her home last night?

The driver continued to tail her, always careful to maintain enough distance, she assumed, to prevent her from getting a good look at him or the car.

The light turned yellow as she approached Spring Street. She accelerated and raced through the intersection. She breathed a sigh of relief when she looked back and saw that the car had stopped at the red light this time.

She parked in one of the drop-off spaces at the preschool's entrance, bundled up the kids, and hurried them inside.

The walls of the entrance hall were resplendent with child-made Christmas doodads and decorations in reds and greens. A string of prancing reindeer and a gift-laden sleigh spanned the ceiling. A four-foot Santa, a bit worse for wear but otherwise festive, stood in the corner near the door.

Miss Kate, the Montessori director, greeted them just inside the entrance. She promptly marshalled the kids to their rooms.

When Cynthia returned to the Suburban, she saw what she thought was same car parked near the Walgreens at the strip mall across the street.

Disquieted but determined not to let it shake her, she pulled out of the Montessori entrance and headed home.

When she got close to Fifth Street, the car was still lingering a block behind. Rather than turn onto Fifth, she continued down Peachtree. Past downtown, she turned left onto Decatur Street and drove the four blocks to the police headquarters, careful not to go too fast lest she betray her disquiet.

She turned into the headquarters lot, pulled into the first available space, and waited.

The car sped past and turned left onto Butler Street.

CHAPTER FOUR
Billy Tarwater

Tuesday, December 15ᵗʰ, 1981

"LARCENY." THE FACELESS OFFICER'S PERFUNCTORY temperament bled through the phone line. Billy pictured him sitting at his desk. Krispy Kreme paunch hanging over his belt. Coffee rings smirching the paperwork strewn across the jumbled work surface. Ashtray overflowing with stale butts. Another goddamned call.

"Sergeant Alford, please," Billy said.

"He's not in."

"Can I leave a message?"

"Shoot."

"Tell him Billy Tarwater called. Please have him call me as soon as he comes in."

"Number?"

"He has my number. Tell him I'm at work."

With the jury selection slated to begin on the twenty-eighth, just thirteen days away, the City Desk was in a frenzy. And Billy was full tilt in the thick of it, as he would be through the trial's duration. Williams was being tried for murder. But of two adult men, not boys.

The disappearances of black children had ended when Williams was arrested. The city rested easier, hoping against hope that the spate of murders was over.

But Billy knew too much to believe Williams was guilty of murdering all, or even any, of the children. That wasn't what the trial at hand was about, though. He would focus on what he'd been entrusted to do. He would fulfill his journalistic duties with vigor. That's what any newspaperman worth his salt does.

In due time, he would reveal to the newspaper his off-duty activities and what he had learned. But only when the time was right. For now, his covert side endeavor would be relegated to evenings and weekends and the occasional break from what was bound to become a gawker's smorgasbord.

On the home front, he and Cynthia would have a lot to fit in through the holidays. He felt no small degree of angst over the bad timing. He was resigned that Cynthia would have to carry much of the load. He knew it was especially hard on her, given what else she was going through. He resolved to do whatever he could to lessen the burden.

On Christmas Eve, they would tuck Billy Jr. and Addie in early with admonitions that under no circumstances were they to leave their bedrooms until morning. No *I saw Mommy kissing Santa Claus* for those two. He and Cynthia would enjoy a bit of free time together—maybe a glass of wine, maybe a little frolic around the tree—before setting out the spoils of the big man's drop-in. There would be the obligatory milk and cookies left on the mantel. The scrawled notes to Santa, more unintelligible scribbles than actual words. The kids would wake early on Christmas morning, race into the living room like little ground cuckoos, and spend the next hour beaming and screaming and reveling in Santa's generosity. After the annual M&M waffle breakfast, they would all pile into the Suburban and head to the grandparents' houses. Billy's mom's first, followed by Adele and Cecil's.

At 3:45, Gary Alford returned Billy's call. "What's up, buddy?"

"Free for a cold one after work? Marnie's?"

"Today? I don't know, Billy. Things are crazy over here. The chief's called an all-hands meeting. Five o'clock. I have no idea how long it'll last. Could be an hour. Could be more. You know how that goes. Can we do it tomorrow?"

"We can. It's just that…well…the sooner the better."

"Is everything okay?"

"Not sure. I'll fill you in when we—"

"What if we meet at the Majestic tomorrow morning? You name the time and I'll be there."

"That works. Six too early?"

"Six it is. And hey, sorry about today. I know grits and hash ain't much substitute for a cold one."

"It's fine, Gary. See you in the morning."

Even though Billy was eager to meet with Gary as soon as he could, a part of him was glad they were getting together at the Majestic Diner instead of Marnie's. Billy was dead tired from little sleep. The last thing he needed was to spend the evening downing boilermakers. And with his upcoming workload, he needed to spend as much time with Cynthia as he could, *while* he could.

* * *

Cynthia was aproned and standing over the stove when Billy walked in. She didn't look up. "He followed me again, Billy."

"Home?"

She wiped her forehead with the dish towel she kept tucked in her apron pocket. "No, but he would have if I had come straight here."

"Where did he follow you from?"

"From here."

"What do you mean from here?"

She turned on her heels to face him. "He followed me when I took the kids to the Montessori. Then he waited for me in the parking lot across the street from the school. You know the one. The strip mall?"

"The one with the Walgreens?"

"Yep. Then he followed me to the police station."

"Why the *police* station? Did something happen?"

"No. Just that he was following me, and there was no way I was coming home with him on my tail. It occurred to me as I was driving down Peachtree that I'd go to the station. Thinking that surely he'd give up at that point, knowing I was on to him. And he did. He took off down Butler Street."

"Did you go inside?"

"No. I waited in the car. As soon as he was gone, I headed home."

"Could you tell anything this time about the car? The driver?"

"I couldn't see the driver at all. He was too far away most of the time. And when he continued down Decatur Street past the police station, he was going too fast. Plus, I had limited visibility because of the other parked cars."

"What was he driving?"

"It looked big. I don't think it was a late model. It was light green with a black top."

"What kind was it?"

"Billy, I'm not into cars like you. I couldn't tell a Ford from a Chevy from a Buick. Or a Gremlin. Well…maybe a Gremlin. All I know is it didn't look new."

"Four-door?"

"I think so."

"I'm meeting Gary for breakfast in the morning. I'll talk to him abou—"

"What are you meeting *him* for?"

"Cynthia, twice now somebody's followed you. I've said from the get-go that I didn't think Kilgallon acted alone back when—"

"Yes, back when. Go on."

"What if his accomplice is out to tie up loose ends?"

"After eighteen years?"

"It's not eighteen years. Kilgallon died *last* year. And it was all because I was onto him. If I hadn't been, he'd surely have gotten off scot-free."

"But he didn't."

"No. He didn't. But what if whoever was in cahoots with him is out for revenge?"

"Against me? Or you?"

"That's what I don't know. But maybe Gary can help us get to the bottom of it."

"Isn't he Larceny? How can *he* help?"

"For one thing, he helped me nab Kilgallon. And even though he's Larceny, he knows his way around the police department. Having had a daddy in Homicide all those years doesn't hurt. The good old boy definitely rubbed off on him. Hell, I bet he knows every regular in that building, even the janitor and the guy that changes the light bulbs. He's just that way."

CHAPTER FIVE

Billy Tarwater

Wednesday, December 16ᵗʰ, 1981

BILLY LOOKED UP AT THE RED NEON SIGN ANNOUNCING FOOD
THAT PLEASES - SINCE 1929. Standing tall above the curved Art
Deco façade with its translucent glass blocks. Its wall of windows
beckoning all who travel down Ponce de Leon, no matter when,
day or night.

He pulled into the Briarcliff Plaza lot and parked in the nearest
space across Cleburne Terrace from the Majestic.

How many times had he sat on one of those chrome knee-
high stools at the red Formica counter, chowing down and shooting
the breeze with whoever happened to be within earshot? He'd lost
count.

Everybody's welcome through these doors, Manny Markos, the best
short-order cook this side of Ol' Man River, used to say. Journalists
and businessmen, pimps and hookers, college students and

Clermont strippers. It didn't matter who you were. Where you'd been. Where you were going. If you had a hankering to snag a plate of sunny side ups or a short stack at three in the morning or in the middle of the day, the Majestic was your go-to place.

Locals called Ponce de Leon the all-night street. Pushers and smackheads roamed around the clock. Hustlers and panhandlers pursued their prey. They were by and large benign. That is, unless you presented yourself as a likely target. In all the years Billy had been going to the Majestic, he'd had a problem only once.

It happened one evening back in the early '70s. He was all of nineteen at the time. Maybe twenty. After leaving the Majestic, he walked by the Soap Suds Laundromat next door and happened to notice a sotted transient standing just inside. She was holding a bottle of Mennen Skin Bracer. She made eye contact with him, unscrewed the top, twisted her face into a granny knot, and began to drink it. Billy burst through the door and tried to stop her. She pulled a pocketknife. Lunged at him, just missing his chest before he pushed her away. He ran to the nearest phone booth and called for help. For her, not for him.

Billy sat in the car with the motor running. The dashboard clock said ten 'til six. The light rain had just ended, and a gentle breeze swept across the parking lot. But it was bitter cold outside, having registered thirty-six degrees when he left home. He flipped the radio to WSB. The early morning host was droning on in monotone about Andres Thomas, some kid from the Dominican Republic, signing on with the Braves as a non-drafted free agent. *It's December for Christ's sake. What about the Falcons? The wild-card playoffs?* He turned to WQXI. "Quixie in Dixie" they called it. REO Speedwagon. *Better.*

Gary eased his car into the space next to where Billy was parked. Gary had the same shit-eating grin that Billy had always found endearing, going all the way back to their East Atlanta playing-army-by-the-creek days. Gary squared his shoulders, tugged at the webbed elastic band of his Sansabelt trousers, and limped over to where Billy still sat, Speedwagon blaring. Even though it had been only a little over a year, he looked a bit stouter, and a little more hobbled, since the last time they got together. But he had the same salt-and-pepper beard. The same horn-rimmed glasses with dark brown lenses. The same birds eye maple cane with the brass wolf's head. The same Braves cap with the frayed visor.

Billy got out of the car and extended his hand.

"No way, buddy," Gary said. "I need more than a handshake." He steadied himself and gave Billy a big bear hug, never letting go of his cane.

"Ready for a biscuit?" Billy asked.

"Hell no. Blueberry fat stack for me. And a coupla eggs and cheddar grits."

"No bacon?"

"Not this time, Billy. He patted his stomach. The missus tells me I need to cut back."

"But pancakes are okay?"

"Of course. A man has his limits."

They took the last table at the far end of the diner.

Gary squeezed into the chair against the wall. He fiddled with the laminated menu.

"What's up?" Gary said. "You sounded iffy on the phone. You okay? I assume you're knee-deep in the Williams shit."

"I am, Gary, but it's not that."

"Is it Finnegan?

"No." The muscles in Billy's nape and shoulders tightened. "Cynthia's being followed."

"By who?"

"I don't know. It's happened twice now, at least as far as she knows, but there could have been more. Of the two times she knows about, one was when she was bringing the kids home from my mom's. Then it happened again on their way to preschool. He waited for her across the street from the school and then followed her downtown."

Gary made swirls in his cheese grits with the tines of his fork. First clockwise, then counter. "So he followed her from two different places."

"That's right."

"Are you sure it was the same person?"

"I'm not positive of anything. Cynthia couldn't identify the driver or the car. The only thing she thinks is that, the second time anyway, it was an older green four-door with a black top."

"Let's assume for now that it's the same person. That tells me he somehow knew where she was going to be at a given time."

"Perhaps. Or perhaps not. It's possible it was random the first time. What if somebody just happened to be driving down the street when she pulled out of my mother's driveway? He follows her home. Now he knows where she lives. Fast forward to the next day. He has time on his hands. He decides to hang around outside The Belmont on the off chance she happens to head out. She does. And he follows her again."

Gary leaned across the table. Peered over his horn rims. "Billy, do you really believe that's what happened?"

"No. Not really. But it's possible."

"A lot of things are possible. But I wouldn't put a plug nickel on ninety percent of 'em. Has she pissed somebody off lately?"

"Cynthia? Are you kidding? I'm the one who pisses people off. Not her."

"Well, let me put it differently. Have *you* pissed anybody off lately?"

"What day is it? Wednesday?"

Gary chuckled. "Okay. I get it. Is there somebody you've pissed off that would go so far as to stalk you?"

"He isn't stalking *me*. He's stalking *Cynthia*."

"Yeah, but he may be trying to get to you through her."

"That occurred to me. I keep thinking about the whole thing with Kilgallon. Somebody was working with him. They had to have been. Whoever it was, maybe I'm their target now. Or Cynthia. Or both of us."

"Would you be willing to set up a trap?"

"A trap? How?"

"The chances are good, assuming it isn't some random thing, that it'll happen again. And probably soon. What if we set him up?"

"What do you mean?"

"You'd need to take your kids to your mom's for few days. Could you do that?"

"Sure. Mom would love that. Especially with Christmas around the corner."

"No, wait. Take 'em to Cynthia's parents' instead. Whoever's doing this knows where your mother lives."

Billy grimaced. "I don't like the kids spending a lot of time alone around either of Cynthia's parents. With Adele's crazy Bible-thumping and Cecil's constant carping about one thing or another. And his incessant alcohol-fueled craps and parlay shit. But I can do that if I have to."

"I think it would be best. Now let's say he shows up again, lurking in wait for Cynthia to leave. Let's say she drives out of The Belmont. But she's not alone this time. You and I'll be crouched in the back. She drives to the preschool like nothing's up. He follows her. She parks as close to the street as she can. He waits across the street. She goes inside. We jump out of the car, run across the street and confront him."

"But you told me to send the kids away. Won't he find it odd that she's entering the Montessori without them?"

"Maybe we don't send them to stay with Cynthia's parents then," Gary said. "Hell, you don't want them to go there anyway."

Billy scratched his head. "Gary, no offense, but sometimes I wonder how you got to be a detective. Don't you think, if he's parked across the street from the daycare, probably with the motor running, that he'll take off when he sees us jump out of the car and head his way?"

"Maybe. Probably. But at least we'll get a good look at him. At the car. And maybe even the license plate."

"And what if he's armed?"

"We'll be too, Billy."

"We?"

"Well, me anyway. Remember when we confronted Kilgallon last year in Alabama? I told you then. I always pack. Just like that American Express commercial. Don't leave home without it."

"And how are we going to somehow know when he's planning to hang around The Belmont? Do you have some kind of sixth sense I don't know about?"

"Of course not. But what if we can make out a pattern? What if it happens another time or two? Then maybe we'll have a pretty good idea when he'll do it again. Then we kick into action."

"Gary, you have a job. How can you just plan to be around whenever the mission calls? And by the way, in case you forgot, I have a job too."

"I can't speak for you, but I took off to help you in Alabama, didn't I? And this ain't even Alabama. I have a lotta leeway as far as where I am in the city. This may not be larceny, but it's a big friggin' deal to me. I'd do anything to help you out, Billy. You know that."

"I know. That goes without saying. And you know I'd return the favor anytime. But this idea of yours, I doubt Cynthia would go along with it." Billy looked at his watch. They'd been there for over an hour. "I need to head out, Gary. Can we continue this in the parking lot?" He held out his hand, palm up. "Give me your check. This one's on me."

Billy paid and they headed back to their cars.

"Gary, this plan you've cooked up doesn't make sense to me. Why don't I just wait until the guy shows back up and confront him?"

"Billy, would you prefer to cause a scene where you live or someplace far from there. You do have neighbors, don't you?"

"Of course I have neighbors. But they—"

"And anyway. If he's just sitting there and you confront him, don't you think he'll deny everything? 'Following somebody?' he'll say. 'I'm not following somebody. I'm just sitting here idling. There's no law against that, is there? Free country last I checked.' But if instead we hide in the back and follow him all the way from there to the preschool, that's pretty damning. Good reason to confront him, if you ask me."

"I guess you have a point, but it still seems out there."

Billy agreed to talk to Cynthia. No promises, though.

"Fingers crossed," Gary said. "By the way, what's going on with Finnegan?"

Billy thought back to his first meeting with J.P. Finnegan. It was in March. Just a day after Gary had said call him. "I'm glad you brought that up. I intended to mention it. I've met with him a few times, but you knew that already. I'm convinced we're onto something, but we need to keep it on the q.t. for now. When it breaks, Gary, I'm telling you the whole damned city may detonate like a Roman candle. And you need to keep as far away from it as you can."

"I know. Plausible deniability, right?"

"Right. If word got out that you were mixed up in this, you could probably kiss your career goodbye."

"Kiss my *ass* goodbye's more like it."

"That too."

Gary put a finger to his lips. "Mum's the word, my friend."

"Gary, do you think there's any way somebody could have gotten wind of my snooping? Of my dealings with Finnegan? And maybe—"

"Billy, no offense, but sometimes I wonder how you got to be a newspaperman." There was that big grin again. "That's not the way those guys work."

Billy stopped at the red light at the corner of Ponce and Argonne.

Traffic crept along. Heavy even for a weekday. Mind-wandering heavy.

He glanced over at the Krispy Kreme. A decade or so ago, Gary's father Gus had suffered a massive heart attack right there on the sidewalk. He was rushed to the hospital, but he never made it out alive. Gary idolized his dad. Billy was sure that he, Gary, had decided at that very moment to become a cop just like Gus.

Life can change in an instant.

Billy thought about Gary's friendship. Until last year they hadn't seen each other in a decade and a half. But when they got together again, they didn't skip a beat. That's the way friends are.

If Gary hadn't become a cop, if they hadn't stayed in touch, if Gary hadn't agreed to help him out last year, he might never have sought out Kilgallon in Alabama. Avenged what happened to Cynthia and the others back in '63. Seen Sam Jepperson walk out of Reidsville State Pen a free man.

Thanks to Gary, Billy was now immersed in the stealth doings of J.P. Finnegan and the scheming of the Vardeman clan.

And now, Billy had called on his childhood friend yet again, to help him track down whoever was stalking Cynthia.

After eighteen years, Jepperson had walked this past June, the same month Wayne Williams was arrested. Williams now seemed on the verge of being sent up for life. Killing two adults, for which he was on trial, was one thing. Killing innocent children was quite another. Even if Williams never ended up having his day in court for the child murders, they would likely be pinned on him. People like a neat and tidy outcome. *Put a bow on it and be done with it.*

Two and a half years ago, Billy had been helping a friend wrap a story about the Klan when he learned of the first black boy to go missing.

* * *

Saturday, July 21st, 1979. He was at the City Desk late into the evening polishing a story that was to run above the fold in tomorrow's *Journal-Constitution*. The result of four weeks of research and interviews, the article dealt with the reemergence of the Klan across the South and beyond.

The principal writer was a *Journal* man, but Billy had agreed to help him out.

The two papers had shared common ownership for almost three decades and had published combined weekend editions since '76. Even though they had been housed in the same building since the early '50s, they kept separate newsrooms. It was rare for a reporter at one paper to collaborate with his counterpart at the other. But Billy never turned down the opportunity to help a friend.

Billy finished reviewing the galley proof. He stared at the photograph that would run in tomorrow's paper. It was of two hundred or so robed modern-day Klan members burning a cross in a field in Texas. In a way, the picture spoke more to conscience than all the words that would accompany it.

He thought back to a similar picture he'd laid eyes on back in '61. It was of ghostly hooded Klansmen carrying flaming torches at a rally somewhere in Georgia. The men looked like something out of a horror movie. It struck fear in a nine-year-old's heart. He had asked Dovey Mae about it. She said, "Binky, them's evil men. And they ain't goin' away. Not in my lifetime."

The fear he had felt as a boy had been supplanted by disgust. Disgust that the evil men had outlived Dovey Mae. Disgust that he was gazing down at a horrifying image not that different from the one Binky had come across twenty years ago.

Billy was about to head upstairs to drop off his comments when he glanced at yesterday's paper, lying on the edge of his desk. It was opened to the Friday Briefing column on Page 2. With everything that had been going on over the past couple of days, especially President Carter's "Georgia Mafia" shakeup, Billy hadn't done a very good job of keeping up with the news beyond his immediate purview.

His eyes fell on the article titled SON OF SAM. The Gannett Westchester Newspapers had reported on Thursday that unnamed police sources alleged David Berkowitz did not commit the last of the New York City murders attributed to him. The NYPD said they would "look into it." He wondered whether the police would give the allegation any more than a perfunctory once-over. Sometimes, when the authorities have put their stake in the ground, they're reluctant to remove it.

Billy was leaning forward, with both hands on his desk, scanning the other articles on the page, when the police radio chimed in with a crackle. The police had been called to the Kimberley Court apartments by a distraught mother. Her fourteen-year-old son had gone missing earlier that day. Some police who happened to be nearby were dispatched, but they didn't stay long. There wasn't anything they could do. The boy had been gone less than twenty-four hours. And he lived in a neighborhood where teenage boys often left home. Where teenage boys were often up to no good—or so it was said. The police ended with a 10-4. The radio went silent briefly before the next audio feed came through.

Billy thought about that boy. And how he would feel if one of his own went missing. Then he headed upstairs.

In the days that followed that evening when the crackle came through the radio, Billy learned a lot about the boy. His name was Edward Hope Smith, but everybody called him Teddy. He had an endearing smile and a self-confident air. He loved football and hoped to join the Therrell High team in the fall. He also loved martial arts.

Billy loaded a sheet of blank labels onto the IBM Selectric's platen. He aligned the typeball with the upper leftmost label and typed the boy's name. He affixed the label to a fresh manila folder and inserted his notes on the boy.

```
SMITH, EDWARD
Disappeared July 21, 1979.
14 years old.
Nickname: Teddy.
Lived in Kimberly Court projects, Cape St.,
southwest Atlanta.
One of the worst/filthiest/most crime-
infested/rundown public housing projects
```

Atlanta. Some residents say there's more garbage on Cape Street than people.

Wanted to escape the projects but hadn't yet figured out how. Had few options at 14. Could run away from home, but where would he go? How would he survive? Maybe move in with friends, assuming their parents would allow it.

Late afternoon July 21, left apartment to meet up with girlfriend. Ended up at Greenbriar Skating Rink. Left skating rink around midnight.

Never made it home. Last seen talking to girlfriend at corner of Campbellton and Fairburn Rds., a stone's throw from the rink.

Four days later, Billy found himself affixing another label on another folder. For another missing boy.

EVANS, ALFRED

Disappeared July 25, 1979.

13 years old.

Nickname: Q.

Left home to go to Coronet Theater, Peachtree St., to see karate movie. Caught a ride with a friend, Randy Joe Heath, to the Glenwood Ave. bus stop near his apartment.

Never reached theater.

Bodies of Teddy and Q were found in a wooded area near Campbellton Rd. by an elderly black woman.

Teddy had .22 caliber slug in his back. Had on a blood-stained black jersey with red letters. Socks and leather sun visor were missing.

Q died of asphyxiation. Wearing a belt that didn't belong to him.

The police claimed, with no proof, that Smith and Evans had been involved with drugs and had earlier been seen at a pot party not far from where their bodies were discovered. The police concluded, again without evidence, that the boys' murders had been drug related.

Then a third boy went missing.

HARVEY, MILTON

Disappeared September 4, 1979.

14 years old.

Didn't run in same circles as Teddy and Q. Parents had moved to a middle-class neighborhood in NE Atlanta, far from his inner-city childhood roots.

Played hooky on first day of school after summer break. Told his mother there was no way he'd wear the lame shoes she'd bought him. Said it was hard enough going to a new school with kids from a world he didn't-couldn't-know. Too embarrassed about wearing the wrong shoes on his first day.

Instead, rode a borrowed 10-speed 3 miles to C&S Bank. Had $100 check his mother had given him to pay credit card bill. Made it to the bank, but never returned home.

A week later, a neighbor found borrowed bike leaning against a pine tree on a dirt road near Charlie Brown Airport.

Five weeks later, his badly decomposed body was found in a trash dump in East Point, [8 miles] from where his bike had turned up. Authorities unable to determine cause of death from skeletal remains, but considered it a homicide.

At that time, the police believed Harvey's death to be an isolated incident, with no connection to Smith or Evans.

But Billy wasn't so sure.

The disappearances of black children had continued. Over and over. Their bodies were found in woodland patches, along roadsides and riverbanks, in the crawl space of an elementary school.

The lives of the dead children's families would never be the same. The city would never be the same.

Chapter Six

Cynthia Tarwater

Wednesday, December 16th, 1981

"NO, BILLY. I WON'T EVEN THINK OF IT." CYNTHIA CAME AS CLOSE as she ever had to slamming the receiver onto the cradle. Then she thought better of it. She'd never hung up on Billy before. And after all, he was just trying to look out for her. But there was no way she was going to take part in some preposterous cloak-and-dagger scheme. "I think you and Gary have been watching too many James Bond movies."

"But Cynthia—"

"Do you want to put me and the kids at even *more* risk? And you and Gary, too? Billy, I think you've gone nuts."

"It was Gary's idea, not mine."

"Well then *he's* gone nuts. When did he cook this plan up? Over too many drinks at Marnie's?"

"Of course not. Over breakfast at the Majestic. I told you I was meeting him this morning before work."

"Ah, that's right. Sergeant Larceny is now Inspector Clouseau. And he has a sidekick."

"C'mon, Cynthia. Be reasonable."

"*Me* be reasonable?"

"I'll be honest. I think it's a crazy idea too. And I told Gary as much. But I'm worried about you. And we somehow need to get a better bead on whoever's following you. It's happened two days in a row now. Did it happen again this morning?"

"I kept Billy Jr. and Addie home today. We haven't been out of the house."

"Are they okay?"

"They're fine. They've been bouncing off the walls all day. They wanted to go out, but I wouldn't let them. I'm just concerned, that's all."

"That's my point, Cynthia. You can't keep from going out. If you have another idea—"

"I don't. Except maybe if it happens again, I can try to get a better look at the car and driver."

"You can. That would be good. But that means going out. And anyway, we need a backup plan."

"What if you just went with me, sitting in the Suburban like a normal human being instead of hiding in the back like a fugitive?"

"My concern is that, whoever it is, if he sees me in the car, he may not follow you. And I can't be with you all the time."

"What about the police? Can we just call the police?"

"They won't do anything unless we have something more tangible to go on than 'I think somebody's following me, but I don't know what they look like, what they're driving, or heaven forbid, who they are.' Will you at least think about Gary's idea?"

"I'll think about it. But give me a few days. Will you be home for dinner?"

"You bet. No more late nights at work. I promise."

Cynthia knew he tried. She knew he meant it—in the moment. A tear coursed down her cheek and made its way onto her blouse. "Billy, the kids are worn out from playing inside all day. I'm feeding them and sending them to bed early. When you get home, can we have a quiet evening together, just you and me, and not talk about any of this?"

CHAPTER SEVEN

Billy Tarwater

Wednesday, December 16ᵗʰ, 1981

A QUIET EVENING. JUST YOU AND ME, CYNTHIA HAD SAID.

Billy hung up the phone wondering whether maybe he had pushed too hard. She was under a lot of stress. He could feel it through the line in the tenor and tone of her words.

He struggled sometimes with the tension between two seemingly disparate Billys. One was his predisposition as a hardnosed journalist to adopt a scorched-earth approach of sorts to get to the essence of an issue. To fulfill a mission. The other was his compassion for the people around him, for the people he cared about most. Even at times for the subjects of his investigations, to the abiding dismay of city editor Dedrick Roberts.

Billy vowed to himself that he would get home at a decent hour for a change.

He returned his attention to the missing and murdered children.

There had been twenty-two boys and two girls in all. Every one of them black. Ranging in age from seven to seventeen. It had begun with Teddy Smith on the twenty-first of July over two years ago. At the time, the police viewed Smith's disappearance and death as an isolated incident. But, as more and more children disappeared, they became convinced that the slayings were emblematic of pattern murder.

Last year, the FBI had joined the Atlanta Police, the GBI, and other local authorities in pursuit of the killer or killers. In keeping with their abiding affinity for acronyms, they had dubbed the initiative Operation ATKID.

For a long time, some people had thought one person was behind it all. Others thought there were multiple perpetrators. Perhaps a few of the killings were random. Perhaps some were the product of copycats.

And now they had their answer. Now they had their man. Or so they said.

The constant clackety-clack of the City Desk's typewriters, the ringing of its phones off the hook, interrupted Billy's thoughts. He turned his attention to the five-by-five Upson-board-mounted map of metro Atlanta on the City Desk wall. In an effort to find geographical commonality among the murders, he had stuck pushpins into the map. Red showing the locations of disappearances. Green for discovered bodies. The pins cut a broad swath across the city. From the Chattahoochee River to Conyers. From Paces Ferry Road to College Park.

He stepped back and pondered his handiwork. Almost all the pins, save for the few you could count on one hand, were inside the expressway that encircles Atlanta. Most were clustered in the inner city and points west and south. Aside from the close-in concentration, no other pattern jumped out at him.

He opened the box of unused pushpins. There must have been twenty of each color, plus a bunch of blues and yellows. He hoped he wouldn't need any more of them.

Billy had immersed himself in the details so much that he could look at almost any pin and know who it was, when it had happened.

There was the red pin at the intersection of Campbellton and Fairburn Roads. That was Teddy Smith. And another at the Glenwood Avenue bus stop. That was Q.

Then there were the two green pins sticking out akilter, vying for the same spot just off Campbellton Road. That was where the two boys' bodies had been found among a grove of trees.

His eyes fell on the red pin where McDaniel and Fulton Streets crossed. And its green counterpart piercing the E.P. Johnson Elementary School on Martin Street. Billy had fashioned a tiny paper pennant, scribed a question mark on it, and attached it to the red pin. No one knew for sure where Yusuf Bell had last been seen before he disappeared. But they sure knew where his body had been found.

Billy shuffled through the folders scattered across his desk. Over months of investigation, he had pieced together the details of this boy's fate.

BELL, YUSUF

Disappeared October 21st, 1979.

9 years old.

Gifted kid.

Left apartment in McDaniel Glenn Housing complex, Rawson St., on eastern edge of West End. Never returned.

A neighbor [Eula Birdsong] had asked him to walk 14 blocks to Reese Grocery, corner of McDaniel & Delevan Sts., to buy pocket can of Bruton Scotch Snuff. She gave him a $1 bill. With his mother Camille's consent, he gladly complied. It was a warm, breezy day. Wore favorite pair of brown cutoff shorts. No shirt. No shoes.

He bought the snuff and headed home.

A witness said she'd seen Yusuf getting into car near intersection of McDaniel & Fulton Sts., 4 blocks from McDaniel Glenn.

Witness said car pulled up along curb near bushes between fenced playground and red brick apt. building. Said driver looked like Yusuf's father John [divorced from Camille].

Camille swore witness was untrustworthy, a "worn-out boozehound with a lying disposition"…should take whatever the "old sot" said with grain of salt.

Witness story kept changing. Car could have been blue or green. Old or new. Sedan or coupe. Driver could have been black or white.

18 days later, John Henry Tye, a school janitor, was looking for somewhere to

```
relieve himself. Found Yusuf's body in crawl
space at elementary school, over 1 mile from
where witness said Yusuf got in car.

Yusuf was in same cutoff shorts he left
home wearing, but a length of heavy tape
was stuck to them.

Had been hit over head twice, but cause
of death listed as asphyxiation by
strangulation.
```

Two years later, Yusuf's one-time babysitter Juanita Saint George disappeared. A city sanitation worker stumbled upon her half-naked body near the Lakewood Fairgrounds. She had been stabbed sixty times. Police surmised that she had been dead about a day when her body was found. She was thirty-two. Her killing was one of a spate of stabbing deaths of young black women that overlapped by a year with the abduction and murders of the black boys.

Camille Bell, desperate to find Yusuf, visited the *Constitution*. The *Journal*. The *Daily World*. She called the local radio and TV stations. She begged whoever had taken her son to let him go. "Please bring my boy back."

The authorities dismissed the murders of Bell and others as the type that "just happen" in poor communities. Yusuf's mother was incensed. She wouldn't—couldn't—abide the city's inaction and apathy. She reached out to the other victims' parents. Something had to be done. So they joined forces to form what became the grassroots Committee to Stop Children's Murders. They would take it upon themselves to find the culprit behind the murders of their children.

Billy tracked the other disappearances across the map, touching each pin, in order, with his index finger. He knew the backstories of those boys and girls as if they were his own.

After Yusuf Bell, Atlanta had experienced a three-month respite, and so a collective sigh of cautious relief began to spread through the city. Some said maybe the ordeal's end is near. But a suspect, or suspects, had not been identified as yet. And mothers and fathers in the inner city's black neighborhoods remained on edge. They knew, even if the authorities wouldn't admit it, that four child murders in four months were not what "just happen" in poor communities.

The three-month respite ended with the disappearance of the first girl.

LANIER, ANGEL

Disappeared March 4th, 1980.

12 years old.

Precocious. Pretty. To mother's consternation, had been receiving attention from enlisted men at Fort McPherson.

She and her mother Venus had relocated to Atlanta from Chicago. Venus wanted daughter to grow up in safe surroundings, with trees and better climate.

At 4 p.m., after finishing homework, left her
SW Atlanta apartment to visit a girlfriend,
where they talked about school and boys.
Watched Sanford and Son. Drank sodas, ate
potato chips.

Left friend's apartment before sunset. Never
made it home.

Body found 6 days later tied to a tree in
vacant lot on Campbellton Rd., near her
apartment. Electrical cord wrapped around
neck and hands. White panties—not hers—
stuffed in mouth.

Wearing the same denim outfit she'd left
home in. Cause of death listed as ligature
strangulation.

Between the eleventh of March and the end of August, eight
more children would disappear and later be found dead. Eleven
boys and one girl. Ranging in age from seven to sixteen. All black.
Most had been strangled or asphyxiated. One died of blunt-force
trauma. One had been stabbed multiple times.

MATHIS, JEFFERY

Disappeared March 11, 1980.

11 years old.

Left West End home in grey jogging pants,
brown shoes, white & green shirt. On way to

Star Service Station to buy cigarettes for mother Willie Mae. Never returned.

Several months later, a girl said on the day he went missing, he got in car with two men, one light-skinned and the other dark-skinned. But she could provide little detail, and what she provided was suspect.

Another witness said he had seen Jeffery in a Chevrolet across from the Stewart-Lakewood Shopping Center.

Skeletal remains not found until eleven months later. Impossible for authorities to determine cause of death.

MIDDLEBROOKS, ERIC

Disappeared May 8, 1980.

15 years old.

Lived with foster parents. Biological mother gave him up when he was 4 months old. Never knew biological father. Half-brother was Atl. police officer.

Phone rang Thursday morning. Eric answered. Soon after, bolted from apartment on his bicycle. Took a hammer with him, he had said to repair bike.

Next day, body and bike found near rear garage of Hope-U-Like-It bar in East Atlanta, next door to Georgia Department of Offender

```
Rehabilitation. Pockets were turned inside
out. Stab wounds about chest and arms. Blunt
force head trauma.
 A fiber was collected from bottom of tennis
shoe and sent to GBI crime lab.
```

At the time, Billy was heartened to learn that, finally, authorities had begun to suspect a link among the children's deaths. To Billy's thinking, it would have been hard *not* to, given that there had been seven children in less than a year. And all of them black.

But his colleagues were skeptical.

Shortly after Eric's Middlebrooks' death, Dedrick Roberts called a morning meeting of the city reporters. He went around the room, pointing to each man, one-by-one, and booming with basso gravitas. "Do you think it's random?" Most said yes. Look at the facts, they said. Look at how they were killed. One was shot in the back with a .22. Three were strangled. One took a blow to the head. Harvey's body was too bad off for the medical examiner to even know how he died. And Mathis hadn't even been found. He may have just run away from home. Is there really a pattern here?

After Middlebrooks, the killings continued.

```
RICHARDSON, CHRISTOPHER
Disappeared June 9, 1980.
12 years old.
Lived with paternal grandparents near
Memorial Dr., DeKalb Cty. Mother had skipped
```

out, nowhere to be found. Father serving 15-year armed robbery sentence at Reidsville. Stepfather also incarcerated.

Last seen on June 9 outside Krystal on Memorial Dr. on way to Midway Rec Center to swim. In blue shorts, shirt, tennis shoes.

Dog found body 6 months later in wooded area near East Point. Wearing swim trunks that weren't his. Various items recovered near body, incl. shotgun shells, Penthouse & Gallery magazines, magnetic recording tape, but none could be connected to his murder. When authorities finally wrapped up their crime scene investigation and departed, accidentally left body parts behind.

No cause of death could be determined.

How the hell do you leave body parts behind? Billy thought. He noted as much with a handwritten margin note.

Thirteen days after Christopher Richardson's disappearance, a second girl went missing.

WILSON, LATONYA

Disappeared June 22, 1980.

7 years old.

2nd black girl to go missing.

Abducted from apartment on June 22. Witness claimed to have seen a man climb into 2nd flr window, depart through back door carrying the girl, and meet up with another man in apartment parking lot.

4 months later, skeletal remains found near apartment, badly decomposed. Cause of death undetermined.

WYCHE, AARON

Disappeared June 23, 1980.

10 years old.

Last seen getting into '70s Chevrolet in front of Tanner's Corner Grocery Store on McDonough Blvd. Car description matched one connected to Jeffery Mathis' disappearance. Witness claimed to have seen Wyche being led away by man with facial hair.

Body found under 6-lane bridge over railroad tracks near Moreland Ave. Wearing red-and-black shirt, blue cutoffs, high-top shoes. Neck broken from presumed fall from bridge. Fall surely not accidental. Tops of guardrails almost as high as him. Acrophobic. Unless trying to escape from something or somebody, would not have climbed guardrail.

CARTER, ANTHONY

Disappeared July 6, 1980.

9 years old.

Disappeared while playing hide and seek with cousin.

Found next day behind warehouse near his home.

Had been stabbed to death.

TERRELL, EARL

Disappeared July 30, 1980.

11 years old.

Started acting up at South Bend Park public swimming pool. Lifeguard threw him out. Disappeared and not seen again.

His aunt said she got a call from a man who sounded middle-aged with white, southern drawl claiming to have Earl and demanding $200 ransom. Supposed kidnapper never called back.

Body found not far from Christopher Richardson's in wooded area near East Point. Missing some clothes.

Cause of death could not be determined.

```
JONES, CLIFFORD

Disappeared August 20, 1980.

12 years old.

Last seen looking for aluminum cans with
cousin. Had been staying with maternal
grandmother, visiting from Cleveland, OH.

Body found beside dumpster next to laundromat,
Hollywood Plaza Shopping Center NW of
downtown. Mouth bruised and cut. Underwear
missing. Wearing red and blue jogging shorts
that weren't his.

Strangled to death.
```

Billy let his index finger linger briefly on the green pin indicating the shopping center where Clifford's body had been found.

It was almost six o'clock. Time had flown by.

He packed up and headed home.

Chapter Eight

Cynthia Tarwater

Wednesday, December 16th, 1981

AS SOON AS BILLY WALKED THROUGH THE DOOR, CYNTHIA sensed something was wrong. Was it the slight stoop in his shoulders? Or the languor in his voice? He put his arms around her. He kissed her. But the ardor was wanting.

"Why don't you get comfortable?" she said. "You're always pouring my wine. Let me treat *you* for once. Merlot?"

"How about a Bombay and tonic instead? With a twist."

"Your personal bartendress at your service." She grinned, hoping to get some semblance of a rise out of him. "I'll even make it a double. Just for you." But the rise didn't come.

Cynthia returned with a double cocktail for him and a generous Merlot pour for her. She sat down beside him. "What is it, Billy?"

"You have enough on your mind, Cynthia."

"But I care about you."

"I fear I was a bit too insistent on the phone with you this morning."

"A bit. I can't argue with that. But I know you're just looking out for me. Is that what's bothering you? If it is, you can put it out of your mind. I need to sleep on Gary's idea, though."

"If I were you, I wouldn't waste my time. The more I thought about it, the crazier it seemed."

"Well okay then. Are we good now?"

He downed half the gin and tonic. "I'm good."

But she knew he wasn't. "What else? There's something else."

"It was a rough day at the office, that's all." He clinked the ice in the empty glass.

"Want another?"

"From my favorite personal *bartendress?* Yes, please."

She returned with another double. "What happened at the office?"

"I spent the entire afternoon reprising the murders of those kids. Trying to thread the needle. It drains the spirit, Cynthia."

"I understand. I know what it's like to replay horrible things."

"More so than I ever will."

"I also know how to get it off your mind. Want to skip dinner? The food's on the stove, but I can put it away. It'll be there tomorrow. And almost as good."

He finally conjured a smile.

"The last time I looked in, the kids were fast asleep," she said. "Why don't you go give them a kiss? I'll meet you in the bedroom. I promise I'll make it worth your while."

CHAPTER NINE

Billy Tarwater

Thursday, December 17ᵗʰ, 1981

THE NEXT MORNING, BILLY ARRIVED AT THE CITY DESK A LITTLE later than usual.

He poured a piping cup and turned his attention back to the children. Where had he left off? He consulted his files.

GLASS, DARRON

Disappeared September 17, 1980.

10 years old.

Last seen getting off church bus at corner of Glenwood and Second Ave. in East Atlanta. Had been to Braves game. Wearing yellow shirt, brown khaki pants, white tennis shoes. Never made it home.

Body never found.

By that time, twelve boys and two girls had disappeared. Most bodies had been recovered. Some had not. A pall hung over the city of one-and-a-half million.

Billy thought about the helplessness he felt, how his heart sank every time a call came in about a missing child or a body found. Memories surfaced. Of Cynthia and the other girls back in '63.

The city's a dangerous place. But damn it, shit like this just shouldn't happen. Not to a black kid from the hood. Not to a thirteen-year-old girl. Not in a civilized world.

And not to a black man framed for another man's crimes.

Billy remembered when he had first told Sam Jepperson's son Rufus that he wanted to see his dad absolved and freed.

* * *

On Saturday, September 20th, 1980, Billy was at Marnie's Tavern waiting to meet Rufus. Billy had taken his usual stool at the bar, at what his buddies called the Billy Roost, when he looked up and saw Rufus walk in carrying a shopworn brown leather briefcase.

Billy got up from the stool and called out to him.

Rufus ran up to Billy and set the briefcase on the floor.

After a long embrace, they removed to the adjacent room, the Sidecar, where they could talk away from prying ears. They took the unoccupied table in the far rear corner.

The waitress came over. Billy held his half-full glass in the air. "I have mine," he said, "but my friend here needs a tall one." He looked at Rufus. "What'll it be?"

Rufus ordered a Miller.

Rufus unclasped the briefcase, which he had placed on the chair beside him. He took out a newspaper and unfolded it. It was the morning *Constitution*. He opened it to page 6 and spread it out on the table. He jabbed the picture at the top of the page. The picture of Fannie Mae Smith. Then the smaller picture to the right. Of Darron Glass, Fannie Mae's foster son.

Rufus said a mama's little boy's gone missing. He searched Billy with pained eyes. He asked him when it was going to end.

Billy knew the pictures well. He knew the article. He had helped write it. He told Rufus he wished he had an answer. What he wouldn't give to see those children back in the arms of their parents. Every one of them. But half of them would never come back. And as for the other half, it didn't look good. Billy remembered saying, "When will it end, Rufus? When evil is behind bars."

"But it won't really end then, will it?" Rufus said. "Not for the families of those children. Not for the soul of this city and its people."

"No, Rufus, it won't end then."

Billy leaned in, elbows on the table. Rested his chin on his interlaced fingers. He asked how Sam was doing.

Rufus said his dad was getting by at the state prison. One day at a time. He reached into the briefcase and pulled out a picture of his father. He pushed it across the table. He said he thought Billy might like to see it. Said the people at the prison had let him take it the last time he and his mother went down to Reidsville.

Billy examined the picture. He told Rufus his dad looked good, considering what he'd been through.

Rufus, now twenty-nine, had been eleven when they took Sam away. He said he missed him every day.

Billy asked how Ruby was doing.

Rufus said she was the one he was most worried about now. She had lost a finger, and another was mangled bad. It happened at the food processing plant. Pinch point on a packing line. They let her go. Said she was negligent. They didn't care that somebody had come along and removed the pinch guard. Rufus had hired one of the best black attorneys in the city to represent Ruby's interests.

He said he was moving back to her place to help her day-to-day. To help pay the bills. Said he could teach snot-nosed fourth graders here as well as he could in Statesboro.

Billy took a deep breath and a boilermaker swig. "It may not be the best time to bring this up, with what you're going through with your mother, but I'd like to talk to you about something else."

"Lay it on, Billy. You know you can talk to me about anything."

Billy told Rufus he wanted to get the '63 murder case that sent Sam Jepperson to prison reopened. To find the killer. To see Sam exonerated and let out.

A big smile came over Rufus. "That would be great, Billy."

Billy left Marnie's that day more convinced than ever that he had to do something to get Sam out.

But he was also in the middle of making journalistic sense of fourteen missing black children, most if not all of them dead. And there was no reason to believe it was over.

And it wasn't over.

STEPHENS, CHARLES

Disappeared October 9, 1980.

10 years old.

Left house after watching TV and drawing. Said he was going to Carver Homes to meet a friend.

Body found on grassy hill near entrance to trailer park. Wearing dark blue pants. Missing shirt and one shoe. Nose and mouth abrasions.

Cause of death asphyxiation.

Dog hairs and 2 Caucasian head hairs found on body, plus 2 pubic hairs, not his, on his boxers 950 feet away.

Before his death, Charles had been accused of dealing drugs. Also known to hang out at Zayre Department Store in Stewart-Lakewood Shopping Center.

On October 24th, Dorothy Allison, a 54-year-old psychic bearing an uncanny resemblance to Edith Bunker, rolled into town from Nutley, New Jersey. The police, desperate to crack the case, had called on her to use her special powers to find the killer.

"We're gonna get the louse that did it," she said. "He's a worm and a rat. I'm not gonna call him an animal because I have a dog that's very nice."

She claimed there would be no more slain children as long as she was in town. And sure enough, three weeks had gone by without another missing child. Billy chalked it up to dumb luck. While Dorothy Allison never found the killer, she left town confident that the killings had ended.

Contrary to the New Jersey psychic's predictions, two more children would disappear before the year's end.

JACKSON, AARON

Disappeared November 1, 1980.

9 years old.

Lived in cinderblock house on edge of Lakewood Hts. with 2 sisters, 2 brothers, and father, a roofer. Mother stayed with 2 other siblings in Washington, DC.

Disappeared from Moreland Ave. Shopping Center. Wearing printed shirt, dark pants, sneakers.

Body found off Forest Park Rd. on bank of South River.

Cause of death asphyxiation.

ROGERS, PATRICK

Disappeared November 10, 1980.

16 years old.

Nickname: Pat Man.

Last seen at bus stop near Thomasville Hts. housing project where he lived with his mother, 3 brothers, 4 sisters.

Body later found caught on cables used by rafters on Chattahoochee River near Paces Ferry Rd. bridge, Cobb Cty.

Cause of death blunt force trauma to head.

Maternal grandmother died the same day his body was found.

Friends with several child victims, incl. Aaron Wyche, Aaron Jackson, Darron Glass.

No other children would go missing in the city until January of '81. That's when Lubie Geter was kidnapped.

EARLY '81

CHAPTER TEN

Lubie Geter

Saturday, January 3rd, 1981

LUBIE GETER WOKE DETERMINED TO TAKE ON THE DAY. THE mouthwatering aroma of hot biscuits and bacon, a treat reserved for Saturdays, wafted through the bedroom and held court over the upper bunk, his bed.

Frankie, two years Lubie's senior, had insisted on owning the lower bunk. Which was fine with Lubie. He liked being up high. So high, in fact, that he could easily reach up and palm the ceiling where Tina Turner lived. Not the *real* Tina Turner, of course, but her poster anyway.

"Chuckie," his mama called out. "Get in here while it's hot."

Lubie hated it when she called him that, especially seeing as he was all of fourteen and a half. His friends and teachers at Murphy High all called him Chuck. His daddy Lubie Sr. called him Chuck. So did Frankie. Why couldn't she?

The kids at school sometimes teased him about his big doe eyes and pudgy brown woodchuck cheeks. *How much wood could a woodchuck chuck?* He didn't mind. He knew they did it because they liked him. He could dish it out too when he took a notion. He was little for his age, but everybody said he made up for it in book smarts. And a quick wit. *Ain't no flies on Lubie.*

He climbed down from his roost and dressed quickly. Green checked shirt, fresh jeans, and polished brown loafers. He grabbed his oversized purple hooded jacket—a Frankie hand-me-down—and bounded to the kitchen.

Frankie was already at the table and had managed to scarf down half his plate before Lubie could even get "Good Morning" past his lips. He sat down across from Frankie and raced to catch up. Frankie had agreed to drop him off at the Stewart-Lakewood Shopping Center with the stipulation that he had to get the family car back in time for their daddy to go to the VA Hospital. Lubie knew that, when his big brother said it was time to leave, he'd sure as hell better be ready.

Frankie rose from the table. Lubie followed suit. He put on his jacket and reached deep into both pockets. He felt around to make sure he had an ample supply of Little Trees air fresheners, which he got from the National Pride car wash. By selling them at a quarter a pop, he could walk away with five dollars on a good day.

Lubie had decided a long time ago that he was going to make something of himself. For as long as he could remember, he'd had money-making jobs. Selling Christmas cards door-to-door. Bagging groceries. Working as a clean-up boy at the car wash. He was proud of his daddy preparing meals at the hospital and his mama running the steam press at the dry cleaners. But he wanted more.

The last words out of Mama's mouth as Lubie walked out the door were "You look after yourself, Chuckie. You don't want to end up like those other boys."

There had been fifteen boys in all, plus two girls. Lubie had known four of the boys. The body of one of them, Aaron Wyche was found six months ago under a bridge. He'd been strangled. Another friend, Aaron Jackson, had gone missing four months after that. They found his body along the riverbank. Strangled. The authorities hadn't found the other two, Earl Terrell and Darron Glass, but Lubie just knew they were dead. If you believed what you read in the paper, so did everybody else in the city.

* * *

The Stewart-Lakewood Shopping Center had been a fixture on Atlanta's southside since '62, just three years before Lubie was born. Lubie remembered shopping there as a little tyke with Mama. It wasn't that convenient to where they lived, but back then it was packed with stores of all kinds. J.C. Penney. Lerner's. Woolworth. Jacob's Pharmacy. It was mostly white at first, but by the end of the '60s, a lot of the white people had started moving out. That's when the main stores began to shut down, mostly replaced by smaller ones. By the time Lubie staked out the shopping center for his air freshener trade, there were more blacks than whites. But it was still mixed. And a good place to do sidewalk business.

Frankie pulled into the Stewart-Lakewood parking lot and dropped Lubie off in front of the Big Star Market. After having tried what other stores were there, Lubie had decided the Big Star was the best for selling. He always stood at the far edge of the sidewalk, close enough to the entrance to grab the attention of people going in but far enough away to escape the wrath of the manager.

Business was slower than usual, and by the time noon came around, the hope of a five-dollar day had faded. But he kept at it. *Don't give up.* That's what Mama always said. Of the nine he'd sold so far, three had been to the same man who bought from him every Saturday, no matter what. The man would always show up soon after Lubie arrived, regardless of the time of day. That struck Lubie as odd, but he didn't give it a lot of thought. The man would reach deep into his pants pocket, take out three shiny quarters, and hand them to Lubie. Not knowing the man's name, Lubie had taken to calling him Mr. Pocket. He was sure Mr. Pocket didn't need that many air fresheners but was doing it to help him out. For that he was grateful. But if he wanted to grow, he needed new customers as well. Every adult who approached the market door, every car that eased past the store, was a potential sale. *Hope springs eternal.* That was another one of Mama's sayings.

Around two o'clock, a Chevrolet four-door pulled up to the curb going the wrong way. Lubie didn't know his cars well, but it looked like it was maybe ten years old. The driver rolled down his window. A cigarette, its inch-long ash hanging on for dear life, dangled from his lower lip. Lubie had a vague recollection of having seen him before.

Lubie brightened, hoping to make a sale. Surely the man needed an air freshener for his smoky car. Maybe the man had bought from him in the past. Maybe that's why Lubie remembered him.

His hopes were dashed when the man snarled. "Get in, boy." The cigarette bobbed up and down as the man spoke.

Lubie ignored him.

"I said get in, boy." The man threw the lit cigarette onto the pavement, opened the car door, and was about to step out.

Lubie took off in a sprint. Down the sidewalk. Around the corner. To the loading dock behind the building. He tried three doors, but they were all locked. He banged on the third one, but nobody came. He crouched behind the dumpster. His heart was pounding something awful. His palms were sweaty.

He waited there, hoping the driver wouldn't come looking for him. Or maybe somebody would bring a load of trash out and he could scurry inside to safety.

He heard footsteps. He rose and swung around. He found himself staring down the barrel of a pistol. The man towered over him. He grabbed Lubie at the elbow with one hand and jabbed the pistol into his back with the other. "Don't say a word. If you do, I swear to God you won't see tomorrow."

The man wasn't very muscular, but his hands were huge. He kept a tight grip on Lubie's arm. So tight that it went numb.

The man escorted Lubie to the idling car, which he had pulled around behind the shopping center. He delivered a swift knuckle slap across Lubie's face and shoved him to the asphalt. He trained the pistol on Lubie's chest. "Try to run and you'll end up in a bloody pool. Understand?" The man opened the trunk with his free hand. He retrieved a roll of duct tape and a large black cloth of some sort. He stuffed the pistol inside the waistband of his pants along with the black thing.

For a split second, Lubie considered taking off. But only for a split second. Everybody said he was a smart kid. He knew better than to do stupid.

"Stand up, boy." The man bent over and grabbed Lubie's arm. He yanked Lubie up and swung him around. He wrenched Lubie's arm behind his back and forced his hand up toward his neck. Lubie felt a pop in his shoulder. He was sure his arm was snapping from its socket. Then the man grabbed Lubie's other arm and twisted it behind him. He gripped both of Lubie's wrists with his massive hand and squeezed them viselike. Lubie felt the duct tape wrap around his wrists. He assumed the man had done it straight from the roll because he heard a swift rip afterwards. He thought he heard the man toss the unused roll into the trunk.

The man threw the black something, a hood, over Lubie's head and tightened it with a drawstring. He picked Lubie up by the waist, hurled him into the trunk, and slammed it shut.

The car careened out of the parking lot. Lubie counted—one thousand one, one thousand two—and tried to keep track of the turns as the car sped away. Out of the shopping center, they turned right, then almost immediately took another right. He assumed they were headed west.

A few minutes later, the car came to a stop and the man turned off the engine. The trunk opened. The man pulled Lubie out and jabbed the pistol into the small of his back. He grabbed Lubie's shoulder with his other hand and pushed him forward. "Time to take a stroll."

Dried leaves crunched under his feet. Tree limbs brushed against him. They couldn't have driven very far. Lubie assumed they were in the woods somewhere in the city. He heard a dog barking in the distance. And the rumble of cars and trucks. A low-flying jet passed overhead.

Lubie now regretted not having run when he'd had the chance. Even if the man had shot him in the back, it would have been better than what he feared he was in for. And at least there would have been people nearby to hear the gunshot and maybe come save him before he bled to death.

The man jabbed the pistol harder and ordered Lubie to stop walking. "Time for sayonara."

Lubie collapsed in a sobbing heap.

The man grabbed him and pulled him up. "Stand up." Something hard—the pistol grip?—struck the right side of Lubie's head through the hood. Enough to almost knock him back down. A warm rivulet trickled down his cheek and to his lips. It tasted sickly metallic.

The man yanked the hood from Lubie's head.

Lubie squinted, struggling to adjust to the blinding light.

The man's mouth was clenched. His eyes were steely under heavy lids. His stare was deep, piercing.

He held the pistol in one hand and a length of rope in the other. He stuffed the pistol inside the waistband of his pants, like before. He ordered Lubie to turn around. He wrapped the length of rope around Lubie's neck.

Lubie squirmed. The rope tightened against his throat.

Tighter.

Tighter.

He gasped for air.

His heart, at first thumping a mile a minute, began to cascade to slow tempo.

His hands and feet jerked.

Images of his mother, his father, Frankie flashed then disappeared.

In an instant, he remembered where he had first met his captor.

He felt an intoxicating rush. Followed by a reeling daze.

He crumpled to the ground, barely clinging to consciousness. He felt it slip away.

Chapter Eleven
Fred Bishop

Wednesday, January 7th, 1981

THE CONSTITUTION HEADLINE READ Missing Youth Sought.

Fred Bishop read on. Fourteen-year-old Lubie Geter had been missing since Saturday. He was described by his parents as an industrious and intelligent kid, like most of the fifteen missing or slain Atlanta children.

Bishop wondered if it would ever end.

Then the fifth of February came.

The Jack Russell was the one that found the body.

Bishop wasn't quite sure how many illegal rabbit traps would turn up, but when he set out that morning, he was determined to find them all. Even if it took the whole day. He planned to search every square foot between Camp Creek and Vandiver Road.

He found the idea of a lacerated and bone-broken animal dying a slow death in the steel jaws of a leg-hold trap repugnant. And on his own damned property. He'd do whatever it took to put a stop to it.

He pulled his pickup off Vandiver Road and parked near where the Camp Creek tributary crosses before it wanders southward, makes a ninety-degree bend, and joins the main creek. He grabbed his Winchester 70 from the gun rack and exited the truck. He preferred blowing the traps to smithereens for two reasons. For one thing, it sent a clear message to whoever was setting them. For another, the last thing he wanted was a bunch of traps to have to dispose of. And if he should happen upon a snared rabbit hanging on with all hope lost, he could put it out of its misery with a single trigger pull.

He started out following the clearing between the tree line and the creek bank. Rabbits spend most of their time where woods meet cleared land. That's where he would find most of the traps.

Bishop was almost to the bend when the dog took off toward Camp Creek. He called out, but it didn't break its stride. He ran after it.

He hadn't gone more than a hundred yards when he heard the dog's frenzied howling. It was standing over something that Bishop couldn't make out. When he got closer, he realized that it was the mutilated remains of a body. The boy was missing all his clothes except his jockey shorts, which had been ripped to shreds. His left cheekbone was bruised. A laceration cut across the right side of his head. His genitals, pelvic area, and both feet were missing.

Bishop raced back to his truck. His first inclination was to head home and call the authorities. But that would take time. And he didn't want to leave the dog alone in the woods with the remains of a dead body.

He threw the rifle onto the back seat and ran to Vandiver Road. He flagged down the first passing car.

Assuming the driver believed him and didn't think he was some crackpot schemer, help should arrive soon.

He grabbed the leash from the truck bed, retrieved the dog, and returned to the truck. There he waited.

The sheriff's deputies were the first to arrive. They were followed by the Atlanta Police, the GBI, Federal law enforcement. FBI agents from the Atlanta office had begun a major investigation into the missing and murdered black children only three months earlier, over a year after the first one had disappeared.

Bishop was instructed to remain on the property but to stay near his truck. He felt like he had been thrown into the middle of a hurly-burly maelstrom. He watched from afar as law enforcement came and went. He listened to the chatter on the police radios, gleaning bits and pieces of information.

A green shirt and brown loafers, presumably the boy's, were found three hundred yards from where the body lay. A pair of Levi's and a brown belt were found in a bag three feet deep in Camp Creek.

The boy appeared to have been strangled, but a final determination would be left to the Fulton County medical examiner.

It was nearing sundown before the body was finally carried away, his identity still unknown.

The next morning, Bishop retrieved the *Constitution* from his front yard. He removed the rubber band and opened the paper to the above-the-fold headline: BODY OF 15TH CHILD VICTIM FOUND. The article said the boy discovered on Bishop's property was Lubie Geter. His mother had identified him the prior evening at the medical examiner's office.

The authorities had determined that he died of asphyxiation by strangulation.

His body had been mutilated by animals.

CHAPTER TWELVE
"J.P. Finnegan"

Thursday, February 5th, 1981

JIM ED TURNER STOOD OUTSIDE AND GAZED ABOVE THE TOPS of the Faircourt Trailer Park double-wides. The sun had just begun to bathe the evening sky with a palette of reds and oranges. He didn't consider himself the kind of guy who would normally go in for that sort of thing—sunsets and the like—but tonight seemed different.

Maybe it was the fact that less than an hour ago he'd gotten a call from Rest Haven telling him his mother had taken an unexpected turn. She was refusing to eat. Refusing to drink. Kept asking when her husband—dead for five years now—would show up with Chick-fil-A from Greenbriar Mall. Turner reckoned hopeful delirium beat nursing home despair any day.

Or was it the untimely death of the ornery but irrepressibly likeable codger two trailers down? They said it was a cardioembolic stroke. Two packs a day surely had something to do with that.

Or the fact that Jean, his girlfriend of two years, had left a message taped to his door telling him she was running off to Reno with a carny. And just ten days before Valentine's. A carny? Who the hell runs off with a carny?

Whatever it was, he took it all in and thought *There's got to be more to life than this.*

When the ghost of the sun had retreated behind the trailers and dark had overtaken the light, he went back inside.

He turned on the TV and adjusted the volume down to nothing. He popped an Old Milwaukee, grabbed a bag of Nacho Cheese Doritos, and settled into the Barcalounger. *Peter Gunn* was on silent. Turner had the same damned black-and-white, and the same damned clicker remote, that his father had had when the old man passed, and his mother moved into the nursing home. Maybe one day, when he had the time, he'd take a drive over to Sears and buy a new one. One day. When he had the time.

He dialed Jean at home. No answer. He dialed her sister. Jean sometimes hung out there. No answer.

He grabbed the Zenith Space Command and clicked to Channel 2. He fixed on the flickering image on the screen. There looked to be half a dozen police cars, maybe more, against a wooded backdrop. The scrolling message at the bottom said BODY FOUND OFF VANDIVER ROAD. He turned up the volume. They had found another dead black boy. The camera zoomed in on a clearing. Close enough to show a huddle of men hunched over what he assumed was the body. But far enough away to show nothing, really. They hadn't yet identified the victim. If they thought they knew who it was, they weren't saying.

* * *

The next morning, the pit of his stomach knotted up when he opened the paper and saw Lubie Geter's name. He knew what he had to do.

For seventeen years, Turner had been a police informer. Seventeen long, tedious years. It was a job of convenience, one that he didn't particularly like. But it kept the authorities off his ass. Kept him out of jail. And that was all that mattered.

He'd gone by a handful of assumed names over the years. Billy Ray Peters. Joe Hardaway. Even J.D. Clampett once as a joke, just to see if he could get away with it. He could. And he did.

Since '78, he'd been J.P. Finnegan, explosives expert. That wasn't a stretch. He knew a thing or two about blowing shit up.

He dialed the police.

Two Summers prior…

Chapter Thirteen

J.P. Finnegan

Friday, July 13ᵗʰ, 1979

FINNEGAN WONDERED WHETHER HE'D END UP REGRETTING having answered the phone. "For Christ's sake, somebody sure as hell wants to talk to me real bad." He picked up on the ninth ring.

"It ain't a city no more." The rasp on the line reminded Finnegan of Roy Rogers' sidekick Cookie, except with a drawn-out drawl. "Ain't been for over two years now."

The man had introduced himself as Graydon Vardeman. Said he lived in Mountain View, the ain't-a-city-no-more city. Said he'd gotten Finnegan's number from Roscoe. Said he needed help with a little job. Something having to do with dynamite.

* * *

Finnegan wasn't much of a reader. In fact, he couldn't think of a single book he'd ever gotten to the end of. But when he'd been a little snot-nosed sprout, his mother—now conscripted to Rest Haven, the Home for the Delusional and Incontinent—would balance him on her knee and read to him for hours. One of the books she read was *Gone With The Wind*. At the time, he wondered why she had chosen *that* book. Did she think he'd really understand a lick of it? And why did the book talk about a stagecoach stop named for the Ruff and Reddy cartoon? He went through adolescence and early adulthood never stopping to think that TV cartoons weren't even around when the book was written. It wasn't until he was "fortunate" enough to do an informer stint in a down-and-out unincorporated community south of town, not far from the airport, that he learned that the stagecoach stop had been named for Rough and Ready, a knockabout tavern on the route to Macon. Nothing to do with the escapades of a smartass cat and a brave but not-too-bright dog. And it wasn't even called Rough and Ready anymore. In 1956, when he was four, Rough and Ready had become the City of Mountain View, so named because on a clear day you could see Stone Mountain. It remained a city until 1978, when it was dissolved, in part because of corruption, public drunkenness, and illegal booze sales. Now it was just a backward vestige of a railroad stop. A down-and-out non-city called Mountain View. An ain't-a-city-no-more city.

* * *

"Head down Old Dixie Highway," Vardeman had said. "Three quarters of a mile past where it goes over the interstate, there's a dirt road to the left. Take it. As soon as you turn, there's a sign says Private – Keep Out. Go 'til it dead ends."

The first thing Finnegan noticed when he neared the end of the road was the Siberian husky, standing rigid and letting loose a spine-chilling growl. The second thing he noticed was that the dog's lips were curled back and his teeth were bared. Finnegan eased the car past the dog. He cut the engine. The dog ran up and lunged on his hind legs against the car window.

The third thing Finnegan noticed was the house—a shabby hooch—and its just-as-shabby yard. A Maytag wringer washer sat on the front porch. Next to a Kelvinator, its bright red door trying to decide whether or not it was hinged. A row of empty Jim Beams, dead soldiers standing guard, lined the porch railing. Three rusted-out clunkers and a stack of bald-to-the-core tires graced the yard. The only objects within sight that appeared remotely operable were two Harley Sporters, a Kawasaki Z, and a seen-better-days Impala. *Deliverance meets Whiskey Mountain*, Finnegan thought.

The fourth thing he noticed was the faded Confederate flag, mounted to an oak tree on a wooden pole and flapping in the breeze. It occurred to him that, had he not become inured over the years to the flag and what it stood for, it probably would have been the first thing he saw, not the fourth.

He tapped his horn.

A man stepped from inside the house and onto the porch. He was rawboned and a little stoop-shouldered, with heavy lids and a low forehead. His hair was disheveled. His Yosemite Sam mustache and beard did little to hide his hollowed jaws. He came down off the porch and pulled the dog by the collar around to the back of the house.

When he returned, he walked up to Finnegan's car. "You gonna sit there, or you gonna get out?"

Finnegan stepped out and extended his hand. "J.P Finnegan. You Vardeman?"

"One of 'em."

"*Graydon* Vardeman?"

"Lookin' at him."

Finnegan followed him to the house. The coir "welcome" mat at the door read COME BACK WITH A WARRANT.

CHAPTER FOURTEEN

J.P. Finnegan

Saturday, July 14ᵗʰ, 1979

BACK AT THE DOUBLE-WIDE, FINNEGAN SET THE CHANNEL
Master portable recorder on the folding tray table beside his chair and adjusted it to 1-7/8 ips. He took a blank two-and-a-half-inch tape reel out of its cardboard box, placed it onto the supply spindle, and threaded it between the capstan and the pinch wheel and onto the take-up reel. He plugged the microphone into the MIC jack and attached its suction cup adapter to his phone's handset.

He grabbed an Old Milwaukee, sank into the Barcalounger, pressed REC, and dialed Roscoe.

"Rosco speaking."

"Who is this guy Vardeman anyway?" Finnegan said.

"What do you mean?"

"I met with him and his two brothers." Finnegan consulted his notes. "Ewell and Dickie. I swear to God, I don't know any more about why I was there than I did before I ever laid eyes on 'em. Who the fuck are they, Roscoe?"

"Graydon didn't tell you what he wanted?"

"Fuck no. He went on and on about how he needed a dynamite guy and you'd told him I was the man. Said he wanted to meet again."

"He's sizing you up, J.P. He needs to get comfortable with you, make sure he can trust you before he'll open up."

"Level with me, Roscoe. Who is he? I don't have time for bullshit."

There was a long pause. "Have you ever had reason not to trust me, J.P.?"

"Are you fucking kidding me? I've *never* trusted you, Roscoe."

"I've always sent you good leads, J.P. I've never let you down."

"Good leads are one thing. Leaning-into-a-left-hook leads are another thing altogether. Shoot straight with me or I don't meet with him and his goddamned racist redneck brothers ever again."

"Racist redneck?"

"Well, the redneck part's obvious. And the battle flag flyin' from the tree? Gimme a break. I suspect you knew that already, though."

"You meet with people like that all the time, J.P. If you've told me once, you've told me a thousand times…it's part of the job. Hell, you can play the part as good as the next guy. It's not like you're taking him to the prom."

"I can hold my own. But I need to know what I'm dealing with. Something doesn't square, Roscoe."

Another long pause. "All I know is he's a member of something called the National States Rights Party."

"That's Klan."

"Pretty much," said Roscoe.

"So that's *all* you know about him?"

"I think he's one of the ringleaders. They're bad news. They've set up camps to teach guerilla warfare."

"Are you fucking kidding me? When were you planning to share that little detail?"

"I'm sorry, J.P. It's just that—"

"Yeah, it's just *that*. You sent me into a fucking klavern without my knowledge. Don't ever do that again, Roscoe. If you do, I won't do another goddamn job for you. And at this point, I don't even know what *this* job is. And where are the training camps, anyway?"

"I don't know. Somewhere in the state."

"You don't know?"

"No. I don't know. All I know is Vardeman reached out to me. He trusts me...or at least he trusts the ones that put him in touch with me. Said he needed somebody that knows explosives. I obviously thought of you. I don't know what he's up to, but I thought you could get in there. Root around. Learn something."

"Why didn't you tell me that in the first place?"

"I should've. I just wanted you to meet with the guy first. See if he's for real. Then I was going to."

"Never again. Capeesh?"

"I understand."

"Are you sure?"

"I'm sure. One other thing. Go armed."

"Always. But thanks anyway for the too-little-too-late advice. What else are you not telling me?"

"They've all done time at one point or another."

"All of them?"

"Correct."

"For what?"

"Burglary. Assault and battery. Wife beating. Drugs. My understanding is that Graydon's wife Sonya also did time. Narcotics."

"Anything else? For Graydon and his brothers, I mean."

"Involuntary manslaughter."

"Manslaughter? Who?"

"I don't know the details, J.P. That's just what I've heard from my sources."

"Anything else?"

"Something about children."

CHAPTER FIFTEEN
J.P. Finnegan

Wednesday, September 5ᵗʰ, 1979

"LAOS," VARDEMAN SAID. "LAM SON 719." HIS STOOPED shoulders rose to attention as he spoke. "MACV-SOG. It changed me."

Finnegan knew MACV-SOG. He wondered how the gaunt and hollow-jawed man who now stood before him in the middle of the Vardeman clan's living room could possibly have fallen in with a special ops unit. *Is he shooting straight? Or is it just so much bullshit?*

Finnegan quickly surveyed the room. He hadn't taken the time to do it on his earlier introductory visit. Perhaps he had been too preoccupied with all the shit outside, or maybe with Vardeman's appearance. But whatever the reason, it wasn't like him to be so unobservant. After all, his stock in trade was about eyes-wide-open awareness. Across the room, near the door leading to the kitchen, was what looked like a double bench seat from an Econoline, positioned atop a shipping pallet. The torn fabric across the seat and back had been repaired with silver duct tape. Finnegan's eyes were drawn to the crucifix nailed to the wall above the bench seat. Against the adjacent wall, to Finnegan's left, was one of those faux-velvet sofas you might pick up on the cheap at a flea market. Above the sofa, ham-handedly installed into the wall and framed in unpainted firring strips, was a window AC unit. Its electrical cord dangled below and disappeared behind the sofa. A Confederate battle flag, like the one outside, was haphazardly draped across the sofa's back. The ashtray on the side table in the corner, between the bench seat and the sofa, was brimming with butts and ashes. A dozen or so folding aluminum chairs leaned against the wall to Finnegan's right. The florist's vase and artificial flowers on the coffee table in front of the sofa seemed out of place, but he assumed they were Sonya's doing.

"Came home two weeks after we hauled ass back across the line to *Veetnam*," Vardeman continued. "Empty handed. Marvin the Goddamned Arvin fucked that one up. And Charlie walked all over them. You do time over there, Finnegan?" Before Finnegan could answer, Vardeman changed the subject. "Hey, Dickie," he yelled toward the back of the house. "Dickie, you there?"

Vardeman's brother Dickie appeared in the doorway from the kitchen, nursing what Finnegan assumed was a generous plug tucked between his gum and lower lip. "What is it, Gray?" The disregard in Dickie's voice was palpable.

"Dickie here spent two years in the Mekong Delta. Hollering through a loudspeaker on a backwater river boat. What kind of crap did you use to squeal out, Dickie?"

"I dunno. Shit like give up before it's too late. They're lyin' to you. Choose life, not death. Shit like that." Dickie shook his head. "Like we were really gonna win over them gooks."

"Dickie came home hooked on boom boom girls and *Veetnam* river boat smack," Vardeman said. "But we didn't hold that against him."

Dickie grinned. "Boom boom girls. That's funny, Gray."

About that time, Ewell appeared in the kitchen doorway. He was even gaunter and more disheveled than his brothers. He looked like he'd just rolled out of bed. His hair was a tangled mess.

Vardeman went on to say that he and Dickie had gotten back to the States within six months of each other. Dickie ended up in drug rehab—not that it did any good—and he, Graydon, took a job as a lineman with Southern Bell. He did that for damned near five years before retiring his boots and hooks and belt holster. "Back couldn't take it anymore."

"And after that?" Finnegan asked.

Vardeman lit a Marlboro then tossed the pack across the room to Ewell. "Damn, man. I just realized I've been doing all the talking and you've been standing there the whole time doing all the listening. I haven't even offered you a place to sit." He pointed to the sofa. "Make yourself at home. Coffee? Brewski? Jack?"

"I'm fine, Mr. Varde—"

Vardeman held up his hand. "Stop right there. I told you before. None of that mister shit. Call me Graydon. Or Gray. Or Vardeman. I don't give a goddamn which. But don't call me mister."

He grabbed the ashtray and moved it to the coffee table, leaving a cloud of fine airborne ash particles in its wake. And a few errant butts that found the floor. He unfolded one of the aluminum chairs and sat down facing Finnegan. "Now, tell me more about *you*. Where you from? Where'd you learn to blow shit up?"

Finnegan had figured out long ago how to craft a story in a pinch. One that fit the current narrative. And that would strike a chord with whoever he was in front of. But that either could be backed up or was sufficiently vague—or far away—in case they decided to go snooping.

He told Vardeman about how he'd had a draft deferment. 1-Y. Flat feet. But he would have gone to Nam if he could have. He told him about how he'd floated around for a few years after high school but eventually ended up at the Thompson Quarry outside Chicago learning all about explosives and blasting agents. About how he had eventually come to Georgia because he heard Rockmart Slate was hiring. Got a job with them. But he got mixed up with a rowdy bunch of bruisers and did two years at Reidsville for armed robbery. "7-Eleven just outside Carrollton."

Finnegan realized, as soon as Reidsville passed his lips, that he may have screwed up. Roscoe had told him that Vardeman and his brothers had done time. Finnegan didn't know where, but he hoped he hadn't hit too close to home. Vardeman didn't react, so he assumed everything was okay. Either that or Vardeman was playing cardless poker.

"Throw me them cigarettes," Vardeman called out to his brother.

Ewell tossed the pack back across the room.

Vardeman lit another one, took a drag, and returned his attention to Finnegan. "You originally from Illinois?"

"Oh no. Grew up in West Virginia. My daddy worked the mines. 'Til he got the miner's lung and couldn't go down anymore."

Finnegan delighted in making up stories. In getting away with it. In watching his audience soak it all in like it was gospel. The only problem was he had to have a damned good memory. One misstep with the wrong individual and he could end up somewhere on the Chattahoochee riverbed.

* * *

He remembered one time when he told his mark he was from Lovelady, Texas. At the time, he knew next to nothing about Lovelady, except he liked the name. He didn't know that only four hundred people lived there. That everybody knew everybody. That there were sixteen students in Lovelady High's senior class the year he claimed to have graduated. Turned out the guy he was pitching to had grown up on a farm just outside Lovelady. Joe Hardaway— that's what Finnegan called himself back then—did his best to fast-talk himself out of the situation, but not before suffering a broken nose and a blown cover. And a bruised ego. That's when Joe Hardaway rode off into the sunset and J.P Finnegan showed up. With a newfound wisdom and determination never to make *that* mistake again.

* * *

"What did Roscoe tell you about me?" Vardeman asked.

Finnegan hesitated. *Never mind that. What has Roscoe told Vardeman about* me? Hopefully nothing that would contradict the tale Finnegan had just spun. But he wasn't too worried. Roscoe was savvy enough to keep his mouth shut and say as little as necessary.

"Nothing really," Finnegan said. "Except that you're looking for a dynamite man. Or something like that."

"He didn't tell you why?"

Roscoe hadn't let on to Finnegan that he *knew* why. Had Roscoe held something back? Had he not told Finnegan the whole story? "No. He didn't tell me anything. Except what I just told you."

Vardeman leaned back and laced his fingers behind his head, revealing a blood drop cross in red and black on his right tricep and the numbers 33 and 6, separated by a lightning bolt, on his left. Vardeman took a deep breath. "I'm going to tell you something, Finnegan. Roscoe says I can trust you." He straightened back up in his chair, leaned forward and placed his palms on his knees. "I sure as hell hope he's right." He shook his head and locked eyes with Finnegan. "Because if he isn't…"

"I didn't come here for any reason other than to help you out. Roscoe's a good man. He and I go back. You can trust him. And you can trust me."

"How far back?"

"Far enough." Finnegan rose from the sofa. "Listen, Vardeman, the last thing I want to do is waste your time. If you don't think I can be trusted, I understand. I can leave now. You just tell me to go, and I'll walk out that door with no hard feelings. I don't have to be here if you don't want—"

"Sit back down, Finnegan. I'll tell you what's what. But you have to swear to me that whatever's said here stays here. What's about to go down will blow this fucking city wide open."

CHAPTER SIXTEEN

J.P. Finnegan

Saturday, September 8ᵗʰ, 1979

FINNEGAN PULLED INTO THE REST HAVEN PARKING LOT AND eased into the space farthest from the building. He grabbed the Chick-fil-A bag and Cocola, as his mother was wont to call it, and headed for the front door.

The slow journey across the lot prepared him for the *delusional and incontinent* ordeal that awaited. He counted off the paces as he strode toward the building. One. Two. Three. This had become his usual ritual whenever he visited, which was seldom these days. The parking lot represented a no man's land of sorts between two disparate worlds.

The nursing home's management had taken to locking the front door. Was it to keep the bad element out? Rest Haven was in West End, not the safest part of the city. Was it to keep in the incarcerated incorrigibles? Finnegan suspected it was both.

He rang the doorbell. The front desk attendant, an ample matronly woman who could surely wrestle the halest of the incarcerated to the floor if need be, buzzed him in. "Good afternoon, Mr. Turner. She expecting you?"

He had gone by J.P. Finnegan so long that the utterance of Turner took him aback for a second. "Uh, no. I thought I'd surprise her."

He signed in and slapped the obligatory visitors label onto his shirt. CHRISTINE TURNER. ROOM 127.

Past the front desk, he turned right and headed down the Memory Wing. Given the average age of the residents—he surmised it must have been damned near eighty-five, ninety— wasn't every wing a memory wing?

The hallway aroma never changed. He called it elder smell. Urine mixed with upchuck mixed with glandular secretions the names of which he couldn't begin to pronounce even if he wanted to. Throw in Ben-Gay and VapoRub, and there you have it.

The door to Room 127 was ajar. He eased it open. His mother's bed was the one near the window. She was staring out at the handmade cedar bird feeder hanging from the oak limb. Her cellmate, a Mrs. Walensky from Collinsville, was asleep.

His mother looked up. "Homer, where have you been? I've searched all over for you."

"I'm not Homer, Ma. He died in '76. Remember? I'm your son. Jim Ed."

She stared back out the window. "See that blue jay there? We talk. When I couldn't find you anywhere, he told me you'd show up soon. He said, 'Just you wait and see, he'll be here before you know

it.'" She retrieved her gaze from the window. "And here you are."
She frowned. "You're not steppin' out on me, are you, Homer?"

He thrust the Chick-fil-A bag at her and set the Coke on the
bedside table. "Ma. I'm not Homer. And, no, I'm not stepping out."

Mrs. Walensky woke with a strained smile. He felt fleeting
remorse for not having brought her a sandwich too. *Maybe next
time.*

He stayed for thirty minutes, long enough for his mother to
chinchilla-nibble through the chicken sandwich, regale him with
stories of her most recent escapades of the mind, and complain
about Mrs. Walensky's gas passing. Her plaints were loud enough
that her poor cellmate could surely hear every word. Intentional?
He wasn't positive, but the result was the same regardless.

* * *

He slid into the driver's seat and cranked the engine. "Is this
what I have to look forward to?" he asked himself. "I'd just as soon
somebody lead me to the grassy field past the factory-builts and
plug me right there. Be done with it."

But it occurred to him as he sat in his car with the motor
running that perhaps reality itself was a delusion. He had spent
fifteen and a half years insinuating himself, undercover and sly of
name, into other people's realities so foreign to his own that he
sometimes wasn't sure when he woke up each morning which world
he was living in.

The dashboard clock said three fifteen. Roscoe had agreed to
meet him at five for a cold one. Roscoe suggested they meet at
a Stewart Avenue nudie bar called the Jolly Fox. Truth be told,
it wasn't Finnegan's cup of tea, but Roscoe had insisted, saying

something about how Finnegan needed to lighten up. He had also said something about a burr up Finnegan's backside, a comment that Finnegan ignored.

The Jolly Fox was down the street from the Stewart-Lakewood Shopping Center and next door to a redneck rock-and-roll honky-tonk called Dee Daley's.

Finnegan had almost two hours to kill. He decided he would grab a beer at Dee's before meeting Roscoe at five. But first, he would run by the Big Star Market and buy a Binaca.

* * *

A cherubic-looking black kid was selling air fresheners curbside in front of the market. For a quarter each.

Finnegan bought one.

* * *

The parking lot shared by the honky-tonk and the strip club was half full even at four in the afternoon.

Finnegan walked into Dee Daley's. He peered through the dim gauze of smoke. A plumpish woman with Edgar Winter hair was working behind the bar. ZZ Top was belting out "Cheap Sunglasses" from the jukebox. A rock-star-wannabe band was setting up in the far corner next to two doors, one labeled Roosters and the other Hens. Three customers sat at the bar. Two more were at one of the fifteen or so tables scattered haphazardly across the room. Three sat at another. That was it. Nine patrons including Finnegan. He took a table near the front door.

The plumpish woman came from around the bar and approached his table. She wore white Nancy Sinatra boots, a two-sizes-too-small mini, and an equally undersized top. When she got close enough, he could read the nametag pinned to her blouse. LIL BIT.

He asked for a Schlitz in a bottle.

She returned with the beer and a bowl of boiled peanuts.

He nursed the beer. Avoided the boiled peanuts—they taste like mush and leave a slimy mess on your fingers. Rehearsed what he would say to Roscoe.

* * *

Finnegan exited Dee Daley's promptly at five. He stood just outside the door for a minute while his eyes adjusted to the bright sunlight.

He saw Roscoe walking toward him.

"What are you doing standing out here?" Roscoe said. He pointed to the Jolly Fox. "We need to get us some eye candy."

Finnegan followed Roscoe into the strip club.

The room was packed with ogling middle-aged men. A few looked out of place in suits. But most were in blue collar working clothes. A bare-breasted curvy brunette was romancing the brass pole that ran from the stage to the ceiling. She made eye contact with Roscoe, gave him a wink, and shed her G-string.

"That's Brandi," Roscoe said. "C-cups so firm you could bounce a quarter off 'em." He headed straight to the waist-high counter that ran the perimeter of the stage and was about to pull out a chair.

Finnegan grabbed him by the arm. "Not here, Roscoe. We need to sit over there, across the room, where we can talk."

"Talk? I brought you here to look."

"If I'm not mistaken," Finnegan said, "*you* chose the venue, but *I* called the meeting."

They found a table way in the back.

Finnegan told Roscoe about his session with the Vardeman clan. About a supposed plan, at least the way Vardeman had told it, to trigger a race riot by killing blacks in the city. They would start with young boys and go from there. All hell would break loose. Vardeman had said it would blow the fucking city wide open. He also had plans to dynamite schools. That's where Finnegan would come in. Vardeman had never gotten beyond talking in generalities. Finnegan had pressed him for details, but no dice.

"Here's the thing, Roscoe," Finnegan said. "They're a bunch of strung-out redneck hopheads living in a rundown piece of shit surrounded by a makeshift junkyard. I saw nothing there that said they were serious. They're fucking clowns parading as big shots. They don't have a plan. They're full of shit."

"But what if they *aren't*?"

"If they aren't, then I deal with it. Don't get me wrong. I'm keeping them under my thumb. The risk is too great not to. But I don't think they have the wherewithal to pull off a tenth of what they're blustering about. I've seen professionals in action for seventeen years. These guys aren't professionals."

"But what about the National States Rights Party? And the training camps?"

"First of all, as for the NSRP, I did my homework. Ed Fields and his cohorts, J.B. Stoner and the like, they were serious shit in their day. Hell, Stoner was indicted for bombing that church in Birmingham back in the fifties. They once were a threat, but even the FBI says they aren't anymore. As for Vardeman, to call him an NSRP ringleader is a stretch to say the least. I doubt he'd know Ed Fields from W.C. Fields if he bumped into him on the street. And as for the training camps, I don't think they exist. They may have at one time, but if they did, it had to be Fields' doing, not Vardeman's. Convince me I'm wrong, Roscoe."

"Are you going to tell the police what you heard? Just in case there's something to it?"

"Are you kidding me? At this stage? I have my own credibility to think about. I didn't get where I am by taking shit to the police before I was sure it was for real. And if it *is* for real and I don't do my own diligence first, the police will totally fu—"

"Lap dance, gentlemen?" Brandi sidled up to Roscoe.

Fifteen months later...

Chapter Seventeen

Billy Tarwater

Monday, March 16ᵗʰ, 1981

THE PHONE RANG. BILLY PUSHED AWAY THE PILE OF PAPERS scattered across his desk and picked up the handset.

It was Gary.

"We're not having this conversation," Gary said.

"What?"

"I said we're not having this conversation."

"What do you mean?"

Gary told Billy that, early one morning five weeks ago, an informer going by the name of J.P. Finnegan had called the Homicide Division. He told them he had information about a man who might be connected to Lubie Geter's murder. And maybe to the others as well. The police asked Finnegan to come in for an interview. He did.

"So why are we not having this conversation?" Billy asked.

"Because my cohorts in Homicide have kept the whole thing under wraps. I'm not supposed to know about it. The media's sure as hell not supposed to know about it. I just found out this morning. People tell me things they aren't at liberty to tell me."

"Hold on, Gary." Billy looked around. Two secretaries were chatting by the water cooler across the room. Everyone else was on assignments or had slipped out for lunch. "I'm back. Shouldn't we be having this conversation in person?"

"Normally, I would say yes. But this can't wait. Every day that another kid goes missing is a day too late. I'm telling you so you can maybe reach out to Finnegan. See what you can find out first-hand. The police, the FBI, the mayor, they're all scared shitless. They aren't doing a goddamned thing about it. Finnegan's frustrated as hell, and I don't blame him. If he thinks you won't turn a deaf ear like the people in charge have, then maybe he'll open up to you."

Gary told Billy about Graydon Vardeman and his brothers. About their Klan connections. About Finnegan's meetings with them over the summer of '79 and through the following year. About their master plan. About how Finnegan was skeptical until he saw in the paper that Lubie Geter had been killed.

"Here's the bottom line, Billy. They have a plan going back two years to kill black kids. The idea is that, once the Klan's killed enough of them and they go public with it, the blacks will take to the streets. There'll be race riots all over the city. Like nineteen aught six. But a hundred times bigger. A hundred times worse."

CHAPTER EIGHTEEN
Billy Tarwater

Tuesday, March 17ᵗʰ, 1981

"MINE'S THE BABY BLUE ONE WITH THE AMERICAN FLAG HANGING off the side," Finnegan said. "And a big ass television antenna on top. And a Bill Elliott No. 9 decal on the door."

When most people say the word *television*, they stress the *tele* part. Finnegan stressed the *vision* part, like the device was a deliverer of some sort of providence from on high.

"Come on over," Finnegan continued. "We'll pop a coupla brewskis. We can talk turkey."

* * *

Billy had called Finnegan from work. He took Atlanta Road out of the city. When he reached Dobbins Air Force Base on his right, he cut west toward Sandtown.

The Faircourt Trailer Park occupies a fifteen-acre expanse of red clay and fatigue-cracked asphalt, punctuated here and there by patches of brown-tinged grass. It lies just off Sandtown Road south of Marietta.

The sign outside the trailer park loomed large. So large, in fact, that Billy knew he had arrived a good two hundred yards before he reached the entrance.

FAIRCOURT – HOME IS WHERE YOU PARK YOUR HOUSE

"Get here before six thirty," Finnegan had said. "We can watch that big ball of fire sink over the trailer tops. My favorite time of day. Then we'll go inside and talk. I'll have a brewski ready for you. Old Milwaukee okay?"

Billy parked alongside the maroon Mustang II in front of the only baby blue trailer within sight. A man appeared at the trailer door. Billy assumed it was Finnegan.

The man approached. He extended his hand. "I'm J.P. Pleased to make your acquaintance."

"Likewise," Billy said. "Nice car."

"Glad you like it." Finnegan grinned. "Mustang Two. Boredom Zero." He held up a finger. "You wait right here."

He returned with two Old Milwaukee 24s. He handed one to Billy and pointed to a couple of lawn chairs planted between the Mustang and the trailer. "Let's sit here a spell and watch the sun go down. Then we'll go inside, and I'll spill my guts all over the floor.

It'll be up to you to mop it all up and do something with it." He tapped the top of his beer can three times with his index finger, pulled the StaTab, and took a big swig. He gazed over the trailer tops at the evening sky. "They tell me I'm a hard ass. And I guess I am when I need to be. But sitting here watching the sky break out like a kaleidoscope when the sun sets, it humbles a man."

After the sun had disappeared behind the trailers, Finnegan ushered Billy inside and had him sit in the Barcalounger near the door. He, Finnegan, sank into the other one—the one with the worn arms and seat.

"That one you're sitting in," Finnegan said. "Jean used to sit there."

Before Billy had a chance to ask who Jean was, Finnegan had moved on. He leaned across the folding tray table. Across the portable reel-to-reel and the open bag of Doritos. "What I'm about to tell you. You have to promise you'll do something with it. Otherwise, I'm wasting my time. And yours."

"If there's something there to run with," Billy said, "I'll run with it."

"You gonna tell the paper about it?"

"If what my contact told me is true…that the authorities have turned a deaf ear, then I—"

"Turned a deaf ear isn't the half of it. They've done everything they can to keep the truth from getting out in the open. They're scared to death of what might happen. They've made me swear to secrecy. If word gets out that I'm the one blowing the whistle, they'll be all over me like white on…let's just say I'll be in big trouble."

What had Gary told Billy? *The media sure as hell isn't supposed to know about it.* It wasn't Billy's nature to dog a story without letting the higher-ups know. But for now, this would be his mission and his mission alone.

"But you want it to come out, don't you?" Billy said. "Keeping the truth under wraps gets you nowhere."

"I want it to come out, but if it's all the same, I don't want to be tagged as the leaker. Mainly about the fact the police, the GBI, even the FBI don't have the cojones to do anything about who's behind the killings."

"I vigorously protect my sources," Billy said. "The First Amendment gives me that right. That's not to say your name won't leak out from somewhere else, though. With a story this big, it's sometimes hard to protect identities."

"I understand. I just have to trust it won't come from you."

"You have my word," Billy said. "So, are you ready to…what did you say earlier…spill your guts all over the floor?"

"I'm ready. But this is a two-beer deal." Finnegan crossed the room to the kitchen, grabbed two more Old Milwaukees from the fridge, and returned to the Barcalounger. He handed one to Billy. He grabbed an Empire Strikes Back spiral notebook with GV handwritten in big block letters on the front. He opened it to the first page. "Okay, here goes…"

> I first met the Vardemans back in July of '79. The thirteenth, to be exact. Graydon, the ringleader. His brothers Ewell and Dickie. I've heard about his wife, but I've never laid eyes on her. I got the impression Graydon was trying to keep me away from her. Or the other way

around. They're all Klan. And Graydon deals narcotics. The whole lot of them are high on drugs most of the time. Needless to say, they're not the kind of people you'd want to have over for cocktails.

Anyway, Graydon wanted to recruit me into the Klan because I know my way around explosives. He told me they wanted to create a mutiny by killing black children. They'd start with black boys and go from there. They might throw in some grownups along the way. All hell would break loose. Race riots and all. Graydon wanted me to help.

At first, I dismissed their boasting and bravado as nothing more than the ravings of a bunch of strung-out racist redneck windbags. They kept talking in generalities but never got down and dirty. And they never asked me to do a damned thing with explosives. I was sure they were full of it. But I kept meeting with them over that summer and through '80 in case I was wrong.

Two things changed my mind. For one thing, in the spring of '80, Graydon took me to a place where the Klan kept a cache of automatic and semiautomatic weapons, explosives, police uniforms. They even had bazookas. It was a two-room cinderblock house. Well, it wasn't a house, really. More like a hideaway. It was way out in the woods near Monroe. The entrance faced away from the road. The windows were boarded up. The door was padlocked. I've seen a lot of arms caches in my day. This was one of the biggest. But I still wasn't ready to believe they were going to pull off a mass killing. Stashing away a lot of guns and shit's one thing. It's a way to feel manly, you know. But using them to murder a bunch of children? No way.

Then the whole thing with Lubie Geter happened.

Finnegan flipped a few pages through the spiral notebook until he found what he was looking for. He ran his index finger a third of the way down the page. "Here it is."

Back in the summer of '80, Vardeman and I visited a man named Sammy. He's a friend of Vardeman's. Lives on the west side. Vardeman parked his Chevy across the street from Sammy's house. These two black kids, Lubie Geter and another boy named Terrell were riding go-karts that I found out later they'd borrowed from a friend. Geter accidentally rammed the go-kart he was driving into the side of Vardeman's car. I didn't think much of it at the time. But then, two months later, Vardeman and I were together again when he spotted Geter. He said, "See that black bastard? I'm gonna get him. I'm gonna wrap my dick around his neck and choke him to death."

"He said that?" Billy said. "The part about his dick?"

"Word for word. As sure as I'm sitting here talking to you and drinking my suds." Finnegan almost let out a grin but caught himself. "He probably has a little one. Sometimes people like that have to talk big to feel big."

"What did you do when he said it?"

"I can put on a good poker face when I need to. Better than most. I didn't react. And I didn't follow up at the time. I thought it was just more bullshit and bluster. But then last month, the fifteenth of February, I saw on television that a body had been found off Vandiver Road. The next morning, I picked up the newspaper and saw where it was Geter. That's when I called the police. They put me through to Homicide. I said I had information about the child murders, specifically the Geter boy's killing."

"Then what?"

The police called me in. They asked me to wear a wire and visit Vardeman again. Which I did. More than once. I got him to talking about Geter. I said, "You killed that Geter kid, didn't you?" He got all puffed up—he's usually sort of a slouchy, stoopy man—and said, "Yeah, we damn sure did."

I assumed by *we* he meant he and his brothers.

Chapter Nineteen

Billy Tarwater

Sunday, June 21st, 1981

ON SUNDAY, THE TWENTY-FIRST OF JUNE, WAYNE WILLIAMS was arrested.

* * *

The prior month, on the twenty-second, police staking out a Chattahoochee River crossing had heard a splash beneath the bridge. They were there because they suspected the killer might dump the next victim into a body of water somewhere. The Chattahoochee was a likely pick, given that it ran through the city with plenty of secluded drop points. The police had staked out twenty-four bridges along the length of the river.

The last car to cross over the bridge, before the splash, was a 1970 Chevrolet station wagon. Two police cars stopped the Chevrolet half a mile from the bridge. Twenty-three-year-old

Wayne Williams was behind the wheel. The station wagon was registered to his parents.

The police noticed suede gloves, a length of nylon rope, and a flashlight on the passenger seat.

Two days later, the nude body of twenty-seven-year-old Nathaniel Cater was found floating downriver from the bridge where police had seen the station wagon. Investigators believed Cater had died of asphyxiation. The ligature marks on his neck matched the fiber pattern on the nylon rope found in the car.

Investigators searched Williams' residence. They collected fibers from his bedspread, his bathroom, his clothes. Rare tri-lobal carpet fiber. Dog hairs.

Williams failed polygraph tests, although the results were not admissible in court.

Witnesses told police that, around the time of the murder, they had seen Williams with scratches on his face and arms. Police theorized they could have been inflicted by the victim during his struggles.

* * *

A grand jury indicted Williams for the first-degree murders of Nathaniel Cater and Jimmy Rae Payne, another black man, who had been murdered in April. Payne was an ex-convict who had recently been released from Arrendale State Prison in Raoul, Georgia, where he had served time for burglary.

FBI Agent John Douglas said that, if Williams murdered Cater and Payne, then he was "looking pretty good for a good percentage of the killings." Douglas was censured by FBI Director William Webster. Nevertheless, efforts were already underway by the police and the media to pin the child murders on Williams, based in part on fibers and dog hairs recovered from several of the child victims' bodies.

* * *

Three days after Wayne Williams was hauled off to jail, Sam Jepperson walked out of Reidsville State Prison a free man.

Rufus, his mother, and his sister Recy were there to meet Sam. So was Billy.

Sam passed through the prison gate with a state-issued outfit— shoes and socks, t-shirt and collared work shirt, belt and trousers— and an ear-to-ear grin.

He was leaving leaner and sturdier than when he had entered. Billy surmised it was thanks to time on his hands and a halfway-decent workout yard. In that sense, and only that sense, a decade and a half behind bars had been good to Sam.

Sam gimp-ran to Ruby and gave her a long and lavish embrace. Tears tracked the contours of his cheeks and fell onto his collar. Onto her summer scarf.

He hugged Rufus, Recy, and Billy, the tears still flowing.

Then he outstretched his arms and beamed. "And this must be your bride, Theda." He reached out to a woman who likely was there to meet another release and happened to be standing near Rufus. He gave her a gingerly hug. She startled and pulled back.

"That's not Theda," Rufus said. "She had to stay behind to tend to her mother."

They all squeezed into Cynthia's Suburban. It being bigger than any of the other vehicles available, Billy had borrowed it for the occasion.

Billy headed north toward Vidalia, then Atlanta. He spoke little on the four-hour trip. Sam and his family needed time to catch up. To laugh and to cry. To sit in quiet contemplation when emotion overwhelmed.

* * *

Thursday afternoon, the twenty-fifth, Billy met with Gary at Marnie's. Gary had called him that morning and said they needed to get together. He had new information based on some ferreting out he'd been doing at police headquarters.

"Bad day for Wayne Williams," Gary said. "That son-of-a-bitch is headed to the chair. But good news about Sam."

"Yesterday was one of the best days of my life, Gary. I wish I could be the one to report on it, but I'm too close to the story. You said you had something big for me?"

Gary told Billy that, back in late February, after Finnegan had tipped off the police about Geter and the Vardemans' plans, they had become convinced that the volatile race situation in the city was on the verge of exploding. *Powder keg* was used more than once. They worried that, if word got out about possible Klan involvement in the child murders, a war in the streets would break out all over Atlanta.

The police called an early-morning meeting with the GBI. They had already learned that Lubie Geter had been friends with at least four other victims: Aaron Wyche, Darron Glass, Aaron Jackson, and Curtis Walker. If they all knew each other, and if Graydon Vardeman knew Geter, then he may have known the other boys, too. And if he knew them, could he have been involved in their murders?

Phil Peters, the GBI director, said it was essential that what they had learned not be revealed to the public. They would continue their clandestine monitoring of the Vardemans and the family's Klan ties. But whatever they did would be done in strict secrecy. They were scared shitless of what they were digging up and where it might lead.

"Pretty much consistent with what I've learned from Finnegan," Billy said.

"I figured as much. But that's not all. Fast forward to this past Sunday. Williams is arrested. They've got their man. I'll be damned if they're not on the verge of closing the case. They're a bunch of wusses if you ask me."

"They may be, but that begs the bigger question. I'm not accusing Vardeman of anything. But what if Williams didn't kill those kids? Are they going to just let a guilty man walk?"

"Exactly. So you're a damned good newshound, one of the best around. What are you going to do with it?"

"I don't know yet, Gary. I'm going to keep meeting with Finnegan. It doesn't matter to me that Williams has been arrested. I've got a lot more digging to do."

"Just be careful, Billy. Watch your back. Some of the higher-ups in the department, they don't take kindly to journalists stepping into their shit. They'll do whatever it takes to substitute your hide for theirs."

* * *

Billy decided he needed to take another trip to Faircourt. The following Monday morning, he phoned Finnegan.

"Come on over," Finnegan said. "I got somebody I want you to meet."

Three hours later, Billy pulled up and parked next to the Mustang II.

Finnegan was standing in the trailer doorway with his arm around a rough looking woman with deep-set green eyes and frizzy strawberry hair tied back in a ponytail. She wore a low-cut denim halter top that left little to the imagination. The smile lines that ran from both sides of her nose to the corners of her downturned mouth belied her solemn demeanor.

"She came back." Finnegan beamed. "Billy, meet Jean."

It took Billy a minute to remember the name. *Ah, Jean. Used to sit in the other Barcalounger.* "Pleased to meet you, Jean."

She crossed over to where Billy was standing and extended her hand. "Pleasure's all mine. J.P.'s told me about you."

"Really?"

"Go on back inside now, Jean," Finnegan called out. "Billy and I have some business to do. Maybe you can whip us up some eats. "You like pastrami, Billy?"

Jean went back inside the trailer.

Finnegan contemplated his shoes. Kicked the ground beside the Mustang, sending a cloud of red clay dust into the air. He looked at Billy. "I need to tell you something. I called on the Vardemans yesterday."

"How's the old clan doing?"

"Graydon brought up the 'nabbin' of that man Williams. Honestly, I couldn't tell whether he was happy or sad about it.

Anyway, that's not what I wanted to tell you. In passing, Ewell happened to mention that he'd seen in the paper about that black man Jepperson walking out of Reidsville a free man. He spit bile when he said his name."

"Did he mention *me*?"

"Oh no. I don't think they have any idea who you are."

"How did *you* know about me and Jepperson?"

"I have my ways, Billy. After all, I'm not new to the hawkshaw game."

"There's no hawkshaw about it, J.P. I got Jepperson freed because he's an innocent man. Fair and square. Nothing to hide there."

"I know that, Billy. Now, where do things stand with *our* deal?"

"Still working on it." Billy told Finnegan about his conversation with Gary. "How hard would it be for you to find out whether Vardeman knew some of the other boys?" Billy said.

"You got names?"

"I'll write them down for you."

"I'll have to figure out how to bring it up without tipping him off."

"Isn't that what hawkshaws do?"

"Give me a week or two."

"I'm worried that, with Williams behind bars, the powers that be will wrap everything up and close the case."

"Yeah, but *you* won't do that, will you?"

"Of course not."

"Don't drop the ball, Willie."

"What?"

"Remember that time Willie Mays dropped Ernie Banks's fly ball?"

"Not really. I was, what, two when that happened?"

"Well, whatever you were, I'm just saying, don't drop the ball, Willie. Ready for some pastrami?"

* * *

A couple of days passed before Finnegan got back to Billy. He said Vardeman had admitted to knowing the two Aarons and Curtis Walker. As for Darron Glass? Vardeman responded with a "what's it to you" and changed the subject. Finnegan didn't want to push it.

* * *

On Monday, the sixth of July, Gary called. "I've been doing some more digging on the Vardemans," he said. "They've got a rap sheet as long as my arm. You name it, they've done it. But one thing jumped out at me."

"What's that, Gary?"

"Back in '68, before Graydon Vardeman shipped out to Nam, he was arrested on suspicion of child molestation."

"Was he convicted?"

"No. The charges were dropped."

* * *

For the next five months, Billy continued to dig on two fronts.

The Wayne Williams part was easy. After all, that was his day job.

As for the Vardemans and their possible involvement in the child killings, Gary provided privileged details about the boys' murders, passed along to him by a friend in Homicide. Billy continued to scour the newspaper archives for background on Graydon and the others. And he occasionally reached out to Finnegan for inside dope.

* * *

On Thanksgiving Day, Billy and Cynthia dropped the kids off at her parents' house, where they would return for dinner that evening, accompanied by Billy's mom and brother. They headed to Carver Homes for a midday feast with the Jeppersons. Cynthia joked on the way there that two gorgings in one day would wreak havoc on the best of midriffs.

Sam, Ruby, Rufus, and Recy were there. And Rufus's wife Theda, whom Billy and Cynthia were meeting for the first time.

* * *

The shopping and holiday preparations that began the next day segued into December without so much as a pause for breath. On Monday, Cynthia took Billy Jr. and Addie to Rich's, where they rode the Pink Pig, and Billy Jr. beseeched Santa with a laundry list of requests, for him and for his little sister.

Then, in mid-December, somebody started following Cynthia.

LATE '81

CHAPTER TWENTY

Billy Tarwater

Friday, December 18ᵗʰ, 1981

WILLIAMS' TRIAL WAS SCHEDULED TO BEGIN IN TEN DAYS. AS soon as jury selection commenced, the courthouse would be Billy's home away from home through the duration of the trial.

Billy would have little time to focus on the Vardemans and their goings-on when the proceedings began, especially given that Christmas was right around the corner.

He pulled the files on the next five boys to go missing after Lubie Geter.

```
PUE, TERRY
Disappeared January 22, 1981.
15 years old.
```

Morning call came through to Rockdale Cty. Sheriff's Office at 8:15 a.m. A man driving down Sigman Rd. on way to work had spotted a body lying near pine thicket along the road. Sheriff's deputies arrived on scene.

Victim was black. Young. Abrasions on arm and bruises on head, likely result of attempt to escape from captor. Wore blue windbreaker with the name Kim in red letters on the back, a yellow T-shirt with Puerto Rico on the front and Washington High on the back, beige knit slacks, blue socks, brown Hush Puppies. Had been strangled to death. Dog hairs found on body.

Even though body was found 20 miles from Atlanta, sheriff turned case over to Atl. police. Suspected he'd been killed in Atlanta and body dumped in Rockdale Cty. Police suspected connection to other child murders based on age, race, nature of death, and string of anonymous calls that had been made to police.

Police identified the boy in part because of surgical scars on right knee.

Two weeks earlier, a man had called the police and said that, if they searched the area around Sigman Rd., they'd find a boy's body there. Sheriff's deputies and police searched area but turned up nothing. Just before body found, the man called again saying he had placed another body there. Police were never able to identify the caller.

Terry had 6 sisters and 6 brothers. Brother Tony said he had seen Terry get on a bus near the projects around 3:00 p.m. the day before his body was found. Terry was last seen late that night in a Krystal on Memorial Dr.

Friends with Lubie Geter. Lived in same housing project as Teddy Smith.

Panic spread throughout the county. Things like this happened in the city, Rockdale residents said. Not in the small-town exurbs.

Between Terry Pue's disappearance and the middle of March, four more black boys would go missing and end up dead.

BALTAZAR, PATRICK

Disappeared February 6, 1981.

12 years old.

Lived with father, stepmother, 2 brothers in 1-room apartment in Vine City, neighborhood rife with heroin dealers, broken windows, abandoned houses. His 7 other brothers and 4 sisters lived with mother in New Orleans.

Industrious. Sold newspapers, cleaned the restaurant where his father worked, washed dishes at another restaurant, sold cotton candy at Omni Complex near his home.

Last seen at Fisherman's Cove Restaurant, where father worked. Had gone there to get money from father. Witnesses later reported having seen him playing arcade games until midnight at Omni.

A maintenance man at an office complex off I85 found body in an overgrown area behind the buildings.

Scrapes, bruises, dog hairs on his body. Had been strangled to death.

A dental assistant who worked in the complex said earlier that morning she had seen an older light green Impala parked in the area with no other cars around. White driver stared at her until she went inside.

Thirteen days after that, another boy disappeared.

WALKER, CURTIS

Disappeared February 19, 1981.

13 years old.

Left apartment in Bowen Homes housing complex early that morning.

Last seen looking for work at Byron's Gun Shop on Bankhead Hwy.

Dogs tracked his scent to rear of nearby elementary school.

Feb. 20, a fireman crossing South River 18 miles away spotted a body snagged on a log. Police ID'd body. Missing all clothes except underwear.

Had been strangled to death.

Witness said he had seen an old green Chevrolet parked nearby around the time he disappeared.

Later that month, the pastor at a nearby church received an anonymous call from someone claiming to have been the killer.

Then another.

BELL, JOSEPH

Disappeared March 2, 1981.

15 years old.

Nickname: *Jo Jo.*

Lived with grandmother. Mother doing time for killing father.

Last seen playing basketball with friend at the school LaTonya Wilson attended. Wearing blue skullcap, jogging sweatshirt, baggy pants.

5 days later, 2 bikers found body in Rockdale County where South River passes Klondike Rd. near where Curtis Walker had been found.

Missing clothes except underwear.

Cause of death undetermined, but authorities suspect asphyxiation.

Word on the street was that he had befriended a black man named Wayne Williams.

And another.

HILL, TIMOTHY

Disappeared March 13, 1981.

13 years old.

Last seen standing on sidewalk talking to 16-year-old girl. Wearing black leather jacket, beige shirt, yellow pants, brown shoes, white socks, white cap.

Reportedly mixed up with a pedophile who went by the nickname "Uncle Tom." Allegedly had sex with Uncle Tom and other men.

Friends with Jo Jo Bell, Patrick Baltazar, Anthony Carter. May have been friends with Alfred Evans, Jeffery Mathis as well.

2 weeks later, canoeists fishing in Chattahoochee River found body about 1 mile S of Campbellton Rd. bridge.

Missing all clothes except underwear.

Cause of death listed as undetermined asphyxiation.

Billy knew the Fulton County Superior Court officials had purposely scheduled Williams' trial to begin the week before New Year's, when no other trials were to begin, in order to allow for a larger potential jury pool.

But early Friday morning, the eighteenth, around sixty prospective jurors had asked to be excused. Most of the requests were denied.

The judge also decided that morning that a closed-circuit television would be made available in the pressroom for the duration of the trial. Billy welcomed that.

Late that day, after much of the newsroom had scattered for the weekend, save for the diehards working on tomorrow's stories, Dedrick Roberts called Billy into his office. "What the hell are you doing, Tarwater?"

"What do you mean?"

"Word's gotten around that you're working on a back-channel story. And I don't like what I'm hearing."

Billy was taken aback. He thought he'd done everything within his power to keep his digging under wraps. But he was reminded of what Benjamin Franklin had said. *Three can keep a secret, if two of them are dead.* He hesitated to respond, not knowing what Roberts did or did not know. Better to let his boss do the talking.

"Kill it, Tarwater," Roberts said.

"Kill what?"

"You know exactly what I'm talking about."

"With all due respect, sir," Billy said, "one of the first things I learned as a newspaperman was the Journalist's Creed. I will remind you that it's memorialized in bronze at the National Press Club. It says the suppression of the news, for any reason other than the welfare of society, is indefensible."

Roberts slammed his fist onto his desk. "Damn it, Tarwater. This isn't coming from me. It's coming straight from my boss. And from Hizzoner himself. Do your goddamn job and dispense with the after-hours bullshit. You have a trial to attend."

Billy left work knowing there was no way he was going to walk away from a story of such import. Nobody—not his boss, not the editor-in-chief, not the mayor—could stop him.

Chapter Twenty-One

Billy Tarwater

Sunday, December 20th, 1981

FIVE DAYS HAD PASSED WITH NO STALKER.

But this hadn't allayed Cynthia's unease.

Billy felt a nudging. He woke to Cynthia propped up in bed beside him. "It'll happen again," she said. "Whoever's following me. I just know it."

"How do you know it wasn't a fluke?"

"Do you really believe it was a fluke, Billy? Twice in as many days?"

"I understand, but five days have gone by since. We can hope, can't we?"

"I don't have much of that left in me right now."

"Cynthia, you have so much going for you. Two wonderful kids. A devoted husband. A teaching career that others would d—"

"You know what I'm saying. That all means the world to me. I'm just talking about *him*. Whoever he is."

"Or if he's even real."

"Oh, he's real alright. He'll be back. Maybe he's just taking some time off to plot his next move."

Their conversation was interrupted by the pitter patter approaching from down the hall.

Billy Jr. and Addie stood in the bedroom doorway.

It was 7:25.

"Breakfast, kiddos?" Cynthia's tone brightened.

Billy Jr. beamed. "M&M waffles?"

"That's for Christmas. How about plain old waffles?"

Billy ate quickly and rose from the table. "I really hate to do this, but I need to go into the office for a while."

"On a Sunday?"

Billy hated not being straight up with her, but he couldn't let on what his real plans were. He wouldn't play the charade if it weren't for her own good. "I know it's out of the ordinary, but I'm working against a hard deadline. I'll be home as soon as I can. Maybe we can bundle the kids up and go for a ride this afternoon. Maybe go to the park. If it gets late enough, maybe we can ride around and look at the yard decorations. Go see that crazy ten-thousand-watt spectacle off Bouldercrest with Santa and the reindeer on the roof."

* * *

Billy eased the car down the dead-end street and pulled up along the curb in front of the parsonage. He cut the engine and gazed across the lawn at the faded canary clapboard bungalow with its washed-out russet shutters. Its gable windows and pitched roof. Its square cupola and rusted rooster weathervane. *What an idyllic delusion*, he thought. *Surface impressions deceive.*

He had come here early this Sunday morning on a quest to make sense of what had happened to Cynthia and the other girls eighteen years ago. To try to process it all. To relive, at least for a moment, what could have been. To treasure the outcome for Cynthia and to mourn what befell the others.

But he had another motive, one that Cynthia would not abide. He couldn't get it out of his head that something didn't add up. How could one man have worked alone? How could he have single-handedly abducted the girls, drugged them, held them captive in the dungeon of that ministerial house, dragged them away and killed them? Or, in Cynthia's case, tried and failed.

And how was it that over a decade and a half had gone by with no one knowing about, or having claimed to know about, the basement prison? Had the Reverend Thomas kept it a secret all those years? Surely he knew of it. After all, he had moved into the parsonage not long after the girls died and the Reverend Kilgallon left town.

Billy looked at his watch. It was 9:40, twenty minutes before the early service was to end. That left him time to drive to the church and park. He would arrive late, as planned, and sit in the last pew in the back. He would seek out Thomas after the service.

* * *

The last time Billy had set foot in Confederate Avenue Baptist was in the Fall of '80. He had arrived on a Sunday at the tail end of the sermon and was planning to speak with Leonard Seymour as soon as the service was over. To ask him why Kilgallon's '61 Valiant had been registered in his, Seymour's, name. But Seymour sneaked out before he could get to him. Billy had followed Seymour home that day, but he hadn't learned much when he finally caught up with him.

Since his adolescent days, Billy had been in the church only two other times. In '77 he was there for his father's funeral. His mother had deemed the injuries from the car wreck too severe, too mutilating, for an open casket. *He would want it that way*, she had said.

The year before that, he had found himself sitting in the sanctuary, wedged between Cynthia and Dovey Mae, mourning the passing of Granny Tarwater. Her casket was anything but closed. She wouldn't have had it any other way.

At both funerals, he had sat in the second row from the front in the same hard pew that his family had always occupied. Now his mind wandered between grieving the loss of a loved one and thinking back to his dreadful Sundays as a kid, having to sit there for hours on end and endure Kilgallon's fevered theatrics, his apocalyptic, guilt-inducing alarums. Had Billy known back then what was to come, he would have searched out Cynthia in the crowd, grabbed her by the arm, and run like hell. *Get out before something bad happens.*

* * *

The congregation filed out at the end of the service. Thomas stood at his obligatory spot just outside the door and greeted the congregants as they left. Billy always found it odd that pastors would do this *after* the service rather than *before*. Wouldn't the flock prefer to be welcomed *into* the house of worship rather than be turned out with a handshake and a beaming glad-to-see-you-go smile?

Billy held back.

Rather than exit through the main door, he padded to the front of the sanctuary, through the door to the right of the pulpit and choir loft and down the hall to the pastor's office, taking in the smell of must along the way. He sank into the splat back chair across from Thomas's paper-strewn desk. The chair with the embroidered seat cushion that read JESUS LOVES ME THIS I KNOW.

He waited.

Soon he heard a shuffle approaching from down the hall. He rose, expecting to be greeted by Reverend Thomas. But it was only Broadus McMillan, the church's part-time sexton. He was also, or so Billy had heard, Leonard Seymour's sometime parcheesi foe and PBR drinking partner. Rumor had it that he and Leonard had become friends shortly after Broadus's arrival at the church years ago.

Broadus had a jagged look about him. He was thin as a bean pole, a stark contrast to Seymour. With ginger hair that radiated in every direction, he looked like a Diamond Strike Anywhere match. Lit.

He slouched against the door frame. He looked Billy up and down. "He know you're here?"

Billy shook his head. "I thought I'd just wait for him."

"I cain't hang around. Late for an appointment. But I'll go find him first. I'll see to it that he comes directly."

Again, Billy waited.

Thomas barreled into the room. He extended his hand.

Billy assumed the reverend wouldn't recognize him after so many years. "I'm Billy Tar—"

"I know who you are. You're Herman and Alice Tarwater's boy." He sat down at his desk. He shuffled some papers around. "What can I do for you?"

"I enjoyed your sermon, Reverend."

"I'm sure you did, seeing as you slipped in after I'd finished. Don't think I don't notice everything that goes on in the Lord's house. At first, I figured you came to see Leonard Seymour. The thing is, he's gone away for a while. Visiting his sister in Sylacauga for the holidays." Thomas peered over his wire-rimmed bifocals. "But that's not why you dropped by today, is it?"

Billy asked the reverend about the parsonage. About the cellar dungeon. How long had he known of it? Had it ever occurred to him to bring it to the authorities' attention when he first learned of it? What had he known about Kilgallon's doings around the time the girls went missing?

Thomas walked around his desk and stood two feet in front of where Billy sat. He jabbed his finger in Billy's face, coming within inches of impaling his eye. "Listen, Tarwater. I don't know what you're up to, but I had nothing to do with what happened to those girls."

Shit, Billy thought. *What the hell's gotten into this guy? He sounds more like Kilgallon than the youth minister I remember.* "I'm not saying you did. I'm just trying to put some pieces of the puzzle together."

"What's there to put together? Kilgallon's dead. Get over it."

"Did you discover the room *after* you moved into the parsonage? Or did you know about it *before?*

"You know as well as I do that the door to that room was hidden behind a heavy metal cabinet. You *do* remember that, don't you? After all, weren't you the one that broke into my house?"

"I'll admit to that, but—"

"I didn't know about it. I never went down there. And I didn't know what was going on with those girls back in '63 either. I had nothing to do with any of it." He walked to the door. "Now, if you'll excuse me, I have an eleven o'clock sermon to prepare for."

Billy got up to leave. "Do you know of anyone else who may have been involved? Might have helped Kilgallon?" Billy hesitated to bring up any names for fear that, if Thomas wasn't playing straight with him, somebody might end up getting tipped off.

"What did I just get through telling you? I don't know anything about it. And anyway, that was ages ago. If you know what's good for you, you'll let the dead sleep." He extended his hand again. "Now, if you don't mind."

Billy grudgingly thanked him for his time and turned to leave.

"Tell the little lady hello for me," Thomas said. "Be grateful that she survived. And don't be strangers. You're both always welcome in God's house."

CHAPTER TWENTY-TWO

Cynthia Tarwater

Sunday, December 20ᵗʰ, 1981

CYNTHIA WORRIED THAT BILLY WAS BEGINNING TO THINK MAYBE there wasn't a stalker after all. That it was just an unfortunate coincidence. At first, he'd seemed enthusiastic about catching whoever it was. But after several days of quiet, he'd called it a "fluke." She didn't buy it. She spent her waking hours fearing that the next time she pulled out of The Belmont, the next time she rounded a corner, or visited the Kroger or the preschool or anywhere really, he'd be there.

Billy had eaten breakfast quickly and gotten up from the table saying something about needing to go to the office for a while. Cynthia remembered replying, "On a Sunday?" From that point on, she hadn't really heard, or processed, what he'd said. Only disembodied wah-wah words. Deadline. Ride. Park. Bouldercrest. Reindeer.

She had no idea when Billy would return. Failed expectations had become commonplace. She'd given up predicting.

The park? What was he thinking? The weatherman was calling for record lows. So frigid, or so she had heard on the radio, that the Atlanta Symphony had canceled a Sunday afternoon concert at the Omni because they feared the bitter cold whipping through the mall would harm their woodwinds. There was no way she was bundling up the kids and going to the park.

But Cynthia needed to get out of the house. And the kids? They needed it more than she did. One of her Agnes Scott students, a practiced soprano, was singing seasonal songs with the First Presbyterian Chancel Choir in the state capitol rotunda. Dare Cynthia subject Billy Jr. and Addie to such urbanity? At their age? Would they be bored stiff? Would they behave? *What the hell*, she thought. *They need to be exposed to a little culture sometime.*

She outfitted them in their warmest winter coats, knit beanie hats, and mittens.

She left a note for Billy. Secured to the refrigerator door with an Atlanta Hawks magnet. In case he got home before they did. He had wanted to do something with the kids. But he'd have to understand that she couldn't just sit at home on a Sunday with no idea when he'd return. Anyway, *he* had left notes for *her* plenty of times. He could handle it.

* * *

Cynthia entered the rotunda with Billy Jr. and Addie, taking a single-sheet program from the attendant stationed at the south entrance.

The choir had set up across the rotunda from where they entered. Folding chairs had been arranged in concentric quarter-circles facing the choir, with an aisle running north-south between them.

The chamber was sparsely populated, probably because of the deep freeze.

They took three seats next to the aisle in the outermost quarter-circle near the south entrance. Just in front of the bust of Abraham Baldwin. Should Billy Jr. or Addie act up, they could all slip out in a hurry and hopefully not attract the attention, or the wrath, of the concertgoers. Cynthia sat as a buffer between the two of them.

Across the aisle, a prim lady in her Sunday best was knitting what looked like a winter scarf in russet and gold. She appeared to be in her mid-fifties. She looked up, smiled briefly at Billy Jr., then turned her attention back to her task at hand. A bow-tied man of similar age sat beside her, pen in hand, working what Cynthia surmised was the Sunday crossword.

Three seats away sat an elderly couple bedecked in matching Christmas sweaters. Heavy fur-collared coats draped over the backs of adjacent chairs. The redolence of Estee Lauder—*Youth Dew?*—drifted in Cynthia's direction from where they sat. The woman reached into her handbag, took out two sandwiches in wax paper, and handed one to her presumed husband.

A homeless woman, bags and all, occupied two seats at the far end of the quarter-circle, near the choir. Even she had managed to turn out in her finest pillbox hat befitting the occasion. A bit worse for wear, two decades past its prime, and no doubt retrieved from some discard pile somewhere. But befitting, nevertheless. Her pursed smile reminded Cynthia of Ruth Gordon's Maude.

The choir opened with "Gentle Mary Laid Her Child." Billy Jr. paid no heed, his neck craned and his concentration focused on the domed ceiling towering three stories above. Addie, on the other hand, bounced in her seat in rough tempo with the music. "Mary" was followed by "Hark! The Herald" and "Oh Come, Oh Come, Emmanuel."

Cynthia looked up and noticed a slim man leaning against the curved third-floor balustrade above the east entrance to the rotunda. Between the portraits of George Washington to his left and, to his right, a dour, black-clad patriot whose identity she couldn't make out.

The man looked curiously out of place, with his khaki work trousers and rumpled button-down. His shirttail struggling to stay tucked in. His scraggly unshaven appearance. His nonchalant slouch against the balustrade. He wore a bushy hat—she thought it was called a ushanka—low on his head, its ear flaps tied below his chin. But he was coatless, at least as far as she could tell. *Maybe he's a capitol employee, perhaps a handyman*, she thought. But he didn't fit the part.

The man fixed his gaze on Cynthia. When she returned his attention, he quickly looked away. She looked down at the program, but she could see out of the corner of her eye that he was staring at her again. He continued to leer, managing a side-glance whenever it was obvious she was looking his way.

After "The Twelve Days of Christmas," Cynthia decided they should head out. Surely Billy would have returned home by now. And the kids were getting fidgety. She gathered them up, helped them with their winter wear, and headed for the exit. She looked up and noticed that the balustrade man was gone.

Chapter Twenty-Three

Billy Tarwater

Sunday, December 20ᵗʰ, 1981

THE LIGHTS WERE OFF. BILLY CALLED OUT FOR CYNTHIA. HE checked the bedrooms. Then the kitchen.

He could have easily missed the 3x3" note attached to the fridge. When he saw it, he had been about to head to the parking deck to see if the Suburban was there.

Penned in blue:

WENT TO A HOLIDAY CHORALE.

BACK LATER.

Followed in pencil:

LOVE YOU.

A holiday chorale? *What* holiday chorale?

The wall calendar beside the kitchen door indicated nothing about a chorale.

Did she take the kids with her? Or had she dropped them off with his mother? Or *her* mother?

He first dialed his mom. She said she hadn't heard from Cynthia in a couple of days. "Billy, is everything alright?" she asked.

He assumed so.

Billy's mom had always been the caring one. The kindly, benevolent guardian.

Thoughts from his childhood redounded.

Eleven-year-old Binky threw his thumb out of joint in the middle of the night. Did it have something to do with the nightmare he'd just had about Leonard Seymour?

> *I buried my thumbs into Leonard's neck. Choking him with all my might. Launchpad Leonard, you've gone and done it now.*

Binky woke up in yeow-inducing pain. With a crooked, throbbing left thumb and a hand-wringing sweat.

His father grabbed his hand way too hard, with a *here let's see if you can move it* indifference and an *it isn't broken* dispassion. "Ouch," Binky screamed, and pulled his hand away. Binky forgave his dad for what he'd done. It was just the way he was. If anything, he was grateful for his dad's attention, which was always doled out in fits and starts.

Mom called Dr. Harper and implored him to visit on a Sunday. Dad advised against it, his penny-pinching proclivities and the doctor's Sunday-house-call fees being what they were. But Dr. Harper obligingly complied, and around three thirty that afternoon, he showed up, black bag in hand.

Sure enough, Binky's dad was right. It wasn't broken. Dr. Harper popped Binky's damson plum of a thumb back in place and applied a splint. The doctor also instructed his mom to make sure he kept his hand elevated with an ice bag on it, at least for the remainder of the day.

While Binky enjoyed no reprieve from school, his mom's priorities being what they were, he did manage to milk his infirmity for what he could every day *after* school, sitting in what he had come to call his convalescent chair and enjoying his mom's attention. At least for a few days while it lasted, until the swelling went down, and the plum was just an eleven-year-old thumb again.

Just two weeks before that, the next-door neighbor Lervene Culpepper, black and blue and bleeding, had shown up at the Tarwater door. Her left eye looked like the back of a bluebottle fly. Her mouth was bleeding through the cloth she held tight against it. She was bruised up something awful.

Her terrycloth bathrobe, barely tied at the waist, fell aimlessly about her shoulders, revealing a hint of her bra whenever she bent over. Binky knew he shouldn't look, especially with her being in the condition she was in, but he couldn't help it. Did Cynthia's bra look like that, lacy around the edge and all? He wondered.

Lervene begged for asylum from another of Ben Culpepper's drunken rages.

Binky's dad wanted to call the police. Lervene begged him not to.

His mom cleaned Lervene up with a wet washcloth. She dabbed peroxide on her cuts, followed by Mercurochrome. She covered the really bad places with gauze and first aid tape.

She brought Lervene a pillow and blanket from the linen closet. "You can sleep here tonight, on the sofa."

Binky's mom was just like that. She cared in a motherly way.

Then again, there were times she did things that didn't seem to make sense. Like when she gave Binky the icy stare for asking why Dovey Mae couldn't sit at Granny Tarwater's dining room table for Sunday dinner. Or when she made sure Binky knew not to interact with the blacks on shopping trips to Rich's and Davison's. Not to look them in the eye. Not to get within touching distance. Binky had to assume her heart was in the right place even though he didn't understand.

Billy's mom wasn't Cynthia's favorite. He didn't know why exactly. Maybe there was some jealousy going on that Cynthia couldn't—or wouldn't—articulate. Maybe she subconsciously yearned for a mother the likes of which she never had. In any event, they managed to get along well enough, but there was a tension.

His mom had come around in her later years on the race issue. Even so far as to stay in the home he had grown up in after white flight had taken hold. Billy suspected that seeing Sam Jepperson exonerated and freed from prison—all because of her son's dogged determination—had something to do with her coming around. And seeing how Dovey Mae had taken Billy under her wing must have factored in.

His dad never did come around and took his sentiments to the grave.

Billy tried to reach Adele, but she didn't answer.

He would wait for Cynthia and the kids to come home. Surely, they would arrive soon. Meanwhile, he would try to focus on other things.

The Steelcase-grey four-drawer file cabinet, jammed into the corner of the bedroom, held sway, along with the Lilliputian secretary desk, over the 5'x6' semblance of a home office that Billy and Cynthia shared. They had reached a meeting of the minds. He took even days, she took odd, as the prospect of the two of them occupying the space at the same time was out of the question. Trade-offs were common, like when he had a hard deadline to meet, or she had a slew of papers to grade in the evenings. In the occasional instance where more workspace was called for, overflow to the kitchen table was an option. It all worked.

Billy wished for more ample accommodations. But it wasn't meant to be, at least for now.

He opened the top drawer, the one with the little CURRENT cardboard label in its little metal frame. They had agreed that he would take the top two drawers, leaving the other two for Cynthia.

He thumbed through the tabs until he came to the folder labeled FINNEGAN, J.P. He settled into the desk chair and picked through the folder's contents until he found his notes from the last time he and Finnegan had met.

He was just about to read them when the phone rang.

It was Adele Hudspeth. How could she have known that he had tried to reach her only twenty minutes prior?

"What time are you coming for Christmas?" she asked.

"I'm not sure, Adele. I'll check with Cynthia. By the way, have you spoken with her today?"

"No. But I need to know when to put the dressing in the oven. And when to brown the marshmallows on the yams."

To hell with dressing. To hell with marshmallows. Billy bit his tongue. "Listen, Adele. I have to run. Let me know if you hear from your daughter."

Billy returned to the file folder. But dusk had settled in with no word from Cynthia, and he was now beginning to worry. Trying to concentrate on FINNEGAN, J.P. was out of the question.

He grabbed the Sunday paper from the kitchen table and pulled out the Arts & Entertainment section. No mention of an afternoon chorale anywhere. There were a couple of church concerts, one in East Point and one in Sandy Springs. But neither started until late in the evening. *Surely not*, he thought.

He called three of her friends. Perhaps they knew where she had gone. Perhaps they had accompanied her. Two said they hadn't heard from her and knew nothing about a chorale. The third didn't answer.

Seven rolled around and still no Cynthia.

Billy dialed Gary at home.

CHAPTER TWENTY-FOUR

Cynthia Tarwater

Sunday, December 20th*, 1981*

CYNTHIA AND THE KIDS DESCENDED THE STEPS LEADING FROM the capitol. Billy Jr. on her right hand and Addie on her left. Addie swung her arms back and forth and capered down the steps singing "and a partree ginna bear tree."

They walked up Mitchell Street to the curbside parking space she had snagged just past Washington.

With the kids secured in the back seat, Cynthia pulled out and headed northwest up Mitchell Street toward Peachtree. Her plan was to take a right on Peachtree and go through downtown and then to Fifth Street, as that would be the most direct route home. Her only concern was the possibility of Sunday shopping traffic, with just five days before Christmas. She hoped it was late enough that the department store crowds would have dispersed.

But she didn't take the right on Peachtree as planned. Less than two blocks from where she had parked, she felt the Suburban pulling hard to the right. She tried to accelerate, but the steering wheel shuddered and shook.

Cynthia was afraid it would be a big mistake to try to make it home. And there were no gas stations that she knew of down Peachtree. She thought she remembered a Texaco up ahead on Mitchell Street, maybe at Northside Drive. She would head there and hope they could make it.

She had just passed the Spring Street intersection, three short blocks beyond Peachtree, when the pulling, shuddering, and shaking was joined by a loud flapping noise coming from the right front of the car. A flat tire? She worried that, if she kept going, it would be just a matter of time before the flapping turned into a grating rasp.

There was not enough room to pull over on Mitchell Street without blocking a lane. Just beyond the large overpass west of Spring, she saw a small street to the right. The sign said Elliott St. She took it.

Cynthia eased the Suburban a few yards down the dead-end street. She looked around. The vacant gulch to her right, roughly the size of a youth football field, was foreign to her. She felt like they had been transported into a modern-day ghost town.

The downtown viaducts, standing watch over dark voids below, surrounded her on three sides. With the overpass that they'd just crossed behind them, she felt hemmed in from all directions. Across the gulch to the right, she could see a railroad track running along the viaduct. A solitary boxcar, forlorn and lonely in the dusk, sat on the track. Near the track just before it passed under the viaduct straight ahead was a small outbuilding. Maybe a railroad shack.

As she gazed across this vast urban desert, she realized these were the same viaducts that had been built over the tracks in the early nineteen hundreds to accommodate cars. But by the seventies, both downtown train stations had been demolished, most of the tracks under the viaducts had been ripped up, and what was left was the bleak wasteland where they now found themselves.

Just a few blocks away, the powers that be in the city had capitalized on the original buildings under the viaducts to create Underground Atlanta. But not here. No standing buildings, except a rundown railroad shack. No restored nineteenth-century storefronts. No tourists. Just dirt and grime and gravel.

In a matter of minutes, she and the kids had gone from *a partree ginna bear tree* to sitting stranded in a vast urban no-man's-land. She realized that driving into a derelict, dead-end barren had been a mistake.

Cynthia rolled down the window. A gust of frigid air engulfed the car's interior, sending a goosebump-inducing chill down her neck. Her shoulders. Her arms.

She remembered the flashlight in the glovebox. But the batteries were dead. *Damn.*

She stepped out of the car, confirmed that the right front tire was hopelessly flat, and quickly got back in. She rolled up the window and locked the doors.

She knew next to nothing about changing a tire. To try to learn now would be of no avail.

She considered bundling the kids and striking out in search of help or a pay phone. Perhaps if they stood along the Mitchell Street curb someone would stop and give assistance. But the sun had set, and the surroundings were ill-boding. And it was bitter cold.

Addie had drifted off, but Billy Jr. was growing restless. "What's wrong, Mommy?"

Cynthia and Billy had vowed to be honest and up front with the kids, whatever the circumstances. As Billy had said on more than one occasion, truth conquers platitudes and sugar coats. "We've had a flat, honey. I'm trying to decide what to do. I'll figure something out."

"I watched Daddy change the tire once. I can help."

"Thanks honey, but I'm not Daddy. And I suspect the two of us fumbling in the dark with a jack and a tire tool, crawling on the ground looking for the lug nuts we'd surely drop, would make for a pretty sad s…" She saw low beams near the rail line. A car eased along the road that ran parallel to the track. It stopped. The headlights went dark.

The light from a match illuminated the driver's face then died as quickly as it had appeared, so quickly that Cynthia couldn't make out much through the murk, except that the driver was a man. A white man, she thought. The bright orange end of a cigarette glowed in the dark. The glow diminished briefly. Then it returned. Its wax and wane continued as Cynthia sat watching, waiting, hoping it remained where it was—across the gravel gulch.

Was this the same man, in the same car, who had followed them before? Who had lurked across the street from the Montessori? Who had tailed them all the way to the police station and then took off? Could it be the same man who had stared at her from the balustrade? A wave of dread came over her. She feared not so much for herself as for Billy Jr. and Addie.

Cynthia, too, had been a mere child, an adolescent but not that much older than they were now, when another man, in another car, took her away. She was grateful that neither of the kids had ever asked her about the scar that graced her thigh, for surely they'd seen it. If and when they did ask, she would have to put *honest and up front* to the test. But she knew how to confront the hard things in a way that gave them comfort and made them feel safe. She sometimes wondered where she'd learned that. Not from her parents. Of that she was certain.

The across-the-gulch pinpoint of orange light died, followed by another struck match. Cynthia tried this time to make out more of the man's face, but the glow from the match was too distant. Too fleeting. The pinpoint returned, alternating as before between bright orange and faint.

Cynthia weighed the few options she had.

Should she drive away on three tires and a rim? Whatever damage the rim might suffer would pale in contrast to what could befall them if they remained where they were. But how far could they hope to get, limping along on three tires and a rim?

Maybe she should try to change the tire after all? Could it really be that hard? In the dark of night, with no prior experience, yes, it could be. And if she screwed up—if she lost the lug nuts in the dark, if she managed to get the flat tire off but for some reason couldn't get the spare on, if the jack collapsed and the rimless wheel went crashing to the ground—she could forget about driving away in any condition.

She returned to the idea of abandoning the car, making her way to the corner with the bundled-up kids, and either searching for a pay phone or flagging down the first driver to come along. The ill-boding surroundings of Mitchell Street at night would surely be no worse than where they now found themselves. But at least they were behind locked doors here.

They could wait it out and hope someone might just happen down Mitchell Street, see the Suburban, and give them assistance. But what were the chances of anyone seeing the car parked on a dead-end street at this hour? And thinking anything of it?

And then there was always the possibility that the driver across the gulch was an innocent party and could provide the help they needed. But was that a risk worth taking?

CHAPTER TWENTY-FIVE

Cynthia Tarwater

Sunday, December 20th, 1981

CECIL WAS CYNTHIA'S DADDY, BUT AS LONG AS SHE COULD remember, she had rarely been able to bring herself to call him by anything other than his given name. Behind his back anyway. To his face, he was Daddy. Otherwise, it was *Cecil this*, *Cecil that*, even in front of her Jesus-obsessed mother. Her mother didn't like it, but there was little she could do other than threaten to tell Cecil. Which she never did, at least as far as Cynthia knew.

Cynthia had no qualms about calling him Cecil in front of others. But she never could do it in front of her own husband. *Why Billy?* Maybe it was because he had a different kind of relationship with his parents. One that was far from *Leave it to Beaver*, but enviable nevertheless. One of mutual respect. One that would never have brooked calling your parents by their first names.

When Cynthia was eleven, maybe twelve, Cecil had made her watch him change the tire on the Fairlane. It was one of the few times he ever took heed of her, unless it was to give her what for. The family had been on their way home from Opelika when the tire exploded just past the state line. Cecil slammed the car into Park and shut it off along the highway's shoulder. He muttered something—the only thing she could make out was *goddamned Firestones*—and hurtled out the door. He called from the rear. *Cynthia, get out here. I'm gonna teach you how to be a boy.*

What she had wanted to say in the moment, but couldn't bring herself to, was *I'm sorry I popped out with the wrong attachments.* If she had, Cecil surely would have wielded his thick leather belt. Right then and there on the side of the road.

Cynthia had paid about as much attention to the tire changing as she did to the Reverend Kilgallon's demented rantings every Sunday morning.

Or to her mother's ravings about one thing or another practically every day.

Like the day she and her mother were riding home in the Fairlane from the A&P. *Mama laid into me.* She accused Cynthia of provoking Leonard Seymour by standing half-naked at the bedroom window so he could gawk like a peep show patron. *You're thirteen*, Mama had said. *He's a grown man.* She blamed Cynthia for the tempting, not Leonard for the gawking. Then she brought up Cecil, Cynthia's own father, saying even he, *a red-blooded man*, wouldn't be able to resist the temptation. She threatened to go straight to Cecil if it didn't stop, saying he would make her go before the whole Confederate Avenue congregation and confess her sin. The standing and the gawking didn't stop. Her mother knew it and surely told Cecil. But he never uttered a word to Cynthia about it.

Cynthia hadn't intended to provoke Leonard Seymour, or anyone else for that matter. But in her thirteen-year-old mind, she had a right to stand in front of her bedroom window any way she took a notion to. Half-naked or otherwise. It wasn't like she showed him anything. Other than her bra and panties.

Why had Cecil never said anything to Cynthia about Leonard and the window? Why was it that her mother was always the one to handle the *talking to* about such things?

When Cecil got mad, he could get really mad. Raging mad. Ply-the-belt mad. But it seemed to happen only when he felt personally slighted. Made fun of. Or offended in some other way. Otherwise, he was content with his booze and betting. And ignoring.

What must Leonard Seymour have made of her preening at her window back then? Her mother had finally confronted him about it. In the front yard among the oakleaf hydrangeas. But to Cynthia's knowledge, nothing ever came of it. He kept looking. Probably couldn't help it. His being a red-blooded man and all.

To this day, I still get the jimjams whenever I visit my parents and happen to run into him next door. More often than not, when that happens, he'll be standing in his yard wooing a can of beer. With his plentiful belly on display. And sporting a twisted smirk. Even just thinking about him gives me the willies.

Cynthia pondered why these thoughts had welled up now, at the very time she needed to focus on the issue at hand. The tire changing episode she understood. But the incident with her mother? And the affair at the window? She chalked it up to an unspoken desire to change the subject. To shift the narrative away from the immediate. She did that sometimes when bouts of anxiety came calling.

The bouts seemed to come calling a lot lately, like a nagging stranger knocking at the door, demanding to be let in, refusing to take no for an answer. They visited when the ugly memories of the Fall of '63 came back. And when a stalker loomed in the rearview. And when she found herself stopped in her tracks in an urban barren with two of the three loves of her life in the back seat.

Cynthia cranked the engine and turned up the heat to cut the chill.

She sat in the dark, contemplating her next move.

Billy Jr. had joined Addie in deep slumber, for which she was grateful.

She wished she had been more attentive to what Cecil had tried to show her that day, on the shoulder this side of Opelika, as he removed the blown-out tire and mounted the spare. If only he hadn't thoroughly pissed her off with his *boy* comment.

She strained hard to remember what he had said and done. Snippets began to crop up through twenty-year-old cobwebs. She remembered about the jack. *Make sure it's secured in place and on firm ground,* he had said. *The hook goes under the bumper bar right here. See?* And the lug nuts. *Don't jack it all the way up at first. Otherwise, you won't be able to loosen the nuts. And when you take them off, put them in the upside-down hubcap. Like this. That way you won't lose them.* That was about it, except for the one other thing that poked through the cobwebs. His under-the-breath *if it kills me* that followed *I'm gonna teach you how to be a boy.*

As a last resort, maybe she could change the tire after all. It was worth a try. Better than waiting for a Samaritan who might never show up. But the flashlight didn't work. Maybe there was another one in the tool kit in the wayback. Or maybe one of those spotlights you plug into the lighter. Or even a road flare. Anything to help her see what she was doing.

She was about to get out of the car and pop the tailgate when she looked across the gravel. The orange point of light was growing closer. It bobbed and weaved, turning bright to dim and back. Then it fell to the ground and disappeared.

CHAPTER TWENTY-SIX

Billy Tarwater

Sunday, December 20ᵗʰ, 1981

THE KNOCK ON THE DOOR CAME AT TWENTY TO EIGHT.

"You got here fast," Billy said.

"I'd break speed records for you, buddy." Gary looked at his watch. "I would have been here sooner, but I had to make a couple of calls. First to the station house. Then to the little lady. She's at her mother's house. Making...what do you call that white sugary candy with the chopped-up pee-cans in it? And half a pee-can on top?"

"Divinity?"

"Yeah. That's it. They're making enough to feed a Christmas throng."

"And your call to the police station?"

"I gave Missing Persons the description of Cynthia and the little ones, of the Suburban...color, make, model, tag, the little dent on the left front fender...all you told me. Normally we wouldn't send out an APB yet, seeing as they haven't been missing very long. But Yours Truly's got pull." He puffed up like a blowfish. "Pretty soon, every beat cop out there will be on the lookout for them."

Gary cane-hobbled across the room and sank into the overstuffed chair, the one Cynthia would have occupied had she been there. He kept hold of his walking stick, with his arm outstretched and his hand gripping its wolf's head. The cane cut a plumb-line presence from his hand to the floor.

"Don't you want to put that thing down?" Billy asked.

"I would, but the last time I was here, you damned near tripped over it. I'd just as soon keep it out of the way. Got any joe?"

"I made a fresh pot. Just for you." Billy lied. He'd been downing it like water for the past two hours. "Black, right?"

"Yep. But some day, when I'm in the right mood, I'm going to ask for it with cream and a single scoop of sugar just so I can say *white one* like they do over there in the mother country."

Given the occasion, Billy didn't appreciate Gary's cavalier joke or his lightsome grin. He retreated to the kitchen.

Billy returned with two cups of arabica. He set them both on the table between the two armchairs and was about to settle into the unoccupied one when he changed his mind. He walked to the other side of the room. "I've been racking my brain, Gary. Trying to figure out where she could've gone…hold on a minute." He headed back toward the kitchen. "I want to show you something." He returned with Cynthia's refrigerator note. He handed it to Gary. "This is what she left."

Gary read the note. "Do you think she may have told anybody where she was going?"

"I called her mother, my mother. I called her closest friends. Reached all but one. They didn't know anything about a concert."

"What about the one you didn't reach?"

"I guess I could maybe try her again. It's a long shot, though."

No sooner had the words passed Billy's lips than he realized his carelessness. *Of course* he could—should—try her again. Cynthia was missing. The children were missing. Wouldn't he go to *any* lengths, long shot or otherwise, to find them? He plumbed Gary's eyes.

"Could? Maybe?" Gary said.

"Must," Billy replied.

Cynthia's friend, whom she had known going all the way back to eighth grade at Murphy High, answered on the third ring. "She called me," the friend said. "Told me she was taking the kids to a chorale. At the state capitol. Asked if I wanted to go. But I couldn't." A pause. "Why do you ask, Billy?"

* * *

Gary eased the unmarked Plymouth Fury—*standard issue, rank has its privileges, he had remarked more than once*—down MLK. Billy sat shotgun, his hands restless about his lap. His stomach churned. His heart quickened. His right hand played back and forth between the folds in his denims and the door's window trim, unable to find a home. He rubbed his thigh with his left.

They took a right onto Capitol Avenue. "We'll circle the block around the capitol," Gary said. "Then down the side streets."

They searched for upwards of an hour and turned up nothing.

"Let's park and go inside," Gary said. "The building's closed, but Security will let me in. I'll call the station house and see if they've turned up anything. And we can ask whoever's inside if they happened to see somebody matching Cynthia and the kids' descriptions. If they saw them leave. And when."

The police had nothing to report.

No one at the capitol remembered having seen Cynthia and the children.

Before leaving the building, Billy called Cynthia's mother again. And his mother. And Cynthia's friends. None of them had heard from her. And Adele was still fretting over her goddamned dressing and marshmallows.

They drove around for another hour, broadening their search, covering an area roughly bounded by Spring and Butler Streets, Edgewood and Woodward. They decided to go back to Billy's and think through what to do next. They headed down Peachtree Street. That was the route Cynthia most likely would have taken. Billy studied each intersecting street, to the left and to the right, as Gary drove to Fifth Street.

* * *

Gary dialed the Missing Persons Unit and gave them Billy's number. "Call me here if anything turns up," he told the night sergeant.

"I'm at my wit's end," Billy said. "I don't know what we can do but wait...and hope to hear something soon. Go home, Gary. Be with your family. I'll let you know if we get a call."

"No way I'm leaving you here by yourself, Billy." Gary sat back down in Cynthia's chair. This time he placed his cane crosswise, straddling the chair's arms. "But I do have a favor to ask."

"What's that?"

Gary picked up his empty coffee cup from earlier that evening. He held it in the air. "More joe?"

They waited.

At eleven forty-two the phone rang. Billy's first, anxious instinct was to answer it himself. But he knew if the call was from the police, they would want to talk to Gary.

Gary lifted the handset. "Tarwater residence." He nodded to Billy. "Speaking. Any news? Hold on a minute." He cradled the handset between his shoulder and ear. He looked at Billy, air-wrote on his palm.

Billy brought him a notepad and a Bic.

Gary returned his attention to the call. "Okay. Shoot." He furiously scribbled on the pad, his countenance becoming more ashen with each pen stroke.

He hung up. Scratched his head. Rubbed his brow. "Billy, they found the car. Abandoned downtown with a flat. Seven blocks from the capitol." He sighed. "We didn't look far enough."

"What about Cynthia and the kids?"

"They're missing. There was no sign of foul play. At least as far as they could tell, but it was dark. They'll be back there in the morning, when daylight comes, and they can get a better look.

"Where's *there*?"

"A dead end called Elliott Street. Off Mitchell. At the viaducts."

"Is the car there now?"

"They're towing it to the impound lot. They may have already."

"Will they call back if they turn up anything more?"

"In a heartbeat," Gary said. He crossed the room with halts and jerks, dropped his cane to the floor, and gave Billy a big bear hug. His body shook. "I love you, man. We'll find them."

Billy felt Gary's tears on his neck. Funny, in all their years growing up together, then reconnecting as adults, searching hand in glove for Cynthia's '63 kidnapper and finding him, then celebrating an innocent man freed, he'd never known Gary to cry.

The burly detective with the cockeyed swagger hugged Billy tighter.

Chapter Twenty-Seven

Billy Tarwater

Monday, December 21ˢᵗ, 1981

BILLY WOKE WITH A START FROM A FITFUL HALF-SLEEP. AND IN a trippy, dreamy state. *Is she back?* He rubbed his eyes. It was 3:52. Monday morning.

He ran his hand across her side of the bed. It was cold.

He donned his bathrobe. He searched every room, careful not to wake Gary, who had crashed on the living room sofa at some point after Billy had turned in. Gary's cane lay beside him on the floor. Granny Tarwater's heather-grey crocheted throw was bunched at his feet. A can of Diet Coke and a plate sporting the crust from a leftover pizza slice were on the table between the armchairs. At least he had felt enough at home to raid the fridge.

Billy staggered back to the bathroom and splashed a healthy dose of cold water across his face and neck. His bloodshot eyes stared back at him, imploring him to try, just once more, to doze off. But he knew that would be a wasted effort.

Late last night, after the call from the police, Gary had phoned all the nearby hospitals. Grady. Crawford Long. Georgia Baptist. Piedmont. *Did a woman with two small children...five-six, brunette, hazel eyes, glasses...and a boy and a girl...show up earlier this evening?* Nothing.

Gary had finally convinced Billy to try to get a little sleep. "You'll thank me tomorrow," he said.

Billy shuffled into the kitchen. The rumpled Arts & Entertainment section from yesterday's paper, opened to page 7, was on the kitchen table where he had left it. Next to it was Cynthia's note. He combed through the paper again, hoping to find the capitol chorale announcement he had surely missed yesterday. But he turned up nothing. He studied the note, hoping to discern anything between the lines that may have escaped him.

He placed a pot's worth of Master Blend into the Mr. Coffee filter basket. He filled the water reservoir and hit Brew. He watched trancelike as the dark liquid dribbled into the glass decanter. The coffee's essence lingered ponderously in the air.

"You're up early." Gary stood in the doorway.

"So are you. Pull up a chair. Coffee's ready."

"How'd you sleep?"

"I tried, but I was visited by a cruel chimera."

"What?"

"Never mind. I'm assuming we haven't heard anything?"

"Nothing."

"Should we call them?"

Gary looked at his watch. "It's not quite five yet. Let's give it a coupla hours. If we haven't heard anything by then, I'll call."

Billy decided to try to get his mind off things, even if only for a few minutes. He trudged into the bedroom, coffee in hand.

He turned his attention back to the FINNEGAN, J.P. file.

MON, MARCH 16, '81 - Spoke on the phone with Gary. He told me about an informer. Goes by the pseudonym J.P. Finnegan (JPF). Gary's recounting of what JPF told him:

SUMMER '79, JPF was introduced by an associate to three brothers named Vardeman. Ringleader: Graydon (GV). KKK-connected white racists. Said they needed explosives man. Associate suspected they were up to no good. GV told JPF about a plan to take out blacks in the city one at a time. To foment a race riot. Would begin with black boys and "take it from there." [direct GV quote]

JPF didn't believe GV. Said they were "just a bunch of racist redneck windbags." [direct JPF quote]

Note—JPF later confirmed the first date of his meeting with GV et al. as Fri, July 13.

SUMMER '79 THROUGH '80 - JPF continued to meet with GV et al. but was never called on to do anything with explosives.

JPF continued to believe they were "full of it." [direct JPF quote]

FRI, FEB 6, '81 - JPF read in Constitution about Lubie Geter body found in woods off Vandiver Road.

Note—I was at City Desk when Geter article went to press.

JPF remembered incident involving JPF, GV and Geter back in Summer '80.

JPF called police.

The phone rang. Billy threw the file onto the Lilliputian desk and rushed into the living room.

Gary had already answered.

CHAPTER TWENTY-EIGHT
Billy Tarwater

Monday, December 21ˢᵗ, 1981

GARY HUNG UP. "GET DRESSED. WE'RE GOING TO GRADY. I'LL FILL you in on the way."

"Gary, you can't do that to me. Are they okay?"

"They're okay. Cynthia's roughed up a bit. They're all obviously traumatized."

"But they're okay? The children are okay? Cynthia's okay?"

* * *

On their way to Grady Hospital, Gary told Billy everything he knew, which wasn't much.

A kind-hearted stranger had brought Cynthia and the children into the ER. Before the woman at the desk could get anything from him—the circumstances behind their condition, who they were, who *he* was—he had exited and disappeared into the dark of night.

"When did all this happen?" Billy asked.

"Sometime after midnight. At least that's what I was told."

"Why didn't they call right away? For Christ's sake, I've been worried sick for hours."

"They said she showed up with no purse. No ID. No nothing."

"But surely she would have given them her name, my name, her number."

"I don't know, Billy. We need to get to the bottom of it. But the most important thing now is that they're going to be okay."

"Were they admitted?"

"They were. But I think it was as much precautionary as anything. Given the circumstances, it was the right thing to do."

"Are the kids with her?"

"I'm sure they're in the Children's Ward."

Billy wondered what Billy Jr. and Addie must be going through, separated from their mother. Having to cope all alone with the trauma they had endured. What could they possibly know about such things at their age? What could they possibly understand?

Gary pulled into the parking lot.

Billy's throat tightened. He had been there before. A déjà vu feeling came over him.

* * *

October '63. Eleven-year-old Binky rode in the back seat of the Hudspeths' Fairlane. Mr. Hudspeth was at the wheel, driving like a madman. Mrs. Hudspeth sat beside her husband. They were on their way to Grady Hospital to visit Cynthia, who had ended up there after barely escaping death's grip. Mrs. Hudspeth had asked Binky's mother if he could come along, knowing how much he cared for their daughter.

Binky's knees wobbled as he exited the car and crossed the hospital parking lot.

Cynthia was asleep when they reached her room. He baby-stepped to the bed. His knees were wobbling even more than they had outside the hospital. His hands were sweating.

Cynthia's eyes were closed. When he touched the bed rail, she opened them. She beamed. "Binky?"

His heart pitter-pattered. *She remembers me.*

* * *

Now, eighteen years and two months later, he was back at Grady.

He and Gary got off the elevator on Cynthia's floor and headed down the corridor. Two uniformed officers were standing halfway down the hall.

Billy studied the officers then looked at Gary. "Are they—"

"Yep." Gary nodded. "They're there for her own good. And to question her when she regains her composure."

"Regains her composure? She not in a co—"

"Oh no, Billy. She's conscious and aware. They just want to give her a little breathing room before they barrage her with whos and whats and wheres."

Back when fourteen-year-old Cynthia had been in the hospital, the police had guarded the door to *her* room too. At that time, they had even insisted that she be admitted under an alias. In an instant, Cynthia Jane Hudspeth became Patti Black. The authorities had feared that Cynthia's would-be killer might come looking for her.

The door to Cynthia's room was ajar.

"He's her husband," Gary said, pointing to Billy. The officers stepped aside to allow Billy to enter. Gary stayed behind with the officers.

Cynthia was awake but groggy. A tinge of blue-black cut across her left brow ridge and around her eye. A rectangle of adhesive-taped gauze coursed her left cheekbone.

A nurse stood at her bedside. "She's on benzodiazepine," the nurse said without looking up. "It helps the nerves."

Billy knew all about benzos. Mother's Little Helpers. This wasn't the first time Cynthia had partaken. Adele had given a bottle to her back when she was pregnant with Billy Jr. Cynthia put it in the medicine cabinet, on the shelf beside the Band Aids and Bactine, without ever taking one. But last October, in the throes of reliving '63, she had succumbed. Billy knew that because he had taken to regularly counting the little blue pills one by one. Shortly after that, the bottle disappeared.

Cynthia brightened. "Billy?" But her cheer was fleeting. She looked around the room. "Are the kids here?"

The nurse drew close to Billy. "Your wife's not totally present right now," she said in a near-whisper. "The medication does that." She left the room.

Billy placed his hand on Cynthia's shoulder. "They're in good care. Just a few floors down." He hoped he was right.

He knelt and took her hand. "Cynthia, are you able to tell me what happened?"

CHAPTER TWENTY-NINE

Cynthia Tarwater

Monday, December 21ˢᵗ, 1981

BILLY BRUSHED THE HAIR AWAY FROM CYNTHIA'S EYES WITH HIS hand.

"It must be a tangled mess," she said.

"It doesn't matter. You're still as fetching as the first time I laid eyes on you."

"You're sweet, Billy, but…" A jabbing pain shot down her right arm. She winced.

"Are you alright?"

"I'm fine." She half-lied. "I'll try to tell you everything. But fair warning. This medication I'm on may end up hijacking my recall."

"Fair warning."

Cynthia asked the nurse to leave the room. To give her a shred of privacy with Billy.

She strained to gather her thoughts amidst the druggy haze.

She told him about the capitol concert. The lurker at the balustrade. The flat tire. The viaducts. Then she described, as well as she could, what had happened next...

I saw the man coming from across the gulch...the great divide. My state of mind ran from high hopes to fear. To high hopes and back again. I watched as the man came closer. At some point, I believe about halfway across the empty lot, he dropped his cigarette to the ground. Or maybe he threw it. It doesn't really matter.

I had been about to get out to see if there was a flashlight in the back. But when I saw him approaching, I stayed put.

He stopped briefly. Lit another cigarette. That's when I realized he had a pistol in the waistband of his khakis.

Fear took over. I made sure the doors were locked. Not that that would have helped much. If he wanted to break in, late at night with no one around, locked doors might slow him down, but they wouldn't stop him.

When he reached the Suburban, he took a deep drag and put the cigarette out with his shoe. He drew the pistol. *Unlock the door*, he said.

I refused.

He began to ram the window hard with the butt of the gun.

That's when I relented. I knew it was just a matter of time before he'd shatter the glass. Or shoot the lock. Or even worse, shoot through the window. And I would pay dearly for resisting.

He yanked me out with such force that I began to tumble to the ground. I seem to recall extending my right arm to catch the fall. Things are a bit of a blur, but it hurts like the dickens now.

I wore my "be-brave" face. Tried my best not to let the fear show.

The kids woke up screaming. *Mommy, Mommy, are you okay?* I don't know whether the man realized, before then, that they were with me. *Stay where you are*, I told them.

The man ordered me to my feet.

Take whatever you want, I said. *Just don't hurt the children.*

I'm not here to hurt the children, he said. He ordered them out of the Suburban.

They ran up to me and wrapped their trembling arms around my waist.

He ordered us to walk across the great divide to his car.

I planted my feet in the gravel and stood my ground. I said something like *if it's all the same to you, we'll stay here.* I don't know what got into me. If you'd asked me before this happened what I would have done, I would have said I'd be a quivering wreck.

The man hauled off and struck my face with the gun.

I fell back against the Suburban.

Then I heard a click. The man pointed the cocked gun at my head. *What'd you say?*

I don't remember walking to the man's car. I guess I was too upset. And worried about Billy Jr. and Addie.

Or maybe the drugs are getting in the way.

The nurse came back into the room. She was holding a small paper cup in her right hand. She extended it. "Here, take this."

Cynthia stared at the round blue pill with the V-shaped hollow down the middle, looking up at her from the bottom of the cup as if to say *I know you despise me, but I'm here to help, not hurt.* She wasn't sure she believed it. She tossed the pill into her mouth. Pretended to swallow it. Let it drop into her cupped hand when "Nurse Ratched" wasn't looking. The haze was fading, and she sure didn't want to blow it now, just as she was trying to muster her recall.

She looked at the nurse and raised her eyebrows. The nurse got the message and went back out with an attitude.

"Doesn't she remind you of Nurse Ratched?" Cynthia said.

"Who?"

"*One Flew Over The—*"

"Oh, her." Billy smirked.

Cynthia continued telling Billy what had happened...

When we got to the car, the man bound my wrists behind my back with tape. He did the same to the kids.

176

He ordered the three of us into the back seat. We did as he said. He slammed the door shut.

The kids sat on each side of me. Nuzzling against me as tight as they could. Trembling. I felt the terror in their faces. The pain in their sad little eyes. I wanted nothing more than to put my arms around them, but I couldn't.

The man drove around for a while. Like he wasn't sure what to do or where to go. He stopped at one point and called somebody from a phone booth.

After what must have been an hour or more, he pulled into the Blue Bird Truck Stop at Pryor and Memorial. He eased up to the pump and cut the engine. He turned around to me and said something like *If you so much as think of running, you'll never make it to the street.* He looked at Billy Jr. and Addie. Then back at me. *Think of your children before you do something you'll regret.*

He got out of the car and told the attendant to fill it up with Regular. While the attendant was pumping, our kidnapper pulled a pack of Marlboros out of his pocket. He shook his head. He crushed the pack and tossed it into the trash. He went inside, I assumed to buy another pack.

Now's my chance, I thought. But my wrists were bound. The window crank handles had been removed. And the little things you pull up to unlock the rear doors had been removed.

"Door lock knobs," Billy said. "What kind of car was it?"

"I could be wrong, but I'm pretty sure it was the same car that followed me to daycare. It said 400 on the side near the front. I don't know my cars...you know that...but maybe early '70s. Light green with a black top."

"The 400 on the front quarter panel sounds like an Impala. There's a little stem that the lock knob screws into. It's hard to lock and unlock the door with just the stem, but you can if you know what you're doing."

Cynthia told Billy about her guardian angel...

I tried to get the attendant's attention but couldn't. Then a stranger pulled up in a big pickup truck. I banged my head on the car window to get his attention. I mouthed "Help." I'm sure the swelling on my face was a dead giveaway too.

He opened the rear door.

He whisked us into his pickup. He removed the tape from our wrists. We took off, squeezed like sardines between him and the passenger door.

I looked back. Just as we were speeding out of the Blue Bird lot, our kidnapper came running out. I could see him yelling at the attendant and flailing his arms about. He didn't follow us, though. At least not that I'm aware.

The stranger brought us to Grady and dropped us off at the ER. He parked and came in. He stayed briefly to make sure we were being taken care of. Then he left without my telling him thank you or getting his name.

"Did you happen to keep the tape? From your wrists?"

"No," Cynthia said. "I should have. It could have had fingerprints on it. But I wasn't thinking straight."

"What did your abductor look like?"

"Thin. Scrawny really. But behind the gaunt there's more than meets the eye."

"What do you mean?"

"He's a lot chippier than he looks."

"What else do you remember?"

"He was scraggled and walked with a bit of a stoop. He smoked cigarettes like a stovepipe. And his hair was a tangled mess. I imagine like mine is right now."

"What color?"

"White."

"I mean his hair."

"Reddish."

"Facial hair?"

"No beard or mustache. Some red stubble was all."

"Anything else you can tell me?"

Cynthia took a deep breath. "I'm not positive, as it was dark outside and I wasn't all there, but I'm pretty sure it was the balustrade man."

CHAPTER THIRTY
Billy Tarwater

Monday, December 21ˢᵗ, 1981

THE NURSE CAME BACK INTO THE ROOM.

"When will my wife be released?" Billy asked.

"Today. That's all I know. But it won't be fast. Discharges around here don't work that way."

"Can I see my children now?"

She straightened her back. "I suppose so, but I don't have control over that. Do I look like an information desk?" Then her demeanor softened a bit. "Here's what you do. Go up the hall to the nurses' station. There's a phone there. Call the main number. Tell them you want the Children's Ward."

"Nurse Ratched indeed," Billy mouthed as he exited the room.

Gary was standing just outside the door. "How's Cynthia?" he asked.

"Getting by. More lucid than I expected. She gave me a lot of info. I'll give you the scoop...but first I want to see the kids."

"I understand. A quick update about the Suburban. Cynthia's purse, ID, car keys were in it. They're dusting it for prints. We can go over and look at it sometime, but only when you're ready."

The walls of the children's corridor were painted bright colors and adorned with crayon drawings affixed with Scotch tape. Construction paper cutouts of various colors and shapes—circles and stars and hearts and such—dangled from the suspended ceiling, swinging to and fro under the sway of the air vents.

The nurses and other staff, sporting patterned pastel uniforms, met him with big smiles. *Nurse Ratched's nowhere to be found on* this *floor.*

Billy Jr. and Addie were in a room by themselves. Two men stood guard in the hallway. Unlike the ones outside Cynthia's room, these men were dressed in street clothes, but as Billy approached one of them, the man showed his badge. Billy surmised that Gary had been responsible in part for their presence. And he also supposed someone had decided that uniformed police in the children's section would have been alarming to some. But the kids in the ward probably would have been delighted, not scared, to see policemen in their presence.

He had assumed the shared rooms in the children's section were single sex. Perhaps the nurses had put Billy Jr. and Addie together because they were brother and sister and knowing what they had been through.

Both kids beamed and sat up in their beds when they saw their daddy. He was sure that they would have given anything to be able to jump out of bed, run across the room, and give him a big bear hug. He bent over and gave Addie a mini-love-blanket hug. Then Billy Jr.

He told them what was going on. That Mommy was okay. That they and she would be leaving the hospital soon. And when they got home, they could each have a big bowl of ice cream. Any flavor they wanted. With sprinkles. He reminded them that Christmas was only four days away. That seemed to help take their minds off what they'd been through.

"Daddy," Billy Jr. said, "is that bad man coming back to get us?"

Truth conquers platitudes, Billy reminded himself. "The bad man's not here, Son. Mommy and I will do everything in our power to protect you two."

Ice cream and sprinkles and Christmas notwithstanding, Billy had little doubt that they'd be dealing with night terrors for many weeks to come.

CHAPTER THIRTY-ONE

Billy Tarwater

Monday, December 21ˢᵗ, 1981

"NURSE RATCHED" HAD BEEN ON THE MARK WHEN SHE SAID *IT*
won't be fast. Discharges around here don't work that way.

It was almost 6:30 Monday evening when *it* finally happened. Before that, Billy had been banished from Cynthia's room for upwards of two hours while the detectives questioned her about her captor. About his car. About the Blue Bird Truck Stop. About her pickup-driving rescuer.

Billy pulled up to the hospital entrance. Cynthia and the kids, each in a wheelchair pushed by its own obsequious looking orderly, exited the main door. Cynthia looked miserable having to be pushed along. Billy imagined she was thinking *I'm perfectly fine walking on my own, thank you.* Billy Jr. and Addie, on the other hand, were cheery and chipper. After all, how often does a kid get to cruise around in a fancy wheeled ride, just the right size and all dolled up with holiday bows? The circuitous ride from the Children's Ward to the car seemed enough to get their minds off bad things, at least for the moment.

Within four blocks of leaving the hospital, they both had drifted off. No doubt the result of an exhausting and emotionally draining twenty-four hours. And of the slow movement of the car, the hum of the engine, as Billy eased down Piedmont Avenue.

Billy broke the news to Cynthia. "My mom's coming over. She's going to stay with us through the holidays to help out."

"What?" She pivoted and stared Billy down. "I'm perfectly fine. I don't need your mom's help."

"Cynthia, Christmas is four days away. You and the kids have been through a lot. There's so much to do between now and then. You don't need to be overexerting yourself. And whoever kidnapped you will surely be on a mission to finish what he set out to do."

"And that was?"

"Thinking about the unthinkable isn't something I relish."

"How do you think Alice is going to protect us? And anyway, where will *you* be?"

"By your side every minute I can. But there are some things I need to take care of before Thursday."

"Work-related?"

Truth conquers. Billy pondered Cynthia's question. Did a vow to be honest and up front, whatever the consequences, stop with Billy Jr. and Addie? Didn't Cynthia deserve as much?

"Well?" she said.

Billy pulled into the Civic Center parking lot and slowed to a stop. It was his turn to pivot. He leaned in, stretched his right arm across the seat back, and placed his other hand on both of hers, which she held clasped in her lap. "It's not work-related. Somebody's out to get you, and I need to find out who. Because of what just happened to you, and with Gary's unfailing advocacy, the police are pulling out all the stops. But I need to do some digging on my own, too."

"Aren't you worried about your *own* safety?"

"I'll be careful. There are some things I need to run down myself. Some things that can't involve the police. At least not yet."

* * *

Billy's mom arrived early the next morning "in all her glory"—Cynthia's words, not his. As soon as Billy was confident that everyone had settled in and Cynthia had accepted his mom, albeit begrudgingly, as her "caretaker pro tempore"—again, her words—he set out on the first leg of his mission—to pay a visit to the Suburban.

* * *

He met Gary and two detectives at the impound lot.

Knowing is one thing. Seeing is another thing altogether. A tautness beset Billy's gut as he stood before the Suburban, jacked up in the lot with its right front wheel missing. The investigators had finished their jobs. Dusting the door handles, the windows, the window trim, the interior for prints. Photographing the car stem to stern, inside and out. Examining the tire for any evidence of foul play.

One of the detectives gave Cynthia's handbag to Billy. "Her keys and ID are in the zipper pocket. Everything seems at this point to be intact."

Billy placed the handbag in his car.

"I want to show you the tire," the detective said. He led Billy and Gary into the garage on the edge of the impound lot. He grabbed a paper towel from a nearby tool cart. Using the paper towel, he retrieved a jagged shard of metal, no more than three quarters of an inch long and flat on one end, from the cart. "This was still stuck in the tread when we got to the Suburban on Elliott Street. If it had been a nail or a screw, it could easily have penetrated the tire but remained there for days, even weeks, with nothing more than a slow leak. But this thing here, it did enough damage when she ran over it that it probably didn't take more than a block or so for the tire to start going flat."

"Do you think it was deliberate?" Billy said.

"It's plausible that somebody placed the shard, flat side down, right in front of the tire. She wouldn't have noticed it, especially with it being on the passenger side. When she pulled out of where she parked and ran over it, the tire would have started going flat quickly." The detective placed the shard back on the tool cart. "But saying it was done on purpose…that's hard to prove."

"Any way to get prints from it?"

"We tried, but we couldn't."

"How about from the car itself?"

"We lifted some. They're not great. They could be your wife's. Or they could be from the perp. We'll have to go through our files manually to see if we can find a match. We don't have access to a database yet, but I'm told they're real close to having one."

After the detectives had left, Billy and Gary stood in the lot and talked for a few minutes.

"Based on the info Cynthia gave the police," Gary said, "they're running the car description through DMV. Green/black Impala four-door. Late '60s to early '70s. We'll see what they turn up."

"Probably a long shot," Billy said. "Don't you think? There must be a lot of green Impalas with black tops."

"They're narrowing it down first to metro Atlanta. Yeah, it's a long shot, but pay dirt sometimes comes from long shots."

"And what about Cynthia's description of the man?"

"That's a longer shot. Unless we have something else to go on, prints or something that we can match to a name. We'll see."

"She said there'd been a man on the balustrade at the capitol. Fit the description. Can we track that down?"

"I'm on it, buddy."

Billy deliberated his next question. "Gary, remember when we were at the Majestic last week, and I asked you whether somebody, like the Vardemans, could be out to get me because of my snooping, and you dismissed it. Do you still believe that?"

"I did dismiss it. But that was before all this happened. At the time, all we knew was somebody might be following Cynthia. Now it's for real. I wouldn't be worth a good goddamn as a detective if I didn't cast a wide net. Trust me, that's what every detective on this case will do now."

Upon leaving the impound lot, Billy stopped at the first phone booth he came to. He consulted his pocket address book, inserted a dime, and dialed J.P. Finnegan.

"Finnegan here."

"It's Billy Tarwater."

"Hello Billy. I was just thinking about you."

"Good things, I hope."

"That depends. What are you doin' to move the Vardeman shit forward?"

"I'm working on it. These things don't happen overnight. You know that."

"I know, but Jesus Christ, it's been…what…nine months now. I'm beginning to worry that you're just another Willie."

"Tell me something, J.P. Didn't you tell me back in March that Vardeman drives a Chevy?"

"I can't say any one of them drives any one vehicle. There's three of them, you know."

"Vehicles?"

"No, Vardemans. Actually, four if you count Sonya."

"Okay, so what do the Vardemans drive?"

"I've seen a Kawasaki Z at their house. And a couple of Harleys. And an old Impala."

"How old?"

"Maybe '70, '71."

"Color?"

"Green with a black roof."

"Four-door? Two-door?"

"Four."

"Is that the car Lubie rammed his go-kart into?

"No. Funny thing is I haven't seen that car since the one time Graydon took me to visit that man Sammy. Sorry I completely forgot to mention that one."

"What kind of car was *it*?"

"It was an Impala too, but it was one of those two-door Sports Coupes. A later model than the other one. Maybe mid '70s. With a fastback look that's sort of like those Chevy bubbletops from the early '60s. Remember them?"

"Color?"

"Metallic blue. Why are you asking all these questions, Billy?"

"I can't say yet. Bear with me, J.P. In time—"

"Don't leave me hanging long, Billy. I'm the one that's on the front line with these guys."

"I understand."

Billy hung up, inserted another dime, and dialed Gary at police headquarters. "Gary, I just spoke with Finnegan. Turns out he saw a green Impala with a black top, early '70s, at the Vardeman house. Please have whoever's running the DMV search be on the lookout for one of their names on the list."

"Sure thing."

Chapter Thirty-Two
Billy Tarwater

Wednesday, December 23rd, 1981

BILLY WOKE FROM A DREAM WITH THE KARPMAN DRAMA triangle stuck in a do-loop. He hadn't given it much thought, consciously anyway, since Psych 101.

Cynthia was sound asleep, her right leg hanging half off the bed. The hem of her silk chemise had ridden up, revealing the P on her thigh.

He rested his head on his hand and reflected upon the scar, faintly visible in the dimly lit room.

Billy respected that Cynthia was determined not to play *poor me*. He respected her resolve. Respected that she would do whatever it took not to be a victim. But he knew how hard it must be, given what she'd just been through, and given that she has to live every day with a physical reminder from her past.

He would do whatever it took to pursue her kidnapper and look after her and the kids. But by trying to protect her, by cosseting her, by insisting that his mother come and stay, was he unwittingly making her into the victim she resisted being? Was he playing Karpman's game?

Billy tried to shake off the thought. But it hung around like an uninvited guest.

Cynthia awakened. She nudged the hem of the chemise down over the P.

"Good morning, beautiful," Billy said. He leaned over and kissed her forehead.

"Good morning. The bed feels so good, I don't want to get out of it."

"You don't have to. I don't have to." For the moment, his mother's presence seemed more a convenience than a cosset. "Mom's here and can take care of the kids for a while."

"What about work?"

"I think I have a pretty good reason to show up late."

* * *

At 10:06, the phone rang. "It's probably for me." Billy reached across Cynthia and answered it. It was Gary. The police had run the DMV report and were culling it. "I have a copy," Gary said. "They're still going through it line-by-line, but I saw no Vardemans on the list. It did turn up something interesting, though."

"What's that?"

"Eight years ago, a light blue 1971 Impala four-door with a black top was stolen. It was never recovered. I was a beat cop then, so I wouldn't necessarily have known about it. Anyway, the insurance company paid out, the police figured the car had ended up in a chop shop somewhere, and that was that."

"That's interesting, Gary, but I don't see the connection."

"The connection is who owned the car and where it was stolen from."

"And?"

"The car was owned by Jephthah Thomas."

"The *Reverend* Thomas?"

"One and the same. And it was stolen from the parsonage driveway before daybreak on Saturday, the third of February. Seventy-three."

"But it was blue."

"Yes, it was blue. But it seems awfully coincidental. Could Cynthia be mistaken about the color?"

"I doubt it, Gary. Three times now she's encountered what she thinks is the same vehicle, and each time she's said it was green. I'm struggling to see the connection."

"Maybe there isn't one. But what if it's the same car? What if it's not blue anymore?"

"I get what you're saying, especially given Thomas's connection to Kilgallon, and by association, what happened to Cynthia and the others. But the car was *stolen* from Thomas."

"If I were you, I'd talk to his holiness and find out more about the car and what happened to it."

"His holiness. Good one, Gary. As much as it pains me to confront the man, I will."

Billy was about to hang up when Gary interjected. "One other thing. You told me Finnegan said he saw a green Impala with a black top at Graydon's. Just because DMV didn't turn up anything, that doesn't mean much, except that none of the Vardeman clan appears to be the owner. You should follow up with Finnegan, too."

* * *

Early that afternoon, Billy told his mother she should go home. He didn't do it in a mean-spirited or uncaring way. He simply told her that, while they all loved her company, a little private time was needed in the wake of what had happened. And anyway, they'd be with her in a couple of days. She understood.

He had briefly considered sending Billy Jr. and Addie home with her but decided against it. They were better off behind locked doors in the security of their own home rather than away.

* * *

That evening, Billy told Cynthia he was going to church.

"You? Going to church? Has my mother wormed her way into your head?"

"No. That'll never happen. I'm going pay a visit to Jephthah Thomas."

"While you're gone," Cynthia said, "I'll keep the deadbolt engaged and not open the door for anybody. That is, unless I'm sure who's on the other side."

Billy donned his coat and prepared to head for the door.

"By the way," Cynthia said. "Jephthah. Is that really his name?"

"Far as I know."

"Do you know who Jephthah was? In the Bible?"

"No. Not really. Truth be told, I don't know jack about the Bible."

"Jephthah of Gilead. From the Book of Judges. He led the Israelites to fight Ammon. Because of the Ammonites' defeat, and because of a vow he made, he sacrificed his daughter, his only child, to God. A human sacrifice. A soul-saving sacrifice. Does that strike you as odd, given what happened in '63?"

On Billy's drive to Confederate Avenue Baptist Church, he thought about what Cynthia, herself an only child, had said. About Jephthah of Gilead. About '63. About soul-saving sacrifice.

* * *

Billy hadn't been to a Wednesday night church supper since he was Binky, and his mother would drag him, kicking and screaming, to the fellowship hall. *What about Ozzie and Harriet* never seemed to work.

He wasn't sure whether they'd make a place at the table for him, since he hadn't called the church and booked in advance. But what the hell—would they really have the audacity to turn him away from God's house just because of poor planning on his part? He'd take that chance.

Billy stood at the entrance to the fellowship hall and scanned the room. It was already half-filled with congregants. It had changed little in eighteen years. Same faux wood shiplap and drab dapple grey LVT flooring. Same six-by-two-and-a-half-foot folding tables covered with disposable plastic tablecloths and adorned with faded fake peonies. Same hard metal hinged-back chairs in institutional beige.

But the red-and-green Lottie Moon Christmas Offering boxes were nowhere to be found, replaced by a pedestaled wooden box with TITHES carved into the front, strategically positioned by the door.

The evening fare was handwritten on a sheet of paper Scotch-taped along the bottom edge of the offering box, no doubt to draw attention to the subtle, or perhaps not so subtle, plea for bestowal. Meatloaf, mashed potatoes, green beans, Parker House rolls, iced tea. And fruitcake.

Billy double-folded a five and dropped it into the box's slot.

He picked up his tray from the serving line, grabbed a red SOLO cup of sweet tea—the only variety they seemed to offer—and found a free space at a table halfway across the room. He wanted to be close enough to the lectern from which Thomas would surely spout forth his supplications before the evening's end, but far enough away so as not to attract the reverend's attention until the time was right.

As soon as Billy sat down, the tableful of eyes set upon him. His tablemates must have wondered who the stranger in their midst was. He introduced himself as just Billy, a member from the church's "distant past." He refrained from giving his last name lest someone put two and two together and excoriate him for what he had done to their esteemed deceased pastor emeritus Kilgallon.

The woman sitting directly across the table welcomed him, with an exacting cavil, back after "so long." "And where is your church home now?" she said.

Billy pointed out that he had no "church home" and that he was just visiting for the evening. He quickly changed the subject.

"I don't believe I caught your name. Are you originally from these parts? How long has this been *your* church home?"

He looked around the room, hoping he might see Leonard Seymour. But then he remembered. The Reverend Thomas had allowed that Seymour had gone away for the holidays.

Thomas swaggered into the room through the side door. He assumed his place at the lectern.

Broadus McMillan appeared right behind him and leaned against the door jamb as if he were holding it up rather than the other way around. He scanned the room and locked eyes with Billy. He approached the lectern and whispered something to the reverend, who then gazed across the room at Billy.

Damn, Billy thought. *Ten minutes here and I'm already busted.*

The reverend's stare lingered. "I had meant on teaching tonight on the Good Lord's arrival," he said, "but something's gotten in the way." He peered over his glasses. "If a dog is asleep, it won't bite. If you wake it, it may." He opened his Bible and riffled through the pages. "I commend Proverbs to you. Chapter twenty-six. Verse seventeen." He cleared his throat with a resounding *chuhuh*. "He that passeth by and meddleth with strife belonging not to him…" He banged his closed fist onto the lectern. "Is like one that taketh a dog by the ears." He slammed the holy book shut, swung around, and left the room in a huff with Broadus following close behind.

Billy scarfed down his meal, skipping the fruitcake. He didn't like it anyway, going all the way back to the days of Granny Tarwater's dreadful tins, kept cool in her root cellar. He conveyed his regrets to the caviller and the others at the table and hotfooted it out of the fellowship hall.

The reverend's office door was closed. Billy knocked. Then again.

The door swung open. It was Broadus McMillan. "He's gone."

"What do you mean, he's gone? He was just here."

"Left in a hurry. Won't be comin' back tonight."

Billy sped out of the church lot and headed to the parsonage.

* * *

He was halfway up the parsonage sidewalk when Thomas swung open the front door and stepped across the threshold. "You just don't know when to give up, do you Tarwater?"

"I'm not here to talk about the girls this time, Reverend. I'm here to talk about a '71 Impala."

"What about a '71 Impala?"

"You owned one? It was stolen eight years ago?"

"That sounds about right. What does that have to do with anything, Tarwater? So I owned an Impala. So it was stolen. So what. Cars are stolen all the time."

"Am I correct that it was stolen from right here in your driveway?"

"It's not *my* driveway. This is a parsonage. It's the *Lord's* driveway."

"So it was stolen from the..." Billy swallowed hard. "...the Lord's driveway."

"That's right."

"And you filed a police report? And collected on the insurance claim?"

"Of course. Wouldn't you?"

"Any idea who may have taken it?"

"How would I know that? Somebody came here at three in the morning. I was roused from a sound sleep. I jumped up and looked out the window. I saw them speeding away in the car. I assumed they hot-wired it. That's the last I saw of it."

"And the police never found it, right?"

Thomas glowered. He backed across the threshold, never relaxing his stare. "I suspect you already know the answer to that." He slammed the door. Billy heard the lock click.

* * *

Billy stopped at a phone booth and phoned Finnegan. "About that Impala you saw at the Vardemans'. Can you get the tag number for me?"

"I'll do you one better," Finnegan said. "I'll even try to get the VIN number if you'd like. But no guarantees. If Vardeman catches me snooping around too much, things could backfire. I doubt that he'll see me before Christmas, though."

Chapter Thirty-Three

Cynthia Tarwater

Friday, December 25th, 1981

CHRISTMAS DAY AT THE HUDSPETHS'. CYNTHIA'S MOTHER plopped down the marshmallowed yams at the edge of the half-empty dining table and put her hands on her hips. "They tell me them little boys that was killed was all mixed up in a sex ring. And Williams, he was the leader of it all."

"Where did you hear that?" Cynthia asked.

"In the paper. And it's been all over the TV too. Don't you ever read the paper? Watch the TV?"

Cynthia had neglected the news lately. She had a good excuse. She turned to Billy. "Is that true?"

He said there had been rumors about some of the boys. But it was all circumstantial.

Her mother didn't buy it. She went on and on about it. "At least they're in a better place now. I just know it. God bless their souls. Saved from predation."

Cynthia was pretty sure her mother meant *perdition*, but she didn't have the heart or the energy to correct her. She wondered how her mother could possibly reconcile what had just come out of her mouth with what had happened to her own daughter, who had been the same age as some of those boys when she was abducted.

Then Cecil had to chime in. "Adele, just put the goddamn food on the table."

Adele shot back. "Don't you ever take the Lord's name in vain. Not in my house you don't."

"Okay, Adele," he said. "Just put the *fuckin'* food on the table, then. Is that better?"

She jingled the keys hanging from her belt loop. She raised her arms to the ceiling and bayed. "Slain in the spirit." Then she withdrew to the kitchen.

So much for a festive Christmas.

On their way here, Billy and Cynthia had swung by and picked up Alice and Chester. Cynthia hadn't been up for a two-meal day of orgiastic gluttony, and Alice didn't seem to want to cook anyway. Adele had said "the more the merrier," just as she had at Thanksgiving, whether she meant it or not.

Cynthia wondered what Billy's mother and brother must have been thinking. She looked over at Alice, who was looking down at her lap, ashen and fiddling with her thumbs. Chester was staring out the window, probably wistfully entertaining the idea of still being on the Mayaguez somewhere rather than with his sister-in-law's insufferable family. Cynthia was grateful that Billy

Jr. and Addie had retreated to her old bedroom to play with their Christmas spoils.

Billy leaned in and whispered, "And I thought the Reverend Thomas was getting ornerier every day. Your dad beats all."

Adele, who had come back into the room, must have heard what he said. She swung around. "That old crackpot Thomas. Pretends to be so upright and godly." She patted her chest. "I've got the Lord right here inside of me. I don't need to go to church and listen to him go on and on. The old racist fool."

Cynthia had never heard her mother call anybody a racist before. It seemed out of character, especially given Adele's own inclinations. She thought back to the time her mother ratted out Sam, who had been hiding in Granny Tarwater's cellar. Adele was convinced "that colored man Jepperson" had abducted and killed those girls.

"Why is he a racist?" Cynthia asked.

"Because he rubs—"

"Adele," Cecil yowled, "will you *please* muffle it and put the damn food on the table."

Cynthia sat on pins and needles at dinner, worrying that somebody would say something untoward, or even perfectly reasonable, and set Cecil off again. It wouldn't take much.

For the first twenty minutes or so, everyone was quiet.

Then Cecil decided to declare that the turkey was "dryer than a popcorn fart."

That's when Billy jumped in and changed the subject. "I understand your next-door neighbor is away for the holidays."

"Are you talking about Leonard?" Adele said.

"Yes, I hear he's in Alabama visiting his sister."

"He's not in no Alabama," she said. "He's been right here the whole time."

"He has?"

"Well, I guess I should know, seeing as how I see him through his window every day."

"Oh. I must have been mistaken."

"I guess so."

"Where's his car?"

"He pulls it around back. Hasn't been goin' out much. Every coupla days, that man from the church comes over on his motorcycle." Whenever she said the word, it came out like *sickle*.

"What man?"

"That man does maintenance at the church."

*   *   *

After dinner, Cynthia and Billy dropped Alice and Chester off at her house, along with the kids, and headed to Carver Homes to visit Sam and Ruby Jepperson. No meal this time. But they had given in and agreed to dessert—Ruby's caramel pecan apple pie— from a recipe passed down from her maternal great-grandmother.

Billy Jr. and Addie would stay overnight with Billy's mom, giving Cynthia and Billy an evening alone. It had taken a lot for Billy to agree to let them go, given what she and the kids had been through and with a kidnapper on the loose, but her arm-twisting did the trick. She had even suggested a reprise of their old Friday-night dress-ups, but Billy didn't bite. He said it was no time for that kind of frivolity. Cynthia half-agreed with him and consented to dispense with the roleplay. But a little holiday cheer was on the menu. She was sure of that.

But first, they would visit the Jeppersons.

* * *

Ruby and Sam greeted them at the door as if they were long lost exiles come back from a decade in the diaspora or something. Sam gave Cynthia an embrace so hard she feared he'd broken her rib.

They ushered Cynthia and Billy through the living room, past the blue spruce adorned with popcorn and cranberries and tinsel, past Ruby's Singer Portable with the cuttings strewn across its platform, and into the kitchen. "I don't sew much anymore," Ruby said, "with one finger gone and another chewed up."

Billy and Cynthia sat at the dinette. Sam and Ruby sat across from them.

"Where are the others?" Cynthia asked.

"Theda had to go see to her mother," Ruby said, "and Rufus went with her. Recy stepped out. I reckon she'll be home directly."

Four perfectly cut ninety-degree pie slices proffered themselves on bright red melamine dishes, flanked by paper holiday napkins on the left and stainless steel forks on the right.

"Eat up," Ruby said.

They dug in.

Cynthia could tell that Sam wanted to bring something up, he was hemming and hawing around so. Billy noticed it too. Finally, Billy said, "Sam, is something bothering you?"

Sam hesitated. "It ain't nothin'. It's just that, you know, ever since I got out, I been tryin' to find good work. It's a shame the barbershop shut down. But Mr. Batson wouldn't a taken me back anyway. He was hoppin' mad, seein' as I just disappeared like I did. If it weren't for Rufus helpin' out with the money, I don't know what we'd a done."

"Have you been able to find any work at all, Sam?" Billy asked.

"I been helpin' out over at the EZ Mart, stockin' the shelves and cleanin' up. But it's not much. My tips was what got me by at the barbershop. No tips doin' what I'm doin' now."

"Sam," Ruby said. "Tell them what's *really* bothering you."

Sam looked at Billy with anguished eyes.

"Sam, go on. Tell them."

He lowered his head as if searching the Formica tabletop for something that wasn't there. He looked back up. "I think somebody's out for me."

"What do you mean, Sam?" Billy said.

"Wednesday, two days ago, I was in front of the EZ Mart sweepin' the sidewalk when a boy rode up on his wheel. He said, 'You Sam?' I said 'Yep, that's me.' He got down off his wheel and handed me a note. Then he rode off." Sam reached into his pocket and passed the note across the table to Billy.

It looked like it had been torn from a spiral notebook.

"Read it out loud," Sam said.

Billy let his gaze linger on the note for a moment. He took a deep breath. "It says Sam Jepperson, you're a dead man walking."

He laid the note on the table. The message had been crafted from letters in various shapes and sizes, pasted onto the paper.

"What did the boy look like, Sam?"

"He was a scrawny little white boy with a ginger top. That's all I can tell you, Billy."

Chapter Thirty-Four

Cynthia Tarwater

Sunday, December 27ᵗʰ, 1981

CYNTHIA SAT SPLAY-LEGGED ON THE LIVING ROOM FLOOR. THE tome-like sections of the Sunday paper were scattered about her. She was determined not to let the news get away from her again.

"Are you picking up the kids today?" she said.

"I told Mom I'd come over early this evening. Not too late, though. Big day tomorrow."

She grabbed Section A and scanned the headlines…debt threatens Georgia farmers, Reagan seeks meeting with Brezhnev, martial law in Poland…down to the article at the bottom of the first page. WAYNE WILLIAMS: THE NEXT CHAPTER BEGINS. Accompanying the article was a picture of Williams, staring dejectedly at the lower right corner of the photograph. The byline credited two *Journal* writers whose names she vaguely remembered Billy mentioning in the past.

Williams would go on trial tomorrow, accused of killing two black men. Their bodies had been found "a month apart in the same brush-choked spot on the Chattahoochee River." But what about the children whose murders had been investigated for over two years? Williams maintained that he was a scapegoat and that those investigations had produced no evidence to implicate him.

She turned to Billy. "Do you think Williams killed those black boys? And the girls?"

He blew the steam from his coffee, the fine mist dissipating into thin air. "I have my doubts. But I fear that, with Williams behind bars and tried and convicted before the jury is even seated, the open child murder cases may dry up fast."

"And if he didn't do it?"

"The killer will walk."

"But the killings did stop when Williams was arrested, didn't they?"

"They did. At least they have. But think about '63. The abductions ended when Sam was locked up. And he was innocent."

"That's true."

"There's something else, though."

"What's that?"

"Every day, I'm less sure that Williams killed those children. If I'm right about who may have been behind the murders, why would they decide to stop, given their purported goal?"

"What are you talking about?"

Billy told Cynthia about the informer named Finnegan. About undercover infiltration of a Klan family named Vardeman.

About the efforts of the police to keep it a secret. About his own involvement in the whole affair for the past nine months.

Cynthia hesitated. She got up, walked into the kitchen, and poured a cup of coffee.

"Billy, who do you think is out to get Sam?"

"I have no idea. There's a lot of crazy shit going on these days."

She sat back down on the floor and continued to read the paper.

Billy was about to walk out of the room when she said, "Truth conquers, Billy. Remember that? Why did you never tell me about what you've been up to? Nine months is a long time to keep a secret."

That evening, Billy left to pick up the kids from his mother's house.

Cynthia decided to take advantage of an hour of quiet to work on her lesson plan. She sat down at the tiny desk she and Billy shared. It was Billy's custom to put away his paperwork before the odd-numbered days—*her* days—but this time he had left a solitary note lying at the corner of the desk. She assumed inadvertently. It was a Xeroxed copy from part of what looked like a typed police report. It read in part:

Anthony Terrell, brother of Earl Terrell:

Anthony and Earl were walking home from school. Their aunt and uncle asked if they wanted to go swimming. RTheir youngest brother was at home with his aunt. The aunt had to leave, so Anthony had to stay back home. Anthony told Earl to go swimming alone. Anthony gave Earl two or three dollars. Earl couldn't find his swim trunks, so he took Anthony's. Earl left to go to the swimming pool. Earl's mother came home later and asked where Earl was. Earl never returned home.

Scribbled in the margin, in blue ink and in Billy's hand:

Contact Anthony Terrell after holidays

Cynthia studied the note. She reread it. She knew the survivor's guilt Anthony Terrell must be feeling. Knew the guilt she, herself, harbored all these years later. For the girls who never escaped Kilgallon's dominion.

CHAPTER THIRTY-FIVE

Billy Tarwater

Monday, December 28th, 1981

TEN 'TIL SIX. MONDAY MORNING. BILLY LEFT THE BELMONT ON his way to the Majestic Diner.

He had decided to get a jump on the day, to grab a bite before heading to the Fulton County Courthouse for what would likely be a long and tedious run of *voir dire*.

Just past Glen Iris, he glanced to his left where the old Ponce de Leon Ballpark had once stood. He had fond memories of going to countless Atlanta Crackers games with Chester and their dad.

Billy pulled over to the curb. For a moment, he could have sworn he heard the crack of Jimmy Williams' bat sending the ball flying to left field and over the wall. He could almost smell the rich aroma of hot buttered popcorn. He took in the *hot dogs, get yer hot dogs* cadence of the vendors in the stands. He looked up and saw the ticketless black kids atop the outfield hill where the railroad tracks ran. He tore open the Cracker Jack box top, reached deep into the box with two fingers, and pulled out a decoder ring, making Sailor Jack proud. Making him the happiest kid around.

In that moment, as Billy sat along the side of the road, he was Binky again.

By '65, when he was thirteen, the Crackers had moved into the newly built Atlanta Stadium. The following year, the old ballpark was torn down, the Braves rolled in from Milwaukee, taking over the city like the usurpers they were, and the Crackers gave up the ghost. *Yer out.*

Billy pulled back into the lane and proceeded down Ponce de Leon. He wasn't far past the Clermont Hotel when he saw the flashing lights ahead.

He turned at Cleburne Terrace, pulled into the lot, and parked in his usual spot across from the Majestic. Three patrol cars had converged at the far end of the parking lot in front of Plaza Drugs. The cars sat facing each other as if they had sped in from three different directions and stopped just short of colliding.

Billy got out of his car and walked toward the drugstore. When he got close to where the police were, he saw that they had apprehended a black man. The man was bent over, face-down, against the hood of one of the cars. He looked like a down-and-out derelict. An officer had wrenched the man's arms behind his back and was cuffing his wrists together.

Billy retrieved his Press ID from his coat pocket and showed it to an officer who was standing nearby. The officer said the man had left the drugstore with a Ho Ho and a Coke, neither of which he had paid for.

All this? Billy thought, as he walked back across the lot to the Majestic. *Three patrol cars, a shakedown and cuff job, all for a snack cake and a soft drink? The man's probably starving.*

Billy stood just outside the diner and waited, on the slimmest of chances that the police would decide to let the man go. If they did, Billy would gladly buy the poor guy a meal. But one of the officers threw the man into the back seat of a squad cars and sped away.

He was about to walk inside when he glanced across the street. In front of the Presbyterian Church, a spike-healed hooker wearing hot pants, spider web hose, and a cheap overcoat was chatting up a man at the bus stop. From the looks of it, she had caught him unawares and was likely offering to sell him her company. *With the place crawling with cops? And at six in the morning? She must be on the tail end of her workday.*

Billy considered taking the table where he and Gary had sat before. It was currently free. But the place was filling up with the purposeful morning crowd. He decided to heed the RESERVED FOR TWO OR MORE placard and sit at the counter instead. Normally, he would have welcomed the counter; he liked chatting up the diners to his right and left. But this morning, he craved time to gather his thoughts before the workday began. He opted for the last stool at the far end. At least he'd have only one patron to politely turn down.

He thought about yesterday. He knew he should have told Cynthia before now about Finnegan and the Vardemans.

Had he kept it from her to protect her somehow, given the stress she was under? Was this just one more example of Karpman shoehorning his way into their lives?

Perhaps. But his side-mission had started nine months before the kidnapper first began dogging her. And he still hadn't said a word about it to her until now.

Maybe he had held back to protect *himself*, not her. But from what? He had no reason to hide anything from her.

Toward the end of their conversation, Cynthia had brought up Sam. Somebody clearly was out to get him. Or at least to scare the bejesus out of him. Billy would give him a call later.

His thoughts shifted to Christmas dinner. Adele had said Leonard Seymour was home the whole time. But Billy clearly remembered what the Reverend Thomas had told him. *He's gone away for a while. Visiting his sister in Sylacauga for the holidays.*

Thirteen months prior...

Chapter Thirty-Six
Leonard Seymour

Tuesday, November 4ᵗʰ, 1980

LEONARD SEYMOUR PULLED OFF THE ROAD. HE HAD JUST LEFT East Irondale Acres outside Birmingham.

He removed the blood-soaked oily rag from his hand. He threw it out the window and into the brush along the roadside. He was in the process of wrapping his hand with the makeshift bandage he'd fashioned from his torn shirt sleeve when he looked up and saw the car pass. Billy Tarwater was driving. The other man was in the passenger's seat.

Seymour had arrived in Birmingham on a mission. To lure Tarwater into a trap. To get rid of evidence and shit so the sumbitch wouldn't get to it first. To save Kilgallon's ass. And his own.

But things don't always turn out the way you hope. Now Kilgallon was dead. Tarwater and the police had found the shit, some of it anyway. And Seymour was headed home with blood on his hands.

On the long trip back to Atlanta, he replayed the events of the last four days. He weighed his options. There weren't many.

The following Friday, he found himself standing over the rusted 55-gallon drum in his backyard. He threw the papers and photos from Kilgallon's house into the drum's belly. Then his bomber jacket, his khaki trousers, his torn work shirt.

He happened to look over at Cynthia Hudspeth's old bedroom window. Someone peered in his direction from inside the darkened room. Was it Adele? Or Cecil? Or maybe it was Cynthia herself.

He doused the drum with gasoline. He lit the match and tossed it in.

When the last flame had died, he crossed the yard and went back into the house. He grabbed another tall boy, his fifth of the evening, and popped the top. He sank into his La-Z-Boy and thought more about what he'd do next.

Earlier that morning, two policemen—a ruddy-faced one and another one so nondescript that Seymour wouldn't even be able to finger the guy in a lineup—had pulled up in front of his house.

They hauled him off to the police headquarters. There, he was questioned in a windowless room for upwards of four hours by two tight-assed Joe Fridays. They peppered him, shotgun-like. He knew the drill. Fire the questions as quick as you can and mix them up. Best way to trip up the guy being interrogated. *Did you know Virlyn Kilgallon? How well did you know him? How did you first meet? When? Where? When was the last time you saw him? What happened to Kilgallon's Valient, the one you came into possession of? How did you end up with it? Did you know the two girls killed in '63? And the one that survived? Did you ever visit the parsonage while Kilgallon lived there? What happened to your hand?*

He refused their offer to give him a ride home, choosing instead to get away as fast as he could. He took the bus.

Had the police believed him? Would they be back?

There was no way in hell he was going to let those miserable assholes drag him over the coals again. Try to pin shit on him.

He knew who he had to call. He lifted the receiver.

EARLY '82

CHAPTER THIRTY-SEVEN
Billy Tarwater

Saturday, January 2ⁿᵈ, 1982

LEONARD SEYMOUR SAT ACROSS FROM BILLY. MUTTERING LIKE an old man in a bingo hall.

Billy was surprised that the man had let him into his house. But he had. And now, Billy wanted to find out what Seymour remembered about the Impala that was stolen from Thomas back in '73.

It was clear, though, that either Seymour was suffering from an extreme case of memory fog or he had decided to play cat-and-mouse.

"Um, Impala?" Seymour shook his head. He let out a loud Launchpad-Leonard eruction. "What about an Impala? You have an Impala?"

"No, Leonard. I don't have an Impala. *Reverend Thomas* had an Impala. It was stolen in '73. You don't remember that?"

Seymour seemed to be a damned near permanent fixture at the church going back two decades or more. Surely, he would remember something as noteworthy as somebody running off with Thomas's car.

Seymour left the room. He returned with two PBRs. He handed Billy one and sat back down. He took in a long, slow swig. He wiped his mouth with his shirttail.

Billy had a déjà vu moment from two Octobers ago. He had sought out Seymour to talk about a different car, Kilgallon's '61 Valiant, which had been transferred into Seymour's name. On that visit, Seymour had taken a long swig and wiped his mouth with the back of his hand. Maybe that was his way of stalling as he came up with more bullshit to spew forth. Billy had left that day having been given a lot of disjointed detail but in the end feeling like he'd gotten the runaround. He feared this visit would bear even less fruit.

Seymour took another swig. "You were saying?"

Billy decided to adopt a more assumptive approach. "Thomas's Impala that was stolen, what can you tell me about it?"

"What color was it?" Seymour said.

"Blue."

"Where was it stolen from?"

"The parsonage driveway. Does that help?" Billy sighed. "Listen, I'm sure you remember."

Seymour tilted his head back and cocked the can in the air, finishing off the last of his beer. "You ready for a recharge?"

Billy shook his head.

Seymour went back into the kitchen and returned with a single PBR. He sat down. "OK, Tarwater. I remember the car. I remember it was filched. But what's that have to do with the price of tea in China? You need to be talking to the reverend, not me."

"I asked him about it. He wasn't much help."

"Why do you think I could be more help than he was. It was *his* car, after all."

"Well, for starters, back when Kilgallon was alive, you apparently got him out of a bind with his Valiant. Took it off his hands, you might say. It ended up vanishing...sort of. I just thought that maybe, given how close you and Thomas are, you had something to—"

Seymour shot out of his chair. "Now you hold on, Tarwater. Are you accusing me of doing something with Thomas's car?"

"I'm not accusing you of anything. I'm just asking questions, that's all. Did you help Thomas file the police report? Make the insurance claim?"

"You've pried enough, Tarwater," Seymour bellowed. "Now get the hell out of my house."

* * *

On his way home, Billy swung by a phone booth and called Finnegan. "Any update on Vardeman's car?"

"Can you come over? I have something I need to show you."

"Now?"

"Yeah, now."

* * *

Twenty minutes later, Billy pulled up to Finnegan's trailer.

Finnegan met him at the door.

"How's Jean?" Billy asked.

"It's the damnedest thing, she up and ran off again. I said, 'Jean, I'm through with you and your goddamned gallivantin' like an alley cat.'"

"Not the carny again, I hope."

"Not this time. Not as I know, anyway. Good riddance if you ask me."

Billy sank into the Jean-used-to-sit-here Barcalounger.

Finnegan left the room and returned with a #10 envelope. "Remember when I told you about the GBI havin' me wiretap the Vardeman phone? Back in February? I just received this from one of my insiders. I thought you might want to read it."

Billy opened the envelope. Inside were two letter-sized sheets, folded together. He unfolded them and read the first page.

March 4, 1981. Partial Transcript. Late-night phone conversation b/t Graydon Vardeman (GV) and ██████████████ ████

GV negotiating purchase of M16 rifles and frag grenades.

GV: "If I threw one of those motherfuckers into a crowd it would have to be somebody I really wanted to do in."

████: "Yeah. I suppose the Klan does shit like that."

GV: "Sure as hell does.

████: "I guess you have people you really want to do in."

GV: "Sure as hell do."

Then the second page.

March 29, 1981. Transcript. Phone
conversation b/t Graydon Vardeman (GV)
and Ewell Vardeman (EV).

EV: "Hello?"
GV: "Hey."
EV: "Yeah."
GV: "What's up?"
EV: "I dunno. What are you doing?"
GV: "Is Dickie around?"
EV: "He just left."
GV: "Where's he headed?"
EV: "I dunno."
GV: "Do you think he'll be back?"
EV: "Oh, yeah."

GV: "When?"

EV: "I dunno."
GV: "I'll give you a buzz later. I might
ride around a little bit."
EV: "Go find another colored kid?"
GV: "Yeah, scope out some places."

"Who's redacted?" Billy asked.

"No idea. I assume it's somebody Vardeman buys his guns and
shit from."

Billy asked Finnegan why it had taken ten months for him to
get these transcripts.

"I'll tell you why," Gary said. "I'm not supposed to have 'em. Even though the authorities have had me keep spying on the Vardemans, they're doing everything they can to prevent stuff like this from leaking. Scared shitless, remember?"

"I do. But I don't understand why they gave it to you now. After so long."

"*They* didn't give it to me," Finnegan said. "My inside GBI source gave it to me. And it's because Williams is on trial now. Even though he's not in the hot seat for killin' those kids, the whole town just *knows* he did it. My source is concerned that, if Williams is convicted, he'll get scapegoated, and all this shit'll get swept under the rug."

That was Billy's concern, too. Assuming Williams didn't kill all those children, the last thing anybody should want would be for him to take the fall, in the court of public opinion or elsewhere, for something he didn't do. And for the guilty to walk.

"But the killings seem to have ended," Billy said. "If the Vardemans have been killing kids to start a race riot, why would they stop now just because Williams is locked up? Doesn't that strike you as odd?"

"Not really. If Graydon and his brothers, and whoever's in cahoots with them, are behind the shit with the children, maybe they're going to lay low for a while, wait for everybody to settle in, let their guard down, assume it's all over. Then they'll hit again. Think of the impact that'll have. These guys may be playing the long game, Tarwater."

"What about the authorities? What are *they* playing?"

"An easy out's all they know. And appearances. If the killings have stopped, they've got their man. That's the story they'll stick to.

Sure, they'll still be keeping an eye on Graydon and the others, but all extra stealthy. Top secret. Out of the public eye. Damn sure away from you and your newshound buddies."

"I get it," Billy said.

"You remember what Mark Twain said, don't you?"

"What's that?"

"I'm not much of a reader, but my mother told me about it once. When he wanted to put something behind him and make it go away, he said he suddenly remembered another appointment. That's what the cops'll do, they'll suddenly remember another appointment."

Billy had read Mark Twain. And *about* Mark Twain. He didn't recall him ever saying that, but he had no way to refute what Finnegan was telling him. It was immaterial, though. Certainly too trifling to bother challenging it.

"Did your source do the redacting," Billy asked. "Or is that the way he got it."

"I don't know."

Billy changed the subject. He asked Finnegan about the tag and VIN numbers on the Vardemans' Impala. He had assumed that was why he had been summoned to come over in the first place.

"I went over there twice," Finnegan said. "Once even to take 'em a rum cake for the holidays. The car wasn't there either time. I'll go back at some point."

"There's something I need to tell you," Billy said. "My superiors at the paper have gotten wind of what I'm up to. I don't know how, when, or from whom, but they have."

"It sure wasn't from me," Finnegan said.

Billy wasn't inclined to rule out anyone at this point. But he also felt the need to acknowledge Finnegan's avowal. "I understand."

Finnegan cradled his cheeks with his palms. "That doesn't mean you're giving in, does it?"

"Not in the least. I'm telling you this just to let you know that I have to be especially vigilant. You do, too. Be careful. Don't let your guard down."

"I've been doin' this for longer than I care to admit. I let my guard down once and it bit me in the goddamned keister. You don't have to worry about it happenin' again."

* * *

On Billy's drive back to The Belmont, he thought about Kilgallon's car. When he had visited back in October of '80, Seymour told him he had *taken the car off Kilgallon's hands*. He'd driven the car to McKnight's Garage and had it painted. Then he made it go away. Not the Valiant per se, just *Kilgallon's* Valiant. But not before popping the VIN plate. *Child's play*, Seymour had said.

CHAPTER THIRTY-EIGHT
Cynthia Tarwater

Saturday, January 2ⁿᵈ, 1982

CYNTHIA GREETED BILLY AT THE DOOR.

"I took the kids to your mom's," she said. "Winter quarter starts Tuesday, but I have to be on campus all day Monday. I told Alice she could have them 'til tomorrow evening. She was delighted, as always. That'll give us some time together before I'm back in the classroom."

"Are you ready?"

"For classes?"

"Yeah."

"Billy, this may come as a surprise to you, but I was born ready."

Billy frowned. "What's *that* supposed to mean?"

"Nothing, really, except that I'm ready. That's all." Cynthia crossed the room and grabbed her wine glass from the side table. "Cecil called this morning," she said, without looking at Billy.

"Yeah? What did he want?"

She spun around. "He asked me what you were doing next door. At Leonard's. What *were* you doing there?"

"Can I pour *myself* a glass?"

"There's an open bottle in the kitchen."

Billy returned to the living room. "I was going to tell you. I just hadn't had a chance yet."

"Were you?"

"Of course. I went to see Seymour because I'm trying to track down what happened to a '71 Impala. It was stolen from the Reverend Thomas's driveway. Years ago."

"Is that the car you were talking to Gary about the other morning on the phone? When we were together in bed?"

Billy nodded.

"I remember you saying something to Gary about me seeing what I thought was the same car three times. You referred to me as she, as if I wasn't even there, and I was lying right next to you. In fact, you had to reach over me to take the call. Then you hung up and didn't share anything with me about the conversation. I didn't appreciate that, Billy."

He said he understood and apologized. He said that, with precious little to go on in tracking down her abductor—a rough sketch of the man, constructed by the police with Cynthia's help, and a description of the car, but no conclusive prints, no tag number, no ID of the good Samaritan who had delivered her and the kids to Grady in his pickup—he was pursuing any angle he could. Was it a coincidence that Thomas had owned a car fitting the description of what Cynthia's stalker-cum-abductor drove, except for the color? It might be. Or it might not be.

"That's why I went to see Leonard Seymour."

"Was he any help?"

"Marginally, before he kicked me out."

"Why did he do that?"

"Because I was asking too many questions."

Cynthia hesitated. "What's up with Earl Terrell's brother?"

"What?"

"I saw the note the other day on the desk."

"Oh, that. I'm planning to contact him."

Cynthia withdrew to the kitchen. She poured herself another glass and sat at the breakfast table.

In a couple of minutes, Billy appeared in the doorway. "What happened? We were right in the middle of a conversation, and you up and left."

"Billy, remember what we talked about on Sunday. About your keeping things from me?"

"I do. But I didn't think you'd care about Earl Terrell's brother."

"This isn't about that. I really don't care what you do in your day job. But when it involves me, that's different."

"It's just that I know you're under a lot of—"

"No, Billy. Don't go there. I don't need to be coddled. I can take care of myself just fine. In fact, I've been doing a lot of thinking. It's a new year. Some things are changing."

"Okay."

"First, I don't want you keeping me in the dark anymore. This is a partnership, not a guardianship, remember? And I'm through slithering around like a craven. I can hold my own. Better than you may realize."

"I understand."

"Truth conquers. You say that a lot. But do you mean it? Or is it a platitude?"

"I mean it, Cynthia."

"Good." She took his hand. "So we have the night to ourselves. Want to change the subject?"

Chapter Thirty-Nine
J.P. Finnegan

Sunday, January 3rd, 1982

FINNEGAN TURNED OFF OLD DIXIE HIGHWAY.

He had returned to the Vardeman place to search again for the Impala.

He eased the Mustang down the dirt road past the PRIVATE – KEEP OUT sign.

Dusk had settled in, but there were no lights on in the Vardeman house, at least as far as he could tell. The Harleys and the Kawasaki were gone. And he wasn't greeted this time by the snarling, curled-lip husky.

But to his surprise, the Impala was there, sitting just about where it had been the first time he'd laid eyes on it back in '79.

Finnegan eased the Mustang alongside the Impala and cut his engine. He got out of the car, took a pad from his pocket, and wrote down the tag number. He checked the door; it was locked. He walked around to the front of the car and felt the hood. It was cold.

In '68, Chevy had moved the Impala VIN from the driver door jamb to a steel plate riveted to the upper dash panel, where you could see it from outside the car through the lower corner of the windshield on the driver's side. For that Finnegan was grateful.

Finnegan leaned over the hood and peered through the windshield. He couldn't see anything in the dusk. He grabbed a flashlight from his car and shined it onto the upper dash panel. The VIN plate was missing. The only way it could have been removed, to his thinking, was by disassembling the dash, popping off the rivets, and putting everything back together. No mean feat unless somebody had the equipment and the knowhow.

He was about to return to his car when he heard a rustling coming from the edge of the woods. He swung around and found himself facing down Ewell Vardeman and the barrel of a shotgun.

Chapter Forty

Cynthia Tarwater

Monday, January 4ᵗʰ, 1982

CYNTHIA PARKED IN FRONT OF THE MONTESSORI. SHE HURRIED the kids out of the cold and the pounding rain and into Miss Kate's eager embrace.

"Happy New Year," Miss Kate trilled with a smile.

When Cynthia returned to the Suburban, she saw the Impala sitting across the street where it had been before, in front of the Walgreen's.

She pulled to the edge of the street and directed her car slightly to the left as if she were going to head south. She looked one way. Then the other. When both directions were clear, she shot across the street and into the Walgreen's lot before the man in the Impala had much time to react.

Cynthia was straining to get a good look at him when he took off heading north, but not before she barely made note of the tag number through the downpour. She grabbed a piece of paper from her purse and jotted it down.

For a moment, a little voice spoke to her. *Follow him.* But her better senses knew *that* couldn't possibly end well.

She sat for minute in the lot, gathering her composure and her thoughts, before exiting and heading south.

She stopped at the first phone booth she came to and called Billy at work. He didn't answer. Then she called the main City Desk number and gave the tag info to the woman who answered the phone. She asked the woman to give it to Billy as soon as she saw him.

Cynthia had one more call to make before heading to Agnes Scott.

She dialed O and asked for the Atlanta police.

CHAPTER FORTY-ONE

Billy Tarwater

Monday, January 4ᵗʰ, 1982

AFTER FIVE DAYS OF WINNOWING FROM A STARTING POOL OF sixty, the court selected a jury for the Williams trial. Eight blacks and four whites. Nine women and three men. Six white-collar, five blue-collar, and one unemployed on disability. Plus four alternates.

Several jurors had said they were somewhat skeptical of the charges against Williams but were all-in and fully committed to doing their jobs with open minds.

Judge Cooper ordered the jurors to report back at three o'clock tomorrow afternoon to find out where they'd be housed for the next several weeks. "Bring your luggage," he said.

Opening arguments would begin on Wednesday.

Billy left the courthouse and headed to the *Constitution* office.

* * *

The pink "While You Were Out" memo on his desk was signed by Judy. It was checked Urgent. The note read YOUR WIFE CALLED. SHE SAID TO GIVE YOU THIS. It was a tag number.

Billy found Judy. "Did my wife say she's okay?"

"She's fine. She called from a phone booth on her way to work."

Billy tried to call Cynthia at her school number, but she didn't pick up.

He dialed Gary.

"I just got back from the courthouse," Billy said, "and to a note from Cynthia. With a tag number. I'm assuming she saw the car again."

"I have it already."

"You have it already?"

"Yeah, she called me when she couldn't reach you. I wasn't around, but I got the same note that I assume you got. As soon as she was finished leaving the information for me, she apparently asked to be transferred to the police operator. The operator put her through to Zone 2. I'm told she gave them all the information, and an APB went out shortly after that."

Billy smiled. *It's a new year. Some things are changing.*

"What about the tag?" he asked. "Who's the owner?"

"I'll know that soon. I'll call you when I have it. It may be a while, though. I've got to get a couple of pressing things off my desk first."

At four forty-five, Gary called back. "I got the report on the license plate."

"And?"

"Bad news. It's a stolen tag. From a '79 Delta 88. Not even close."

"Shit. What else can we do?"

Gary told Billy that detectives had been dispatched to the Blue Bird Truck Stop to see if anyone there remembered the incident and could perhaps help identify either the Impala driver or the man in the pickup.

"I'll let you know what they find out," Gary said. "I wish we had them on closed-circuit camera, but it's not like they're everywhere."

At five-fifty, Billy left the newsroom.

* * *

After dinner, Cynthia put the kids to bed and returned to the living room.

"You've become quite the sleuth," Billy said.

"What?"

"The car? The license plate? The police?"

"That doesn't make me a sleuth. I did it out of necessity. It wasn't by choice. That's for sure. The car came to me, not the other way around."

Cynthia told Billy about seeing the car again across the street from the Montessori. About how she sped over to where the driver was parked. How he took off, but not before she got the tag number. For a second or two, she had considered following him, but then thought better of it. His windows were a bit fogged up, so she hadn't gotten as good a look at him as she had wished. But from what she could tell, she was pretty sure he wasn't her kidnapper. "This guy looked sort of like him. Same facial features. Same disheveled look. But different."

"How so?"

"Well, for one thing, this guy was younger, and his hair was a little redder."

"Did you tell the police that?"

"I did."

"That was a bold move, confronting him like that" Billy said. "You put yourself in danger."

"I wasn't necessarily planning to confront him. My decision to cross the street wasn't well thought out. Frankly, Billy, I was pissed."

"I understand, but regardless of how thought out it was, or how pissed you were, it was a damned risky move."

"Be that as it may, I'm safe and sound. And I got the tag number."

"Unfortunately, it's a stolen plate."

"Damn. I thought we had him, whoever he is."

"I did too. Or at least I hoped so. But in the end, Cynthia, the risk you took notwithstanding, I'm proud of you for what you did."

"I'm proud of me, too."

Just when Billy had begun to tell Cynthia about the APB and the detectives' planned truck stop visit, the phone interrupted.

Cynthia answered it. "It's for you," she said. "It's Sam." She handed the receiver to Billy.

Sam asked if Billy could come over to Carver Homes tomorrow.

"Tomorrow's a good day, Sam. After that, it's anybody's guess. Is everything okay?"

Sam said he wasn't sure. That he had more information about the kid on the bike.

No sooner had Billy hung up than Cynthia said, "So, are you going to tell me what that was about?"

Chapter Forty-Two
Billy Tarwater

Tuesday, January 5th, 1982

BEFORE LEAVING HOME TUESDAY MORNING TO VISIT SAM, BILLY phoned Gary. "Got anything for me?"

"Yep," Gary said. "Want the good or the bad first?"

"Give me the bad. Might as well get it out of the way."

Gary told Billy that, when the detectives visited the truck stop, an attendant remembered having waited on the man in the Impala and seeing a woman and two kids get into the pickup. He couldn't remember anything about the Impala driver, beyond the description Cynthia had already provided, except that the guy was "all het up" when he came out and saw the pickup leaving.

The attendant couldn't remember much about the pickup driver, except that he was damn near six and a half feet tall, fair-skinned, clean shaven and wearing jeans and a plaid shirt. As for the pickup, all the attendant remembered was that it was white and of recent vintage. He couldn't recall the make or model.

The truck stop manager looked for any credit card charges that may have been processed right around the time the Impala and the pickup were there. He found nothing. He could only assume that both men had paid cash.

"And the good news?" Billy said.

"Yesterday morning, around nine o'clock, a Cobb County sheriff's deputy thought he spotted the Impala with the stolen tag. Near Lake Allatoona. The driver saw him and took off. The deputy called for backup and gave chase. Unfortunately, the driver got away."

"Help me understand how that's good news."

"The deputy saw the car. That in itself is a start. It won't be long before he's found."

"I don't understand how he could let something like that slip through his fingers."

"The roads were slick from the rain. And it was foggy as all get-out. He said he had a helluva time making out the tag, given the visibility."

"What the fuck, Gary? He has the man in his sights and he loses him? I don't get it."

"I'm told the guy in the Impala almost spun out when he veered off the main road and proceeded down a rutted dirt side road at a high rate of speed. It was muddy and surrounded by dense woods. The deputy took the byway in pursuit. But he got mired, and the muck slowed him down. He searched all over but couldn't find the driver or his car. The damned Impala got away."

"Don't you think they could have found him on a country road, which I assume was poorly traveled?"

"Turns out the side road cuts through to Highway 41. They think that, when he reached the highway, he took off, probably headed north. Now the Bartow sheriff's in on it too. They're scouring the area and all up and down the highway."

"Gary, I'm sorry, but that sounds like bullshit to me."

"I know. To me too. Unfortunately, things don't always work out."

"I guess not." Billy shook his head. "Damn."

"I hate it as much as you do."

* * *

Billy pulled off Pryor Road and into Carver Homes. His thoughts turned briefly to the projects. The public housing complex had opened in '53, when Billy was just a year old. It had been built to provide low rent housing for African Americans.

He seemed to recall Sam saying he and Ruby had moved in sometime in the late '50s, maybe '60. Billy had fond memories of going there with Dovey Mae back in '63 to meet Rufus for the first time. The apartments were nice back then, as nice as projects could be, but by the time the late '70s rolled around, they were getting long in the tooth.

Two Octobers ago, ten-year-old Charles Stephens had been headed to Carver Homes to meet a friend before he went missing. Before his strangled body was found on a grassy hill near a trailer park.

Ruby met Billy at the door with her hair in a bun, her crisp white apron tight around her waist, and her hands on her hips. "Don't even think of comin' inside," she said, "less you plan to eat a biscuit."

The aroma wafting through the apartment reminded Billy of Granny Tarwater's house back in the day.

She led him into the kitchen. "I'll leave the two of you to talk."

Sam was at the breakfast table. He seemed in deep thought, as if meditating over the want ads from the morning paper. A cup of coffee and a half-eaten biscuit, slathered with butter and what looked like strawberry jam, sat on the table in front of him. He looked up. "Hello Billy. Come sit a spell."

Billy sat down across from Sam at the place Ruby had dutifully prepared for him. He took in a big gulp of coffee and had just bitten off a good sized mouthful of biscuit and jam—raspberry, not strawberry—when Sam asked him how he was getting along.

Billy held up an index finger as he struggled to swallow his mouthful in a hurry. He washed it down with another coffee swig. "Sorry about that," he said. "You caught me off guard. I'm doing well. I'm keeping busy. The trial starts tomorrow." He considered the want ads spread in front of Sam. He leaned in with his elbows on the table. "I'm more concerned about *you*, though. How are you doing, Sam?"

Sam looked around the kitchen and at the doorway leading to the living room. He spoke so softly that Billy had to strain to make out what he was saying. He said he was "fair to middling."

"You told me on the phone that you had more info about the kid?"

"It's not good, Billy."

"What is it?"

Sam said that yesterday afternoon, fifteen minutes before he was to get off work, he was in the front room of the EZ Mart sweeping the floor. Mr. Rutledge, his boss, was in the back. The same kid rode by again on his bike. Just as the kid passed by, he threw a brick through the plate glass window, sending shards of glass flying every which way.

"What time would that have been, Sam?"

"Little before five thirty. I went running out the door. I tried my best to chase the boy down, but I can't run too fast with my leg and all." Sam rubbed his thigh. "I don't know what I was thinking. Him on a wheel and me with a gimp."

"Did Rutledge report it to the police?"

"Yep. They came when I was sweeping up the glass."

"Where's the brick now?"

"I guess Mr. Rutledge put it in the back room. That's unless the police took it."

"Can you call him?"

"I'll be at the store in an hour. I'll see him then."

"Okay. Mind if I go with you?"

"Sure, Billy. That'll be fine. Ruby was going to drop me off. If it's just the same, I'll hitch a ride with you." Sam scanned the half-eaten food in front of Billy. "But you better finish that biscuit first. Cause if you don't, there'll be hell to pay."

"I heard that, Sam." Ruby was standing in the doorway.

"That's okay, Ruby," Billy said. "I was going to finish it. How could I not? This has to be the best pinch biscuit I've ever put in my mouth. Even better than my grandmother's, and that's saying a lot."

She beamed. "It's the buttermilk, Billy. Mathis Dairy. Straight from Rosebud's udder. None better."

"Well, I suspect you played a bigger role than you're letting on. But if it *is* the buttermilk, as you say, it sure does make good biscuits."

She beamed even wider. "Can I tell you something funny? When Rufus was a little boy, he thought spotted cows made buttermilk and brown cows made chocolate."

On the way to the EZ Mart, Sam told Billy he had let Mr. Rutledge know he wasn't going to be able to work there anymore. He said he'd work the week out, but that was it.

Billy asked Sam what he was going to do.

"I don't know, Billy."

"Have you told Ruby?"

"I can't. I just can't."

"I'm sorry, Sam. I can help you out 'til you get back on your feet."

"Appreciate that, but we have Rufus. He's a godsend."

"Is there any more you can tell me about the brick thrower?"

"No, not really," Sam said. "Just what I told you before. Skinny little white boy. Maybe twelve. Thirteen."

"And his bike?"

"It looked like a Schwinn. Red. With one of them banana seats."

"About the brick," Billy said. "Was anything attached to it? Like a note or something?"

"Nothing was stuck to it. But it had words on it."

"What did it say?"

Sam looked at his lap. "It was big black letters, like it was done with a Magic Marker. It said Die Nig...I don't want to say that word, Billy."

Chapter Forty-Three
Cynthia Tarwater

Tuesday, January 5ᵗʰ, 1982

CYNTHIA ARRIVED AT AGNES SCOTT EARLIER THAN USUAL AFTER dropping the kids off at daycare. It was the first day of the semester, and she wanted to be well settled in before the second period bell rang.

She parked in the faculty lot and carried her bagful of books and lesson notes across the lot and up two flights of stairs to her office.

She was gathering up the paperwork to take with her to class when she looked up and saw Belinda Nettles, a junior and one of her best students, standing in the doorway. "Can we talk?"

Cynthia looked at her watch. "I wish I could, but I have class in ten minutes."

Belinda winced. "After class?"

"Of course. Meet me back here at a quarter past ten. That work?"

* * *

Cynthia arrived back at her desk at five after.

Ten twenty-five rolled around and Belinda, always the prompt one, still hadn't showed up.

Finally, a little after ten thirty, Cynthia looked up and saw the girl hesitating in the doorway.

"Come in," Cynthia said. "Shut the door and pull up a chair."

Belinda sat across the desk from Cynthia. She fidgeted and didn't make eye contact.

"What is it, Belinda? Is something wrong?"

Worry lines creased the girl's forehead. She took in a deep breath and let out a sigh. "Mrs. Tarwater, I've told you about my past."

Two semesters ago, Belinda had confided that, when she was five, her father had skipped out on her mother, leaving the poor woman to raise her and her brother alone. Belinda spent the next six years yearning for the father figure she didn't have. Her maternal grandfather had died when she was less than a year old, and her mother had barred her from seeing her deadbeat father's parents. There was no man in the family she could turn to. Then, when she was eleven, her dream finally came true. Her mother married a boarder she had taken in less than a year earlier. But things didn't work out as Belinda had hoped, and her dream became a nightmare. A week before her twelfth birthday, her stepfather "took advantage of her." More than once. And it continued for years. Belinda carried the secret with her, fearful that no one would believe her. Not her mother. Not her brother. Certainly not the pastor at the church they attended now and then. But on her eighteenth birthday, thinking that finally her mother would believe her, but still terrified of the consequences if she didn't, Belinda got up the courage to bare all. Her mother summarily kicked her stepfather out of the house and filed for divorce.

But the damage had already been done.

If it hadn't been for a full-on scholarship and loads of therapy, Belinda never would have ended up at Agnes Scott.

Not a day went by, though, that she didn't feel some degree of regret for not telling her mother years earlier. Perhaps her mother would have believed her back then. Perhaps Belinda would be different person today had she not endured what she did at the hands of that sick man.

Belinda had never told Cynthia what she meant when she said her stepfather "took advantage" of her. Cynthia didn't need to know. Imagining was enough.

Cynthia nodded.

"Something happened this morning," Belinda said. "In the parking lot. It brought back bad memories." She looked at Cynthia as if waiting for her cue to proceed.

"Go on," Cynthia said.

"I was getting out of my car when a man approached me. He reminded me of…" She looked down.

Cynthia walked around her desk and placed her hand on Belinda's shoulder. "It's okay. I understand." She understood more than Belinda would ever know.

Belinda breathed deeply again. "The man said he was a friend of yours."

"Of mine?"

"Yeah. From high school."

"Did he say his name?"

"I asked, but he wouldn't tell me. He said he hadn't seen you in years. He started asking a lot of questions about you."

"What kinds of questions?"

"Things like what kind of teacher you are, what classes you teach, whether you hang out with your students sometimes. When you get to work. When you leave. Things like that. I tried to put him off. I lied and told him I was late to class. Then he came closer. He reached out and ran his hand through my hair. That's when I took off running. Mrs. Tarwater, it scared the…it scared me to death."

"Did you see what kind of car he was driving?"

"I never saw him get out of a car."

"What did he look like?"

"Real thin and hollowed out. Messy looking. He had a scraggly mustache and hadn't shaved in a few days. He looked like somebody that might've come right out of the backwoods somewhere. Not like those guys from *Deliverance*. Not that bad, but close."

Chapter Forty-Four

Billy Tarwater

Wednesday, January 6th, 1982

BILLY WAS SURPRISED THAT HE HADN'T HEARD BACK FROM
Finnegan. It wasn't like him to go so long without following up.

Billy phoned him early Wednesday morning before heading to
the courthouse. There was no answer.

Then he rang Gary.

"Could you write something down for me?" Billy said.

"Lemme grab a pen. Okay, shoot."

"You know the EZ Mart on Moreland where Sam Jepperson
works."

"I do."

Billy told Gary about the kid on the bike, the brick, and the
words printed on it. "The EZ Mart owner filed a police report. They

took the brick with them. Can you follow up? Maybe get a copy of the report?"

"Sure thing, Billy."

"And there's something else you need to know. Yesterday morning, one of Cynthia's students was accosted by a man in the Agnes Scott parking lot. He said he knew Cynthia. It may be the same man who abducted her."

"Did they call the police?"

"Cynthia called campus security. The girl gave them a description of the man. But he was long gone by then."

"Even though Decatur's outside our jurisdiction, do you think the girl would be willing to come in? We could construct a drawing, like they did with Cynthia at the hospital."

"I'll let Cynthia know. Listen, Gary, she's already told the police this, but the man she saw on Monday driving the Impala…she said he resembled her kidnapper, but it wasn't him."

* * *

Billy popped into the newsroom after court had adjourned. He had four phone messages, but none from Finnegan.

He tried Finnegan again, but to no avail.

He called Cynthia and said he'd be late getting home, that he needed to run by the Faircourt trailer park first.

Before heading out, he made one more call, to the Terrell residence. He had been trying to reach Anthony for a couple of days, but no one ever picked up.

* * *

Finnegan's trailer was dark, and the Mustang wasn't there.

Billy was sitting in his car, composing a note to leave on Finnegan's door, when a man walked up.

The man motioned for Billy to roll down the window. "He ain't home," the man said.

"Do you know when he's expected back?"

"Nope. He left Sunday and ain't been back since. I got his newspapers when they started pilin' up." The man sized Billy up and down. "You ain't the law, are you?"

"Oh no," Billy said. "Just a friend."

Chapter Forty-Five

Cynthia Tarwater

Thursday, January 7ᵗʰ, 1982

THIS SEMESTER, BOTH CYNTHIA'S CLASSES WERE MON/WED/FRI. *Convenient.* Tuesdays and Thursdays were reserved for downtime, lecture prep, and office hours.

Thursday morning, she sought out Belinda and asked her if she would be willing to go to the police headquarters and work with a sketch artist there to create a rendering of the man who accosted her in the parking lot. Last evening, Billy had said Gary could make it happen.

Belinda said sure. Anything to help catch "that loathsome creature."

Cynthia called Gary at work.

"Give me an hour," Gary said. "If I can arrange it, is there any way you can bring the girl in late this afternoon."

* * *

At 3:30, Cynthia and Belinda arrived at police headquarters.

Gary met them in the main lobby, signed them in, and escorted them to the third floor, where the sketch artist awaited them.

He instructed Cynthia to have him paged when they were through so he could come back and escort them downstairs. No wandering around the building.

As if I would ever do that. Cynthia grinned as Gary walked away.

Cynthia waited in the anteroom while Belinda met with the sketch artist behind closed doors. Cynthia was glad she had thought to bring reading material. The room was sparse, not like a doctor's or dentist's waiting room, which surely would have been replete with stacks of tattered back issues of *People, Good Housekeeping, Newsweek*. Not that she would have found those to be of much interest, though. *Playgirl*, on the other hand? Maybe. She chuckled to the otherwise empty room.

She opened to the bookmarked page of her current read, *Memoirs of Alexander Campbell,* and settled in for what she assumed would be a long wait.

At 4:45, the sketch artist opened the door and motioned for Cynthia to come in.

She took the seat next to Belinda and across the table from him.

He explained that the decision he had made was "above my pay grade." But, seeing as he was doing Gary a favor outside the normal course of business, he would make an exception and share the sketch with Cynthia.

He eased the sketch across the table, oriented right-side-up for her benefit.

She took one look at the drawing and froze.

* * *

Cynthia and Belinda were both uncharacteristically silent on the drive back to Agnes Scott.

She assumed Belinda's reticence was borne of a forced reliving, through the drawing, of her parking lot encounter with the man. And of her past by association.

And as for Cynthia? She had just seen, in stark black and white, the spitting image of her kidnapper.

CHAPTER FORTY-SIX

Billy Tarwater

Thursday, January 7ᵗʰ, 1982

WHEN BILLY ARRIVED AT THE COURTHOUSE ON CENTRAL AVENUE
early Thursday morning, the throngs of spectators had begun to
gather along the sidewalk and up the steps leading to the courthouse
door. Opening arguments had begun yesterday, and the crowds
outside the courthouse then had been just as large, if not larger.

He flashed his press ID, entered the courthouse, and climbed
the stairs to the fourth-floor courtroom. He took a seat in the
section reserved for the press. He watched as the spectators filed
in. And witnesses, attorneys, court officials, other interested parties.

Williams' defense attorney turned briefly to scan the gallery.
She looked tired. Stressed. Three months earlier, give or take a
day or two, she had summarily dismissed her co-counsel. That
same day, she sent a letter to the court advising of the dismissal

without saying why. But Billy and his newspaper colleagues knew why. The two lawyers had been feuding over who should direct Williams' defense. Their dispute reached the boiling point when her co-counsel tried to convince Williams and his parents that he had more experience than she and should be the lead attorney. She convinced them otherwise and gave her co-counsel the boot. She replaced him with an experienced but brash and abrasive white lawyer from Mississippi. But it was made clear from the outset that she would be the lead attorney.

Billy wondered whether the defense team reorganization, along with her protestations of being overworked, with a lack of funds and insufficient time to interview hundreds of prosecution witnesses, may have contributed to a degree of anxiety. He felt empathy for her and for what she would surely endure over the next two months or so, especially given that she was up against a crack prosecution team.

Wayne Williams was escorted into the courtroom in shackles. His orange jumpsuit presented a sharp contrast to the suits and ties and otherwise staid attire throughout the room.

All rise.

Judge Clarence Cooper entered the courtroom and assumed his place at the elevated mahogany bench from which he would hold court for the duration of the trial. He instructed the bailiff to bring in the jury.

The jurors filed into the courtroom and took their assigned positions in the jury box.

Over the course of the morning, stakeout officers testified as to the events of the twenty-second of May, when they heard a splash in the water and spotted Williams on the James Jackson Parkway bridge over the Chattahoochee.

Prosecutors attempted to show that both Cater and Payne were likely dropped from the same place on the bridge, which has an unusually low railing.

One of the stakeout officers, Freddie Jacobs, testified that the headlights of Williams' station wagon were not on when it moved across the bridge at about "three to four to five miles per hour." He said another officer had radioed that he heard a "big, loud splash" in the river.

After the lunch recess, the lead defense attorney's fatigue and stress seemed on display when she cross-examined Jacobs. She attempted to trip up Jacobs on the stand, but in the process tripped all over her own gaffes.

"Isn't it true," she said, "that you testified last year that he radioed he had heard a loud splash, Mr. Campbell?"

"My name is Jacobs," the witness replied.

"I'm sorry. I have a bad habit of calling people the wrong names. I called the task force commander, Morris Redding, Otis Redding once. Does your memory improve with time?"

"It improves all the time," Jacobs said.

Jacobs told her that he had spoken with her private detective in November about what he had seen and heard.

"And this is December?" she said.

"No, this is January," he replied.

The spectators in the courtroom broke out in laughter, eliciting a stern admonition from the judge.

In an apparent effort to show that Jacobs had not been paying attention during the bridge stakeout, she asked him if he hadn't tried to read a book to relieve the boredom. Jacobs reminded her that the stakeout had occurred in the dark, making it impossible to read a book.

She raised her voice and said, "Now, Mr. Jacobs, you're a scary person, aren't you? Isn't it true that at least ten times you radioed that you heard ghosts out there?"

"No," he said. "It's not true. I don't believe in ghosts."

"You never saw Wayne Williams stop on that bridge, did you?" she asked.

"I never saw a car stop," he replied.

Billy thumbed through his notes. At the onset of Jacobs' testimony, he had clearly stated that he'd seen the car drive slowly across the bridge, not that he had seen it stop.

The afternoon heat buildup in the courtroom was so oppressive, notwithstanding the fact that it was January, that sweat beaded on Billy's forehead. He looked around the room. He wasn't the only one sweating.

The judge instructed the bailiff to open two tall windows. The traffic noise from the street below drowned out the cavernous and acoustically challenged courtroom, making it impossible for Billy to hear the witnesses as they left the stand temporarily to testify around a scale model of the bridge. Billy looked around the gallery. Several people were leaning forward and cupping their hands to their ears. He hoped the jurors could hear the witnesses better than he and the others could.

Billy left the courthouse at the end of the day wondering whether the afternoon fiasco was an indication of how the trial would unfold in the coming days.

* * *

He swung by the newsroom, typed up a recap of what went on after the lunch recess, and handed it off to his colleague Pete, who would polish it and prepare it to go to press. He had already phoned in the events of the morning during the court's lunch adjournment.

He headed home.

* * *

Cynthia was standing in the middle of the living room when Billy came in. She was in her bathrobe and holding an unopened bottle of Merlot in one hand and a wine key in the other. "You're going to drink this bottle with me, Billy, and then we're going to bang each other's brains out."

Once Billy had regained his ability to speak, he said, "Damn, Cynthia, what's gotten into you? Not that I'm complaining, but—"

"New year. New me. Remember?"

He looked around the room and down the hall. "Where are the kids?"

"I called Alice again. She came and got them. They're spending the night with her. It's all good."

"What about tomorrow morning? Is she taking them—"

"No. They're staying home with your mom. They need a break. And she can use the company. I'll call Miss Kate in the morning and let her know."

She raised the bottle and the wine key. "You or me?"

"Why don't you? If you don't mind."

As Cynthia was uncorking the bottle and filling two glasses, he thought back to their Friday dress-ups from the past? Why had they stopped? He wasn't sure. Maybe it was because of the kids. But if his mom was willing to have the little ones over more often, maybe, just maybe… A mere two weeks ago, Cynthia had tried her best to engage his interest in a dress-up reprise. He had turned her down. *But it* is *a new year.*

Billy was about to settle into his usual chair when she said, "Let's sit on the floor."

They sat pretzel style across from each other with the bottle between them.

She raised her glass. "Cheers."

He raised his, and they clinked their glasses.

"Clinking and kissing," she said. "You know, it's a tradition in some quarters to kiss after a toast."

He leaned over and kissed her. He eased his free hand between the panels of her bathrobe and up her thigh.

Cynthia pushed his hand away. "Not yet, Billy. There's something I need to tell you. And we have a bottle to finish. No need to rush things. We have all night."

She told him about taking Belinda Nettles to police headquarters. About waiting in the anteroom until the sketch artist summoned her. About her staring at the drawing when he eased it across the table. "It was him, Billy. A dead ringer."

"Your kidnapper?"

"Yes. I bet if you put the two sketches side-by-side, the one they did with me and the one they did with Belinda today, they'd look like identical twins. I froze for a minute. But the surprise wore off quickly. And then I thought okay, we have one more witness to what the man looks like. And he's been spotted in another location."

"Did you say anything to Belinda or the artist?"

"No. I put on my best poker face. But before Belinda and I left, I did take Gary aside and told him."

"I haven't even seen the sketch they did with you at the hospital."

"Maybe you should stop by the police station and look at it sometime."

Cynthia led Billy by the hand down the hall.

He wondered if the change that had come over her was perhaps an acting out, a way of coping with the angst she surely was feeling. This wasn't the first time he'd wondered that, but the change seemed to have become more vigorous overnight.

Billy dared not bring it up, though. Not now.

CHAPTER FORTY-SEVEN

Billy Tarwater

Friday, January 8th, 1982

THE ALARM BUZZED WAY TOO EARLY.

Billy's knee-jerk inclination was to hit Snooze. But if he did, he might end up hitting it more than once. And he couldn't afford to do that.

He wasn't disposed to springing out of bed this morning. For one thing, he had dialed back the wake-up time by an hour to allow him to drive out to Finnegan's place before he had to be downtown. And for another, more importantly, Cynthia had worn him out.

He would also call Gary at some point to follow up about the sketches.

Cynthia was sound asleep and curled up in a near-fetal pillow embrace.

"Tonight," he whispered. He slipped out of bed and headed to the shower.

* * *

When Billy pulled into the Faircourt trailer park, he had a nagging sense that, after several days of unanswered calls, Finnegan wouldn't be there.

Sure enough, Finnegan's place was pitch dark, and the Mustang was gone. But the man who had come up to his car the other day was there again, walking away from Finnegan's trailer with a paper under his arm. Billy assumed it was Finnegan's morning *Constitution*.

When the man saw Billy, he came running up. "I know you," the man said. "You was here the other day."

Billy asked the man if he'd seen Finnegan since last Wednesday.

"Nope," the man said. "No hide and no hair. You said you was a friend of his, right?"

Billy nodded.

"You worried about him?" the man said.

"A little." Billy wrote TARWATER on a slip of paper and handed it to the man. "If you see him, please have him call me. He has my number."

Since Billy didn't have to meet with Finnegan, he had time to stop by the newsroom and call Gary before heading to the courthouse.

* * *

Gary picked up on the first ring.

Billy told him Finnegan was nowhere to be found.

"There's a man named Roscoe," Gary said. "Finnegan ever tell you about him?"

"No. Never heard of him."

"He's the one that connected Finnegan with the Vardemans in the first place. Maybe he knows something. Hold on a minute. I'm gonna put the phone down."

Gary returned to the phone. "I pulled his card from my Rolodex. I don't know the man. I got his name and number from Finnegan. Word on the street is he's well-connected with a bunch of…let's just say he knows some unsavory characters."

"The Vardemans…case in point, I guess."

Gary gave Billy the phone number.

"Does he have a last name?" Billy asked.

"Of course he does, but I don't know it."

"Thanks. I'll try him."

"Oh, and by the way," Gary said. "Word is he likes to hang around titty bars."

"Wonderful. That's the last thing I need."

"And one other thing. I wouldn't let on that you're a newspaperman. Tell him you're a friend or something. And if he asks where you got his number, give him the runaround. Maybe tell him Finnegan gave it to you. I don't want him connecting any dots back to me."

Billy told Gary he'd call back later to talk about the sketches.

He hung up and dialed Roscoe.

"Speak," the voice on the other end of the line said.

"Is this Roscoe?"

"Depends. Who's this?"

"My name's Billy. I'm a friend of J.P. Finnegan. He gave me your number a long time ago. I've been trying to reach him for almost a week now and I thought maybe you—"

"Billy who?"

Billy's eyes landed on the Littrell Ace Hardware calendar hanging on the wall next to the Upson board pushpin map. "Littrell," he said. "Billy Littrell."

"He gave you *my* number? Why the hell would he give you my number?"

Roscoe likes strip clubs, Billy thought. "Um, I dragged him once to the Gaslight Follies. On Luckie Street. Know it? We started talking there, and he said you were the only person who loves a little nudie action as much as I do." It was all Billy could do to get the words out. "He gave me your number and said I should call you sometime."

"And here we are, I guess. So you're calling me because you want to get together? Tell me, who's your favorite dancer at Gaslight?"

Shit. "Honestly, I was too inebriated to remember their names. I think one of them was Amber. I can't say I'm a regular there."

"Where *are* you a regular, then? I know them all."

Am I digging a hole I can't get out of? Billy thought back to the strippers he'd sat next to at the Majestic. "I'll be honest with you, Roscoe. I'm a creature of habit. I settle on a place I like and that's where you'll find me."

"And?"

"I'm a Clermont Lounge man myself. You know Blondie?"

"Blondie? Of course. Everybody knows Blondie. Who else do you know there?"

"Barbie?"

"I know her, too."

"We should meet there sometime. But what I'm calling about now is I've been trying to find Finnegan for over a week. I owe him some money and I promised to pay him back before the end of the year. Obviously, I missed that, but I'd like to settle up. Problem is, nobody's seen him."

"I can't help you there. We haven't spoken in eight, nine months. Now, when are we going to the Clermont?"

"I'll have to get back to you on that, Roscoe."

* * *

The morning trial proceedings were consumed with the same old same old as yesterday, but without the babble and blunder.

More witnesses attested to the splash "very similar to a body hitting the water," to Williams' white station wagon creeping across the bridge, to Nathaniel Cater's body later found one and a quarter miles downstream from the bridge, near where Payne's body had turned up a month earlier.

As soon as the lunch recess commenced, Billy found the nearest available phone and called in his notes. Then he dialed Gary.

Gary said he'd examined the two sketches. "Cynthia's right, they're virtually identical," he said.

"Could there be any implicit bias going on?" Billy asked. "The same artist doing sketches for two people with an obvious connection to each other, and only two and a half weeks apart?"

"This guy's a professional, Billy. What you're suggesting is longer than a long shot."

"Just asking, not suggesting. Does the guy in the drawings look familiar to you?"

"Yeah. He resembles about half the ones that come across my desk. The white ones, anyway."

"What about the EZ Mart police report?"

"I got a copy of it, but it doesn't have anything of value in it. A racist kid on a bike threw a brick through the window. The kid wasn't ID'd. The police took the brick. Tried to lift prints. I could've saved them time. It's almost impossible to lift prints off a brick. Rutledge got a copy of the report to file an insurance claim. That's about it."

There was silence on the line.

"Gary, you still there?"

"I'm here." He cleared his throat. "I have more bad news."

"Please don't tell me the Keystone Kops fucked up again."

"Are you sitting down?"

"No, Gary. I'm at a bank of press phones at the courthouse, and there are three people behind me waiting to make calls. Just tell me what it is."

"The Cobb County detectives stopped a car with the stolen tag."

"That's good news, isn't it?"

"Not really. It's on a different car now. A '79 Buick LeSabre."

"What?"

"Seems the guy we're out to get, once he knew we were on to him, switched out the plates with the Buick as soon as he could. The owner of the Buick thinks it happened last night while it was parked in his carport."

Chapter Forty-Eight

Cynthia Tarwater

Saturday, January 9th, 1982

CYNTHIA PULLED THE DUVET CLOSE TO HER CHEST. SHE TOOK A sip of chamomile with lemon and cardamom. *Liquid ambrosia, perfect for a cold winter Saturday.* Its spicy citrus teased her palate. Its heat coursed down her throat and warmed her body. *My morning frill.*

Her current read, opened to Chapter Fourteen, lay face-down on her lap.

Billy was still asleep. Uncharacteristic for him, even on a Saturday.

He stirred and slowly opened his eyes with a squint. "What time is it?"

"Half past seven. Pretty late for an early bird like you."

"I'll say. What are you reading?"

"A boring tome. Dry as a bone. I wouldn't have dipped into it in the first place were it not for my day job."

"What is it?"

"It's called *Memoirs of Alexander Campbell*. It's about the American Restoration Movement. Part of the Second Great Awakening." Cynthia told Billy about Campbell and his evangelical cohorts, and their obsession with scriptural infallibility, a mandatory weekly Lord's Supper, believer's immersion as the only baptism.

"Sounds a little too close to home," Billy said.

"Are you referring to my mother?"

"I was actually thinking about Kilgallon. You can throw Thomas in there, too. And, of course, your mother."

"This character Campbell got so wrapped up in his dogma that, when he was on a roll, he couldn't stop himself. He had a penchant for whole-page sentences. Faulkner would have delighted him." She thumbed through the pages. "Listen to this."

> Of all the vices which have ever disgraced human nature; of all the extremes of madness and folly to which mankind has ever run; of all the irreverent, irreligious deeds which have ever blackened human character, there is none more horrid, flagrant or profane; none so presumptuous, arrogant and irreverent, as carelessly, heedlessly and impiously to invoke the sacred name of Him whom angels worship, saints adore, and before whom devils and wicked men shall tremble with horror, anguish and dismay— to invoke the sacred majesty of heaven on every light, frivolous and wicked occasion—to

call God to witness every lewd, base, mean or trivial action they perform or perpetrate; and, still worse, to supplicate that pure and righteous Being to damn, curse or punish a fellow-creature, a fellow immortal, or, it may be, some brute or inanimate thing.

"The part about damning, cursing or punishing a fellow-creature...that makes sense," Billy said. "The rest is nonsense."

"This is tame compared to some of his drivel."

"Such as?"

"For one thing, he espoused white supremacy, using lofty deception to justify it. And he went so far as to say that America... *white* America, that is...was divinely favored. So much for not punishing a fellow creature."

Billy pulled himself up and sat on the edge of the bed. "Can we continue this in a couple of minutes?"

He returned from the bathroom and slipped back under the duvet. He arranged his pillow behind him. "Since we're on the subject of religion, how much do you know about the Klan's Christian roots?"

"More than I'd like. Ever heard of a guy named William Simmons?"

Billy shook his head.

"An itinerant preacher. Early twentieth century." Cynthia told Billy about how, in the Fall of 1915, Simmons and a dozen or so men climbed Stone Mountain. They built an altar on the mountaintop. They erected a cross, set fire to it, and took an oath of allegiance to the Invisible Empire. At the foot of the cross, they laid an American flag, a sword, and a Bible, and announced the revival of the KKK. Simmons appointed himself Imperial Wizard.

"How do you know these things?" Billy asked.

"Think about it. We're in the deep South. I teach religion and philosophy. It comes up. Plus, I'm the scion of an evangelical nutcase who claims, disingenuously, not to have a racist bone in her body."

"Yeah, right."

"Did you hear what she said about Thomas the other day?"

"Refresh my memory."

"She called him an old racist fool. I'm sorry, I know she's my mother, but what sanctimonious hypocrisy." Cynthia took another sip. "I'm assuming you're asking about all of this because of the Vardemans?"

"That's right. I was looking through my Finnegan file and I ran across something that, frankly, I hadn't paid enough attention to before."

"What's that?"

Billy crossed the room to the Lilliputian desk. He returned with a sheet of paper. "This is a note from a meeting Finnegan had with the Vardemans back in September of '79." Billy perused the note. "Finnegan said he noticed a crucifix on the Vardemans' wall. And a blood drop cross in red and black on Graydon's right tricep. And the numbers 33 and 6, separated by a lightning bolt, on his left." He looked back up. "Do you know anything about what the numbers might mean?"

"I don't know about the numbers," Cynthia said. "The blood drop cross has evolved over the years. It's obvious what the cross stands for. And the blood drop symbolizes that which is shed to protect the pure white race. God's chosen. Sounds like Campbell, doesn't it." She reached over and placed her book on the nightstand. "I feel like it's a weekday and I'm in the classroom."

"Sorry. Didn't mean to drag us into a long, drawn-out conversation about this."

"That's fine. Anything to help the cause. What does your day look like?"

Billy told her that he needed to find Finnegan. "I'm worried, but I'm hoping he just went away for a few days and failed to tell anybody. I'll phone him again this morning."

"And if you can't reach him?"

"The last thing he said to me was he was going to the Vardemans' Sunday evening. I may take a ride over to their place. But I have to come up with some kind of cover before I do. I can't just show up. I'll talk to Gary first and see what he thinks."

"You came down on me the other day for taking risks. That sounds dicey to me."

"I'll be careful."

She reached over and ran her fingers through his hair. "You'd better."

Chapter Forty-Nine
Billy Tarwater

Saturday, January 9th, 1982

"MOST DOUBLE-WIDE LOCKS ARE EASY TO PICK," GARY SAID. "Unless Finnegan's installed a deadbolt. Still can do it, though, with the right tools."

After not being able to reach Finnegan, Billy had called Gary, saying he remembered Finnegan's spiral notebook with The Empire Strikes Back and GV written on the front. Maybe there was something in it that would clue Billy in as to where Finnegan might be. And maybe there were other notes in the trailer that could provide clues. Maybe a scribble near his phone. Maybe something on his wall calendar.

"You realize, don't you," Gary said, "that we can't just break into his home without a warrant unless contraband is in view. Or if there's some kind of emergency, like a fire or something. Far as I know, none of that applies."

"Not to my knowledge," Billy said.

"Or a trapped pet." Gary chuckled. "Finnegan have a pet? Maybe a bloodhound?"

"Never saw a pet there," Billy said. "So, do you have the right tools?"

"I do. Are you asking to borrow them?"

Billy wasn't keen on having to call in another favor, especially after all Gary had done for him. But his sense of urgency prevailed. "I was hoping maybe you'd help me."

"Notwithstanding that you wouldn't go along with my stalking plan, you *do* like to live on the edge, don't you, Billy?"

"You might say that. When it makes sense. I think it goes all the way back to when we were eleven and used to cross the quicksand creek in pursuit of the Nazis. Remember that?"

"Like it was yesterday."

"We go way back, don't we, Gary?"

* * *

They waited until dusk to go to Faircourt. Gary drove. He said it would arouse less suspicion if people saw the unmarked Plymouth Fury instead of Billy's car. Billy questioned why that mattered. After all, Gary's car was unmarked. Gary said don't kid yourself. People can recognize detective wheels from a football field away.

"Why will it arouse less suspicion?" Billy said. "It seems to me that a cop car would arouse *more* suspicion, not less."

"Maybe less problematic's a better way to say it. If anybody asks what we're doing hanging around, busting into Finnegan's trailer, I can flash my badge, point to the Plymouth, and tell them we're on official business."

They pulled up to Finnegan's double-wide. It was dark inside, and the Mustang wasn't there as before.

Gary put the car in Park. "Let's sit here for a minute. So here's the deal, Billy. I'll get Finnegan's door unlocked." He looked up at the trailer. "I don't see a deadbolt. That's good. You'll go inside. I'll come back to the car and watch for anybody that might be moseying down the street."

Billy looked out the window, thinking Finnegan's neighbor might be hanging around.

Gary reached under his seat and retrieved a small flashlight and a pair of latex gloves. He handed them to Billy. "You'll need these."

Billy searched through the trailer for the spiral notebook, but it was nowhere to be found. *He must have taken it with him.* There were no random notes lying around, no calendar entry to clue him in. There were a couple of other notebooks. They appeared to be related to non-Vardeman jobs Finnegan was working on. Billy felt like a voyeur as he skimmed through them. Nothing jumped out at him, so he quickly put them back where he had found them.

Nothing seemed out of place in the trailer. The unmade bed, the dirty dishes in the sink, and the half-empty Doritos bag on the folding try table didn't strike Billy as the least bit out of the ordinary, given what he had come to know of Finnegan's ways.

Billy waited until they were back in Midtown and parked at the Belmont entrance to broach the subject of visiting the Vardemans.

"I wouldn't advise it," Gary said. "Those guys don't take kindly to strangers. Armed and dangerous is an understatement. Anyway, you don't even know where they live."

"I have a general idea. Maybe you can fill in the details."

"And send you into a minefield? I don't think so."

"You know I can find them on my own. We journalists know how to dig."

"Yeah, you'll need to know how to dig your way out of a hot mess."

* * *

Sunday morning, after finally convincing Gary to save him the trouble of digging, Billy prepared to leave the apartment and head to the location off Old Dixie Highway that Gary had given him.

Gary had offered to accompany him, but Billy had said no. He figured he had asked enough of Gary already. And if Billy was headed into a minefield, he wanted to do it alone. Against his initial protestations, he had borrowed Gary's spare .22 revolver.

Last night, after a couple of gin and tonics and some helpful back-and-forth with Cynthia, Billy had finally come up with a cover. He wasn't sure it would work. He was prepared to tack if he had to.

He consulted his FINNEGAN, J.P. folder one more time, particularly the details Finnegan had provided regarding the Vardemans' *shabby hooch* and its surroundings. He wanted to get a feel for being there before *actually* being there.

He headed for the door.

Cynthia gave him a peck on the cheek. "Please be careful, Billy."

* * *

Billy eased to the end of the road and onto the dirt patch in front of the Vardeman house. The whole area was a patchwork junkyard, empty Jim Beam repository, and vintage appliance museum. There were two motorcycles, a Harley and a Kawasaki, parked near the house. And an Impala, but it was a two-door Sports Coupe, not the one Billy was hoping he might encounter. There was no sign of Finnegan's Mustang.

The Siberian husky, the one Finnegan had mentioned in passing, lunged onto the side of Billy's car and clawed at the window.

A man stepped from inside the house and onto the front porch. He was wearing a camouflage hunting vest and khaki cargo pants. Billy assumed he was one of the Vardeman brothers. A young boy in dungarees and with a sock cap pulled down over his ears came running out of the house behind the man. The man stepped down into the yard and approached the husky. He grabbed the dog by the collar and told the boy to carry it around back.

The man stuck both hands into his pockets.

Billy reached across the seat and grabbed the borrowed pistol. He slipped it into the interior pocket of his jacket. He stepped out of the car and extended his hand. "Mitchell Goodenough. Summerwood Real Estate."

The man kept his hands in his pockets. He didn't say his name. He gave Billy the once-over.

"This your property?" Billy asked.

"Maybe."

"Want to sell it?"

"Maybe."

"What's your name again?"

"I didn't say."

Billy apologized for showing up out of the blue on a Sunday. He said he was working with a buyer looking to purchase several tracts of land in these parts. "He's willing to pay top dollar."

The man said his name was Dickie. He said he owned the property with his brothers.

Billy assumed *top dollar* must have done the trick.

"Are they around?"

"They're not here. You got a card or something?"

Billy pretend-searched the pockets of his pants and jacket. "Damn, you know what, Dickie? I must've left my cards behind. I can't believe I did that. There's a first time for everything, I guess."

Dickie looked Billy up and down again. "You come back with a card. Maybe I'll talk to you then. Maybe my brothers will be here."

Billy was headed back to his car when he decided to do something he might live to regret. Or worse. He swung around. "By the way, I forgot to tell you. A friend of mine named J.P. Finnegan's the one who sent me out here. Said you might be interested in selling. Know him?"

"I know him."

"Funny thing is, I tried to call him a few times before heading over here, just to let him know I was coming, but I never could reach him. Have you talked to him lately?"

Dickie stuffed his hands back into his pockets. He shook his head.

Billy turned his car around and headed toward the dirt road. He looked in the rearview mirror. The boy had come back around from behind the house. Dickie pointed to the porch. The boy went running up the steps and into the house, the screen door slamming behind him. A woman stepped out onto the porch. Billy could barely make out the silhouette of another man standing inside, just beyond the screen door.

Billy eased his car along the dirt road. About halfway between the house and the highway, something caught his attention. It was an out-of-place purplish-red splotch poking through the scrub. He pulled his car to the side of the road and stepped out. He approached the tangle and pushed it out of the way to get a better look.

A forsaken maroon Mustang II, camouflaged by cut and broken brushwood, sat in the clearing, its front pointing toward the dirt road.

CHAPTER FIFTY

Cynthia Tarwater

Sunday, January 10ᵗʰ, 1982

BILLY BOUNDED THROUGH THE DOOR AND HEADED FOR THE telephone.

Cynthia held up her hand. "Excuse me. Can you please slow down and tell me what's going on?"

"It's not good." Billy told Cynthia about discovering the Mustang II in the brush. "I need to call Gary."

Cynthia moved to Billy's side as he punched Gary's number into the phone. She leaned in when Gary answered. Billy moved the receiver slightly from his ear so she could hear the other end of the conversation.

Billy told Gary that, when he came upon the abandoned car, his first inclination was to return to the Vardeman house and confront Dickie. But no telling what "hot mess" he would have walked into had he done that, especially given that somebody else was lurking inside.

Billy said he went back to his car, grabbed the borrowed pistol, and returned to the Mustang. He tried the driver-side door, but it was locked. Same on the passenger side. He peered into the car. Nothing seemed amiss. He then walked around to the back of the car to take down the tag number. But the plate was missing.

"Can you meet me at the Majestic?" Gary said.

Cynthia touched Billy's forearm and mouthed, "Have him come here."

"Why don't you come here?" Billy said. "Cynthia can whip us up some lunch."

"Sounds like an offer I can't refuse," Gary said.

Billy hung up.

Cynthia stared at him through narrowed eyes. "Whip us up some lunch? Really?"

"I'm sorry. That was inconsiderate of me."

Cynthia nodded. "It was. I'll do it, but you owe me."

"That's okay. I can order Domino's."

At twelve twenty-five, the doorbell rang. Cynthia opened the door expecting Gary. It was the pizza guy. "That was quick," she said.

"Thirty minutes. That's our promise."

"How much do I owe you?"

"Four ninety-nine plus tax. That comes to…" The pizza guy consulted the sales slip. "…five fifteen."

Gary arrived twenty minutes later. "Cynthia, knowing you, I bet you've whipped up something good."

"Of course, Gary," she said. "I hope you like pepperoni. I whipped it right up." She pointed to the Domino's box on the kitchen counter.

Gary took a big bite of pizza. "It's a dicey situation."

Billy frowned. "What do you mean?"

"So, we know Finnegan's been spying on the Vardemans for the police. Then he goes missing. You discover Finnegan's vehicle…at least you *think* it's his…hidden in the scrub at the Vardeman place. But the police don't know what you're up to. Why would you have even been there? See where I'm going with this?"

"I do, but the police may know more about what I'm up to than you think."

"Why is that?"

"The higher ups at the paper know I've been doing something on the side. Apparently, so does the mayor. I don't know how much they know. Roberts told me to kill it. I obviously didn't. And I won't."

"Here's the problem," Gary said. "If you go to the police, they'll start asking questions we don't want them to ask. And *I* can't get involved. Remember what you told me last month about kissing my career goodbye."

"I think you changed it to your ass."

"I did. And as for you? You'll be in a heap of trouble if the police know you were snooping around at the Vardemans'."

"Again, that's assuming they don't already know."

"I understand," Gary said. "But is that a chance worth taking?"

Cynthia, who had remained quiet, spoke up. "What about that fellow Roscoe you've told me about, Billy? He knows Finnegan. And he knows the Vardemans, right? Maybe you could finagle your way into getting him to go over there. Let *him* find the car. Let *him* be the one to call the police."

Gary looked at Billy with his trademark grin. "I hate to say it, you being my close friend and all, but when it comes to smarts, I think you may have married up."

Billy laughed. "I've never denied that."

"So," Gary said, "what do you think about getting Roscoe involved?"

"It might work. I could meet with him. He did say he wanted to get together at the Clermont Lounge sometime."

Cynthia pulled a face. "The Clermont Lounge? Oh, great."

"Sacrifice in the call of duty. I promise, no lap dances. And I won't touch."

She reached across the table and smacked Billy's wrist.

He recoiled with a feint. "Damn, that hurt."

"Deservedly so," she said. "Maybe I should go with you. Who knows? It might titillate me. And even if it didn't, I could at least keep you an honest man."

For a moment, Cynthia was lost in the thought of accompanying Billy and Roscoe.

All three agreed that Billy would reach out to Roscoe and plan to meet him at the Clermont. Chat him up. Somehow figure out how to get him to visit the Vardemans and discover Finnegan's car himself. It was a long shot, but it was the best they—Cynthia, that is—had come up with so far.

"What was it like at the Vardemans?" Gary said. "Before you discovered the Mustang."

"Dickie was standoffish, cagey. But I didn't expect otherwise. I don't know whether he bought into my ruse. He could have been on to me the whole time and been just playing me. There was a woman there. I think it was Sonya. And somebody just inside the house. Probably Graydon or Ewell. And then there was a little boy, maybe ten or eleven."

"A little boy?" Gary said.

"A little boy. And it's the damnedest thing. There was something about him that looked oddly familiar. I've been trying ever since to put my finger on it."

Chapter Fifty-One

Billy Tarwater

Sunday, January 10ᵗʰ, 1982

WHEN THEY HAD TALKED ON THE PHONE BEFORE, ROSCOE SAID he hadn't seen Finnegan in eight or nine months, which surprised Billy. He thought they were closer than that. Roscoe had been the one who connected Finnegan and the Vardemans in the first place. Billy assumed they would have stayed in touch. And Finnegan had seen fit to give Roscoe's number to Gary. In any event, Billy had no way of knowing whether Roscoe was shooting straight with him when he said eight or nine months.

Billy rehearsed what he would say before dialing Roscoe's number. The more he had thought about meeting at the Clermont Lounge, the more concerned he became. He had let on to Roscoe that he knew a few of the strippers there. If he and Roscoe walked in, and the dancers recognized him not from the strip club but from the Majestic lunch counter, or worse yet, they didn't recognize him at all, his cover would be blown in a heartbeat.

"Speak," Roscoe intoned through the line.

"Roscoe, it's Billy Littrell."

"Hello, Billy. Long time no talk." Roscoe chuckled. "What's up?"

"When we spoke on Friday, you mentioned the Gaslight Follies. I haven't been back since I took J.P. there. I wouldn't mind checking it out again. Want to join me?"

"You bet I do. When?"

Billy and Roscoe agreed to meet there after work on Tuesday.

Roscoe said to park at the Dinkler Plaza Hotel next door to the Gaslight. "Where the Playboy Club is. Pull into the garage off Luckie Street and drive up to the third level. Your car'll be safer there. I'll be waiting for you."

"No Clermont?" Cynthia said when Billy had hung up.

Billy explained why he had changed the venue.

"You know I'm crestfallen, don't you?" Cynthia feigned a pout. "I was so looking forward to tagging along, if for nothing else just to see Blondie do her thing."

That evening, Billy was about to walk out the door to go pick up the kids from his mom's when the phone rang. "It's Adele," he said. He handed the phone to Cynthia.

"Is he okay?" she said to her mother.

Billy edged closer.

She cupped her hand over the mouthpiece and whispered, "It's about Cecil."

"I will," she spoke into the phone. "But you need to call an ambulance *now*. Don't take no for an answer. And whatever you do, don't wait for me to get there." She hung up.

"What going on?" Billy asked.

"Cecil may be having a heart attack. He needs to get to the hospital right away, but he's refusing. She asked if I could come over and 'knock some sense into him.' Her words. I need to get there as soon as I can. I may end up staying the night."

Billy put his arm around Cynthia. "I'm so sorry. What can I do to help?"

"Nothing. Except take care of the kids. Maybe your mom can keep them for a night or two since you've got to be downtown early in the morning."

"I'll call and see. I'm sure it won't be a problem. And the kids will love it. They always do."

Cynthia packed her overnight bag and headed for the door.

"I should go too," Billy said.

"There's not a thing you can do. I'll be fine. Stay near the phone. I'll call you."

"Please do. And tell Cecil I'm thinking of him. I hope everything's okay."

She opened the door to leave.

"Cynthia, I'm just a few minutes away if you need me."

CHAPTER FIFTY-TWO

Cynthia Tarwater

Sunday, January 10ᵗʰ, 1982

CYNTHIA PULLED UP TO THE CURB IN FRONT OF HER PARENTS' house. The ambulance had already arrived, and the paramedics were carrying Cecil out on a gurney. Adele was loping behind them, flailing her arms and yelling something about driving the devil from the afflicted.

Leonard Seymour's front door flung open. He came running out holding a beer can and with the stump of a cigar poking out of his mouth. He was wearing a denim work shirt under a bomber jacket. Even though it was bitter cold, his jacket was open in the front, exposing his considerable midriff. The buttons on his shirt looked like they could pop any second. He stopped short of the property line and just stood there, staring at Cynthia, then at the ambulance, then back at Cynthia. He threw the cigar stump to the ground, took a swig, and wiped his mouth with the tail of his shirt.

Adele climbed into the back of the ambulance with Cecil. Before the paramedics secured the door, she yelled out to Cynthia. "Put the leftovers away."

"Shouldn't I come with you?" Cynthia said.

"No," Adele replied. "Stay here. I'll call you when we know something."

The ambulance sped off on its way to Grady Hospital.

Cynthia stood in the darkened living room. On a fair September day in '63, she had awakened and found herself all alone in the same darkened house. She had stumbled into the kitchen, grabbed a Coke from the fridge, spread a huge glob of peanut butter onto a Ritz cracker, and gobbled it down before donning her favorite denims and bounding out the door. A week and a half later, she ended up at Grady. She was finally discharged and returned home a different person.

Leftovers was an understatement. The kitchen looked like Hurricane Dennis had passed through, throwing shit every which way in its path. The kitchen table was strewn with half-eaten Chinese takeout and opened packets of soy sauce and hot mustard. An upended Schlitz bottle lay prostrate at the table's edge, its contents having spilt all over the floor. The counter was no better, its surface covered with dirty dishes, empty containers, and kitchen detritus.

Cynthia was nonplussed. While what lay before her was not out of keeping with Cecil's habits, it was wholly uncharacteristic of the mother she knew. *What the hell? Is this the aftermath of a struggle to save a man in the throes of a coronary, the kitchen be damned? Or maybe my delusional mother has finally been overcome by the rapture soon to be, to the neglect of all worldly things in her midst.*

Cynthia set about cleaning up. Storing the lo mein and egg foo young leavings. Rinsing the plates and loading the dishwasher. Mopping up the mess on the floor. Discarding the empty to-go boxes. Wiping down the Formica tabletop and counters.

When she had completed the task of "putting the leftovers away," she went out to her car, grabbed her overnight bag, returned to the house, and withdrew to her old bedroom.

Adele, for whatever reason, had decided to preserve Cynthia's room as some sort of shrine to her only child's adolescence. No idea why, unless it was borne of a desire to hold onto some semblance of what had been lost when Cynthia grew into her adult self and found truth.

Cynthia surveyed the room, with its Arvin portable record player and stack of 45s on the three-legged table in the corner. The Murphy High pennant, with Go Eagles in white and royal blue, thumbtacked to the wall. The twin bed, with its popcorn stitch bedspread and pink chenille dust ruffle. The framed Lord's Prayer holding court above the headboard. *Was this really me?* For a second, she thought Scalawag, the well-worn stuffed sock monkey propped against the pillow, winked at her as if to say *Yes, my darling, it was you.*

As she stood in the middle of the bedroom, she found it interesting that very little in the way of sentimental feelings or nostalgia came calling. She guessed she had finally moved on.

Then her eyes fell on the window. The curtains were closed. How many times had she stood there while Leonard Seymour gawked from across the narrow driveway? Her mother had threatened to have Cecil take her before the church congregation to confess her sins if it didn't stop. It took the kidnapping in '63 for it to stop.

Cynthia walked slowly across the room. She carefully pulled back the curtains.

The light was on in Leonard Seymour's bedroom, but the room appeared empty.

As she was standing there, recalling nights long past, he sauntered into his room still holding a can of beer. He set the beer on his dresser. He unbuttoned and removed his work shirt, revealing a sleeveless undergarment.

She was about to turn away, fearing that he might expose more than she had bargained for, when something on his arm caught her eye. She leaned in and strained to get a good look.

A blood drop cross in red and black occupied his right tricep.

Chapter Fifty-Three

Leonard Seymour

Sunday, January 10ᵗʰ, 1982

LEONARD SEYMOUR FELT HER EYES ON HIM. IT WASN'T THE COY, adolescent glance he remembered from the past. Her gaze now was intense. She didn't look down in the coquettish way of an adolescent. She locked onto him.

He covered the tattoo with his hand and backed across his bedroom, never losing eye contact. He quickly put his shirt on and retreated to the kitchen.

He didn't have to look up the phone number.

"I think she may be on to me," he said.

"*Who* may be on to you?"

"The Hudspeth…sorry…the Tarwater girl."

"Why?"

"She saw my tattoo. She just stood there in the window staring at it."

"It's just a tattoo, Leonard. People get tattoos all the time."

"It's not just *any* tattoo."

"Shit, I bet if you asked half the goddamn state, they'd say they have one, or one like it. Or they'd like to get one. You got it at Jimmy's downtown, right? Do you have any idea how many blood crosses he's done? Probably thousands. It's a badge of honor. Like Mom. Or Popeye."

"That's not the only thing. You know Billy's been snooping around the church. He even dropped by here one day."

"How soon can you get here?"

"An hour. Maybe sooner."

"Just get here. We have work to do."

One week prior...

Chapter Fifty-Four
Graydon Vardeman

Sunday, January 3rd, 1982

GRAYDON AND DICKIE VARDEMAN RETURNED HOME WELL AFTER sundown.

Ewell met them at the door. He handed Graydon the spiral notebook without saying a word.

The notebook was well-worn, with tattered pages and a coffee cup stain on the front cover just to the right of the GV. The stain reminded Graydon of a dog chasing its tail.

Inside the front cover was J.P. Finnegan's handwritten name and phone number.

Damned near half the book was filled in. The top of the first page read:

MEETING WITH GRAYDON VARDEMAN, JULY 13, 1979.

Graydon read the first few pages. "The goddamn son-of-a-bitch." He looked over at Ewell. "You may be slow, little brother, but you had that motherfucker pegged from the get-go."

He leafed through the pages. About a third of the way in, the header jumped out at him.

MEETING WITH BILLY TARWATER, MARCH 17, 1981

Graydon read this page. Then the next. He threw the notebook onto the coffee table. "Are you telling me Finnegan and that nigger-loving son-of-a-bitch are in cahoots?"

Ewell nodded. "Looks like it. *Were* anyway."

"What do you mean, *were?*

Ewell led Graydon and Dickie to the shed behind the house.

Chapter Fifty-Five
Graydon Vardeman

Monday, January 4ᵗʰ, 1982

ROSCOE HESTER LIVED IN A 1920S CRAFTSMAN BUNGALOW ON
Hartford Avenue in the Capitol View section of town. A stone's
throw from Stewart-Lakewood Shopping Center. And right next
door, so to speak, to Sylvan Hills, where the Geter boy rammed
Graydon Vardeman's car that time with his go-kart.

Graydon eased the Impala onto Roscoe's ribbon driveway. The
grass between the concrete strips was weedy and crabgrass infested.
The yard itself didn't look much better. The other yards didn't either,
for that matter.

He remembered when Capitol View was the epitome of
picket-fence pride. Before the "undesirables" started moving in, as
Sonya liked to say. Of course, Capitol View was still a far sight
more "presentable" in the eyes of John Q. Public than his own place.
But he and his brothers, and his old man before him, had never

claimed to be anything other than the badass shitkickers they were. Badge of honor. *If you ain't one, you'll never understand.*

Graydon hadn't been to Roscoe's house before. He didn't know what to expect. How would he be greeted? Or would he be greeted at all? He had decided not to call first. The thing is, he wanted to confront Roscoe face-to-face, man-to-man.

He climbed the three steps onto the porch and tapped his knuckles on the door stile.

He tapped again. This time harder.

He thought he heard a rustling beyond the front window.

Two eyes peered through a slight break in the drapes. Then they disappeared.

He heard the lock disengage.

The door swung open.

Roscoe's substantial presence filled the doorway. He was dressed in what looked like a Hugh Hefner smoking jacket. He stuffed the last of a Snickers bar in his mouth, crumpled the wrapper and deposited it into his jacket pocket, and swallowed hard.

"Graydon, this is a surprise. What are you doing here?"

"We need to talk."

Roscoe stepped back. He invited Graydon into his living room with the sweep of his hand.

The room was fitted out like a Roman brothel. Graydon had never seen anything like it outside of an honest-to-god whorehouse. A tasseled floor lamp on the other side of the room let out a soft red glow, competing only with a sliver of light poking through from beneath a nearby closed door. The chairs and loveseat were crimson, with deep padding and gold button upholstery. The drapes were gold brocade with pinch pleats—at least that's what Graydon thought they were called.

He expected Madam Désirée herself to waltz into the room any moment, her hair French-twisted and her silk gown flowing. If that were to happen, "Boom Boom Dickie" would never forgive him for coming alone.

Roscoe motioned toward the nearest chair. "Take a load off, Graydon." Roscoe took the loveseat. "Talk about what?"

"About Finnegan."

"What about Finnegan?"

"Who the hell is he?"

"Finnegan's an explosives expert. He knows how to blow up shit. You know that. That's why I connected you two in the first place."

"How long have you known him?"

"Long enough."

"He's an informer, Roscoe. A fucking informer. You sent me a fucking informer."

Roscoe's face blanched. He started stammering and stuttering like a damned fool. Said something about how he had no idea. About how, in all the years he'd known Finnegan, the man had never betrayed him.

Graydon didn't believe him, but he decided to let it go for now. "What's Finnegan's connection to Billy Tarwater?"

"Billy who?"

"Don't play dumb with me, Roscoe. Tarwater."

"I don't know a Billy Tarwater."

"Well, Finnegan sure as hell does. I've been on to Tarwater for six months now. But about something else. Not in my wildest dream did I think those two were in cahoots to fuck us over."

"Fuck you over how, Graydon?"

"It doesn't matter. What *does* matter is you owe me big. And you're gonna pay big."

* * *

Graydon let a week pass while he mulled over what to do.

Late in the day on Sunday the 10th, he called Roscoe.

"Speak," Roscoe said.

"Who's Billy Littrell."

"All I know is he's a friend of Finnegan's. Been looking for him. Asked if I wanted to go titty bar cruising with him. I'm meeting him Tuesday night at the Gaslight."

"Roscoe, you're a bigger dumbass than I thought."

"Why's that, Graydon?"

"Ain't no daylight between Littrell and Tarwater."

Chapter Fifty-Six

Billy Tarwater

Tuesday, January 12th, 1982

BILLY AND ROSCOE HAD AGREED TO MEET AT SIX O'CLOCK SHARP in the Dinkler Plaza parking garage. Third level. Next to the stairs. *But how will I recognize him?* It had occurred to Billy, too late, that he had no idea what Roscoe looked like. And he assumed Roscoe didn't know what *he* looked like.

During the lunch break from the trial, Billy stepped out and tried to reach Roscoe by phone. No answer. He'd have to take a chance that they would connect without a hitch. After all, how many people would just happen to be at that particular place? At that particular time? On that particular day?

Yesterday, the prosecution had poked holes the size of a Mack truck through Williams' alibi as to his whereabouts during the hours before police spotted him on the bridge. And today, a star witness testified that she had seen Williams and Cater sitting together on a park bench on Verbena Street the Friday before a canoeist found Cater's body hung up on a low-lying tree branch along the Chattahoochee riverbank. She said she recognized Cater because he had dated her niece.

By the time the day's adjournment rolled around, a lot was preying on Billy's mind in addition to the trial. The meeting with Roscoe, and how Billy was somehow going to contrive a visit to the Vardemans'. Cecil's situation, and whether he'd pull through. What Cynthia had shared Sunday evening about Leonard Seymour and the tattoo.

The weather was dreadful. The biting cold that held a tight grip on the city had turned into a massive snowstorm. Billy wondered whether his meeting with Roscoe was still on. And even if it was, would the Gaslight be open? He tried Roscoe again but couldn't reach him. He then called Cynthia to check on her and to tell her of his plans to soldier on. Fortunately, Agnes Scott had shut down early. She had managed to pick up the children from daycare and get them home before the worst of it hit. Cecil was still hospitalized, and Adele was by his side.

Billy would soldier on to Luckie Street on the assumption that Roscoe would be there as planned. The last thing he wanted to do was stand him up. He would take his chances and weather the elements, assuming the roads were passable enough for him to make it the seven blocks from the courthouse to the parking garage.

He pulled the collar of his overcoat tight around his neck and descended the courthouse steps. The relentless snow and sleet pelted his face. He held his head low to ease the sting. Within seconds, his hair was soaked. The melting show crept into his shoes, sogging his socks and insoles. He had left home this morning prepared for the record-setting cold, but not for this.

When he reached his car and turned on the radio, he learned that the city was paralyzed. It had all happened so quickly. The governor had declared a state of emergency in all of Georgia north of Macon. The airport was virtually shut down, with thousands of travelers finding themselves grounded there. Hundreds of elementary and high school students were stranded on school buses.

He pulled out of the parking space on Central Avenue and headed north. He crept along at no more than five miles per hour. A snarl at the Decatur Street intersection brought traffic to a standstill. A policeman and a couple of men were working to help extricate a car that had mired in the ice and snow in the middle of the intersection. Every time the car's driver put on the gas, the rear wheels spun in place.

Billy put his car in Park and jumped out to help. One of the men had a Jeep with a trailer hitch. The man retrieved a length of chain from the back of the Jeep and wrapped one end around the hitch, the other around the bumper of the stranded car. Billy and the others got behind the car and pushed as the Jeep driver eased the car out of the intersection.

Billy got back into his own car and cranked the engine.

It was five 'til six. There was no way he was going to make it to Luckie Street on time, even under the best of conditions. He still had five blocks to go. But surely Roscoe would be dealing with similar setbacks, assuming he would show up at all.

It was six twenty when Billy finally reached the Dinkler Plaza.

An attendant greeted him at the entrance to the parking garage with a skeptical stare. "Checking in?"

Billy explained that he wasn't a hotel guest, that he was accompanying a friend to the strip club next door.

"Good luck with that," the man said. He gestured to the street with a wave of his hand as if to emphasize the obvious. "Worst storm in years. Everything's shut down."

Billy asked if anyone had entered the garage within the past half hour or so.

"Three men came in a few minutes ago. Claimed they were here for the gift show at the Merchandise Mart and were staying here."

"Anybody else?"

"That's it. A lot more leaving than entering."

Billy drove up the ramp to the second level. Then the third.

A solitary light bulb flickered fitfully in the far corner of the garage. An illuminated emergency exit sign above the door to the stairs provided the only other light.

He parked near the stairwell and got out of his car.

He heard a scurrying across the way. He called out, "Roscoe?" but no one replied. A brown rat, maybe a foot or so long, scampered toward him before disappearing through a one-inch hole in the concrete wall.

He decided to wait a few minutes to see if Roscoe would show up. If not, he'd take a chance on making it home. As a last resort, if the streets seemed too treacherous, he could always hunker down in a hotel room, assuming one was available, and hope tomorrow would prove more cooperative. He was sure that all government offices, including the courts, would be shut down, even if the storm had moved on.

The last thing he had said to Cynthia when he called her from the courthouse was that, with the weather the way it was, he didn't plan to stay out late. And if he ended up having to check into a downtown hotel for the night, he'd call right away and let her know.

He waited.

Soon, he heard footsteps from across the way.

He saw, under the light from the flickering bulb, three men approaching at a rapid clip. They were wearing heavy black coats and three-hole ski masks. Two were thin. One was stocky.

The stocky one held something in his hand.

As they neared, Billy realized it was a tire iron.

CHAPTER FIFTY-SEVEN

Cynthia Tarwater

Wednesday, January 13th, 1982

MAYBE IT WAS THE CRICK IN HER NECK THAT WOKE HER. OR THE bitter nip in the room.

A sliver of incandescence passed through the crack in the kitchen door.

Cynthia's half-drunk glass of Merlot sat on the table beside the chair where she now half-lay, one leg sprawled on the ottoman and the other planted on the floor. Her head and neck were contorted against the chair's wing.

She raised up and squinted at her wristwatch. It took a few seconds for her eyes to adjust. It was a quarter to two.

When had she dozed off? She remembered having put the kids to bed, pouring herself a glass, and returning to the living room to wait for Billy to get home.

Had he come home? Maybe he had seen her sleeping soundly in the chair and decided to leave her be rather than rouse her. But it wouldn't be like him to do that.

She shuffled to the bedroom. The bed was undisturbed. The leather valet tray, where Billy always places his wallet and keys and such, sat empty on the dresser.

She remembered Billy telling her about waking up and searching for *her* three and a half weeks ago, only to realize she wasn't here.

She parted the curtains and peered out the window at a blanket of white. *It's probably okay*, she thought. *He just checked into a hotel somewhere and forgot to call.* At least, she wanted to believe that. But the last thing he had said on the phone was that he'd call if he couldn't make it home. Things just didn't add up.

Or maybe they *did* add up, and she couldn't bear the thought of what they might presage.

Her first inclination was to call Gary at home. What a godsend he had been when she herself had gone missing. But at this hour?

She thought about calling the police. But they wouldn't do anything until more time had passed. Without Gary's pull, anyway.

She phoned a few hotels, but no one would tell her anything.

She decided to await the arrival of a decent hour before calling Gary.

Given the ice and snow, daycare would surely be closed today. And surely Agnes Scott would be, too. Regardless, she would call and cancel her own classes. There was nothing that couldn't wait a couple of days. And her students always welcome a break. Especially on a day like this.

She sat back down and waited.

* * *

At 7:15, the phone broke Cynthia's dead-tired fog. *Billy?* She jumped from the chair and ran to answer it.

It was her mother. "They're springin' him from that hoosegow of a hospital, praise the Lord," Adele said. "They just called and told me to come and get him."

"How is he doing?"

"He's all right."

"What do you mean, he's all right? Forty-eight hours ago, you didn't even know whether he'd pull through."

"I didn't think he would, but you know Cecil. Yesterday he was all down in the mouth and sayin' it was over, that his ticker couldn't go on any longer. But then I guess them sawbones knocked a little sense into him."

"And?"

"Said he'd had a mild myocardial…um…"

"Infarction?"

"That's it. They said go home. Get some rest. Come back in a week. I'm supposed to make him take his damn medicine, as if he's ever listened to me about anything." Adele hesitated. "You want to know what I think? His carryin' on and all and sayin' it was over. It was just Cecil bein' Cecil. The ornery cuss. Oh, the things he puts me through."

"Do you need help getting him home?"

"We'll get by. They tell me the roads are plowed and passable now. But it'd be good if you could come over later and carry us some dinner."

Cynthia couldn't bring herself to mention her own predicament. Adele never understood situations like this and had a penchant for shifting the conversation to herself. Or erupting into one of her evangelical rantings. *Reborned again*, Cynthia could hear her mother saying. *If you know what's good for you, you'll get reborned again.*

She hung up, but not after obligingly agreeing to drop by later with KFC. She reckoned it was the least she could do, given the situation. Somehow, she would fit it in. *Heart-healthy KFC?* She knew not to try to foist fruit and vegetables down Adele's throat. *Little good that would do.*

Upon confirming that Agnes Scott had delayed opening until early afternoon, well past the time her classes would have ended even if she *hadn't* canceled them, and the Montessori would be closed for the day, she called Billy's mom and arranged for her pick the kids up and keep them, maybe even overnight. She refrained from mentioning that Billy hadn't come home last night. But unlike with her own mother, in Alice's case, it was because Cynthia didn't want her to worry.

She dialed Gary. He said he would come over.

Then she called the City Desk on the off chance that maybe Billy had shown up for work. He hadn't. She told Judy what was going on.

* * *

Gary sat across from Cynthia in the living room. "When's the last time you spoke to him?"

"He called me when he was leaving the courthouse. Said he was headed to that strip club on Luckie Street next to the Dinkler."

"The Playboy Club? That's not a strip club."

"No. The Gaslight Follies?"

"Our Billy? Why in God's name would he go there? That place is even sketchier than the Clermont."

"He made plans to meet Roscoe there instead."

Gary dialed the Dinkler Plaza. He covered the mouthpiece. "Being that I'm a detective, they'll tell me what they wouldn't tell you."

They said nobody named Billy Tarwater had checked into the hotel. Gary then called a half-dozen other hotels in the area. None claimed to have a guest by that name.

"I'm going down there," Gary said.

"Down where?"

"To Luckie Street. To snoop around. See if I see his car somewhere. But I promise I'll do a better job than Billy and I did when we searched for *your* car."

"I'm going with you," Cynthia said.

"No, Cynthia. This is not a job for a wom—"

"I'm going with you, Gary. I won't take no for an answer."

"But Cynthia—"

"Don't sell me short, Gary. I'm tougher than you think. I'm not some meek and fawning housewife."

"I know that, but what we're dealing with here…this is a man's job."

"How many women are on the police force? How many are beat cops?"

"A few. Enough, I'd say."

"I bet what you really mean is *more* than enough."

"I didn't say that."

"Well think of me as just another one of the few. I can hold my own."

* * *

Cynthia and Gary found Billy's car parked on the third level of the Dinkler Plaza garage.

They asked the parking attendant whether he remembered Billy having entered last night.

"I just got here," the man said. "But the night guy that was here, he just clocked out. He may still be around. Check inside."

Cynthia and Gary went inside the hotel. The desk clerk said the man was in the back. She went to get him.

The parking attendant said yes, he remembered a man fitting Billy's description entering the garage.

"Did anyone else enter around that time?" Gary asked.

"Yep. Three men came in a few minutes earlier. Said they were here for the gift show. Said they were checking into the hotel."

The desk clerk chimed in and said no one had checked in last night. "Not surprising, given the weather."

"Do you recall what the men were driving?" Gary asked the attendant.

"I do," he said. "Impala four-door. Green."

Gary and Cynthia searched every level of the parking garage looking for the Impala, but they turned up nothing.

They drove around in the vicinity of Luckie Street. Nothing.

They then returned to The Belmont.

* * *

Gary called the station house. Signal 56. White male, five-eleven, 170 pounds, brown hair, green eyes. Name, Billy Tarwater. Last known location, the Dinkler Plaza parking garage on Luckie Street. He then asked that a tow truck be dispatched to retrieve Billy's car and take it to the police impound lot to be checked out.

Gary hung up the phone. He asked Cynthia to recount for him all that had happened going back to mid-December. The first time she was followed. Then again the next day. Her trip to the capitol. The balustrade man. Her kidnapping. And now Billy's disappearance.

"I know finding Billy is the most important thing right now," he said, "but do you find it odd that somebody, somehow, seems to have known your comings and goings? When you left home? When you went to the capitol? When you showed up at daycare?"

"I've thought about that a lot, Gary."

Gary looked over at the phone. "Cynthia, is it possible that somebody's been listening in on your calls? And Billy's?"

"Like somebody's tapped the line?"

"Yep."

Cynthia thought back. "Come to think of it, last October, I was home on an off-day when a man from the phone company showed up saying there was a problem and he had to check it out. He was inside no more than thirty or forty-five minutes. While he was here, I asked if he could replace the three old rotaries with touch-tones. At first, he seemed reluctant. Perturbed, actually. Like I was putting him out. But I persisted, and he finally said he didn't have any in his truck but could get me some. He returned the next day and replaced them."

"What did he look like?"

"Honestly, I couldn't tell you."

Cynthia said she was busy with other things and just didn't pay much attention to the man. She let him get on with his work and went about hers. All she could remember was that he had on a work shirt with a Southern Bell logo. Otherwise, she wouldn't have let him in. And he wore a wide-brimmed Braves baseball cap pulled low, casting a shadow over his face.

"I think he was clean-shaven," she said. "I guess I should have been more mindful of what he looked like. I'm sure Billy would agree with that. Later, when Billy found out I had let a stranger in, logo or no logo, he wasn't happy, but I thought little of it at the time."

Gary walked across the room to the phone. He picked up the handset and unscrewed the transmitter cap. "Come here, Cynthia."

He pointed to a small disc stuffed inside the handset. It was about a half inch in diameter and wafer thin. Two tiny wires, one red and one green, were connected to it. "Right there," he said. "That's all she wrote."

"So that's a phone tap?"

"Technically, it's called a bug. It's a radio transmitter. It's hard-wired to the microphone, so it'll pick up everything both parties are saying and transmit it through the air to a receiver close by."

"How close by?"

"Obviously within range of the transmitter. But that could be as far away as a football field. Maybe in a van parked nearby."

Cynthia recalled the car parked across the street on more than one occasion. Maybe it had been there at other times, and she just hadn't noticed. Or maybe there had been different vehicles. Or different locations. In the city, parked vehicles go unnoticed all the time.

"But somebody would have to sit out there for hours," she said, "just waiting for a call to be made. Who has time for that?"

"Somebody with a lot of free time on his hands, I guess. And an agenda." Gary checked the other handsets. There was a radio transmitter in each one. He removed them all. "I have a duty, as an officer of the law, to take this to the proper authorities, but we shouldn't do that just yet."

Cynthia said she understood.

"Whoever did this would have known where Billy would be last night," Gary said, "assuming he called Roscoe from home."

"He did. I was with him when he made the call. But the thing is, he used an alias. Roscoe didn't know he was meeting Billy *Tarwater*. He thought he was meeting somebody named Billy *Littrell*."

"But your electronic interloper would have known who it was."

Gary said Roscoe may have been the last person to see Billy before he disappeared. "We need to find him."

"Do we know his surname?" Cynthia said. "Or where he lives?"

Gary said no, they didn't. And his number's unlisted. But the phone company could trace the number to its owner. They wouldn't do it, however, without a court order.

He dialed Roscoe, but no one answered.

He then called the station house back. A wide net had been cast, but so far, no news.

He told Cynthia he was thinking about taking a ride back to Luckie Street, before it got dark, to search in and around the parking garage for any clues.

"I'm going with you," Cynthia said.

Gary's sigh spoke volumes. He had made it clear he didn't want her to tag along before, and he obviously didn't now. But staying behind was not an option she would abide.

"Let's take the Suburban this time," she said. "You can drive if you'd like. But after Luckie Street, we have to go by KFC."

"Why KFC?"

* * *

Gary and Cynthia hadn't turned up anything else on or near Luckie Street.

He eased her car close to the curb and parked in front of her parents' house.

"Stay here," Cynthia said. "I don't want to arouse suspicion. If my mother sees I'm with you and not Billy, there's no telling where her twisted mind will wander off to. I shouldn't be long." She took the KFC bag and exited the car.

She climbed the porch steps, careful to avoid the ice on the treads, and opened the front door without knocking.

Her mother greeted her in the living room. "Cecil's in bed. He just dropped off. I reckon he'd want to see you, though."

Cynthia handed her the KFC bag. "I wish I could stay, but I have a lot to do before nightfall. Tell him I'm thinking about him. I'll be back to visit later."

Cynthia stepped onto the porch to leave. She happened to look to her left. Leonard Seymour was standing on his own porch with another man. They seemed to be in animated conversation. She stared at the man. As soon as the two saw her, they turned and went inside Seymour's house.

She swung around and went back inside her parents' house.

"Who is that man next door?" she asked.

"Leonard Seymour?" her mother said.

"No, the other one."

"Oh, that's the maintenance man from church, Broadus McMillan. They're like two beans in the same pod. Except Leonard's a butter bean and that other one's a pole bean."

By the time Cynthia had traversed the fifty feet from the porch to the Suburban, her heart was pounding in concert with her fear. She slid into the seat next to Gary.

"Are you okay?" he said. "You look like you've seen a ghost."

"Worse," she said. "Remember when I told you about the second Impala man? Across the street from the Montessori?"

"The one that looked sort of like the one that kidnapped you, but wasn't?"

Cynthia nodded. "I think I just saw him."

319

Chapter Fifty-Eight
Billy Tarwater

Wednesday, January 13ᵗʰ, 1982

BILLY AWOKE COLD AND WITH A THROBBING HEAD. A BLINDFOLD covered his eyes. His ankles were bound. His wrists were tied behind his back. He stretched his fingers and ran their tips along the prickly husk of what he thought was jute or sisal.

The last thing he had remembered was the big guy hitting him across the side of the head with the tire iron. And one of the others jabbing a needle in his arm.

Now he found himself, wherever he was, slumped over where one of the men had silently ordered him, with a shove, to sit. He could feel the seat springs yearning to poke through the upholstery. They let out a loud squeak with the least movement.

A mingling of Old Spice Classic, acrid sweat, and mustiness filled the room. The cologne brought back memories of his father.

The must suggested the smell from his maternal grandmother's gas space heater when dust got in it.

He could hear people moving around. The floorboards creaked as they paced back and forth. No one spoke.

He heard a door open and close. And a lock turn.

The room was quiet now except for a low humming sound—here one minute, then gone, then here again—like the too-frequent cycling of a refrigerator with a dirty condenser. It sounded like it was coming from another room.

The Old Spice and sweat, but not the must, soon faded.

He listened carefully for a sign. Breathing, a floorboard creak, anything that would tell him one or more of the men had stayed behind. There was nothing. He was pretty sure he was now alone in the room.

He tried to wrench his hands free, but to no avail.

If he slumped over to the side, maybe he could catch the blindfold on one of the arms of the seat and somehow pull it off his head. He leaned far to his right. Then to his left. But he couldn't find anything to catch onto.

Maybe if he tumbled forward and out of the seat, he could worm his way across the room. But then what? What could he do with his wrists and ankles tied?

Maybe he could fall to his knees, reach down and behind, and untie his ankles. Maybe he could find something to catch the blindfold on. At least then he'd be able to walk and see. And, after that, it would just be a matter of finding something sharp, maybe the corner or edge of a table, that he could rub against to break his wrists free.

He played the scenario in his head. While he considered himself reasonably fit, a contortionist he was not. Did he really think he could reach behind his back with his wrists tied, make contact with his ankles, and loosen whatever bound them? It was a long shot. And what if the men returned and found him on the floor? What would they do then?

He decided it best, without a clear plan and a reasonable chance of success, to stay put and continue to vet his options, meager as they were.

His thoughts turned to Cynthia. She must have been worried sick when midnight passed and he hadn't come home, with a cold fear twisting in her gut and panic rising in her throat. He had been in her position before. He knew the feeling. The helplessness. Your mind goes to the darkest place.

He pictured Billy Jr. and Addie, their eyes glued to the frost-etched window, waiting.

And what about work? The trial? He imagined the rhythmic clatter of typewriters echoing across the smoke-filled newsroom. A frenetic energy captivating the room full of caffeinated newshounds pursuing the next big scoop. Had Roberts seen to it that the authorities were canvassing the city in search of him? If anybody had influence, if anybody knew how to grease the skids, Roberts surely did.

Had Roscoe waited last night, for what seemed like an eternity, in the blinding snow and brutal cold? Finally packing it in and thinking *that goddamned no-show stood me up*?

In time, Billy heard muffled voices from afar. Maybe from another room. Even though he could make out only a word here and there. *Deadweight* or *headway* or something like that. *Wheel.* Something about a message. He could tell from the register and lilt that it wasn't men speaking. Then a radio came on. Patsy Cline, "I Fall To Pieces." Somebody turned the volume up loud enough to drown out the voices.

A lock turned. A door opened. The floor creaked.

"Please," Billy called out. "Water."

One of the men trod heavily out of the room and soon returned. The man held a cup of water up to Billy's lips and tilted it slightly. The cool liquid—nature's elixir—washed down his bone-dry throat.

Billy caught another strong whiff of Old Spice. He leaned in and half-whispered. "Why am I here?"

The man didn't respond.

Chapter Fifty-Nine

Cynthia Tarwater

Wednesday, January 13th, 1982

"ARE YOU SURE?" GARY ASKED CYNTHIA.

"Not a hundred percent, but close. When a stalker stalks you, and you get within a few yards of him, you never forget his face. Even with a partially fogged window."

"Who is he?"

"My mother says he's Broadus McMillan, the maintenance man at the church." Cynthia could see Gary's mind racing. "What do we do now?" she said.

"I don't think we should confront him. Not here anyway. Not in Seymour's house. And not unless you're a hundred percent."

They were sitting in the Suburban, pondering their options, when Leonard Seymour's car came barreling from behind his house and onto the street. Seymour was driving. The other man was in the passenger's seat. Seymour headed east and turned right onto Gresham.

Gary cranked up and slammed the Suburban into Drive. He made a sharp U-turn and followed Seymour, being careful to stay several blocks behind.

Five minutes and one and a half miles later, Cynthia and Gary found themselves lurking in the Suburban a block from the Confederate Avenue Baptist Church. Behind the dense woody brush of an overgrown forsythia.

The church lot was almost full. She assumed it was because of the Wednesday night supper.

Leonard Seymour and Broadus McMillan parked and entered the church's side door.

Gary placed his hand on Cynthia's wrist.

Cynthia and Gary were at a crossroads with diverse paths forward. Would some converge? Would some bring pay dirt? Others just wasted effort? The weight of decision felt heavy.

Billy was missing, and all they had to go on was the last known man who may have seen him. A man they knew only as Roscoe. Gary had said he wasn't convinced that a judge would grant a court order to reveal his identity. Especially with the only basis being a missing person, who had been gone less than twenty-four hours in the middle of a major snowstorm, no clear evidence of foul play, and a planned meeting with a casual acquaintance.

Cynthia thought she had just seen, ten minutes ago, one of her pursuers. And now he and Leonard were ensconced inside the church. And what about the Vardemans? J.P. Finnegan, their only connection to Graydon and the others, was also missing. And the Impala? Who did it belong to and where was it?

On top of it all, earlier this morning they had discovered that Cynthia and Billy's phone had been bugged.

The city was bracing for another major snowstorm tomorrow. Maybe even worse than yesterday. So bad that the whole city was poised to shut down again. So bad that a trial the likes of which Atlanta had never seen had been postponed for another day. At least that's what the papers were saying.

Cynthia and Gary had to act wisely. With the storm brewing, every step mattered.

Confronting Seymour at church seemed even more imprudent than doing so at his home. Especially with the fellowship hall full of people. They would wait for the right time. First and foremost, right now, was finding Billy.

They were about to leave when Cynthia looked across the way at the parking lot.

A green Impala pulled into the lot from Woodland Avenue and parked next to Seymour's car.

Broadus McMillan exited the side door of the church. He walked over to the Impala and eased into the passenger's seat.

Cynthia and Gary waited.

After five minutes, both men got out of the car and went inside. Cynthia tried to get a good look at the other man, but he was too far away, and he never turned his face in her direction.

A couple more minutes passed without Cynthia or Gary saying a word. She was trying to process it all. She assumed he was too.

Finally, she spoke. "The silence is killing me, Gary. What do we do?"

"We wait. Let's give it a few more minutes. I have an idea."

"And it is?"

Gary looked at Cynthia. "You don't want to know."

The sun had begun its slow descent. The Impala still sat in the church lot.

Gary asked Cynthia if she had a flashlight.

"In the glove box," she said.

Gary retrieved the flashlight and flicked the thumb switch on and off. He reached into his coat pocket and produced the blue-steel burl-handled revolver that he had claimed to carry with him everywhere. He held the revolver up to the light from the streetlamp and spun the cylinder. He opened the Suburban door. He stepped out and reached back in to grab his cane.

"What are you doing?"

"Stay here," he said. "I'll be back."

Cynthia watched as Gary stalked haltingly past the patch of dirt and weeds she knew from her childhood as Confederate-Woodland Circle. He crossed Confederate Avenue and headed toward the parking lot and the Impala, cutting a stark silhouette in the waning full moon.

He looked all around, then approached the front of the car. He leaned in on the driver's side and shined the flashlight through the windshield. He circled around toward the rear, shining the light into the car along the way. He was crouching along the side of the car doing something—Cynthia couldn't make out what—when Leonard Seymour came out of the church.

Cynthia's heart seized up like a clenched fist.

Chapter Sixty

Leonard Seymour

Wednesday, January 13th, 1982

LEONARD SEYMOUR WALKED OUT THE SIDE DOOR AND HEADED to his car, which was parked two spaces down from the Impala.

Out of the corner of his eye, he caught a glimpse of movement on the far side of the Impala. He approached slowly. He was almost to the hood when a man stood up from behind the left rear fender. He thought he looked vaguely familiar but couldn't put his finger on it.

Before he had a chance to say anything, the man spoke. "Definitely not the one I was looking for."

"What are you doing here?" Seymour shouted.

The man gimped forward and produced a badge. "APD Larceny. Got a tip on a stolen '70 Impala four-door we've been lookin' for. But this ain't it. A year off."

Seymour wasn't about to take the word of some swingin' dick just because he had a badge. "I need more than a piece of brass."

"This piece of brass here should be enough. If you've got a problem, you can take it up with headquarters."

Seymour looked around. He didn't see the supposed detective's car anywhere.

"Just a minute," Seymour said, and went back inside to get the others. If the man decided to leave, surely he couldn't go far. He was crippled with a cane, for Christ's sake.

When Seymour and the others came back out, the detective was gone. They fanned out looking for him but returned empty-handed.

As Seymour stood in the parking lot under the light of the moon, it suddenly hit him why the supposed detective looked familiar.

Back in October of '80. He was the sidekick who showed up in Irondale with Billy Tarwater. The day Virlyn Kilgallon died.

CHAPTER SIXTY-ONE

Cynthia Tarwater

Wednesday, January 13th, 1982

ONCE CYNTHIA REGAINED HER COMPOSURE AFTER SEEING Leonard Seymour come out of the church, she moved to the driver's seat in case she needed to rescue Gary.

The two men stood in the church lot, next to the Impala, talking. Then Seymour went back inside.

Gary came hobble-running back to the Suburban. He jumped into the passenger seat. "We need to get the hell out of here."

Cynthia did a three-point turn in the middle of the street and raced down Woodland Avenue away from the church.

As they barreled down the street toward East Atlanta, Gary told her the VIN plate was missing from the Impala. "There's another one on the engine block, but no way I was gonna get under the hood right then and there."

"What happened when Seymour came out?"

"I showed him my badge. Made up a story about looking for a stolen Impala. Not much of a stretch, don't you think? I said it was the wrong year. Then he went back inside. That's when I took off." Gary rubbed his thigh. "Haven't run this hard since I got the gimp."

"Surely they'll come looking for you."

"That's why we needed to bolt. By the way, I'm pretty sure that's Rev. Thomas's Impala. The one that was stolen from the parsonage driveway."

"How do you know?"

Gary told Cynthia that, right before Seymour came out, he bent down and scraped some paint off the left rear fender with his pen knife. "It was blue underneath."

"What do we do now?"

"Billy had a hunch about the reverend's Impala. About who might have painted it, assuming it was painted. We'll go to McKnight's Garage. Hopefully they'll still be there."

Cynthia turned off Gresham and onto the alley that ran to McKnight's. She pulled in front of the Oil and Lube bay and put the car in Park. The bay door opened. She sat there for a moment staring at the men huddled around a kerosene heater in the far corner of the garage. She assumed Cecil would probably have been right there shooting craps, and shooting the bull, with the rest of them, if the heart attack hadn't made him prisoner to her mother, his live-in nursemaid and grudging protector.

She and Gary got out of the car and approached the bay. She didn't see Mac McKnight anywhere. But she did see the son, whose name escaped her.

Gary walked up to the man, extended his hand and introduced himself. "And I imagine you already know Cynthia, here."

The man approached Gary with his grease-covered hands in the air. "I'd shake, but I don't think you want to. Pleased to meet you. Name's Shane. McKnight. I think we may have met at some point. Aren't you Billy Tarwater's friend?" He looked over at Cynthia. "Gosh, how long has it been? I don't think I've seen you since…I'm sorry about what happened to you way back when." He returned his attention to Gary. "Now, what brings you out on this godawful winter day?"

"Your dad around?" Gary said.

Shane said his "old man Mac" had retired last year. "Maybe I can help you."

Gary told Shane about the '71 Impala. He and Cynthia suspected it had been painted around eight years ago. It was a long shot, but they wondered whether McKnight may have done the painting.

"We don't do a lot of paint jobs here," Shane said. "You probably know that, though, seeing as we're mainly a grease house. But when a friend would come by asking for a favor, the old man couldn't say no."

"Do you remember painting a blue '71 Impala around that time?"

"Like it was yesterday. Only reason I do is I did the painting. At least the first time."

"The first time?"

"Yeah. Totally fucked it up. I didn't know what I was doing. My old man had to completely redo it. Boy, was he pissed."

"What color did it end up?"

"Light green as I recall."

"Who brought it in?"

"Leonard Seymour. The one used to hang out here a lot. Ain't been around much since my old man retired."

CHAPTER SIXTY-TWO
Billy Tarwater

Wednesday, January 13th, 1982

BILLY COULDN'T TELL HOW MANY OF THE MEN WERE STILL IN the room. Old Spice for sure. But as for the others? He listened carefully for floor creaks, footfalls, anything that might clue him in.

The muffled voices from afar had waned, replaced by what sounded like the intermittent clanging of metal on metal.

In what seemed like an hour but could have been no more than a few minutes, someone came into the room. The footsteps were light. Nimble. Not the men's ponderous thuds. Following behind was an erratic click-clack. Like a dog's nails on a hardwood floor.

Billy felt a gentle touch against his shoulder, pulling him ever so slightly forward. Whoever it was reached behind him and untied his wrists. Then they splayed the fingers of his left hand and placed a warm bowl in his palm. He cradled the bowl with both hands.

Felt its warmth. Took in the aroma issuing from its recess. He ran his thumb along the bowl's rim until he found the spoon.

For a moment, with his hands unbound, he considered ripping the blindfold off. But he knew that if he were to do that, it might end up being the *last* thing he did.

The thin broth was intoxicating to his senses. He tried to deconstruct it. Chicken stock. Onion. Fennel perhaps. He rolled a carrot slice between his tongue and palate. A chunk of celery. Tastier and more inviting than the finest feast.

When all was done, he blindly searched the bottom of the bowl for the last few drops, hoping the feast would persist but knowing it was over.

The silent hand took the bowl from him, guided his wrists behind his back, and rebound them. The footsteps trailed into the distance.

Billy had a meager sense of where he was, of who had abducted him, and why, but in the moment, as he sat in this cold room, blindfolded and bound, he was appreciative of the little things. A cup of water, a bowl of broth, a kind hand. In the midst of trial and hardship they meant everything. They and the thought of Cynthia and the children kept hope alive.

He passed the hours preoccupying himself with these enduring thoughts, punctuated by trivial mind exercises. Reciting the states and capitals in alphabetical order. The presidents and vice presidents since FDR. The Supreme Court justices. Stopping by Woods on a Snowy Evening.

Later in the day—Billy assumed evening was beginning to settle in, as the room had grown more frigid—the front door opened and closed. At least, he thought it was the front door. The heavy, thudding footsteps were back. The men—more than one—passed by where he sat and seemed to have retreated into the other room where the high-pitched voices had come from earlier. The door to the room slammed shut.

Soon he heard yelling and what sounded like a scuffle coming from the other room. He strained to hear words but couldn't make out what was going on. He thought surely it would abate soon, but it only got worse.

He called out for water, but no one responded.

He ran his fingertips along the rope that bound his wrists, just as he had done before. But this time, it felt different. He stretched his fingers, grabbed onto the rope's knot, and tugged. The knot gave a little. It gradually yielded under his touch. With each twist and turn, it relinquished its hold, until finally it came undone, releasing him from its grasp.

Had the gentle hand intentionally left the knot undone? He didn't care. All he knew was this was his chance to escape.

The men were still in the other room arguing.

Without betraying his freedom, he called out again with muted voice. Again, nothing.

The chance to flee was one worth taking.

He slipped off the blindfold and surveyed the room. There was no one there. A lamp, sitting on a side table beside an ashtray filled with butts, provided the only illumination.

The heavy black overcoats that Billy recognized from last night were piled in the corner near the front door. An ushanka—it looked like rabbit—sat on the coffee table before him.

He climbed down from where he had been sitting and made for the door, careful to cross the room with lightened steps so as not to arouse attention from the adjacent room.

Once outside, he realized where he was. The green Impala sat at the edge of the house's clearing. A red Schwinn lay on the ground between the car and a stack of bald tires.

He took off toward the dirt road that led to the highway. Halfway up the dirt road, he looked back. No one was following him, but he knew it was only a matter of time. He quickened his pace.

Traffic was light on the highway and the sun was setting. He tried to flag down three passing cars, but they didn't stop.

He heard gunshots from somewhere down the dirt road behind him.

CHAPTER SIXTY-THREE

Cynthia Tarwater

Wednesday, January 13ᵗʰ, 1982

CYNTHIA AND GARY RETURNED TO THE BELMONT.

He called the station house. There were no leads on Billy's whereabouts.

Cynthia poured two glasses of Merlot, handed one to Gary, and planted herself in her chair, bereft and exhausted. "What now?"

Gary was about to answer when there was a banging at the door.

"Who is it?" Cynthia called out.

"It's me."

Cynthia threw open the door. Billy was standing at the threshold, disheveled and out of breath. She mined his bloodshot eyes. She rushed forward and embraced him.

He nodded to Gary before stumbling into the room, weary and wobbly, and sinking into the sofa.

Cynthia ran into the kitchen and returned with a glass of water. She sat beside him, her head resting on his shoulder.

He took the glass in both hands, wrapped his fingers around it, and raised it to his lips.

"We've been worried sick," Cynthia said. "What happened?"

Billy said he would lay it all out in detail. But first he wanted to steal into the kids' bedroom and give them a big kiss.

"They're with your mother," Cynthia said. She hated that they weren't here for Billy, but she knew they were in good hands with Alice. And there would be plenty of time for reunion. Hopefully soon.

Billy recounted the events of the past twenty-four hours. "I was waiting for Roscoe in the parking garage when three men in masks overtook me. They drugged me. That's all I remember until I woke up in a cold room, blindfolded and bound. Somebody, I don't know who, showed me mercy. Either that or they were incredibly careless. If it weren't for whoever did it, I wouldn't have been able to break free. I ran out the door. The green Impala was outside. I took off toward the highway. Five or six cars passed before an elderly black couple picked me up and brought me here."

Gary said he was going into the kitchen to call home and to give Cynthia and Billy some time alone.

Cynthia ran her fingers through Billy's matted hair. "I have some things to tell you, too." She told Billy about recognizing Broadus McMillan as the second Impala man. "Not a hundred percent, but close." She told him about following McMillan and Seymour to the church. About seeing the Impala there. About visiting McKnight's. About the phone tap. "Remember the man from the phone company that time?"

"I do. And I have a hunch I know what went down with that."

Gary came back into the room. "I called the station house. I let 'em know you're okay."

"Did you provide any details?" Billy said.

"No. Just that you're safe and sound. I told them we'd follow up with all the nitty gritty. When you're ready."

Billy rose from the sofa, crossed the room, and peered out the window as if in deep thought. "The Vardemans. They drugged me and took me to their house." He turned to face Cynthia and Gary. "This is all a big fucking mess. I'm still not ready to get the police involved."

"But Billy," Gary said, "this is serious shit. You were kidnapped."

"Cynthia was too, remember." Billy walked back to the sofa and sat beside her. He placed his hand on hers. "But here's the deal. The police have done everything they can to cover up the Vardemans' involvement in the child murders."

"*Potential* involvement," Gary said.

"Okay, potential involvement. But if Finnegan's right, the authorities sure as hell think Graydon and his clan are involved. And they're scared shitless it'll get out, and all hell will break loose."

"Speaking of Finnegan, was his Mustang still in the brush at the Vardemans'?"

"Gary, all I was thinking about was getting the hell out of Dodge. I couldn't tell you whether it was there or not." Billy went on to say that, with Wayne Williams captured and indicted, and now on trial, the police had their man. Regardless of Williams' guilt or innocence, they could sweep the Klan under the rug, wipe their hands of it all, and go on about their business. And the public would be none the wiser for it. The killer's locked up. Riots are averted. "Case closed. Move on."

"But you were kidnap—"

"I understand. It's serious shit, as you said. But that's even more reason to get to the bottom of it without anybody, especially somebody with a hidden agenda, gumming it up."

"You know what they say about taking the law into your own hands."

"What's that, Gary? What do they say?"

"You do it at your peril."

"Well, my response to that is the danger's been here for a while. Do you think the police will protect us from a renegade cabal that they themselves are scared shitless of? Hell, they've apparently done everything they could to snuff out what J.P. Finnegan, their number one informer, was trying his damnedest to tell them. Kill the messenger. Right?"

Cynthia spoke up. "For what it's worth, I agree with Billy."

"So, what do we do now?" Gary said.

"Cynthia filled me in while you were making your calls. About McMillan and Seymour. And the Impala."

"And the phone tap," Cynthia said.

Gary went back into the kitchen and returned with the bug retrieved from one of the phones. He was holding it with a paper towel. He held it out for Billy to see. "Best not to touch it with your bare hands. Prints, you know."

"I'll be back in a minute," Billy said, and got up and retreated to the bedroom.

He returned with a sheet of paper. "This may explain the phone tap. These are notes from one of my meetings with Finnegan. Seems Graydon Vardeman was a Southern Bell lineman. For four-plus years."

"But linemen mainly work outside, don't they?" Gary said.

Billy said generally, yes. But Vardeman would have been with the phone company long enough to learn the ins and outs of home wiring jobs. And with a little outside guidance, he could have learned how to install a bug. Plus, he may have kept his Southern Bell uniform. Just in case he ever needed it. Billy asked if Gary could get prints lifted and examined on the sly.

Gary said he'd try. No promises. "Back to my earlier question, what do you think we should do now?"

Billy said he wanted time to process it all before they went off half-cocked. Plus, he reminded Gary and Cynthia that he still had a day job. Somehow, in the midst of all that was going on, he needed to find time to get back into the trial.

Always the workaholic, Cynthia thought. "You haven't missed much. Everything's been at a standstill because of the dreadful weather."

"One other thing," Billy said. "Cynthia, didn't you tell me the balustrade man was wearing an ushanka?"

CHAPTER SIXTY-FOUR

Leonard Seymour

Wednesday, January 13th, 1982

AFTER THE OTHERS LEFT IN THE IMPALA, LEONARD SEYMOUR
drove up and down the side streets near the church looking for Billy's
sidekick, the supposed detective. Then he drove up Confederate
Avenue all the way to where the old Soldier's Home used to be.
Nothing. He finally gave up and headed back to his house.

* * *

When he pulled into the driveway, he looked over and saw
Adele sitting on her front porch. The yellow porch light, shining
down on her and the KFC box on the table beside her, made her
look like a jaundiced baby elephant. She glanced his way briefly but
quickly looked away.

He sank into the La-Z-Boy with a PBR in one hand and a
freshly fired-up stogie in the other. He puffed hard, with long, deep

draws. He watched the smoke as it curled to the ceiling and crept across the room, cloaking his surroundings in a sullen grey.

Why had he first gotten deep in it with the Vardeman clan in the first place? He reckoned it went all the way back to that day in '63 when Virlyn Kilgallon handed him a slip of paper and said call this number. Ask for a man named Graydon. "He's got the goods." Then he slipped Leonard a fifty, saying this should cover it.

But it wasn't Graydon Jr. back then. It was the old man. The father.

Two days later, Leonard was pulling off the dirt road onto the Old Dixie Highway with a baggie of syringes and a coupla vials of phennies. Bingo Barbies.

Leonard wasn't the one that shot up the girls, at least not at first. Kilgallon started off doing it. But over time, Leonard got used to doing it himself.

Leonard learned quickly enough that he could always count on the old man and his three boys when push came to shove, whether it was drugs, ammo, or a little good old-fashioned protection. The thing is, though, the Vardemans' help always came with strings attached. They had a way of sucking a man in. Just like Kilgallon had done, with his holier-than-thou *we're doing this for the Lord* bullshit. Even when it came to killing those girls. Leonard remembered thinking Kilgallon was some kind of modern-day Svengali.

Kilgallon was bad. Evil bad. But the Vardemans took the whole damned thing a step further. They had figured out how to commingle God and racialism and end up with some twisted shit that said it's okay to kill black boys because they were black.

And Leonard had fallen for it. Deeper and deeper. Even to the point of getting ink on his arm that would never come off. And bloodstains on his hands that probably wouldn't either.

What a fool. He flicked a long, fat ash into the ashtray before taking another draw.

Old Man Graydon had stroked out and given it up right in front of the boys. What year was that? '65? '66? To this day, every year on his birthday, the boys made sure a new battle flag—Blood-Stained Banner on a little stick that you can push into the dirt—got put on his grave. Good boys to their daddy at least. Leonard just wished they were as good to everybody else.

When the war came, Graydon and Dickie were shipped off to Nam. Ewell was spared. Word was he had bone spurs, but Leonard knew better. Truth be told, he just didn't have the smarts to pass the test. Leonard had heard stories from Graydon Jr. that Old Man Graydon wasn't Ewell's father. Ewell and the others' mother had slept with some fellow who ended up imbecilic in the Central State Hospital in Milledgeville. The acorn doesn't fall far, Leonard supposed.

Almost as soon as Graydon got back from Nam, he took a job as a telephone lineman. He lasted four years or so. Then, not even a year later, they hauled his ass off to prison for drugs.

Dickie came back from Nam strung out on who knows what and bounced around from rehab to halfway house and back to rehab again.

In '73, Ewell, being the dimwit that he was, was looking all over the place for work so he could put food on the table for his son, who'd just turned three. That's when Leonard got him the job.

It was good that he had, because two years later, the little boy's no-account mother flew the coop to follow the Grateful Dead from pillar to post, leaving Ewell holding the bag—and the boy. Fortunately, Sonya, who had shown up on the scene, was there to help out.

In the Summer of '79, Graydon walked out of Reidsville more hardened and more racist than when he went in. He would have made his daddy proud. Leonard had heard Graydon had gotten mixed up with the Aryan Brotherhood in there, but that was hearsay. What wasn't hearsay was that he was getting in even tighter with the Klan than his daddy had been.

There was a lot of racial shit at Reidsville back then. About a year before Graydon was let out, racial fights had erupted at the prison, and an inmate even got killed. It was so bad that a US district judge ordered a cooling-down period during which the prison dorms would be segregated. Leonard hadn't learned this from Graydon. It was all over the papers.

As soon as Graydon had *resettled*—his word—he dialed up Leonard. *You know a thing or two about killing kids, don't you?* Graydon had said. Leonard remembered the blood draining so quickly from his face that Graydon surely felt it over the phone line. Leonard hedged. Graydon went on to lay out his plan for the black boys.

Leonard had lain low for a few months, refusing even to talk to Ewell about it.

Then November of '80 came, and Leonard made the call to Graydon that would change everything. He had returned from Irondale with Kilgallon dead and blood on his hands and the law on his ass. He picked up the phone and called the one person who could protect him. The attached strings came out in a big way. *What's in it for me?* Graydon said. Funny thing is, Graydon always wanted to know what was in it for him, but he had a way of getting his brothers, and now Leonard, to do the dirty work. So his own hands would be clean. Even going as far as foisting evidence off on Leonard so it wouldn't be traced back. Graydon was clever like that.

Leonard clipped another stogie and lit it, feeling the heat from the newborn flames as they leapt with each deep breath and dissipated just as quickly. He had fallen in hard with the Vardemans all right, but what happened this evening was more than he could stand.

After looking high and low for Billy's sidekick, he and the others had gone back inside the church. They retreated to the Reverend Thomas's office, knowing he would be in the fellowship hall chowing down with the flock.

Graydon told Leonard that Billy was being held, bound and blindfolded, back at their place. Sonya and the kid were watching over him until they returned. Leonard asked where Dickie was. Graydon said he was there too, but he was back in the shed behind the house taking care of some other business. Leonard didn't ask what that meant. He didn't want to know.

Leonard thought back to last June, when he had told Ewell about Sam Jepperson being freed thanks to Billy. When Graydon found this out, he was livid. Jepperson had been sent up for killing those girls back in '63. And to Graydon, it was justice served. Just another black man turning prey on those poor, innocent white girls with their whole lives before them. And the way Graydon saw it, Billy was no better than Jepperson. He had called Billy a goddamned nigger lover. Leonard made the mistake of reminding Graydon that Cynthia had been an intended victim but had escaped and was now Billy's wife. Graydon's response was that she was just like her worthless husband and probably deserved what would have come to her, given that she got in the car with Jepperson in the first place. Rode around with him. His lily-white jailbait. It had all come out in the trial. No hiding from the truth.

Funny thing is, Graydon *knew* it was Virlyn Kilgallon, not Sam Jepperson, who had kidnapped and killed those girls. And Leonard Seymour had helped. That had come out early on in one of the Vardemans' lets-grill-Seymour sessions. But none of that mattered to Graydon as long as Sam was rotting in prison. A closed mind is a powerful thing and can convince a man of pretty much anything.

Then Graydon had learned, through Finnegan's spiral notebook, that Finnegan and Billy were in cahoots to fuck him and his brothers over because of their involvement in the black-boy killings. Especially that *nappy-headed Lubie Geter.* That was the straw that did the camel in, as Graydon said.

What are you going to do to Billy? Leonard had asked Graydon as they stood inside Thomas's office.

Ice him, was Graydon's response. *But only after he squeals his guts out.*

Leonard had seen a lot, been through a lot, gone along with a lot. But when Graydon said that, he decided he'd had enough. He couldn't see Billy losing his life, with Cynthia left to raise those kids alone, just because of what Billy had done or not done. It wasn't that Leonard liked the guy. But too far is too far.

And he told Graydon as much. *Ice him,* Leonard had said, *and* I'll *be the one doing the singing.*

The last thing Graydon had said to Leonard before leaving in the Impala was, *You can run, but you can't hide.*

Leonard dozed off in the La-Z-Boy thinking about those last words.

He was rousted from a deep sleep by somebody knocking at his door.

CHAPTER SIXTY-FIVE

Billy Tarwater

Wednesday, January 13ᵗʰ, 1982

BILLY, CYNTHIA, AND GARY SAT QUIETLY. HE ASSUMED THEY were pondering, like he was, the next thing they should do.

At 8:45, the phone broke the silence.

Billy got up and answered.

It was Adele. From the moment she said her name, the tremble in her voice spoke fear. "I just heard gunshots next door."

"At Seymour's?"

"Yes." As soon as she had heard them, she ran to the front door and peered through the sidelight in the direction of Seymour's driveway. There was a car parked there. She thought it was the one she had sometimes seen Broadus McMillan driving when he would visit Leonard Seymour. "Then I called you."

"What kind of car was it?"

"I don't know. It's long. With a big grille on the front. And the back swoops down from the top a little."

"Color?"

"Green."

"Is it still there?"

She said yes.

Billy told Adele to stay put with the doors locked and, whatever she did, she wasn't to open the door for anybody. "I'll be right over."

Billy hung up.

Cynthia came and touched his arm. "What is it?"

"It was your mother. She heard gunshots from next door." He looked over at Gary. "Ready for some adventure?"

"For you, buddy, always."

"I'm going, too." Cynthia said.

Billy pushed back.

"No, Billy. We've been through this before. And it's my mother, not yours." She looked at Gary. "Tell him, Gary."

Gary looked down at his shoes. Then back at Billy. "She's right, Billy. You'd best go along with whatever she wants."

* * *

The Impala—Billy had suspected that was the car based on Adele's description—was still parked in Leonard Seymour's driveway.

Gary dropped Billy and Cynthia off in front of her parents' house, saying he was going to park his detective car a block up the street so as not to arouse suspicion.

Adele met them at the front door looking like she was staring into a stiff wind. Her rumpled blouse and mismatched slacks screamed afterthought. "He's out back."

"Who's out back?" Billy said.

"That McMillan man. He's been going in and out of Seymour's house through the back door."

"Any sign of Seymour?"

Adele said no. She hadn't seen him since before the gunshots.

Gary arrived and came inside. He shut the door and locked it.

Cynthia looked around the room. "Where's Cecil?"

Adele laughed nervously. Fidgeted and fiddled with her blouse buttons. "He's asleep. The old crank's driving me batty, if you want to know the truth. I gave him a couple of valiums and sent him to bed. Told him they were his heart medicine. He didn't know the difference."

Billy, Cynthia, and Gary repaired to the back of the house, with Adele following close behind. Cynthia turned off the kitchen light. Billy pushed back the kitchen curtains and peered across the way to Seymour's backyard. "Do you have binoculars?" he asked Adele.

She retreated to the other room and got them. "Here."

Under the faint glow from the incandescent bulb over Seymour's back stoop, Broadus McMillan was standing in the snow, chucking something into the half-rusted-out 55-gallon drum in the far end of the yard. Billy thought it was clothes. And a box full of something, the contents of which McMillan dumped into the drum. He reached into his overcoat and retrieved what looked like a box of matches. He lit a match and tossed it in. He lit another. Then another.

He went back inside and returned with a gas can. He tilted the almost-empty container over the drum, a meager trickle of gasoline surrendering to gravity. He shook it upside-down then tossed it to the ground. He threw in another lighted match. Flames danced in the air, illuminating the contours of his face.

Adele, inexplicably and without warning, threw open her back door. "Drive them demon spirits from that hateful man."

Just as she did, McMillan reacted with a start and ran back into Seymour's house.

"Why did you do that?" Cynthia screamed.

Adele clinked the keys to the kingdom hanging from her belt loop. She raised her arms in exaltation. "The Lord made me."

A shaft of light broke the darkness between the two houses. Billy craned his neck and peered out the kitchen window toward the front of the house. Someone—he assumed Broadus—had started the Impala and was barreling in reverse out of the driveway.

Billy's first inclination was to take off and follow him. But by the time they could get to Gary's car, McMillan would be long gone. Plus, they may have a crime scene on their hands next door.

Gary agreed. He said, "Wait here."

He returned with his car and parked in the Hudspeth's driveway. He came back inside, holding two flashlights and two pairs of latex gloves. He handed one of the flashlights and a pair of gloves to Billy. "Sorry Cynthia, that was all I had. Anyway, somebody needs to stay here with your mother. And Cecil."

Down the hall, the door on the left was closed. "That's Seymour's bedroom," Billy said. Gary eased the door open. He and

Billy cautiously stepped into the dimly lit room. The air hung heavy with the acrid scent of gunpowder. An eerie silence blanketed the room, broken only by the sounds of their footsteps.

Leonard Seymour was sprawled on the floor, face up and in a pool of crimson. Two dark holes, ragged at the edges and spattered with blood, marred his forehead. His lifeless eyes stared blankly at the ceiling.

Billy and Gary exchanged knowing glances in silence.

Gary knelt and felt Seymour's pulse. He stood back up and shook his head. "He's gone."

Not until they were about to go summon the police did they see the bloody footprints leading to the bedroom door. The prints continued down the hallway to the kitchen at the rear of the house, where they ended.

Billy walked over to the sink. There was residual water in the porcelain basin, tainted by the unmistakable hue of blood. But the counter surface was clean. A gallon jug of Clorox sat on the far end of the counter between the staple cannisters and the toaster.

"Don't touch anything," Gary said. He removed the handset from the telephone on the kitchen wall and struggled to dial the police through his gloved hand.

J.P. Finnegan

Thursday, January 14ᵗʰ, 1982

J.P. FINNEGAN KNEW RIGHT AWAY WHERE HE HAD BEEN sequestered. The bone-chilling cold, tempered by only a musty wool blanket and the intermittent blast of warm air from what he assumed was a nearby space heater. The smells. Sawdust and turpentine. Motor oil and gasoline. The sounds. Snow pounding on the tin roof. The door's rusty, creaking groan whenever the men came and went. The soft crunching footfalls as they passed before him. The space heater's on-off cycling. They were all dead giveaways.

How long had he been here? Bound and blindfolded, without the ability to see night or day, he didn't know for sure. But he guessed it had been a little over a week, based on the like-clockwork visits of someone bringing him dry toast for breakfast, broth for dinner. And the occasional cup of water. And the trips to the pail across the room.

Finnegan was pretty sure, based on the distinctness of the footfalls, that different people were coming and going during the day.

Each day, between the toast and the broth, somebody—he was sure it was one of the brothers—would show up and grill him mercilessly, resorting to swift blows to his head and torso when he refused to answer their questions.

This morning, whoever brought him food every day had just arrived.

With wrists unbound, Finnegan savored the toast and water, drawing out the process for as long as his food deliverer would allow. The person then retied Finnegan's wrists and departed without ever uttering a word. Finnegan heard the door creak and close.

A surge of adrenaline coursed through his veins now that he discovered he could wrench free from the rope that bound his wrists. Desperation sometimes calls for bold action, danger be damned. He yanked the shroud from his eyes with no concern for whether anyone was in the shed with him.

Finnegan let his eyes adjust. A sliver of morning light from the crack between the door and the outside wall pierced the dark, tiny dust particles dancing in its path.

He surveyed the darkened shed. How many times had he been here? Before Ewell forced him back, blindfolded and at gunpoint? Half a dozen at least. He knew the shed well. He knew where the guns were hidden. The munitions. The explosives.

I know a thing or two about blowing shit up.

CHAPTER SIXTY-SEVEN
Billy Tarwater

Thursday, January 14th, 1982

BILLY WOKE EARLY AND CALLED THE CITY DESK. HE SAID HE was okay and would be in later, half-jokingly telling Dedrick Roberts that he, Billy, had found himself on the wrong side of the story. "I'll fill you in later." He knew he'd have to come up with an explanation that would pass muster without raising Roberts' ire. *Kill it*, Roberts had said just a month earlier.

Roberts said Billy was lucky. He had timed his disappearance well, given that the Williams trial had been postponed because of the weather and wouldn't resume until Monday at the earliest. *He doesn't know how lucky I am*, Billy thought.

Billy hung up and went back to bed, where Cynthia was still fast asleep. They didn't get up until almost two hours later. Sleeping in was a rare luxury, but one they deserved, given the last few days.

Midmorning the call came. They had just finished breakfast. Billy was clearing the table, and Cynthia was in the bedroom preparing to go pick up the kids from Billy's mom's.

It was Gary. Billy assumed he was calling about what had happened last night. The two of them had been questioned for over an hour by the police. Investigators had scoured Seymour's house for evidence. The coroner had hauled Seymour's body off on a gurney. The crime scene had been cordoned off with yellow line tape.

"You're not gonna believe this," Gary said.

Billy could feel in Gary's voice a mix of exhilaration and distress. Shock and disbelief.

"There's been an explosion. At the Vardemans'. The whole damned house is blown to smithereens."

Billy struggled to process what he'd just heard. "What? When did it happen?"

"This morning. Around nine."

"Were the Vardemans there?"

"I don't know who was there and who wasn't. I'm learning things on the fly. I can tell you this. They've found at least two bodies. Parts of bodies anyway. They're still combing the property, but it's a mess, and the fire's still smoldering. I'm told it's busier than a beehive."

Billy asked if Gary thought they could get close to the beehive.

"I need to stay as far away as I can," Gary said. "Given that I'm larceny, for me to show up would raise all kinds of questions. You, on the other hand. You're with the paper. I'm sure you could get a lot closer than I'd want to be."

Cynthia walked into the room. "What's going on?"

Billy covered the mouthpiece. "It's Gary. There's been an explosion at the Vardemans'."

Cynthia winced when Billy said he was planning to go over there. "Do you really think that's a good idea?"

"Given the circumstances, yes. Don't get me wrong. It's not that I want to, but I *have* to."

Cynthia asked Billy which hat he was planning to wear. His dogged reporter hat? His escaped prisoner hat?

"A little of both, I guess, but the only way I can get past the cordon is in pursuit of the story. That's my job."

"Are you going to tell Roberts? Or, better yet, ask permission?"

"There's no time for that, Cynthia. I'll ask for forgiveness when the opportunity presents itself." Billy knew there would be hell to pay with Roberts, but first things first.

* * *

Billy drove past the line of squad cars ranked along the edge of Old Dixie Highway. He parked on the shoulder just south of the dirt road. He grabbed his notepad and pen and headed toward the Vardeman place, or what was left of it. An officer stopped him halfway between his car and the entrance to the dirt road. Billy knew a lot of the policemen, but he'd never seen this guy before. He whipped out his press ID. The officer examined it like he was perusing a rare and delicate manuscript, his finger tracing every detail. He finally handed it back to Billy and sent him up the dirt road.

"Rookies," Billy muttered under his breath as he made his way toward the crowd.

Legions of squad cars, first responders, and fire trucks surrounded the clearing where the house once stood. On the right edge of the clearing sat the Impala, its driver's side scorched from the explosion and fire. The Harley and the Kawasaki lay on the ground between Billy and the car.

A horde of forensic investigators, medical examiner and crew, and law enforcement surrounded the charred rubble and human remains, some of which had been blown fifty yards or more from the house's foundation.

Billy felt compassion for the dead, regardless of their infamy or inevitable lot. A life is a life. As he stood amidst the smoldering ruins, a chilling realization crept over him. He couldn't shake the haunting thought that, if he hadn't escaped, he would have been among the victims.

He walked up to the officer who was standing at the periphery of the crowd. "Any ID on the bodies yet?"

"Not yet," the officer replied.

Billy decided to wander around the property, away from the crowd.

The solitary wooden shed stood defiantly amidst the wreckage like a lone sentinel. Despite the explosion that had leveled the house, it remained remarkably intact, its weathered panels bearing testament to resilience.

Billy approached the shed with no small degree of hesitance. He eased open the door and peered into the partial darkness. He felt along the wall on the door's strike plate side until his hand landed upon a light switch.

A solitary bulb hung by a cord from the ceiling. Upon the flick of the switch, it dimly lit the shed's interior. A bulky oaken chair—it looked almost like an electric chair without the essential paraphernalia—sat in the center of the shed. Next to the chair's front right leg lay a black blindfold and a two-foot length of sisal. A white five-gallon pail sat in the rear corner of the shed. As Billy stood just inside the door, taking it all in, he noticed a long workbench to his right, along the shed's front wall. A bunch of large boxes on the workbench's surface were overturned and in disarray. Spilling from the boxes was ammunition of various kinds and calibers. Small handguns. A few dynamite sticks. Billy's eyes fell on the workbench's lower shelf, upon which was arranged an assortment of weapons. More handguns, semi-automatic rifles, a double-barreled shotgun.

One box remained upright. Billy walked over to it. Inside were three rolls of two-inch grey duct tape and a roll of three-eighth-inch twisted sisal.

Billy headed back to his car to get a small camera from the glove box.

He passed by where Finnegan's Mustang II had been the one time Billy visited of his own accord. He stared into the brush. The car was still there, covered in snow and barely discernible through the tangle. He heard a noise coming from the far side of the car. His first thought was that it was the Vardeman husky. But then he heard a psst and the whisper-quiet utterance of his name.

He approached the Mustang with the same hesitance as he had the shed. "Who is it?" he called out.

He heard a stirring. A figure appeared from the other side of the car through both sets of windows, which were covered with a delicate veil of snow mixed with grime.

It was J.P. Finnegan. His face was cut and bruised. His left eye was swollen. He stepped around the car. He had what looked like a semi-automatic Glock stuffed in his waistband. "Please get me out of here," he muttered.

Billy knew he and Finnegan couldn't just walk down the dirt road, past an army of police officers, and expect to get away with it. He told Finnegan as much.

"Head south down the highway," Finnegan said. "You'll come to another dirt road and a clearing on your left. Go there and wait for me. I'll make my way there through the woods. It shouldn't take me more than twenty minutes, if that."

* * *

"Get down," Billy shouted, just before they drove past the police cars lining the highway.

Finnegan crouched low in the seat. "It's not what you think," he said.

"What do you mean, it's not what I think?"

Finnegan sat back up. "I had to do it. I heard too much, Billy. Knew too much. Those were the evilest of men. And they were just waiting, biding time, knowing complacency had settled in. It wasn't over. Not even close. If I hadn't done what I did, God only knows what would have happened."

Suddenly things were out of kilter. Billy bore down on the gas. He struggled to make sense of it all. "Are the Vardemans all dead?"

"All but the kid."

"What kid?"

"Ewell's kid."

"Ewell had a kid?"

"Yeah. I'm surprised you didn't know. I thought I'd told you."

Finnegan told Billy about being confronted by Ewell when he returned two and a half weeks ago to get the VIN number from the Impala. About being tied up and blindfolded ever since. Interrogated. Beaten. Until he finally broke free.

Finnegan said that, when he'd swung open the shed door in his escape, the kid was just outside on his Schwinn. Finnegan leveled the pistol at the boy and told him to take off down the road. Don't look back if you know what's good for you, Finnegan said. Then he went back inside and grabbed several sticks of long-fuse dynamite and a torch lighter from the bench.

As soon as the boy was well on his way down the dirt road, Finnegan ran past the house, turned around to face it, lit a stick and threw it as hard as he could. Then another. And another. He was, at that moment, grateful for his high school quarterback days.

And that was that.

Chapter Sixty-Eight
Ewell's Boy

Thursday, January 14ᵗʰ, 1982

HE PEDALED LIKE HELL DOWN THE HIGHWAY AMIDST THE SEA OF traffic. Everything was a blur. The ice-cold wind whipped through his hair. His cheeks were numb. The passing trucks, their engines roaring, sent rumblings through the asphalt beneath him. Almost blew him off the road. But he pressed on.

When he had left the house, at gunpoint and terrified, a few minutes ago, he heard the blast behind him before he even made it to the highway. He knew then that it was probably over. After the things they had done to those two men, and to the others, it must have been time.

The others. He wondered how many there had been. He thought back to that little boy, only a couple of years older than him. Why did they have to kill that little boy? Daddy said it was because the boy ran into Uncle Graydon's car with his go-kart, but he knew it was more than that. He knew it was because the boy was black.

Why had Daddy sent him off that time to bike across town and throw the brick through the window where the black man worked? Why did his whole family hate those people so much? What had they ever done to Daddy and the others?

Miss Willkie used to say there were bad people and there were good people in this world. There were bad deeds and there were good deeds. He wanted to be known for doing good deeds.

As he pedaled down the Old Dixie Highway, he thought about those two men who had been tied up, one in the house and one in the shed. He sure hoped they got away okay.

It took him over an hour to make it to the church. He parked his bike in the lot and walked up the front steps. The big wooden doors were locked. He walked back down the steps and around to the side of the building. He tried that door. It was locked, too.

He banged on the door as hard as he could.

An old man with a little bit of a stoop opened the door. "Can I help you, son?"

He told the man he had left home. He had no place to go. He needed help.

The man took him back to his office. Gave him water. "How did you end up here?"

"I came here because my Daddy works here. He's always told me if I got in trouble, you could help me."

"Your daddy works here?"

"Yes, sir. His name is Broadus Ewell McMillan, but he sometimes goes by Vardeman."

CHAPTER SIXTY-NINE

Billy Tarwater

Thursday, January 14ᵗʰ, 1982

BILLY AND FINNEGAN WENT TO THE BELMONT.

As soon as Billy crossed the threshold, Cynthia ran up to him. "Are you okay?"

"I'm okay, but Finnegan here may need some first aid for his cuts and bruises."

Cynthia retreated to the bathroom and returned with first aid cream, Mercurochrome, adhesive bandages. She had Finnegan sit on the sofa. She doctored his face just like Billy remembered his mother doing for Lervene Culpepper, the next-door neighbor, when he was a boy.

"Any word from Gary?" Billy asked Cynthia.

She said he'd had to go to the station house to do some "day job" work. "It seems a rash of car thefts happened last night somewhere near Stewart Avenue. He said he'll report back with any news on the explosion as soon as he can come up for air."

He asked her if she had heard anything from her mother about the investigation next door.

"She said only that the place is still crawling with police, but they're all inside the house."

Cynthia finished doctoring Finnegan and said she'd be in the bedroom working on tomorrow's classes, that the timing was awful, but she couldn't let her students down.

"I don't think that's a good idea," Billy said.

"Preparing for classes?"

"No, *going* to your classes. I know how much you care about your students, but think about your own safety."

"I have to go, Billy. They're already behind."

Billy and Finnegan spent the rest of the day rehashing with each other everything that had happened since back in March of '81 when they'd first met. Finnegan said he was convinced the Vardemans had set their sights on Billy last year because of his efforts to free Sam Jepperson. It was almost more than they could stand to know a black man, sent up for killing those girls, had been set loose. They didn't care a whit about whether he'd really done it. "And then when they found out you were mixed up with me," Finnegan said, "that was the last straw."

"Why were they after Cynthia?" Billy said.

"They weren't, at least not directly. She was an easy target to get to you?"

"And what about the killing of the black kids?"

"We may never know how many they had a part in," Finnegan said. "Maybe every last one, for all I know. Another black man's locked up in the crossbar hotel and on his way to the chair as soon as the trial's over. Seems pretty convenient, don't you think?"

"It is, but if we have evidence that the Vardemans were involved in even one of the murders, you or I will have to have to take it to the authorities."

Finnegan reminded Billy that all the evidence they had was circumstantial or hearsay. "Think about it." And he had beat his head against the wall, too many times and to no avail, trying to get the authorities to act. Furthermore, Williams wasn't even on trial for killing any of the children and probably never would be. "Give it up, Billy. It won't go anywhere."

Billy asked Finnegan how he intended to deal with his complicity in the Vardeman bombing, but Finnegan remained silent.

It was late in the evening before Gary showed back up. "They recovered three bodies. All men. It may be tomorrow before they have IDs on them. Dental records'll help. But I think we already know who they are."

"And Graydon's wife?" Finnegan asked. "Sonya?"

Gary said they hadn't recovered a woman's body, but they were still searching through the ruins. It might take a few days.

* * *

Two days passed before they got word on the bodies.

Graydon Lee Vardeman, forty years old.

Richard Lee "Dickie" Vardeman, thirty-nine.

Broadus Ewell McMillan aka Vardeman, thirty-five.

The body of a husky was found. Police surmised it had suffered from the blast and had run away, getting no farther than the edge of the woods before succumbing to its injuries.

There was no sign of the woman.

* * *

On Sunday, Billy and Cynthia drove to his mother's house to reunite with the children.

The ordeal looked like it might finally be behind them.

Cynthia sighed. "We've earned the right to hope again."

Chapter Seventy

Billy Tarwater

Monday, January 18ᵗʰ, 1982

WHEN BILLY HAD RETURNED TO THE CITY DESK ON FRIDAY, HE took a dressing down from Dedrick Roberts, followed by a perfunctory *I'm glad you're okay*. He left Roberts' office glad it was behind him and with the confidence that he *was* okay.

But it wasn't *really* behind him. He would still have to deal with the prospect of Wayne Williams' near-certain conviction in the court of public opinion for the killing of every last one of the black kids. And there was the issue of Finnegan's complicity in the murder of three people, regardless of how guilty they may have been for their own wrongdoings.

* * *

Now, Monday morning, he found himself back in the courtroom, sitting on the rock-hard press section bench and listening to the droning testimony from an FBI agent. Billy had a difficult time focusing on the task at hand, given everything that had happened away from the courtroom over the past week. But at least he still had a job. And he was free. He'd take rock hard and drone any day.

The agent laid out the discrepancies between the Wayne Williams account of the bridge incident, which Williams had shared in a marathon session at the FBI Atlanta office in June, and what Williams had told two FBI agents when they visited his home the month before.

In the afternoon, a cameraman from WAGA Channel 5 played a 35-minute tape recording of a May news conference at Williams' home, corroborating the inconsistencies set forth by the agent.

Billy glanced over at the defense table. Wayne Williams sat passively, his hands in his lap, his eyes trained on the papers scattered across the table.

Court recessed to wait for the anticipated submission of fiber evidence tomorrow.

* * *

As the trial continued through the week, it was becoming clear to Billy that the determination of the guilt or innocence of Williams in the killing of the two black men would come down to a few strands of fiber. The prosecution claimed these had been found on the bodies of the men and matched a rug in Williams' car and a blanket in his home.

Billy tried to recall another incident where fiber evidence had been the linchpin of a murder case. Where so much rode on notoriously unreliable evidence. But he couldn't.

Aside from a few dog hairs, there wasn't much else. No reliable witnesses. No recovered weapon. No fingerprints.

It was also becoming apparent to Billy that the prosecutors would try to link Williams to the child murders without his ever standing trial for killing even one kid.

* * *

Saturday morning the twenty-third, Billy, Cynthia, and the kids paid a visit to Sam and Ruby Jepperson at their Carver Homes apartment. Rufus and Theda were there. So was Recy. It felt like old times.

Ruby had scared up a bountiful breakfast complete with M&M waffles. She had heard through the grapevine that they were Billy Jr. and Addie's favorite. Everybody dug in.

After breakfast, Billy and Sam stayed behind in the kitchen while the others congregated in the living room. Billy brought Sam up to speed about everything that had happened.

He asked Sam if he had gotten any other threatening notes. "Nary a one," Sam said.

Billy smiled. "I suspect you won't."

Should Billy reveal that Sam's release from prison had set the Vardemans off on a vendetta against him and Cynthia? He didn't have the heart.

* * *

On the drive home, Billy and Cynthia decided to swing by her parents'. The kids hadn't seen them since Christmas. And Cynthia had suggested that, after what had happened a week and a half ago, Adele could use some checking in on. Her insufferability notwithstanding.

Adele met them at the front door with a scowl and her hands firmly planted on her hips. "Well bless your heart. You've brought the whole darned family."

"That's not very nice, Mother."

"Well, I wondered when you'd be back. After all I've been through, I feel like I was put through the wringer washer and left out to dry."

"Would you care to say hi to your grandchildren?"

Adele bent down with a half-smile. She wrapped her ample arms around both kids. "Come on in, you little scamps. Want me to whip you up some beanie weenies and tater tots?"

Cynthia shook her head. "They had a big breakfast, Mother. They don't need anything."

"Well, let me put a blanket on the floor and get the wooden blocks out, then. It'll give 'em something to do."

Adele returned with the blanket and blocks. "You children play quiet, now, so your mama and daddy and I can talk turkey."

"Talk turkey?" Cynthia said.

"It's about Cecil. I can't look after him anymore."

"What do you mean you can't look after him?"

"Just what I said. I can't look after him. The Lord A'mighty didn't put me on this earth to be a keeper of a crazy man. He's got bigger plans for me than that." She looked to the ceiling. "Don't you, Lord?"

"But Mother, you can't just—"

"Don't *but Mother* me. I'm telling you the way it is."

Billy grimaced. Once upon a time, he would have rushed to Cynthia's defense, but he had learned, ever since her it's-a-new-me revelation, not to get in the middle of it. "I'm going outside for some fresh air. Want me to take the kids?"

Billy Jr. and Addie had gotten a routine going. He would stack the blocks as high as he could. She would knock them down. He would let out a little pout. Then they would start the whole thing over again.

"They're having fun," Cynthia said. "Just leave them be."

Billy walked out onto the back stoop. Over in Seymour's yard, the yellow line tape had been removed. The weather was unseasonably warm for a change, pushing into the low fifties. The midday sun peeked through the clouds and cast a warm glow. The snow had melted away. If Billy didn't know better, he could have easily assumed nothing out of the ordinary had ever happened over there, nor would it today.

Billy descended the steps and crossed into Seymour's yard. He peered into the bedroom window. The room was a wreck. He assumed the police had pretty much ransacked the place looking for evidence. He walked around to the back door. He jiggled the knob. He was surprised to find it unlocked. For a moment, he considered going in, but he decided against it. He and Gary had done that once before, only to come upon Seymour's dead body. The police had surely scoured the place; he doubted he would stumble upon anything noteworthy this time.

He walked over to the drum and gazed into its belly. There were several objects in the bottom. The clothes he had seen Broadus aka Ewell toss in were gone. Either they were ashes, or the police had taken what was left of them as evidence. *Probably the latter*, he thought, remembering the mere trickle from the gas can.

The clouds threw down shadows onto the drum, making it difficult for him to make out what was in the bottom. He wrapped his arms around the drum's rim and pulled hard toward him, upending the drum and causing it to tumble to the ground just as he got out of the way. He knelt and looked inside.

He pulled the objects out one-by-one and laid them on the ground before him.

Four empty PBR cans.

A pearl-handled three-inch pocketknife.

A boy's brown leather shoe with SIZE 7J stamped inside.

Three Little Trees air fresheners.

Billy knew what he had to do.

He was about to head back to the house and tell Cynthia what he had found when he noticed something else in the drum. He reached in and pulled out two weathered and blurry black-and-white Polaroids stuck together, singed in the middle and burned around the edges. The top Polaroid was a picture of the lower torso and legs of a nude girl lying face-down in the dirt.

He pulled the bottom Polaroid off, careful not to damage it any more than he had to. He froze. It was a picture of 13-year-old Cynthia. Her eyes were closed. Her mouth was stuffed with a rag.

He examined the first picture more closely. On the back of her thigh, ever so faint, was a ragged P.

Chapter Seventy-One

Sonya Vardeman

Saturday, January 23rd, 1982

SONYA VARDEMAN HAD SPENT NINE DAYS SEARCHING HIGH AND low, calling around, looking for the boy. She knew he had survived the blast because she saw him speeding up the dirt road on his bike just before it happened.

She had barely gotten out herself. She had been standing at the kitchen sink, looking out the back window, when she saw J.P. Finnegan approach the house with the dynamite sticks in his hand. He headed around the house toward the front. Just before she ran out the back door, she called out to Graydon and the others to run like hell. But they ignored her just like always.

She had run around the side of the house opposite where Finnegan had gone. She crouched behind the Impala and peeked around the car. That's when she saw Ewell's boy speeding up the dirt road.

After the explosion, she hightailed it through the woods in the opposite direction from the highway, knowing it was just a matter of time before God-only-knows-who would show up, probably the whole damned county. She wandered through the woods until she came to Jester Creek. She followed the creek north until she reached the first road. She straightened herself up all nonchalant-like and stuck out her thumb. Within five minutes, somebody picked her up and took her into town, where a friend let her sleep on the couch.

She thought about Tarwater and Finnegan and how they both had managed to escape. At first, she wondered how that could be. But the more she thought about it, the more she knew how. It had to have been the boy. He'd always been a caring kid. Unlike his daddy. Unlike his uncles. Maybe more like his mama before she ran off with that hippie band, or whatever the hell she did.

At least Roscoe hadn't gotten away. She wondered whether anybody would ever dig him up.

Saturday afternoon, she was about to give up on finding the boy when she thought of the church where Ewell worked. She took the Soldier's Home bus from downtown and got off at the corner of Confederate and Woodland. As she approached the church, a man came out of the side door and headed to a car. She approached him. "Are you the preacher?"

"I am. Reverend Thomas. And you are?"

"I'm Ewell Vardeman's sister-in-law."

"You mean Broadus McMillan's."

She nodded. "I'm looking for his boy." She extended her arm out, palm down. "About this high. I think he's twelve. Goes by Brody. He's missing. I'm worried sick."

The reverend looked down at his feet, then back at Sonya. "I'm sorry, miss. But nobody like that's come around here."

Chapter Seventy-Two
Brody McMillan

Saturday, January 23rd, 1982

BRODY MCMILLAN GRASPED THE EDGE OF THE CURTAIN AND pulled it back just enough to create a sliver of an opening. He squinted through the blinding afternoon sun and peered out onto the church parking lot. He saw the reverend go out the side door and head to his car. The reverend had said, *I'll be back. What flavor do you like?* Brody said chocolate.

He remembered his daddy once saying *the reverend's a good man*, as if Ewell would know a good man when he saw one. But he must have been right. After all, the reverend had taken Brody in. Fed him. Bought him some new dungarees and a flannel shirt from Sears Roebuck. Gave him a place to sleep in the basement of the parsonage. Let him do some of the chores Ewell used to do. And now even went off to buy him ice cream.

The reverend was about to get into his car when Sonya came running up and started talking to him. She was all agitated like she got sometimes. Brody couldn't make out what they were saying, but he was sure she was looking for him.

The reverend shook his head.

Sonya started walking slowly toward the street.

Just as Brody was closing the sliver in the curtain, the reverend came back in. "Did you see that woman?" he asked.

Brody nodded.

"Do you know her?"

"She married my uncle. Half-uncle anyway. I think that's what you'd call him."

"Well, she's trying to find you. Do you *want* her to find you?"

"No way. She's as bad as the others."

"I told her I hadn't seen you. I think she believed me because she up and left." The reverend turned to leave.

Brody hadn't roamed around all by himself in the church before. He hadn't even *been* in a church 'til last Thursday, at least as far as he could remember. The building was cold, dark, and musty. Everything seemed so strange to him. He wondered if all churches were that way. He shambled up the hall, feeling a mix of dread and wonder, toward the sanctuary. That's what the reverend called it, anyway.

He eased into the front row and gazed up at the awesome cross on the wall. Jesus was nailed to it, his head slumped, his arms outstretched, his legs bent slightly at his knees. The sun shined through the stained glass windows onto Jesus' face, making it look like he was lit up or something.

The closest thing he'd ever seen to anything like that cross was the one that hung on the wall in the old living room. And maybe the tattoos on Ewell's and his uncles' arms. If that stuff was so important that they hung it on the wall and stuck it on their arms, why did they never go to church? Never took him to church. Never talked about it.

Six days ago, Brody had sat in that very same spot and listened while the reverend preached about sin and salvation. About damnation and mercy. It didn't make a lot of sense to him, except it reminded him of what Miss Willkie had said about bad people and good people. About bad deeds and good deeds. Except she was sort of quiet when she said it. The reverend yelled a lot.

Brody had almost drifted off when he heard a noise coming from somewhere in the back of the sanctuary. He thought it must be the reverend. Then he heard her call his name. It was Sonya. The hairs on his arms stood up straight.

He sank down in the pew. He raised his head just high enough so he could see over the back, but she wasn't there. She must have been in that little room between the front door and the sanctuary. The reverend called it a vestibule.

He slithered to the altar and crouched behind the pulpit, curling up into a little ball like a roly-poly. He listened as her footsteps grew closer. Louder and louder. Then they began to fade until he couldn't hear them anymore. He stood up slowly and looked around. She wasn't there. But she was still in the church—he was sure of that.

He opened the door that led up the stairs to the big old tank of water. The first thing the reverend had done when Brody showed up at the church last Thursday was take him up there and show him the tank. *Have you been immersed in the name of Christ?* the reverend had asked. Brody said he didn't know what that meant. Even after the reverend explained it, he still didn't get it.

Brody thought about the carnival that came to town once a year. And the Dunk Buffo tank. For seventy-five cents, you got three balls and the chance to hit the target and plunge the clown into the water. The crowd would cheer and whoop and holler. And you got to go home and tell your friends all about it.

This past Sunday, he had sat in the pew and watched as a boy and a girl, both about his age, got dunked. It didn't look nearly as fun as Buffo the Clown. He figured that, if the reverend had *his* way, he'd be next.

He decided to wait in the tank room until it was safe to come out. Surely, the reverend would be back soon and save him from Sonya.

After a while, when the reverend hadn't shown up and everything had gone quiet, he crept down the stairs, across the altar, and down the hall. That's when he heard her calling his name again, this time from what the reverend called the fellowship hall. He grabbed his overcoat from the hook by the side door and ran outside. The reverend's car wasn't there.

He took off running up the street. He didn't know where he was headed or where he'd end up. But anywhere would be better than going back to *her*. Even if he had to sleep in an alley or somewhere.

It was cold, but a whole lot warmer than the day he'd run away from home. He was glad of that. At least he wouldn't freeze to death.

He hoofed it up Confederate Avenue. At the corner of Moreland, he gazed up at the larger-than-life ice cream cone on the sign above the Zesto hamburger joint. His mouth watered. He cupped his hands against the plate glass window. His breath fogged the glass. He wiped the condensation away with his palm and stared inside, hoping that maybe, just maybe, the reverend had come here to buy the ice cream. But no luck.

Brody felt bad leaving the reverend behind. He was sure the reverend would be worried sick when he got back with the ice cream and nobody was there. For a second, he thought about going back to the church, but he knew he couldn't. Not with Sonya snooping around.

He went behind the store, past the dumpster where he wouldn't be seen from the street. He sank onto the pavement and sat with his back against the building. He needed some time to figure out what to do next. Where to go.

Brody was five when his mama ran off and never came back. He didn't remember her much. After all, he was just a little kid. Everybody said she was no good for leaving him and his daddy like that. But Brody got it. He would have left, too, knowing what he knew now.

Sonya thought she could take Mama's place. No way. He remembered the time he bit down on Sonya's finger so hard he drew blood. She slapped him across the face with the back of her hand. Even though the slap hurt like hell, Brody came out ahead that day. He taught Sonya a lesson. She learned she'd never take Mama's place, and she shouldn't even try.

Sometimes Graydon and the others, Sonya included, would get together in the living room and talk all serious-like about what they were going to do to the blacks when they had the chance. Sometimes, other people would come over for meetings. Lots of people. Brody would help Sonya put the folding chairs out, and the men would all sit around and talk about bad things. Ewell always made Brody go into the other part of the house when they were meeting, but more often than not, he'd sneak into the kitchen and listen from behind the door. One time, Sonya came into the kitchen and found him hunched down on the floor just inside the door. She said, *Better keep your little mouth shut if you know what's good for you.* She also threatened to tell Ewell if she caught him listening in again. Ewell never found out, at least as far as he knew. And Brody learned to be more careful. But he didn't have to listen in much to know those bad things were happening.

He thought back again to the time he threw that brick through the store window. That man hadn't done a thing to hurt Graydon. Or Dickie. Or Brody's daddy Ewell. Not a thing.

And that little Geter boy. Graydon had come back from *settling up scores* with somebody on the west side of town. Brody didn't know just what settling up scores meant, but Dickie and Ewell did. Graydon bragged then about how he was going to kill Lubie Geter. Called him a name Brody couldn't bring himself to say, not then and not now. Sometime after that—Brody couldn't remember how long—the kid went missing. Then they found his dead body. What had Lubie Geter ever done to Graydon except accidently hit the car with his go-kart? Nothing except being the wrong color.

Brody thought about how, when it comes to the family you're born into, you don't have any say in the matter. He could just as easily have been born into a family of good people. But he wasn't. Lubie Geter could have been born into a family that Graydon and the others didn't hate. But he wasn't. If God was all about looking after everybody, like the reverend said, he sure didn't seem to be doing a very good job.

* * *

Brody woke with a crick in his neck. He was still slumped against the rear wall of the building. He rubbed his eyes with his knuckles. It was pitch black out. There was a chill in the air. *What time is it?*

He rounded the corner of the building. The parking lot was empty. The store was dark inside. He pressed his face against the window and strained to read the wall clock across the room. He thought it said 3:15.

He saw headlights approaching. A policeman drove by. Brody crouched down until the patrol car passed. He ran back to the rear of the building beyond the dumpster, where he would wait until the sun came up.

He dozed off again.

CHAPTER SEVENTY-THREE
Billy Tarwater

Monday, January 25ᵗʰ, 1982

MONDAY MORNING, BILLY ARRIVED AT THE OFFICE BEFORE sunup. He had planned to get a leg up on the day before heading to the courthouse.

Even this early in the morning, the City Desk was a cacophony. Telephones ringing. Keyboards clacking. Journalists shuffling papers and scurrying about.

The adrenalin in the air. The surging electricity. The excitement of the next big scoop. These were the things that drew Billy to the paper business in the first place. And it never got old.

There was a lot of breaking local news today. The Majik Market convenience store magnate's son had been charged with hiring an undercover FBI agent to knock off his ex. The fate of a thousand Cuban refugees, fingered as criminals and being held in the Federal Pen just a stone's throw across town, hung in the balance. The state attorney general was on a crusade to enforce the death penalty, which hadn't been carried out in Georgia since '64. One of the people sitting on death row was Andrew Legare, who had killed a man when he was seventeen. His case had just been sent back to the state by the Supreme Court in light of last week's ruling on capital punishment for minors. Then there was the legal secretary who had been charged with murdering a Cobb County lawyer. The man's bullet-riddled body was found on the floor in her house. They had once been lovers.

And, of course, there was the Wayne Williams trial. After a week of perfunctory technicalities and plodding testimony from expert witnesses, today's proceedings promised to be gripping. The Fulton County medical examiner was expected to present evidence about the deaths of ten other victims, all black children. Nine of them had died of asphyxiation, just like the two men Wayne Williams was on trial for killing. The prosecution intended to implicate Williams in the child murders, even though he wasn't being tried for them.

Billy had gotten wind that Lubie Geter was one of the child victims to be showcased. This was one day Billy didn't want to miss.

He was about to walk out the door and head to the courthouse when the phone on his desk rang. It was the receptionist. "There's someone here to see you," she said, with a healthy dose of hesitancy.

"To see *me*? Who is it?"

She said it was a little boy. He wouldn't say who he was. Just that he had come to see a man named Tarwater. "Be prepared for a shock," she whispered into the phone. "The kid's a wreck."

The elevator doors opened.

The boy, maybe ten, eleven, was sitting on the banquette across the room. His unkempt hair was a tangled mess of dirty red locks that hung limply around his face. His red flannel shirt was rumpled. A fresh rip and what looked like mud stains adorned the right knee of his dungarees. A bunched-up overcoat lay beside him.

He was fidgeting with his hands. His eyes, red-rimmed and weary, flitted around the room. Their dark circles betrayed a lack of restful sleep.

When he saw Billy, he jumped up, grabbed his coat, and approached. He fixed Billy with anxious, imploring eyes.

"May I help you?" Billy said.

Before the boy could respond, Billy flashed back to two weeks ago yesterday when, posing as *Mitchell Goodenough, Summerwood Real Estate*, he had visited the Vardeman place. A young boy in dungarees and sock cap had come running out of the house behind Dickie Vardeman.

Was that the same boy who now stood before him?

Then Billy remembered the conversation with J.P. Finnegan as they barreled down Old Dixie Highway in the aftermath of the explosion.

Are the Vardemans all dead?

All but the kid.

What kid?

Ewell's kid. I'm surprised you didn't know he had a kid. I thought I'd told you.

"You're Ewell's son, aren't you?"

The boy nodded. "Is there a bathroom somewhere I could use?"

Billy ushered the boy to the restroom just off the lobby.

When the boy came out, they took the elevator to the third floor. Billy knew better than to make their presence known to the gaggle of City Desk reporters. He secreted the boy in the small room, just past the elevator bank, reserved for one-on-one meetings.

The boy said his name was Brody, he was eleven, and yes, he was Ewell's son. He had run away a week and a half ago when the explosion happened. The preacher took him in. He'd seen on the preacher's television that his father and uncles got killed. But not Sonya, no. She was still alive. When he learned she had come to the church looking for him—and had even gotten inside—he knew he had to find somebody who would protect him. Somebody who would maybe understand.

"I remembered your name," Brody said. "And that you worked for the paper. Daddy and the others hated you, you know."

Billy looked down at the dungaree rip. At the mud stains. At the blood-smeared abrasion peeking through the tear in the fabric. "Does that hurt? We need to do something about it." He looked back up at Brody's tangled mop and dirt-smudged face. "We'll get you cleaned up. And I bet you're starving, aren't you?"

Billy drove the boy to The Belmont after telling Dedrick Roberts that something unexpected had come up and he had to go home right away. Roberts had demurred. *What about the trial?* Billy knew he might be out of a job come sundown, but he had to do the right thing.

Billy opened the door to a dark apartment. Cynthia was at Agnes Scott. The kids were at daycare.

"Why don't you shower first?" He grabbed one of Cynthia's terry robes from the hook on the bathroom door. "You can wear this while I wash your clothes. I know it's big, but it's the closest I've got to your size." He opened the medicine cabinet. He took out a bottle of hydrogen peroxide, a tube of antiseptic cream, and an adhesive bandage, and set them on the counter. "Then we can treat that abrasion."

"Can I do it myself?" Brody said.

"Of course."

While Brody was showering and his clothes were in the wash, Billy cooked up a breakfast that would make Ruby Jepperson proud.

Brody appeared in the doorway swallowed by the folds of Cynthia's bathrobe, its sleeves hanging past his fingers, the hem pooling at his feet.

Billy watched as Brody scarfed down the food to the last morsel without uttering a word. He wondered why the boy had sought *him* out. Was it really for protection? After all, why would Billy, of all people, protect the son of one of the men who had set out to do him in? Or was it more than that? Had something else drawn Brody to the newspaper office?

When Brody had finished breakfast, Billy handed him his clothes, fresh out of the dryer. "Sorry I can't mend the rip, kid. Cynthia could if she was here. She's better at that kind of thing than I am."

Brody frowned. "Cynthia?"

"My wife. That's her robe you're wearing."

Brody ran his hand across the terrycloth folds. "Please thank her for me."

"I will. But you'll have a chance to meet her, I suppose."

After getting dressed, Brody sank into the overstuffed chair beside the window. Cynthia's chair. He fixed his eyes on the hole in his overalls. He wrung his hands. "They would have killed you," he said with a tremble. "Just like that Hester man. If it hadn't been for…" A tear dribbled down his cheek.

"Just like that Hester man?"

"I think his name was Roscoe. I didn't know him, really. He was mainly friends with Uncle Graydon."

A shiver climbed from Billy's heels to his scalp. "They killed him?"

Brody looked up and fixed across the room. "Uh huh."

Billy placed his hand on Brody's shoulder. "I'm sorry, kid."

The boy fell into himself, sobbing.

Billy knelt and held Brody's hands. "I know it's hard, what you've been through."

When Brody had regained his composure, Billy said, "You were about to say something earlier. You said if it hadn't been for…"

Brody locked eyes with Billy. "If it hadn't been for me."

"You're the one who left my wrists unbound, aren't you?"

The boy nodded and looked back down at the tear in his denim.

"And that other man," Billy said, "Finnegan?"

Brody nodded again.

Billy's heart swelled. He thought back to his own eleven-year-old self. Binky had gone through a lot that year, with what happened to Cynthia and the other girls, and Sam. But it all seemed to pale against what the kid who sat before him had experienced, and done, at such a young age.

For the next two hours, they talked.

About what it was like for Brody to grow up in a family of haters. And how hard it is sometimes to accept the one you're born into.

About hiding at the kitchen door, listening in as his father and uncles plotted their awful plans with those other men.

And the brick through the window.

And Lubie Geter. Was he the first? Brody didn't know for sure.

About Sonya. And the preacher.

About Miss Willkie.

About good people. And bad people.

About deeds. Good and bad.

Chapter Seventy-Four

Brody McMillan

Monday, January 25ᵗʰ, 1982

BRODY PLOPPED INTO THE BIG, SNUG CHAIR. MR. TARWATER said it was the one his wife always sat in. The soft cushion wrapped around him like a cocoon. Made him feel safe for the first time in a long time. Maybe ever.

Mr. Tarwater said, "Please call me Billy." But Brody couldn't bring himself to do that. It felt wrong.

Just like it felt wrong to cry. But when Brody told Mr. Tarwater about that Hester man being killed, and then when Mr. Tarwater put his hand on his shoulder, Brody couldn't hold it in anymore.

Daddy and the others had always told Brody never to cry. *Real boys don't cry*, they said. *Sissy boys cry*. Sometimes, Brody would cry in bed at night, but he knew if Daddy ever caught him, he would whup the daylights out of him just to teach him a lesson. Brody made sure Daddy never did.

When Brody told Mr. Tarwater about saving his life, he thought he may have seen a little tear in the corner of Mr. Tarwater's eye. But maybe not. Maybe it was just a speck or something.

Mr. Tarwater seemed like a really good man. Like he really cared. Brody was so glad he'd left the rope loose that day. But he knew if Daddy and the others had found out about *that*, he might have gotten more than just a whuppin'.

Anyway, Mr. Tarwater wanted to know what it was like growing up in that house, hiding behind the door and listening in when those other men came over.

Brody told him all about it. And he talked about how he had taken off from home on his bike, pedaling as fast as he could, after he'd freed Mr. Finnegan. He just knew Mr. Finnegan had shooed him off to make sure he got away before the explosion happened. To protect him. He told Mr. Tarwater about showing up at the church and about how the reverend took him in. But then Sonya showed up, and he knew he had to leave.

"Where's your bike now?" Mr. Tarwater asked.

"At the reverend's house. We took it there in the back of his car. It's in the basement. That's where the reverend let me sleep."

When Brody said that, Mr. Tarwater did a little shiver like he was cold or something. But the apartment was really toasty, unlike the church. Or the reverend's basement.

Mr. Tarwater was the one who first brought up Lubie Geter's name. He said he'd been doing a lot of research for the paper about all those black boys that had gone missing. But he seemed most interested in the Geter boy.

Brody told Mr. Tarwater about Graydon coming home one day saying he was going to kill that boy. About Brody finding out the boy had died. And he just knew, then and there, that Graydon did it.

Mr. Tarwater asked about the other boys. Did Brody know whether his daddy and uncles had killed any of *them*? Brody said he didn't know for sure, but based on what he'd heard the men talk about when they had their meetings in the living room, he didn't doubt they'd killed a bunch. Mr. Tarwater asked if Brody would be willing to go into the newspaper office and go through the files he had on the boys. Just see if maybe Brody might remember something.

"Do I have to look at dead bodies? 'Cause if I have to look at dead bodies, I'd rather not do it, if it's all the same."

"I'll make sure you don't have to," Mr. Tarwater said.

After a little while, a woman—Brody assumed it was Mrs. Tarwater—arrived with two children. She looked confused when she walked in and saw Brody. He jumped up and apologized for sitting in her chair.

"No, no. That's okay," she said. "And to whom do I owe the pleasure?"

Brody thought she talked funny, but he assumed she wanted to know who he was. Before he could answer, Mr. Tarwater spoke up. "This is Brody McMillan," he said. "And Brody, this is my wife Cynthia. And Billy Jr. and Addie." He told the children to go to the other room and play, then he told Mrs. Tarwater all about Brody and how he had ended up in their apartment, even ended up wearing her bathrobe and sitting where she always sat.

Later that evening, Mrs. Tarwater ordered a big pizza with everything on it, even things Brody had never eaten before, like black olives and goat cheese. It was so good, Brody thought maybe he'd died and gone to heaven.

After dinner, Mrs. Tarwater put sheets and a blanket on the sofa and said he could sleep there. She even brought him one of her old tee shirts and a pair of her pajama pants with a draw string. The shirt was way too big, and Mrs. Tarwater had to pin up the pants legs. But that was okay. He was grateful for something to sleep in besides his street clothes. She even said she would sew up the rip in his dungarees before morning. She was so nice. Unlike Sonya.

After everybody had gone to bed, Brody lay on the sofa, wide awake, thinking about everything that had happened the past week, wondering how he'd get by with his whole family except Sonya dead and with no place to go. No money. No nothing. He'd heard his daddy sometimes talk about the poorhouse. Is that where he'd end up? Or maybe at some orphans' home somewhere? Or sent away to live with his aunt back in Arkansas, the one Graydon used to call Crazy Myrtle? Maybe he could find Miss Willkie. Maybe she'd take him in.

Then he thought about all those poor black kids. He was lucky to even be able to worry about where he'd end up, given where *they* ended up. He wondered how many his daddy and uncles killed. All of them? Or just some of them?

It didn't matter. One was too many.

* * *

The next morning, Brody awoke to the best smells ever. Coming from the kitchen. He folded the sheets and blanket and moused to the bathroom.

In the bathroom, he found his dungarees and flannel shirt neatly folded on the little table between the washstand and the bathtub. He unfolded the shirt and held it out with both hands. All the wrinkles were gone. He brought it up to his nose and breathed in. It smelled the way he imagined fresh flowers straight from a garden would smell. And the rip in his dungarees had been fixed. They were just like new. He dressed, folded Mrs. Tarwater's tee shirt and pajama pants, and placed them on the little table just like she did his clothes.

Brody sat across from the kids. Billy Jr. sat at the table. Addie was in a high chair. Mrs. Tarwater was putting food on the table. Bacon. Eggs. Grits.

But Mr. Tarwater wasn't there. Brody heard him in the other room. Talking harsh-like to somebody on the phone. But Brody couldn't make out what he was saying.

Mrs. Tarwater sat a platter full of waffles on the table and took the seat at one end.

Billy Jr. got a big grin. "M&M waffles! Is it Christmas again? Already?"

"No, Billy, it's not Christmas," Mrs. Tarwater said. She looked over at Brody. "But special guests deserve as much."

"The only time I ever had 'em when it wasn't Christmas," Billy Jr. said, "was when we went to visit that black family."

Mrs. Tarwater looked over at Brody, then at Billy Jr. "That *black family*, Billy, are the Jeppersons. Your daddy and Mr. Jepperson go way back."

As soon as Brody heard the name Jepperson, he knew he'd heard it before. He searched his memory, but it didn't come to him.

Mr. Tarwater came into the room and sat down at the end of the table across from his wife. But he didn't eat. He seemed upset about something.

After everybody had finished eating, and Mrs. Tarwater was helping the kids from the table, Mr. Tarwater looked over at Brody. "I have to go into the office this morning. I want you to go with me."

* * *

Brody was nervous on the way to Mr. Tarwater's office. Maybe not as nervous as yesterday. But nervous enough that he had a hard time not shaking a little. Sure, he was worried a little about seeing the files for those little black boys. But that wasn't why he was nervous this time. He had a question for Mr. Tarwater. "Who is Mr. Jepperson? Mrs. Tarwater said y'all go way back."

"We do, Brody. We go back ten years or more. All the way back to when I was younger than you are now."

Brody thought about that. He'd never had a black friend.

"He got in some big trouble," Mr. Tarwater continued, "and I helped him out."

When they stopped at a red light, Mr. Tarwater looked over at Brody. "You've crossed paths with him, too, in a way, but you don't know it."

"I have?"

Mr. Tarwater nodded and continued through the intersection. "Yesterday, you told me about throwing the brick through the window?"

"I did."

Mr. Tarwater kept looking straight ahead. "That brick was intended for Sam Jepperson."

CHAPTER SEVENTY-FIVE

Billy Tarwater

Tuesday, January 26th, 1982

BRODY GRIPPED BILLY'S HAND TIGHT AS THEY CROSSED THE room of reporters on their way to Dedrick Roberts' office. Every City Desk eye was trained on the boy.

Billy could feel Brody's anxiety, undoubtedly borne of fear. Fear from being in a strange and unfamiliar place, full of loud noises and watchful men. Fear of authority and the prospect of meeting Billy's boss. Fear of having to look at the pictures of the boys and confronting the reality of their deaths. And all of this in the wake of the deaths of his own family members.

Billy would see to it that Brody was shielded from any crime scene eight-by-tens. Looking at the innocent, unharmed faces of kids near Brody's own age, and knowing they were gone, would surely be bad enough. But Billy wanted to find out which of the children might have fallen at the hands of the Vardemans. And he needed Brody's help. He would do whatever he could to protect the boy in the process.

Roberts winced when he saw the boy walk into his office, then he looked at Billy through close-knit brows. "Who is this?"

"This is the kid I told you about on the phone this morning," Billy said. "The Vardeman boy. Actually, McMillan. Brody McMillan."

Brody's hands fidgeted. His gaze, fixed on the floor at first, slowly lifted to meet Roberts' eyes. Brody nodded ever so slightly.

"What's he doing here?" Roberts said.

"I brought him in to look at the files on the children."

Roberts rose from behind his desk. "Billy, can we have a moment alone?"

Billy ushered Brody back out into the main room. "Sit here," he said. "This is my desk. I have to go talk to Mr. Roberts in private. I'll be back soon." Before Billy turned to walk away, he noticed Brody staring at the Upson-board-mounted map, with its array of red and green pins, some with little paper pennants attached. Billy sensed that Brody knew, in an instant, what those pins represented.

Billy reentered Roberts' office and shut the door behind him.

"Have a seat," Roberts said.

"If it's okay with you, I'd rather stand."

"Suit yourself." Roberts rose and leaned in with his hands splayed on the desktop. "You're a slow learner. Aren't you, Tarwater? I told you a long time ago to leave that shit alone. They caught Williams. He's going up for life...or worse. He killed those children. Mark my word on that. And anyway, the Vardemans are dead. Give it up."

"But what if I have it on good authority that the Vardemans killed at least one of the black boys?"

"Whose authority? That of an unreliable gamin. From the same disreputable family he's accusing, no less. Are you kidding me?"

"It's not just the boy's word I'm going on. I have another source."

"The informer?"

Billy frowned. "What informer?"

"You know exactly what informer I'm talking about. J.P. Finnegan."

This was the first time Billy had heard Roberts utter Finnegan's name. "So, you know about him."

"I know about him, Tarwater. I know more than you *think* I know."

"One thing you may *not* know is that Finnegan came within a razor's edge of sacrificing his life to get to the bottom of the plot to kill black kids. So did I, by the way. Anyway, perhaps that's neither here nor there. But if you know about Finnegan, surely you know about the Vardemans' plans."

"The authorities don't want to dredge any of that shit up. Especially not now. *I* surely don't want to. And if you know what's good for you, you won't either."

"I get that, but let's just say, hypothetically if you wish, that Wayne Williams didn't kill *all* those kids. Let's say the Vardemans killed one, probably more. Don't you think we owe it to those kids' families to seek the truth? Doesn't justice deserve as much?"

Roberts sat back down. "Tell me something, Tarwater, let's say you *could* implicate the Vardemans. Incontrovertibly. What would you do, then? Take it to the authorities and let *them* deal with it from that point on? Mount a campaign to get one of the big wheels upstairs to splash it all over the front page of the paper? Try to get evidence thrown out of the Williams trial? Good luck with that."

Billy thought back to what Finnegan had said last year when they first met. *What I'm about to tell you, you have to promise you'll do something with it. Otherwise, I'm wasting my time. And yours.* And the commitment Billy had made to Finnegan. *If there's something there to run with, I'll run with it.*

Billy locked eyes with his boss. "I'd bring it to you first, but only if you'll commit to doing something with it. Not just letting it die."

"Do whatever you have to do with the kid, Tarwater. But get on with it. You need to get your keister in the courtroom bright and early tomorrow morning. The trial's going on, in case you forgot, and your stand-in needs to get back in here to write obituaries." Roberts smirked.

Billy was about to leave Roberts' office when he thought of something else Finnegan had said. *If word gets out that I'm the one blowing the whistle, they'll be all over me like white on rice. I'll be in big trouble.* He turned to face Roberts. "One other thing. Finnegan's a good man. And he's a reliable source. A source worth protecting. If it gets back to the authorities that he's been talking to me for almost a year, I'm worried for his safety."

"That train's left the station, Tarwater. But what do you mean anyway, his *safety*? Who do you think would do him harm? The Vardemans are dead."

"I don't know. I'm just worried."

Billy returned to his desk and grabbed the banker's box full of murder files. He said, "Come on," and headed to the one-on-one meeting room with Brody trailing behind him.

Brody settled in at the conference table.

Billy brought him a Coke and a pack of cheese crackers and sat across from him. "I appreciate that what you're about to do is hard," Billy said. "If you want to stop at any time and take a break, let me know."

Brody nodded.

Billy steeled himself. "You said you didn't know for sure whether your daddy and uncles had killed any of the boys, other than Lubie Geter, but based on what you heard them and the other men talk about, it was likely they did. Did I get that right?"

Brody nodded again.

"As we go through the names of the children," Billy continued, "I want you to think back and try hard to remember what you might have heard. A name. A description. Anything."

Brody took a swig of Coke. He opened the pack of crackers and popped one into his mouth.

For the next hour, Billy shared with Brody the names of the victims, their backgrounds, the whys and wherefores of their deaths—sparing Brody the nonessentials—and their pre-kidnapping headshots.

Brody took a deep breath when he heard Aaron Wyche's name. "I bet they killed him," he said.

"Why do you think that?"

"I heard 'em say his name a coupla times. Daddy and the others talked a lot about planning to strangle black boys and just leave their bodies wherever somebody could find 'em, like on the side of the road or something."

"Did you hear them say that specifically about Aaron Wyche?"

"No. They just said it like it was something they wanted to do."

Billy asked Brody how Aaron Wyche's name had even come up.

Brody waited a couple of minutes, as if in deep thought, before speaking. "Uncle Graydon said he knew him from somewhere. I don't know where. Maybe from Lubie Geter. Maybe my uncle got friendly with him somehow so the kid wouldn't be scared before he was done in."

Brody recognized two other names, nine-year-old Aaron Jackson and thirteen-year-old Curtis Walker, but he couldn't remember any details. Just that their names had come up in the men's conversations.

"And you don't recognize any of the others?" Billy said.

Brody shook his head. "No, but that doesn't mean my daddy and uncles didn't kill *them, too*."

When they had finished going through the files, Brody brought up Sam Jepperson again. "Mr. Tarwater, on the car ride over, you said that brick I flung through the window was for that black man."

"That's right. He was upset and scared at the same time. He's a good man, that Sam Jepperson. He didn't deserve what happened."

Brody sat with his hands in his lap and his head hung low.

"But then again," Billy continued, "you didn't know what you were doing. You were just following orders."

Brody looked up with mournful eyes. "Do you think, if I told him I was sorry, he would forgive me?"

CHAPTER SEVENTY-SIX

Cynthia Tarwater

Tuesday, January 26ᵗʰ, 1982

CYNTHIA WAS CLEANING UP IN THE KITCHEN WHEN THE CBS
Evening News with Dan Rather came on in the living room. She
continued with her work, paying sporadic attention to the news
coverage. President Reagan's anticipated State of the Union address.
Two World Airways passengers believed dead in the recent Boston
Harbor crash. An accident at the Ginna nuclear power plant in
New York. Surprise testimony in the Wayne Williams trial.

She stopped what she was doing and ran into the living room.
Dan Rather was reporting that two surprise witnesses, one a
teenager and the other a middle-aged woman, had allegedly linked
Wayne Williams to the murder of Lubie Geter.

The teenager claimed he had seen Williams with Geter the day
Geter disappeared from the Stewart-Lakewood Shopping Center.
He also said Williams had given him $2 in late 1980 after fondling

him, then drove him to a wooded area, where he ran away when Williams went to get something out of the trunk of his car. But the boy's testimony was suspect. He couldn't seem to get his story straight. At times he claimed two black men, not one, had taken him to the wooded area. And he claimed to have been at work on another occasion, but his boss had said he wasn't.

The middle-aged woman said she *believed* she had seen Williams with Geter at the shopping center, but her recall was suspect, given that she couldn't provide any detail.

When the Cadillac commercial came on, Cynthia returned to the kitchen.

At 6:35, she heard the front door open. She greeted Billy and Brody at the door. "It's late," she said. "Dinner's waiting on the table, but you may need to heat it up. Where have you two been?"

Brody beamed.

"I'm so sorry I didn't call," Billy said. "We visited Sam and Ruby."

"Sam and Ruby?"

"Brody wanted to meet Sam face-to-face. To apologize for what happened."

"How did *that* go?"

"It went great," Brody chimed in. "Mr. Jepperson is such a nice man. He even hugged me and told me he forgave me."

Cynthia's heart warmed. "I'm so happy for you, Brody.

Billy looked around. "Where are the kids?"

"They're in the bedroom playing before tuck-in time. Brody, why don't you go wash up before dinner?"

Brody scampered to the bathroom.

As soon as Brody was out of earshot, Cynthia said to Billy, "Have you heard the news about the testimony today?"

Cynthia told Billy about the surprise witnesses.

Billy scratched his head. "Maybe I'm chasing a wild goose. Maybe the Vardemans didn't have anything to do with Lubie Geter's death after all. It's hard to know who to believe. It's just a big mare's nest."

"From what I heard on TV, it seems like the witnesses are not the most reliable," Cynthia said. "And it's all circumstantial, anyway."

"Yes, but the only thing I have on the Vardemans is circumstantial, too. Just because they said they wanted to kill the boy doesn't mean they did it. I think I'll call Finnegan and see if he can meet after work tomorrow. I want to get his take on all of this."

Cynthia went to tuck in the kids.

When she returned, Brody and Billy were chowing down.

She asked Brody about school. "How many days have you missed now?"

"Two weeks, I think. Miss Willkie must be worried sick about me."

"Do you want to go tomorrow?" Cynthia said. "I can drop you off in the morning on my way to work and pick you up afterwards."

The anguish in Brody's eyes spoke volumes. "Do I have to? It's not that I don't want to go to school, ma'am, but I'm scared."

"Scared of what?" Cynthia said.

Brody looked at Billy. "Does Mrs. Tarwater know about Sonya?"

After Brody had fallen asleep on the sofa, Cynthia and Billy retired to the bedroom for the evening.

"Sonya sounds like a piece of work," Cynthia said.

"How could she *not* be," Billy said, "given the family she married into."

"Do you think Brody's fears are warranted?"

"It's hard to say. It's obvious the kid's been traumatized. He was scared enough to run away from the church and sleep on the street somewhere. Would she physically harm him? I don't know. But it's a chance not worth taking."

They both agreed that Brody should be kept out of school a little longer. Just in case Sonya were to come looking for him. But where would he go during the day? Cynthia had classes in the morning. And Billy's job hinged on his showing up at the courthouse. They couldn't leave him home alone.

"I'll call my mom," Billy said. "Maybe he can stay there during the day."

"Or maybe he can stay with *my* mom." Cynthia laughed. "Maybe she can finish what the reverend started. Hell, Brody might come back another Marjoe Gortner."

"That's a good one, Cynthia, but I think we'd better stick with *my* mother."

Billy picked up the phone and called his mom.

He covered the mouthpiece with his hand. "She's available all day," he said to Cynthia. "Can you drop him off on your way to Agnes Scott?"

* * *

Early Wednesday morning, as Cynthia cleared the breakfast table, and Brody got ready to go to Billy's mother's house—*you can call her Miss Alice*, Cynthia had said, *she'll love that*—Billy dialed Finnegan at home.

There was no answer.

CHAPTER SEVENTY-SEVEN

Billy Tarwater

Wednesday, January 27ᵗʰ, 1982

BILLY LISTENED AS THREE WITNESSES CLAIMED TO CONNECT Wayne Williams to Yusef Bell. One witness testified he saw Bell get into Williams' car near an elementary school in West End. But he couldn't remember the date. Williams' defense attorney accused the witness of rehearsing his testimony ahead of time with three detectives. The witness said the detectives "just refreshed my memory of what I seen."

One of Williams' associates, a local songwriter, testified that, when the subject of the slain kids had come up, Williams said, "They ought to keep their damn asses at home."

All circumstantial, granted, but Billy began to doubt his own conviction that the Vardemans had been behind a master plan to kill black children. Then again, look at all the evidence Finnegan had collected—and the accounts Brody had shared. They pointed the finger squarely at Graydon and his brothers.

Maybe, Billy thought, the authorities had zeroed in on one suspected perpetrator, whereas in reality, there had been multiple killers. With different motives, but with the same outcome. Some people had believed this to be the case all along. Maybe Wayne Williams had killed some, but not all, of those kids.

During the last recess and after his third attempt to reach Finnegan, Billy stepped outside the courthouse for a brief respite from the scrum inside. Even though he knew the temperature had plummeted from a high in the fifties yesterday to almost freezing today, he forgot to put on his coat. The chill enveloped him. With each breath he took, his warm exhale created a fog that hung in the air before dissipating.

He glanced down the street. He thought he saw Finnegan in a bomber jacket, standing on the corner with two men in trench coats. The two men were doing most of the talking, and from what Billy could tell, it didn't look like small talk. One of these trenchcoated men then wrenched Finnegan's hands behind his back, and they led him up the street toward Billy. When they got halfway up the block, Billy saw it wasn't Finnegan after all. They threw the man into the back of an idling sedan and sped off.

* * *

When the trial had adjourned for the day, Billy left the courthouse wearied and concerned. Wearied from the full day of testimony and trying to square it with what he knew of the Vardemans. Concerned that, after having phoned Finnegan three times, he hadn't been able to reach him. Sure, it hadn't been even twenty-four hours, but after all that had happened recently, and after his experience during the last recess, he was doubly uneasy.

He drove to his mom's to pick up Brody, all the while unable to get Finnegan off his mind.

He called Gary from his mom's. "Do you ever feel like you have a sixth sense?" he asked Gary.

"You mean ESP? Psychic shit and all that? Like Miss Cleo? Or that Madam Ludowici woman you've told me about?"

"I mean more spontaneous. Unplanned. Unscripted and unfaked. Like a nagging feeling that something's not right."

Billy shared the story of one time back in his college days. He'd gone home for the weekend, probably to do laundry if nothing else. That Saturday night, he dreamed his dorm had flooded and he and his dormmates were floating down the hall in three-foot-deep rushing water. When he returned to campus the next day, he learned that a pipe had broken and the dorm had, indeed, flooded. Not three feet. More like an inch. But enough to make him wonder. Was it a coincidence? Or was there more to it?

"I've never had anything like that happen to me," Gary said. "Not that I remember, anyway. So did you have another dream or what?"

"No, not a dream. More like a waking premonition. About J.P. Finnegan."

"What about Finnegan?"

Billy told Gary about trying to reach Finnegan three times, once from home and twice from the courthouse.

Then he related seeing the trenchcoated men and the Finnegan lookalike.

Gary said it was probably nothing. Maybe detectives cornering a pimp or a drug dealer or something.

"It could be," Billy said, "but whatever it was, my thoughts quickly returned to Finnegan, because the man I saw looked just like him from a distance. It gave me pause and no small dose of angst. I know it's irrational to project any of this onto Finnegan, but I sure hope he's okay."

"Yeah, he's been in pretty bad straits before, hasn't he? So have you, though. Wanna pay him a visit?"

"Later tonight?"

"Why not?" Gary said. "The missus is staying overnight with her mother. I'd probably just be at home watching *WKRP*.

"I'm at my mom's picking up Brody. Let me get him home and settled in. I'll call you after Cynthia and I talk."

* * *

Billy looked over at Brody, who was sitting quietly in the passenger seat with his hands tucked under his thighs. The boy was looking out the window as Billy drove down Moreland Avenue. Billy wondered whether Brody may have been thinking about how he had fled the church and made his way down this street just a few days ago, stealing sleep God only knows where and ending up at the newspaper office.

"How did it go today?" Billy asked.

Brody perked up. The question must have jolted him back to the present from wherever his mind had been. He slid his hands from under his thighs and rested them on his lap. He paused for a moment. "Miss Alice is a really nice lady. We made a bunch of oatmeal cookies." He made a sweep with his index finger. "She even let me scoop out what was left in the bowl. Then we watched TV."

Oh God, Billy thought, *surely not* Days of Our Lives. "What did you watch?"

"Cartoons and stuff." Brody looked up at Billy. "Did you know Miss Alice likes cartoons? She said they didn't even have 'em back when she was my age. Didn't even have TV." He shook his head. "Did you know that?"

Billy chuckled. "Well, I can't say I know she likes cartoons, if that's what you mean. But as for not having TV, it didn't come around 'til not long before I was born."

"Wow. I can't imagine."

"Do you want to go back to Miss Alice's tomorrow?"

"Can I?"

* * *

Back at The Belmont, Billy tried Finnegan at home again. Still no answer.

After dinner, Brody asked if he could play with Billy Jr. and Addie, "seeing as I haven't ever been with little kids and all."

Once Brody was out of earshot, Billy told Cynthia he needed to go out for a while. "Probably nothing," he said, "but Gary and I need to go over to J.P. Finnegan's to check on him. I shouldn't be late getting home."

Cynthia sighed. "Billy, you two be careful. Okay?"

"We will. I feel a lot safer than before, with the Vardemans out of the picture."

He dialed Gary.

"I'll pick you up in fifteen," Gary said. "No, better give me twenty."

When Billy hung up, Cynthia asked him about Brody. "Is he going back to your mom's tomorrow?"

"She said she'd be glad to have him. Apparently, they hit it off, although I seriously doubt she likes *Scooby-Doo* and *Plastic Man* as much as Brody thinks. Could you maybe drop him off again on your way to Agnes Scott?"

"Tomorrow's Thursday. I don't have classes. Remember? But I can run him over there anyway." She walked over to the kitchen table and gestured to the empty chair. "Have a seat."

"Okay. But I need to watch the time. Gary's picking me up in a few minutes."

She leaned across the table. "Where's Brody going to go?" she said in a near-whisper. "I mean long-term. Given that he has no family left."

"Well, technically, he does. There's Sonya. But she's not blood-related, and he doesn't want to have anything to do with her anyway. And then there's his mother, but nobody knows where she is. Except that she's off somewhere with the Dead."

"They're not touring right now," she said.

Billy frowned "How do you know *that*?"

She grinned. "I get around."

"No, seriously. How do you know that?"

"I heard it on the radio. Their tour starts next month and runs through December. Maybe you could turn into a Deadhead and chase his mother down. With a headband, some rose-colored glasses, and a tie-dyed tee, I think you'd fit right in."

Billy half-laughed.

"I'm sorry," Cynthia said. "I know this isn't something to make light of."

"Actually, Cynthia, a bit of levity is good."

Chapter Seventy-Eight

Billy Tarwater

Wednesday, January 27ᵗʰ, 1982

BILLY THOUGHT BACK TO HIS FIRST PHONE CONVERSATION WITH
Finnegan almost a year ago. *Mine's the baby blue one with the
American flag hanging off the side. And a big ass television antenna on
top. And a Bill Elliott No. 9 decal on the door.*

Gary was barreling down Sandtown Road past the Faircourt
– Home Is Where You Park Your House sign. But somebody
had sprayed over the last three letters, so it now read Where You
Park Your Ho. Gary's chuckle lightened their tension a bit. Billy
wondered whether the sign had been that way the last time they
were there, two-and-a-half weeks ago, when they had come looking
for Finnegan. Maybe they had been too preoccupied to notice it.

The baby blue trailer was dark inside. Just like before. But the
door was wide open, banging in the winter wind against the trailer's
metal siding.

Gary pulled the Plymouth Fury into the space where Finnegan used to park his Mustang II. Before it ended up covered with brambles and brush at the Vardemans' place. He cut the engine.

Billy had opened the door and was about to step out when Gary stopped him. "Wait, buddy." Gary reached into the glove box and grabbed his pistol and flashlight. "You stay here. Lemme go in first. I'll let you know when it's safe."

"No way, Gary."

Gary stared at Billy with narrowed eyes and pursed lips. "Do *you* have a gun?"

"Of course not," Billy said.

"I didn't think so. Look, I don't have a spare this time. And if you ain't packin', you'd best stay right where you are 'til I check things out. This is the kind of stuff I'm trained for, you know. I'll go inside. When I wave you in, then you can join me. Okay?"

"But—"

"Last time, *I* stayed in the car. It's *your* turn now."

Billy watched as Gary, caneless and with his pistol in one hand and flashlight in the other, hobbled up the steps to the open door. Gary stopped at the threshold, bent forward, and peered inside. "Anybody there?" he called out. He cradled the flashlight on his neck the way a seasoned secretary would a telephone. Billy could see him feeling along the inside wall of the trailer, near the door jamb, until he found the light switch. He turned on the interior light and stuck the flashlight in his back pocket. He entered the trailer, holding the pistol with both hands, one gripping the handle and the other supporting it from below, in what Billy had come to know from his newspaper work as the Weaver stance.

Within a couple of minutes, Gary reappeared at the door and motioned for Billy to come quickly.

Billy jumped out of the car and ran to the trailer. He followed Gary inside, past the dirty dishes in the sink, the half-eaten food on the counter, the empty Doritos bag and Old Milwaukee can on the TV tray, and into what had to be Finnegan's bedroom.

Finnegan was on the floor, face-up. He was naked except for his boxers. Just below his sternum was a gaping hole rimmed in charred flesh. The skin around it was seared, the mark of a close-range shot. The edges of the wound were dark, almost black, where the bullet had torn through muscle and bone, leaving a jagged circle. He was lying in a congealed pool of dark red. Blood was spattered on the wall at the head of the bed like a burst of shattered glass.

Other than Finnegan's lifeless body and the powder burns and blood, nothing looked to be out of place in the room. The clothes strewn haphazardly across the floor didn't strike Billy as noteworthy. There was no outward sign of struggle. No overturned furniture. No broken objects. Nothing to suggest a fight.

Billy knelt beside Finnegan.

Come on over, Finnegan had said on the phone that day in March before Billy hung up and headed to Sandtown Road. *We'll pop a coupla brewskis, watch that big ball of fire sink over the trailer tops.* He loved his brewskis. And he loved his sunsets.

"J.P. was one of the good guys," Billy said to Gary. "Just out to make things right. He didn't deserve this."

Billy looked around for evidence. All he saw of note was a used condom peeking out from beneath the edge of the bed.

Billy and Gary returned to the main room. Gary grabbed a dishcloth from the kitchen counter and reached for the phone. He lifted the handset with the cloth and dialed 911.

"They're on their way," Gary said. "We're gonna be here a while. You may want to let the little lady know."

Billy phoned home.

Cynthia didn't pick up.

He tried three more times, in succession, but to no avail.

It wasn't like her to not answer the phone. Especially after multiple calls in short order.

Maybe she was tied up with the kids. Or dealing with Brody. Or otherwise indisposed. He wanted to head home to make sure everything was okay. But he knew he couldn't. He'd first have to deal with a plethora of questions from the Cobb County police. He understood.

"No luck?" Gary said.

"No. I'm worried."

"One of those sixth sense things again?"

"Maybe," Billy said. "I don't know."

Gary ran the palm of his hand down his cheek, fingers brushing against the stubble on his chin. "Listen, I may lose my job for this, but..." He handed Billy his pistol. "Here, take this." Then his car keys. "And take the Fury. Get outta here before the police arrive. I'll deal with them. Cop-to-cop. They'll understand."

"Are you serious?"

"I'm serious." Gary flicked his hand like he was shooing a fly away. "Go."

"But—"

"I said go. It'll all be okay. I'll see to it."

Billy made for the door.

"Just come back and get me," Gary called out.

* * *

Billy drove down Sandtown Road, careful not to exceed the speed limit lest he arouse suspicion in an unmarked cop car. A dead giveaway. Halfway to Atlanta Road, he passed the Cobb County squad car coming his way, with its lights flashing and sirens blaring. Probably on their way to the trailer park. A pang of guilt passed over him for leaving Gary to deal with them on his own. But he was appreciative, as always, of Gary's generosity, reckless as it was.

Billy swung into the Belmont courtyard and parked at the front door instead of in the parking deck. He stuffed Gary's pistol into his coat pocket and rushed to the fourth floor.

The door to the apartment was ajar. Billy eased it open and called out.

He searched every room. Nothing looked amiss.

Then he heard a rustling coming from the bedroom closet. Pistol in hand, he threw open the closet door. Cynthia, Billy Jr., and Addie were huddled on the floor. Their mouths were muted by silver duct tape. Their hands and feet were tied.

Billy quickly but carefully removed the tape from Cynthia's mouth and untied her arms. He was about to do the same for the kids when she screamed, "Go Billy. Now. They just left with the boy. We're okay. I can take it from here."

"Who is *they*?"

"Two women. Brody knew one of them."

Billy ran into the living room. He was headed to the front door when he looked out the window and saw a weathered and dull maroon Mustang II, looking like a battled-hardened warrior fresh from the fray, idling across the courtyard. The car eased toward Fifth Street at a leisurely pace. Not what Billy would have thought if something nefarious was at play. But now was not the time to take chances. After all, how many maroon Mustang IIs were there in the city.

Billy hurtled down the stairs two steps at a time. He made sure he was out of sight of anyone in the Mustang—whoever *they* were—before bounding out the lobby door and to the Plymouth Fury. He sped out of the courtyard to Fifth Street. To his left, he saw the Mustang up the street at the Peachtree intersection. It turned right. He followed two blocks behind.

After a circuitous route through the city, the Mustang pulled to the curb in front of a weathered clapboard Cabbagetown house on Carroll Street, a stone's throw from the old Fulton Cotton Mill, which had closed in '77.

Billy knew the houses well. Back in the late seventies, he had visited a friend who had bought one for a song and planned to refurbish it. The houses had been built in the '20s and '30s to house the mill workers. What they lacked in size they made up for in character, with steep gabled roofs and broad front porches. But by the time Billy had visited his friend, the well-worn steps sagged and the planked flooring creaked. And things had continued to go to seed ever since.

Billy watched from the corner of Carroll and Gaskill Streets a half block away. The driver, a woman, stepped out of the car. She then opened the rear door on her side, and another woman got out with a boy in hand. Billy couldn't make out much in the dusk, but he could tell it was Brody.

It wasn't until the three of them began to climb the stairs onto the porch, with the overhead light shining down on them, that Billy realized who the women were.

One was the woman he had seen that time at the Vardeman place. He assumed it was Sonya.

The other one was Jean. J.P. Finnegan's on-again-off-again girlfriend. The "ran off to Reno with a carny" girlfriend.

All three went into the house. Jean and the boy first. Sonya inches behind.

Billy eased Gary's car up Carroll Street and parked behind the Mustang. He slid the borrowed pistol into his coat pocket and got out. He approached the porch.

Someone pushed back the curtain in the front window, but the house was dark inside, and he couldn't tell who it was.

The front door eased open. A third woman, thick and rough-hewn, stood in the doorway with her feet shoulder width apart and her hands firmly planted on her hips. "What do you want?"

"I'm looking for the two women who just entered. With the boy."

"Why do you want 'em?"

Billy's inclination was to lay it all out for the woman. *They came into my home, tied up my wife and kids, and abducted the boy. Need I say more?* But he didn't know her from Adam. And he didn't owe her an explanation.

"Send them out with the kid or I call the cops."

"Wait here." The woman went back inside and shut the door.

Billy stood on the sidewalk. His hands were clammy. His heart was beating hard. He reached into his coat pocket. He gripped the handle of the pistol and eased it halfway out. Not far enough that it could be seen. But enough that he could draw it in a hurry if he had to. He hooked his index finger around the trigger guard.

He waited.

The door flew open.

Sonya stood in the doorway, squeezing Brody's arm tight with her left hand and, with her right, holding what looked like a semi-automatic Glock. Similar to the one in Finnegan's possession after he had escaped from the Vardemans'.

Brody was trembling. His eyes were fixed on his shoes. Billy could feel the boy's fear, palpable and intense.

Sonya pointed the Glock at Billy.

His grip tightened on the pistol in his coat pocket. His finger moved from the guard to the trigger. He eased the gun out of his pocket, holding it close to his waist.

"Leave now if you know what's good for you," she said.

Billy steeled himself. "Not without the kid." He drew his pistol and leveled it at Sonya.

She slowly brought the barrel of the Glock around and jabbed it into Brody's right temple. "Try me, Tarwater. You want to see what I'm made of? Go ahead. One wrong move and there won't be a kid left for you to leave with."

Brody broke down crying.

Sonya jabbed the Glock harder.

When Billy looked into her eyes, even in the faint glow of the porch light he could see all the way through to the black hole of her soul. He knew, then and there, that she was serious. He slowly pulled Gary's pistol back.

"Sonya, please," he said. "Think about the kid. Think about—"

A single gunshot pierced the night air.

Sonya crumpled onto the floor planks. Her muscles spasmed. Her body writhed.

Jean came running out and embraced Brody, who fell into himself, sobbing.

Billy ran onto the porch and bent down next to Sonya, now lying in a growing pool of blood. Her pulse was gone.

He ran inside and dialed 911.

He instructed Jean, Brody, and the other woman to sit and wait until the police arrived. "And whatever you do, don't disturb anything."

Jean sat alone in the corner of the living room, sullen and silent. Her fingers were wrapped around the handle of a small handgun. Her head was hung low.

Brody was curled up in a ball at Jean's feet.

The other woman paced back and forth between the kitchen and the living room, clutching what looked like a rosary.

The woman told Billy the house was hers—"well, not *mine mine*, but rented"—and that she was a friend of Sonya's going back to their childhood Holy Spirit days. Her name was Phyllis.

Billy needed to reach Gary. He dialed Finnegan's phone, hoping against hope that Gary would answer.

CHAPTER SEVENTY-NINE
Billy Tarwater

Friday, January 29th, 1982

ON FRIDAY AFTERNOON, AFTER TWO MORE DAYS OF TESTIMONY in which prosecutors attempted to tie Wayne Williams to the murders of children and adults for which he was not being tried, Billy headed to the Fulton County Jail next door to the courthouse.

* * *

Gary had shown up at the Carroll Street crime scene late Wednesday evening, courtesy of a Cobb County patrolman. Billy guessed cop-to-cop really did have its privileges, even if it crossed jurisdictions. Upon arrival, Gary asked Billy for the gun and the keys to the Plymouth. He had entrusted Billy with both, which he said he'd do again in a heartbeat if he had to. But he said the sooner he got them back, the sooner he could rest easy knowing—or at least hoping—that he hadn't been caught. He said he had managed to talk his way through everything with the Cobb County police, so they didn't suspect a thing. As far as they knew, Gary had been at Finnegan's alone. "None the wiser," Gary said to Billy.

Well after midnight in the wee hours of Thursday morning, after the paramedics had hauled off the body and yellow line tape had been stretched across the Carroll Street yard, two Atlanta policemen had thrown Jean, in handcuffs, into the back of a squad car and sped off on their way to the county jail, where she was later booked for killing Sonya Vardeman.

Two other officers had taken Brody into protective custody and placed him into a second patrol car in preparation for transporting him to an undisclosed Child Protective Services location. Billy reckoned that, had it been earlier in the day, CPS would have sent a caseworker to the scene. But not after midnight. Brody, sitting forlorn in the back seat, looked to Billy as the car was about to pull away. The pain on Brody's face was evident. Billy mouthed "Hang in there" just as they were leaving. He hoped Brody knew he would do everything in his power to secure the boy's well-being.

* * *

Now, Billy entered the jailhouse and checked in at the front desk. He had arranged yesterday morning to meet with Jean today. The authorities had approved the visit, and Jean had agreed to it. It otherwise could have taken a few days, or longer, to get administrative sign-off for the visit, but Billy's persistence and Gary's contacts helped grease the skids.

The jail attendant led Billy into the stark, windowless inmate visitation room.

The harsh fluorescent lighting cast a cold clinical glow over the room. The institutional green walls, with their chipped and peeling paint, their stains in hues of yellow-brown, belied better days.

Billy sat on the heavy metal chair bolted to the floor, on the free side of the thick glass partition. The glass was scratched and clouded from years of use. A corded telephone was mounted on the wall to the right of where Billy sat. He could see one on her side, too.

A matron brought Jean in on the interned side of the glass. She was handcuffed and shackled and in a khaki jumpsuit.

She and Billy made eye contact, then she quickly looked away.

"Hello, Mr. Tarwater," she said. Her staticky voice creaked through phone equipment Billy assumed had been in use since '69 when the jail opened.

"Hello, Jean. Thank you for meeting with me."

Her pursed smile dissipated. "You know I would do anything for that little boy."

"You knew him?"

"Listen," she said, "when somebody…I don't care who it is… sticks a gun in the side of a little boy's face and is about to pull the trigger, I'll do whatever it takes to protect him. Sonya was a friend of mine. We went way back. I even hooked her and Graydon up. I hate what I did, but I had to do what I had to do."

"Didn't we meet at J.P.'s? You were his girlfriend, right?"

"Off and on," she said. "Sonya hooked *us* up. Funny how that works."

Billy was confused. Jean and Graydon? Sonya and Finnegan? It didn't make sense. What was he missing? He quizzed Jean.

She told him about how, way back, Graydon was going through some hard times. "He'd been back from Nam for, I don't know, maybe three years? He was fucked up from dope and war nerves.

He was workin' for the phone company but having a hard time gettin' back into the groove." Jean said she hooked Sonya up with Graydon hoping Sonya could give him some stability. "But then what happens? A year later the SOB fucks it all up and lands in the clink. I felt sorry for Sonya. But I was dealin' with my own problems. I didn't have time to worry about hers."

"How did you get hooked up with Finnegan?" Billy asked.

"Well, around the time Graydon got hauled off to prison…not that it was related…I up and split. I ended up wandering around trying to get my own damned head on straight. That went on for four years. Graydon got paroled. Then Sonya looks me up one day and says she wants me to get involved with something. I said 'Sonya, I ain't comin' back.' She said, 'Oh no, Jean, I'm not askin' you to come back. I've got this guy I want you to meet.' Little did I know at first that she wasn't doin' it out of the goodness of her heart. Seems he'd been snooping around and stickin' his nose where it didn't need to be, and Sonya wanted me to spy on him. Nothing like a little hanky-panky under the sheets to get a guy to wag."

The guard on the free side came to where Billy was sitting. "Ten more minutes," he said. "Then you'll have to wrap this gabfest up."

"The thing is," Jean continued, "I was never made to be with any one man for long. That's why I was on-again-off-again with J.P. God rest his soul."

"Who killed J.P.?" Billy said.

"I didn't do it. I swear I didn't. It was all Sonya's doing." Jean and J.P. were in bed in the double-wide, "doin' the bump nasties, if you know what I mean, when Sonya came bustin' through the front door, all hot and het up. J.P. jumped up and put on his boxers. Sonya kept yellin' 'you sumbitch killed my old man.' She pulled out a Glock and pointed it at him. I tried to reason with her, but she told me to shut up. To stay out of it. She said she wouldn't think twice about usin' it on me too.

"J.P. lunged at Sonya and tried to wrench the gun from her hand. She shoved him back onto the bed. He raised up and held his hand out. 'Don't do it, Sonya,' he said. Then she pulled the trigger.

"That's when I knew it was all over. Sonya told me to get dressed. 'You're coming with me,' she said. She forced me to the car at gunpoint. Somehow, Sonya had found out where Brody was. Or maybe it was just a hunch. Anyway, she made me ride with her to get him. She said, 'don't pull no shit if you want to live to see the boy.'"

Jean said she hadn't seen Brody in a long time. Didn't know if she'd recognize him. Or if he'd recognize her.

She then recounted how she and Sonya had hightailed it to The Belmont and managed to finagle their way into the apartment.

Billy wondered why, in God's name, Cynthia had opened the door for them. Had it been Brody's doing? Had he had a change of heart and decided Sonya, the only link to family he knew, wasn't so bad after all? *A long shot at best.*

Jean didn't let on she knew why. All she said was that Cynthia wouldn't open up at first. But Sonya pleaded, saying she was Brody's aunt. Jean heard Brody say something she couldn't make out. Then Cynthia let them in.

"You realize, don't you," Billy said, "that you're going to need good counsel. Do you have access to an attorney?"

"Are you kidding? I can barely make rent."

"The court has to provide one if you can't afford it on your own. The good news is that, under Georgia law, the defense of a child is justification for deadly force. If you believed Brody was in imminent danger of death or bodily harm, you could protect him. Do you think you can make a case for that?"

Jean said yes. And that she had Phyllis and the boy to back her up.

"If you can show you had to do what you did to save Brody's life, and that the threat was immediate and serious, the DA may not press criminal charges. And even if he does, it's likely you won't be convicted. But it'll be a tough slog."

Jean welled up. "I love that boy so much. I ask myself every day why I left, but I just couldn't deal with those people anymore."

"What do you mean?" Billy said.

She retrieved a tissue from the pocket of her jumpsuit and wiped her eyes. "I've been keepin' something from you. Something you need to know. When you asked to see me, you asked for Jean Parks, right?"

"That's right. Phyllis told me your name."

She took a deep breath. "Well, that's the name I was born with. And that's the name I go by now. But back in the day, before I ran off, I went by another name."

"What was that?"

She searched her lap. "McMillan." She looked up. Tears streamed. "I'm Brody's mother."

CHAPTER EIGHTY

Billy Tarwater

Friday, January 29ᵗʰ, 1982

BILLY LEFT THE JAILHOUSE WONDERING HOW JEAN, IF SHE loved Brody as much as she claimed, could have abandoned him and his father and not looked back. No matter how fucked up the family was. How can a mother do something like that?

And why did she agree, four years later, to get mixed up with Sonya and Finnegan in the convoluted ruse? Was it to insinuate herself back into the family she had abandoned?

Did Ewell and his brothers know about the ruse? Or had Sonya cooked it up on her own? Ewell was so pissed off with Jean for leaving, surely he never would have gone along with it.

Jean had told Billy, as they talked through the glass partition, that Brody hadn't recognized her when she and Sonya showed up at The Belmont. She said maybe those years on the road with The Dead, and then with the "ride jock carny," had rendered her unrecognizable to the boy. And after all, he was only five when she split.

Jean said Sonya made her distract Brody in the living room while Sonya ushered Cynthia and the kids into the bedroom, tied and taped them up, and stashed them in the closet.

While Jean and Brody sat on the sofa, she told Brody who she was.

What must Brody have thought? Was he happy? Mad? Confused? Jean didn't let on what his reaction was. And I didn't ask.

Now, Brody was off somewhere in a place he didn't know. With people he didn't know. And struggling to understand why. *He must be scared to death.* Billy vowed to find him. Nobody cared more than Billy about the kid's fate. Not even his own mother.

Chapter Eighty-One
Billy Tarwater

Sunday, February 28th, 1982

A MONTH HAD GONE BY SINCE THAT FATEFUL THURSDAY WHEN all hell had broken loose.

Yesterday, the Wayne Williams trial had ended after an eleven-hour jury deliberation. He was convicted of murdering both men.

Billy needed a break. And after all that had happened over the past two-and-a-half months, he was sure Cynthia did too.

"How about that Florida trip?" Cynthia said. "Spring break starts March nineteenth."

Billy conjured images of him and Chester in their PJs in the Brookwood Wagon. Of campfire breakfast by the roadside. Of the unfortunate loblolly pine, somewhere this side of Hazelhurst, that had suffered his and Chester's irrigations all those years.

"Let's do it," he said. "I wonder if Brenner's Motor Court's still there?"

"What's that?"

"It was in Ormand Beach. We always stayed there when I was a kid."

Billy looked over at Brody, who was sprawled on the floor reading the Sunday funnies. "Hey, Brody, ever been to Florida?"

Brody shook his head.

A month ago, Brody's fate had hung in the balance. His mother, his only remaining kin, had ended up in a jail cell with no guarantee that she wouldn't spend the rest of her life in prison for killing Sonya. Finnegan, a good man, was dead. Gary had somehow managed to squeak through an egregious infraction of department protocol and decorum. And Billy and Cynthia needed to get on with their lives.

But oh, what a month can bring.

Jean had managed to get out on bail, thanks to a savvy public defender and Billy's largesse. But Billy knew she couldn't take care of Brody. She had never been the mothering type. She'd admitted as much. And especially now, with her facing the prospect of doing time, it didn't make sense for her to take Brody in, wherever *in* might be.

With Cynthia's blessings and encouragement, Billy had approached Jean. *What if we adopt the boy? You'll always be his mother. You can see him anytime.* Billy knew, as soon as these words had left his lips, that Jean would not be able to see him *anytime* if she ended up behind bars. But hopefully, if that were the case, Brody could visit her on occasion. *I know how much you care about him. And Cynthia and I have the desire, and the wherewithal, to see to it that he's taken care of.*

It hadn't taken long for Jean to agree.

Over the next month, Billy had worked diligently to make it happen. Gary's indirect access to higher-ups had helped.

On this Sunday morning, Billy, Cynthia, Brody, and the two little ones were getting ready to visit the Jeppersons for one of Ruby's now famous and heartily anticipated breakfasts.

There was a faint knock on the door. At first, Billy wasn't sure whether it was really a knock or just a noise coming from the fourth-floor vestibule.

When he opened the door, there was no one there. He thought he heard someone treading down the stairwell.

A Thom McAn shoebox lay at his feet just past the threshold. He picked it up and took it into the kitchen. He set it on the table and removed the lid. Inside was a scrawled letter:

> BEFORE THE COPS GOT TO PHYLLIS'S, I WENT OUT TO THE MUSTANG TO LOOK FOR MY SWEATER. I FOUND THIS BOX IN THE TRUNK. I ASKED HER TO HIDE IT FOR ME. NOW THAT I'M LEAVIN, YOU CAN HAVE IT.
>
> I'M OUTTA HERE. GOIN BACK TO THE CARNY. FAR AWAY AS I CAN GET BEFORE THE LAW AND THE BONDSMAN COME LOOKIN FOR ME.
>
> TAKE CARE OF MY BOY. TELL HIM I LOVE HIM.
>
> JEAN

Beneath the note were some newspaper clippings. Articles, chronicling the discovery of the black boys' bodies.

Beneath the clippings was a stack of Polaroids.

Billy fixated on the first one. It was a picture of a little boy lying on the ground in nothing but his underwear. A length of rope was wrapped tight around his neck. There were bruises about his neck and throat. His tongue was distended. Graydon was standing over him with his arms folded and a smug grin, like a big game hunter standing over his fresh-killed prey.

Billy recognized the kid in the photograph. He was pretty sure he recognized the others, too.

He thought back to the time, not that long ago, when he found the pictures of thirteen-year-old Cynthia in Leonard Seymour's backyard trash drum. And to the pictures of the dead girls he and Gary had found in the Reverend Kilgallon's house back in '80.

He phoned Gary. "We need to call the DA first thing in the morning. There's something he needs to see."

Postscript

ON FEBRUARY 27, 1982, AFTER ELEVEN HOURS OF DELIBERATION, the jury found Wayne Bertram Williams guilty of murdering Nathaniel Cater and Jimmy Rae Payne. He was sentenced to two consecutive life terms in Hancock State Prison in Sparta. He is currently serving out his sentence at Telfair State Prison in Helena.

Two days after Williams' conviction and sentencing, the Atlanta police claimed, with little direct evidence, that twenty-one of the other murder cases could be linked to Williams and declared them to be closed. As of this publication, the only charges filed against Williams are from the Cater and Payne cases, and Williams continues to maintain his innocence.

Suppose Wayne Williams is innocent of killing all or some of the children. Then what? Not everyone thinks he's guilty.

One boy who knew several of the murdered children allegedly has nightmares in which he sees his best friend's death, each time a different way. By strangulation. By gunshot. By stabbing. And then he's left with one image—of a man, always the same man, with long hair, a beard, and scary eyes.

On March 21, 2019, Atlanta Mayor Keisha Lance Bottoms and Atlanta Police Chief Erika Shields announced that officials would retest crime evidence, which would be gathered by the Atlanta Police Department, the Fulton County District Attorney's Office, and the Georgia Bureau of Investigation.

In July 2021, Mayor Bottoms announced that DNA had been identified and sampled in two cases that would be subjected to additional analysis by a private lab. Also, investigators had combed through 40% of the original DNA evidence and had sent that to the same private lab for testing.

Mayor Bottoms' tenure ended in 2022. She chose not to run for a second term.

Andre Dickens, Atlanta's current mayor, has continued the efforts started by former mayor Bottoms, including pushing for advanced forensic analysis to potentially identify additional suspects or provide new insights into the cases.

As of this publication, no DNA results have been made public, despite numerous requests from the victims' families.

Williams' new defense attorney continues to challenge the original investigation, arguing that the case against Williams was built on public perception rather than solid evidence. Although the Atlanta Police Department has confirmed that the case remains open and active, there is apparently still no conclusive DNA evidence to either confirm or disprove Williams' involvement in the child murders.

In 2015, *Spin* Magazine ran an extensive article, "A Question of Justice," laying out the case for the Klan family's involvement in the children's murders.

Nothing ever became of it.

Acknowledgments

YOU WOULD NOT BE READING THIS IF IT WERE NOT FOR MY fellow writers Glen Heefner, Julia Sennette, and Dru Sumner. I will forever be indebted to them for helping me through every chapter, every page, and every word of this book. They inspire me every day.

Caren, my wife of forty-seven years, has been by my side and provided encouragement each step of the way. She has endured my writing obsession, countless hours heads-down at my laptop, and general inattentiveness. And all with a smile. She is my soulmate.

I am also indebted to my family and friends who continue to support and encourage my passion for writing.

Dea Shandera, my publicist, has provided inestimable expertise and guidance, for which I am grateful.

Much of my writing was done with our precious Bella by my side or nearby. While she may not have realized it, she provided inspiration beyond measure. She will be missed.

Bottom line, I had a lot of help writing this book. I could not have done it alone.

About The Author

MIKE COBB'S body of literary work includes both fiction and nonfiction, short-form and long-form, as well as articles and blogs. While he is comfortable playing across a broad range of topics, much of his focus is on true crime, crime fiction and historical fiction. Rigorous research is foundational to his writing. He gets that honestly, having spent much of his professional career as a scientist. He vehemently refuses to box his work into a specific genre.

Mike splits his time between Atlanta and Blue Ridge, Georgia.

MGCOBB.COM

MGCobbWriter

@mgcobb

cobbmg

About The Type

This book is set in Adobe Caslon, a typeface designed by Carol Twombly and based on William Caslon I's original design dating to the mid 1700s. Caslon, a trained London engraver and typefounder, is widely credited for creating the first original typeface of English origin and establishing a national typographic style. Caslon's self-titled typeface is know for its enduring style and legibility.

In the late 19th century the Caslon typeface was adapted for hot metal typesetting with the gaining popularity of mass-market printing.

Made in the USA
Middletown, DE
14 January 2025